D0847005

CARETAKERS

TABITHA KING

A SIGNET BOOK

NEW AMERICAN LIBRARY

A DIVISION OF PENGUIN BOOKS USA INC.

NAL BOOKS ARE AVAILABLE AT QUANTITY DISCOUNTS WHEN USED
TO PROMOTE PRODUCTS OR SERVICES. FOR INFORMATION PLEASE
WRITE TO PREMIUM MARKETING DIVISION. NEW AMERICAN LIBRARY.
1633 BROADWAY. NEW YORK. NEW YORK 10019.

This is an authorized reprint of a hardcover edition published by Macmillan Publishing Company. For information address
Macmillan Publishing Company,
866 Third Avenue,
New York, N.Y. 10022

SIGNET TRADEMARK REG. U.S. PAT. OFF. AND FOREIGN COUNTRIES
REGISTERED TRADEMARK—MARCA REGISTRADA
HECHO EN DRESDEN. TN. U.S.A.

SIGNET, SIGNET CLASSIC, MENTOR, ONYX, PLUME, MERIDIAN
and NAL BOOKS are published by New American Library, a division of
Penguin Books USA Inc., 1633 Broadway, New York, New York 10019

First Signet Printing, September, 1984

6   7   8   9   10   11   12   13   14

PRINTED IN THE UNITED STATES OF AMERICA

This is for Kay McCauley

My husband and co-conspirator, Stephen King, read and reread this story in manuscript and gave both advice and support, for which I thank him. Domo also to George Walsh, whose editorial advice was invaluable.

PART ONE

Joe Nevers climbed out of his truck in front of Fogg's General Store. Scanning the sky, he blinked once as if to ward off a flake of snow. He stamped his boots.

He could smell and feel the storm coming as well as see it. Clouds seeming low enough to touch engulfed the mountains in the west. They drew vapor up in slow trails like attenuated ghosts from the smoked glass mirror surface of the lake, glimpsed in fragments from the height of Nodd's Ridge. They blotted up the thin light of April so that at midmorning, it seemed like four o'clock in the afternoon. So it would seem all day, as if that hour only was sufficiently mournful for snow, and all the hours of a snowy day must imitate it. Joe Nevers guessed the first flakes would fall before noon.

He said so to George Fogg as soon as he was inside and had taken off his cap.

The storekeeper looked out the window, still plastered with outdated posters announcing last summer's church fairs and last fall's county fairs, and unhappily agreed. The whole weight of the incipient storm seemed to settle on his shoulders as he slumped behind the cash register, wondering why he had ever left Manchester, New Hampshire. It had never snowed on Easter weekend there.

But he had lived on Nodd's Ridge long enough to

know Joe Nevers, as his senior, rated first guess at the weather.

"How many inches do you think, Joe?" George asked.

"Well," Joe Nevers answered, "I don't know."

He seemed surprised, as he always did, that anyone thought his opinion worth the asking. He scratched thoughtfully behind one ear.

"Leastways a foot," he finally said, then hedged. "Maybe two."

George hissed like a deflating baloon. "That's what the radio said, too. You plow me out, Joe?"

Joe Nevers' faded blue eyes sparked. Here was something new and curious.

"Why, sure, George."

He paused to pat down his pockets for smokes. He knew he was out of cheroots. But he was a careful man, the sort of man who checks three times to make sure he has locked a door. And he was old enough for routine to have hardened into habit, and then into ceremony.

George Fogg had done his own plowing, however inexpertly, for several years. Clearly, he had a tale to tell about why he couldn't plow himself out of the coming storm. Likely it was a tale of woe involving some kind of aggravating mechanical breakdown. A lengthy discussion of the faults and virtues of four-wheel-drive vehicles and plow attachments might ensue, or a debate on methods of plowing. Whatever the tale, it was only courtesy not to rush it. Indeed, there was pleasure in the anticipation and in the deliberate pace of the conversation.

At last Joe Nevers interrupted the ceremonious search of his pockets to ask the question George Fogg was busting to answer.

"Something wrong with your Jeep, George?"

The storekeeper leaned over the cash register. His lower lip trembled indignantly.

From the back of the store, where a pair of unemployed loggers lounged at the lunch counter, watching and listening, there was a rude anticipatory bray of laughter.

"What's wrong with my Jeep," George sputtered, "is that last night Torie Christopher came in here to buy booze and goddamn if that crazy old bitch didn't go right out a here and drive her goddamn fatass Cadillac right into it." George stopped to take on air, then complained querulously, "Bust the headlights all to shit."

The two men at the lunch counter pounded it hysterically.

"Should a seen it, Joe," one of them managed to wheeze.

The other was not to be outdone. "I hear she's got six, seven, old Caddies, down to Portland." He looked significantly at his buddy. "Keeps 'em for the parts."

Joe Nevers stood silent, ignoring the boys in the back, who couldn't be expected to know any better. But his eyes, slitted under reptilian old-man lids, were as bleak and unforgiving as the frigid waters of the new-thawed lake.

George Fogg's red-faced outrage wavered.

Joe Nevers was known to dislike bad language in reference to or in the presence of women. No more did he countenance bad-mouthing his employers, of whom Torie Christopher drunk or sober was one, behind their backs. If a body had something to say, he held, it was best said face to face. But his silence was his own favored and angriest reproof and that he turned on George Fogg.

Fool that he might have been to have left Manchester, George Fogg was not so stupid as to miss how Joe

Nevers' lips had thinned and tightened, or the sudden jagged blue lightning of veins pulsing in the old man's temples. Suddenly spitless, the storekeeper was seized by the conviction that Joe Nevers was about to have a stroke or a coronary on him and he would be held to blame. If the old man's eagle eyes were unbearable, what George found himself staring at as he looked away was not much more of a comfort: the bright orange sticker that bore the telephone number of the Rescue Service, on the side of the pay phone.

"Sounds like you got off lucky," Joe Nevers said.

George sucked in a big breath and relaxed a little. "I guess so." He was prepared to agree with anything Joe Nevers said from then on.

The loggers settled down to snickering and slurping their coffee.

George looked out the window as if there were something there to see besides the old blue truck with its neatly lettered door: JOE NEVERS/CARETAKER. The old man still fixed him with that ironic expression, making him squirm inside like a kid at school. Joe Nevers didn't need to say out loud that George, purveying alcohol to a known abuser, was not strictly innocent of his own misfortune. As a licensed agent of the state, privileged to peddle the state's booze, George was duty bound to refuse to sell to the obviously incompetent. But he had been content to pocket his share of the profits and never mind the consequences until they happened to him.

"I'll have a packet of cheroots," Joe Nevers said, in a voice as mild as Ivory soap.

Fixing his face in the brave grin of a man much tried but treating his troubles as a cosmic joke on himself, George looked round again at the old man. "Sure, Joe."

Tucking his change and his cheroots into his mackinaw, Joe Nevers promised, "I'll come by as soon as there's something to scrape."

"Great," said George, too heartily.

Joe Nevers stopped short at the door.

"Missus Christopher. Don't suppose she picked up anything to eat, did she?"

George's smile slipped. He shook his head. Fresh embarrassment heated his face. He hadn't so much as urged a Twinkie on the woman. He felt a new rush of anger at Torie Christopher. It wasn't enough she had smashed hell out of the front end of his Jeep, she had also caused him to feel small and mean. Goddamn but it wasn't his business to run a soup kitchen for drunks. Truth was, Joe Nevers wasn't exactly a Good Samaritan. It was his living, coddling rich people. But this time George kept his lip buttoned and his resentment to himself.

As soon as the door closed on Joe Nevers, the storekeeper hauled out a bandanna handkerchief and mopped his forehead.

"Key-rist," he blurted to the loggers. "I thought the old fart was going to drop right here." He laughed hopefully.

The two men stared at him as if he were something from outer space.

One of them dug deep in a pocket of his green wool pants and produced a dime. He held it 'twixt thumb and index finger and drawled, "Ol' Joe Nevers was borned right here in this town. A good gaddamn long time ago, too. But ain't nobody ever made a dime," and the man slapped the coin flat-handed onto the counter top, rattling the thick china mugs, "bettin' on when ol' Joe'll buy the farm. I seen quite a few strong young bucks thought they was going to live forever and got a big surprise, and ol' Joe Nevers puttin' a shoulder to their coffins."

George Fogg sank back onto his stool with a sigh and popped a Rolaid into his mouth, with the glum thought that these people were as uncomfortable as their goddamned weather.

Outside, in his truck, Joe Nevers sat smoking a cheroot and staring out across the Ridge toward the invisible mountains. No matter what the weather, the view was a masterpiece. Sometimes the neat houses dotted along either side of Route 5 as it traced the spine of Nodd's Ridge seemed to have been placed there solely to give scale to the composition. And every day was different. In all the decades he had looked at the same vista of sky, mountains, and shining lake, he sometimes thought he had seen every shade of blue. Now and again, he still opened his eyes to see it, surprisingly, all new. But this day, the sky had fallen in the west. Nodd's Ridge was the edge of the known universe.

Joe Nevers thought about Torie Christopher and the way she had of turning up in his life when he least expected it, like a blizzard in April. No doubt she had parked the Cadillac in a ditch, or halfway up a tree, and he would have to put it back on the road. There would be one mess or another to clean up all weekend. The woman had a real antagonism to the furniture, liked to take an ax to a chair now and again. The toll on the dishes was something awful too, when she was drunk-clumsy, or having a temper tantrum.

He would try to feed her, with uncertain results. Years past he had stocked the house with frozen food. After finding the remains—dinners thawing in a cold oven because she had forgotten to turn it on, and then forgotten she was hungry, or reduced to unidentifiable charcoal because she had left them at 500 degrees for a day or two—he had stopped, worried about electrical fires from an overheated oven, and unable to stand the waste. Since then, he cooked for her, telling himself his home cooking was more nutritious than store-bought anyway. If he got half of it into her, coaxing and wheedling, and she kept half of it down, he figured to have staved off malnutrition for that weekend, at least.

The weekend was a road oft traveled, no question about it. And he was anticipating it as if there was something new at the end of it. That a weekend with a combative drunk looked so much better than another by himself hinted he was lonelier than he had ever admitted to himself. Perhaps he had been wrong to scorn retirement. Was there really any special value in not migrating to Florida each winter with his sister Gussie and her second husband and so many others of those who survived from his generation? Truth might be, he was afraid to pick up and go, another useless old man exiled to a soft, exotic nursing home of a state. He had always been alone. It was not living alone that troubled him so much as the fear of a strange land, a place where no one knew his name.

But the day's chores waited on him. Opening the truck's window, he pitched out the butt of his cheroot. Perhaps it was only the grayness of the day that made him fret about such things. It was a relief to see the first flakes make cat's paws on the windshield. The snow was not waiting for noon.

By then he was home again, punching down the bread dough that had risen on the ledge over the kitchen range all morning while he rode the miles of dirt road, only recently bared of winter's snowpack, to check the day's schedule of houses and cottages. He did accounts while the bread rose again, then cleaned up while the loaves baked. There was Maggie the cat to feed and put out, the parlor stove to bank, the thermostats to set so if the stoves went out in the night the little emergency furnace would come on and keep the pipes from freezing.

It was exhilarating to go from the comfortable domestic warmth, the smell of new bread, into the crisp air that was thick with swirling, blown snow. The cold stirred his blood and cleared his head. Long since Joe Nevers had recognized the snow was going to outlast him. It would fall and fall and fall again, long after he and the yellow plow blade on his truck, and his old blue truck too, had melted back into the earth. But a body still felt the good of pushing the snow before the blade, reclaiming a patch of earth from the obliterating white.

There were only small plowing jobs—the town office, the post office, Needham's diner, a few driveways of widows, elderly or infirm folks—as the grammar school was out for the Easter vacation, not in session again for ten days and by then there was a good chance the snow would have melted away, and the town saved the price of his services, so he would leave that one go.

Fogg's lot was cluttered with the vehicles of storm-panicked shoppers that hampered the work of clearing the accumulation. It was coming down fast and heavy. A quirky wind half-blinded him, and undid the job even as he was doing it. A fool's errand, he thought disgustedly, like the ones that brought folks out to the store in such weather, or kept George open in the face of it.

When he had done what he could, he lifted the plow blade as far clear of the road as it would go, and headed north on Route 5, out of the village and nearly to the town line. He turned down the dirt road that led to the Christopher place, dropping the blade to plow his way in.

There were other houses on the road in his care but the light was already failing. It would be easy enough to look in on them the next day. Ten inches of untracked snow on the road testified that no one had passed over it since the forenoon. It looked as if no one except Torie Christopher was in residence this Easter weekend. And the thieves and vandals that made his job necessary were pretty much fair-weather fiends.

The road was one he classed, in the privacy of his mind where none could take offense, as an upsy-downsy old whore. It took him the best part of an hour to plow his way to the Christophers' driveway.

The driveway made the road in look like a freeway. In winter it was a slippery slide of ice. The spring melt nearly always tore up great chunks of it and washed them away. At any time of year, the zigzag breakneck plunge down the hill was best approached with caution. Joe Nevers had not lived so long by being either careless or hasty. He stopped his truck at the top of the driveway to have a look at it.

Below him the steep granite ledge that formed the hillside sheltered nearly five acres of fine shorefront. A few lifetimes ago, the lot had been a lush wilderness meadow. Before that, it was a bit of lake bottom, when the lake was much greater. But within the short memory of the white man, represented by the Nodd's Ridge town records, it had been the site of three dwellings.

The first was a hunting camp, a crude log cabin that once abandoned had quickly decayed and disappeared.

The second was a summer house, built at the end of the last century by a shipping merchant from Portland, the first Albert Christopher. It was his son Albert who fathered Guy, who in his time married and widowed Torie. The whimsical towers and turrets of that house survived only in a few old photographs and in the memories of the oldest citizens of Nodd's Ridge. Joe Nevers remembered it better than anyone except Torie, not only because he had had the caretaking of it for many years, but because he nearly died in that house, not once but twice.

He was just a tyke the first time. It was the summer after young Albert married a Boston debutante named Frances Burr. The bride's mother-in-law, Mrs. Albert Christopher, Sr., gave a tea to introduce young Mrs. Albert to Nodd's Ridge.

IT WAS LIKE SUNDAY MEETING with games and lemonade thrown in. In white lawn and linen, the ladies fluttered over the green, green grass like nightshirts on the line. They flocked along the broad front porch where the lemonade was served, and where they might sit in wicker chairs, imagining a breeze from the lake.

He rolled in the grass like a puppy, watching a game of croquet from the bug's viewpoint, and staining his elbows, knees, and stocking toes where they peeked out of his Roman sandals, green. He was not old enough to be embarrassed by his sailor suit or the fussing of his mother, nor bold enough to chase after the other children in their games, even if she would let him, but he was drawn to those joyous mysteries, and bored by the grown-ups.

Most of what the grown-ups did was talk. That was nothing new. It went on all the time, in the village and on the road, from the backs of horses and the seats of buggies; in farmyards over stock, and at the Meeting House, all dressed up in Sunday best; on the lake in fishing skiffs; and over the cracker barrel in his father's store.

He knew already that talk wasn't as easy as it sounded. His grandfather, Old Will, was wont to say any fool could run his gums. The trick was not to Put Your Foot In It. Anybody who expected to do business with his neighbors had to Get On with them first, and if you always had Your Foot In It, you wouldn't. Most times the talk fetched up with a laugh or a chuckle that meant everything was okay, nobody had Put Their Foot In It.

He listened carefully, not because he knew he had a lot to learn, though he was told often enough that he did, but because sometimes he heard something he had never heard before, something new and curious. But the talk at this party was too much like the talk after Meeting, too much weather and politeness. The laughter of the women had that tautness to it that meant they were worried, probably about Putting Their Foot In It.

Later on, he understood why. Mrs. Christopher, the kindly, plump lady who wore pince-nez under her broad-brimmed straw hat, was giving this tea because of what he would learn in high school French to call *noblesse oblige.* That was a fancy way of saying that Mrs. Christopher was treating the ladies of Nodd's Ridge as equals, precisely because she was somebody and they weren't. Not that the farmers' and shopkeepers' wives, the maiden aunts and widowed grandmothers of the Ridge thought for a moment they were nobodies.

It was pride, pure and simple, that brought them to the tea all dressed in Sunday best. Their Sunday best was carefully altered each spring with new ribbons, buttons, ruffles; let in or out; hems raised or lowered, so it would do three, four, five seasons before being made over for a daughter, younger sister, or age-shrunken mother. Summer demanded white, just because it was so easily soiled, so fragile. The good women ruined their hands in their washtubs, and sealed the ache in their backs bending over flatirons in the dog day heat. If it was vanity and pride, it was bought and paid for. The women of Nodd's Ridge knew they were hardworking, respectable, virtuous, and proud. And Mrs. Christopher knew it too. But what *noblesse oblige* meant was it didn't matter.

His mother had her own reasons for nervousness. He knew she was; her hand in his was moist and trembling. When she bent to straighten his collar, to smooth his hair, he could see the dew of perspiration at her hairline and on her upper lip. The heavy floral perfume she wore did not quite smother her natural scent, so well learned while snug against her milk-heavy breasts more recently than he would admit. Like the pink and white peonies that bloomed at the foot of Mrs. Christopher's porch steps, she was bitter-sweet to smell and as silky to the touch.

She had come to the tea in defiance of her mother's and mother-in-law's best advice, five months gone with his baby sister. It was a time when a modest married woman did not flaunt her condition. Pregnancy still ended, for public purposes, not in labor but in "confinement." As the wife of the town's most successful storekeeper, she was one of the few who could afford a new dress for the occasion. Her mother-in-law, put out with herself for coddling her once-widowed son's much younger second wife, determined to make the best of the situation. Taking a pattern from the latest women's fashion book from Boston, she had modified it cleverly to disguise Josie Nevers' embarrassing belly. But a waistless dress could not hide the nervousness, or diminish the nausea and faintness that the sun and too many people evoked; Josie had to mask that herself, not so much from her neighbors as from her mother and mother-in-law, the pair of them watching her sternly from their chairs on the porch. She tired quickly. When she dared their scrutiny to seek the shade of the porch, she found the chairs all taken by the infirm, elderly, or her seniors. Mercifully, there were pilasters to lean against, in an unobtrusive way.

The boy was delighted with the crowded, noisy porch. It was a cinch to slip in and out among the chattering women, sampling the trays of exotic treats with impunity. He had a bite of everything going, while his mother made brave small talk with young Albert's bride.

It was an oyster, unexpectedly slick and a little bit rubbery, that he choked on. His mother seemed to know almost immediately, alerted by the first faint sound he made, the only one he managed, or by some spastic movement at the corner of her eye. She moved so quickly that only Frances Christopher realized what was happening.

Josie told him, some years later when he was almost a big boy, that she meant to seize him and turn him upside down, the standard procedure in those days for choking. But he was back-to to her and she was clumsy with fright. Her arms encircled him from behind; she clasped him to her with more strength than she intended. The sudden pressure of her arms across his diaphragm popped the oyster out of his mouth and onto the floor. A small puddle of undigested hors d'oeuvres followed the oyster.

The hum of conversation on the porch dipped briefly as the ladies noticed the unpleasantness he had committed and then, in the best tradition of the day, did not notice. At Frances' signal, one of the local girls hired to help out at the party removed the mess in as little time as it took him to make it. The bride reassured herself he was all right, then suggested to Josie that a glass of lemonade might settle his stomach.

Plucking a glass from the neat ranks of crystal on the lemonade table, Josie Nevers seized the nearest sweating pitcher and poured it—not into the glass in her shaking hand, but into the lap of the stiff old spinster seated hardby. There was a chorus of squeals and hisses from the women on the porch. Only Josie, so stunned she continued to pour lemonade into Miss Esther Linscott's lap, and Miss Esther herself were rendered speechless.

Young Albert's bride stepped into the breach, as she had been bred and raised, calmly placing her hand over Josie's, guiding the by then empty pitcher back to the table.

With a single all-purpose exclamation of "Good Lord!" Mrs. Christopher senior descended on Miss Esther and whisked her into the house, where she was able to restore that antique virgin's dampened dignity while preventing the onset of rust.

The bride kept Josie Nevers' hand in hers. Scooping him up in passing, she led his mother through the buzzing gauntlet of women, who fell silent in the face of her easy untroubled smile. Once inside, beyond the eyes and ears of her neighbors and relations, Josie gave way to tears.

Young Joe Nevers was deposited in the kitchen in the care of Cook; the young women disappeared up the back stairs. Cook introduced him to the interesting upset stomach remedy of Coke syrup in soda water. When bride and guest reappeared, half an hour later, the two women were giggling, though Josie Nevers' eyes were still puffy from weeping. Mysteriously, so were Frances'.

It was the beginning of a relationship that lasted the remaining seven years of his mother's life. One treasured memento had passed in time to Joe Nevers—the photograph his father had taken with his new camera a little later at that same tea. Young Albert's bride Frances stands tall, slim, dark of eye and hair, entirely self-assured. Hand in hand with her by the old sundial on the lawn, Joe Nevers' pale-haired mother, round of face and limb, glows with the pregnancy her dress was meant to disguise. They might have been a pair of schoolgirls, so wonderfully young do they seem now to Joe Nevers' eyes.

Frances Burr Christopher was just turned twenty before her wedding; she would live to be seventy-nine and was foolish the last twelve years. Joe Nevers' mother Josie, married and a mother at sixteen, was three months from her nineteenth birthday. She would be taken off by the Spanish influenza after the Great War. It had all happened a lifetime ago.

The old man stomped around the truck, clapping his gloved hands. He shivered not with cold but with pleasure at the clean chill air, and the tickle of snow on his face and down the back of his neck, between his cap and his muffler. He crunched the snow under his boots just for the sound of it and for the sight of his boot treads stamped in the satiny white. Sparkling and luminous in the truck's headlights, flakes showed themselves like ghosts and winked out again in the twilight. The tracks he made filled up again quickly.

From the top of the hill he could see the house, lit up like a lighthouse. If he were blind, he could sniff his way to it, smelling the money Torie was burning up on electricity. Of course, it was her money to piss away if she liked, her right and privilege. If she didn't have more money than she needed to hold body and soul together, she'd not have a house like this one just to use for her binges. And he'd be out the work.

Truth be told, he was prejudiced against the new house, now twenty-five years old. From where he stood, Torie's house was six wedges of varying size, stuck together in a construction that seemed incomplete, as if a single movement of one of its elements was all that was necessary to reveal its true shape. The damn thing made him uneasy. Houses should look like houses, not one of those cubes the kids fidgeted with nowadays, when they wasn't plugged into one of those video games.

Scratching thoughtfully behind one ear, he allowed it might be just, the new house wasn't the old one, that bothered him. He liked to tell the old farts he knew, the Good Old Days was never as Good as all that, because he was an honest man and liked to remind himself too, and also to get their goats, which needed getting now and again. But the truth was, nostalgia came all too easy. It was harder and harder to get a proper hold on the present.

This sudden attack of philosophizing came of walking down this road again, to where he had been too often. There was hardly a foot of it that wasn't haunted.

Fall, 1956

THE AFTERNOON WAS SLIPPING AWAY when Joe Nevers turned down the road to the Christophers' house. The last place he was due to check, it was also the last on the road, which petered out to a rough logging road beyond it. Not only had the summer traffic to the half-dozen homes and cottages on the shore done its share of damage to the road, but logging trucks harvesting in the woods thereabout had further broken and rutted it since Labor Day. He took it slow and easy, in part because he was trying to baby the old Ford pickup through one more winter. He was on guard as well against meeting a logger coming out. When the big sloppy trucks were loaded as high as they could be without tipping over, with logs that were whole trees severed from their roots and shorn of their branches, all tied up with thigh-thick chains and a claw as wide as the Ford's bumper for a bow, they were nothing with which a prudent man would care to tangle.

Nor was there any rush. Since Marion had left him there was no one waiting at home except his animals, and they were a patient lot. He had it half in mind that the sun setting from the Christophers' house would be a treat to see. A little distance from the driveway, at the crest of a long hill, he stopped to check a culvert showing through the gravel. He found it dented a little, but not broken as he feared by the passage of the big trucks. Not likely to be a problem come spring runoff.

He had been cooped up in the cab of the old truck too long on this fine day. Admiring the hard-edged indigo of the lake water and the mountains through the wide breaks in the evergreens where the leaves of the hardwoods blocked the view in summer, he strolled the few yards to the Christophers' driveway. The smell of the lake and the dead leaves and the sun-warmed cedars and pines tickled his nose and lungs as he drew it in deep. The lake sounded angry, crashing and smashing on the rocks below. And in the ebb of that sound, he heard a woman's voice, a mocking, distinctive voice he knew well.

Instinctively he peered through another crooked window in the evergreens and saw the flash of her hair, the color of the sun setting on a cold winter day. Then he saw a darker head and heard a deeper voice, also known to him. Slowly, carefully, soundlessly, he backed away. When he reached the truck, he took off his cap and wiped his forehead with the sleeve of his shirt. As brisk a day as it was, he was sweating a bitter musky sweat.

Gently, he pryed open the cab door, hauled himself up and in as if he were climbing rope, and closed the door with a click no louder than the sound of a party line receiver being surreptitiously hung up. He threw the truck into neutral without starting it, and backed down the hill. It rolled over the gravel, crunching and whispering its secret passage. At the bottom of the hill he realized he was holding his breath, and laid his head on the wheel, suppressing the sudden need to laugh. He switched the key in the ignition, hoping if they heard the sound of the motor, as he backed to the nearest neighbor's driveway to turn around, they would think whoever it was had not come all the way down the road.

It was not the first time he had stumbled upon a secret. He told himself it was none of his business. Nothing to keep him up nights. He concentrated on holding the truck to a sedate pace, fighting the urge to flee. It wouldn't do to be seen tearing out onto the highway as if his pants were afire.

Joe Nevers shivered again, this time with the cold that was rooted deep in the frozen heart of the earth, climbing slowly from his toes in their woollen socks and heavy boots toward his core. The lights of the house became a beacon that promised warmth and shelter. He realized he was tired with a too familiar weariness that no amount of sleep remedied anymore.

The walk down the hill would do him good. As bright as the house lights were, they illuminated only shapes and shadows this far away. Not good enough light to risk jockeying the truck down the unplowed roller coaster of the driveway. That was his excuse, though he knew full well it wasn't the light that wasn't good enough, but himself. He didn't trust himself to take the pickup down the hill in the dark, in blowing snow.

It was safe enough to leave the truck standing at the side of the road. No one would pass this way before morning. Joe Nevers reached into the cab to turn off the headlights and ignition, and haul out his basket of provisions. He pocketed the keys. The smell of fresh-baked bread escaped even the plastic in which he had bagged it, and was somehow intensified by the cold air.

Leaning into the wind and the hillside to keep his balance, keeping a firm grip on the basket, he took each step with utmost care. The wind tugged at the fringe of his muffler, then whipped it across his dried and cracking lips.

The driveway was blurred by windblown and drifted snow. If it were not for the lights from the house backlighting an occasional landmark boulder or tree, and his own sense of direction, he might easily have wandered off the driveway. There was no evidence of Torie's passage, the tread marks in the new-thawed earth erased by the newer fall of snow.

Around the first bend in the driveway, he sighted the Cadillac, fetched up against a battered oak at the second sharper bend. It had been claimed by snow and darkness that blurred its hard machine edges. In the spill of the house lights the snow that frosted it twinkled as coldly as distant stars. Its glossy blackness was a denser shadow in the night, a black hole in space through which he might be drawn into the mystery of itself.

It was easy to see what had happened. She had skidded, lost control of the skid, and slued into the ditch to be stopped by the tree, an old adversary of hers. Three of the Cadillac's wheels were up to the top of their hubcaps in drifted snow. Like a matron's rump, the tail end of the car hung over the far edge of the driveway. The fourth wheel, right side rear, was out of contact with terra firma by a good foot.

The oak leaned wearily over the hood. It looked as if this time it had sustained a mortal injury in the undeclared war with Torie-driven Cadillacs. Tree and car together had the stance of a pair of winos supporting each other along some skid row Stations of the Cross.

Leaving the basket in a snowdrift, Joe Nevers groped his way along the high right side of the Cadillac. The old dinosaur shivered and groaned when he leaned full weight into it and pushed down. He tried to peer into the car but the opaque windows only reflected his face as a blurred ghost. The fingers of his gloves stuck to the lacy ice that had formed on the glass and chrome. The first door he tried, the right side rear, was frozen shut. But the front passenger door had been left not quite closed, and was now not as solidly frozen as the other.

Inspecting the interior with a quick pass of his butane lighter, he found it empty even of bottles. The key was still in the ignition, turned to on. The shift was in drive, the lights, heater, and defroster lifeless but still at on. Torie had simply crawled out and abandoned the bitch. The drain on her battery had surely killed her beyond immediate resurrection. She would need a jumping from his truck, at least, and no guarantee that would work.

No doubt the key was frozen in the ignition. Come morning he would free it with the lighter and bring the truck down the hill to jump her. For now she could be left; there was less likelihood of anyone stealing a dead car than his truck. Even after he hauled her out of the ditch, there was no way Torie would be driving her back to Falmouth Sunday night. Not with the battery deader than last Fourth of July's fireworks, the hood crumpled, the grill shattered, and the headlights smashed. That was only the damage that showed.

She would have to let him ferry her back. Once there, he could round up the necessary parts and have Reuben Styles cobble the Cadillac back together. If it weren't for the fact that Torie had a standing order with the used parts dealers in town for everything and anything from this make and year, the old heap of bones might never run again, for the last of her kind had rolled out of the showrooms a decade ago. Indeed, so many of her parts had been replaced by Reuben and other mechanics that it could be argued the original Cadillac had long since ceased to exist. What Torie had slammed into the abused oak was a mechanical

Frankenstein's monster, created from the used parts of dead cars.

Abandoning the patchwork Cadillac to the right and its storms, Joe Nevers reclaimed his pie basket and set off down the hill. He stomped onto the back porch feeling much better than he had any right, considering what a bitch of a job it was going to be to unditch the car, come morning. Assuming he didn't give himself a heart attack getting her out, it would be a long day. A long drive, after the car was out, and no guarantee that Torie would be any more tractable than usual.

The surprise was the mild excitement he felt at the thought of seeing Torie's place in Falmouth again. It would only be his fifth time there, and none of the previous visits counted among his most cherished memories, though one was among the most enduring.

The first occasion had been Bert Christopher's funeral, at a church in Falmouth in 1932, which he had attended with his father. Afterward there had been a reception at the house. With the crowd and the attendant confusion, he had come away with only a hazy impression of a fine stone pile, massive and romantic. Meaning unheatable. Years later, he came again, uninvited, with Marion, his first wife. It had been a mistake, not an unforgivable one, but still a mistake; he had long since encapsulated the memory. And the third and fourth times were for the funerals of Guy and his mother Fanny, separated by only a few months.

At the last, Torie had seen him to the truck. He could tell the degree of her drunkenness by the straightness of her spine; the further gone she was, the more she seemed to brace herself against it. She was like a ramrod that day, one hand falling lightly on his forearm, as they stood next to his truck.

"Now don't wait for somebody else to die before you come again, Joe Nevers," she said severely, and tipped him a slow outrageous wink that must have been visible to the people spilling out of the big house behind them.

She had such a talent for finding his weak spots, and in those days he was still trying to hide them from her. And she was still looking for them. It was not shock that made him pat her arm and turn away but pain and the fear of hers. In time he had come to think that was the moment he most failed her.

He knocked at the back door and waited patiently for half a minute. It was unlocked, he knew. In all the years he had known her, he had never known Torie to lock a door. It was a surety she would not answer. If she heard his knock, she would know it was him. He could not recall when she had stopped answering his knock, but it was a long time ago anyway. He might just as well walk in unannounced. But it was not in him to do such a thing. This was not his house. If its walls had fallen, leaving only the door standing in its frame, he would still have knocked. A single breach of that rule had been enough for him to take the lesson. Having given Torie the option of answering if she so desired, then and only then would he let himself in.

Once inside, most of the first floor was visible to him at a glance. As he stood in the hall that led leftward to Fanny's old rooms, a bedroom and bath that formed its own small wing, and rightward to the master bedroom and the stair spiraling through the upper stories of the house, Joe Nevers could look straight past the galley kitchen into the outsized multistoried room that was most of the first floor, the sitting room.

There he saw what he had just left, through the far wall of the room, all glass, meant to open the interior of the house to the light, the lake and the mountains. Instead it was like the mouth of a tunnel leading directly into the stormy night. Into the frame of light it

cast into the dark, a white confetti of snow spilled out
of the dense black of the night, piling up on the deck,
spitting against the glass. The cold outside leeched the
heat in the house through the glass almost as quickly
as it was generated by the electric radiators. The glass
had begun to frost on the inside.

At the table in front of the glass wall, Torie worked
a jigsaw puzzle. Cocooned in layers of clothing, out-
door and in, she exposed only her small white face
and waxen hands to the cold. She had turned her
mink coat inside out, so the gray satin lining, glimmer-
ing in the electric light, was outside. The fur was a
silvery fringe at hem, cuff, and collar. Surprisingly the
effect was not ludicrous at all, only eccentric and
romantic, somehow foreign and antique, as if the coat
were the exotic outer garment of some exiled Russian
czarina.

When Joe Nevers spoke to her, she neither answered
nor looked up, as though she were deaf. She wasn't;
she heard as well as anyone and better than some. It
was only Joe Nevers she couldn't hear, when she was
drinking.

Her hands, livid in the cold, moved slowly and
painfully over the pieces of the jigsaw puzzle she was
working as if she were also blind, trusting to her sense
of touch to identify the mysterious fragments and how
they fitted together. She found the bottle of bourbon at
her right hand in the same fashion, as if by memory of
a world no longer seen but guessed at with uncanny
accuracy.

So as not to track in the snow, Joe Nevers took off
his boots and jacket, though he felt at once the cold,
the marrow-deep chill of unlived-in space. The base-
board radiators, still set at the minimal level necessary
to keep the pipes from freezing, could not penetrate it.
Leaving his basket in the kitchen, he turned up the

thermostats and then built a fire in the old tiled stove in the sitting room, filled the kettle with bottled water stored under the sink, and put it on to boil.

In the master bedroom's smaller Jötel, he built a second fire. The quilted spread was crumpled on the unturned bed. Evidently, Torie had rolled herself up in it the night before.

The bed linen, made up by Ruby Parks after Torie's last visit—he struggled to recall just when that was—had long since grown musty. He stopped to strip and remake the bed with comparatively fresher linen from the closet. As he shook out the top sheet, it came to him; it had been ten months. How the time had slipped by him; he was getting old. Of course, she had not come at all the past summer, not since June. Had to be, since he had made wild strawberry jam for her. She had thrown it at him, in the jelly glass. About what he might have expected. She came and went as she pleased. There was no reason for her to account for her comings and goings to him.

It was his own failure to notice, one more evidence of decline, that bothered him. He had been uneasy, the way he was in '79/'80, the winter without snow. It wasn't until the middle of the following winter that he looked out of his bedroom window and felt the change, not in the world, but in himself.

New snow overlaid the accumulation of half a dozen previous snows on the back fields, and the lake and mountains dazzled in the distance. The day outside was new and bright. When he cracked the window an inch or two, the air was sweet-smelling, almost balmy, the way it often is after heavy snow, At that instant, he felt the wholeness of the world and his part in it. Only then did he understand how disturbed he had been by the inexplicable disruption of the natural cycle, the winter previous. When he heard from George Fogg that Torie was back, he felt much the same thing, a sudden surge of good cheer that he could now identify as relief from that shapeless unease.

There was no more use fretting after Torie than after the weather. The weather he had learned to feel in his bones and through his skin, but Torie had always remained unpredictable. She changed and changed again; he had never established if and how her seasons cycled.

Forgotten too was when and how the woman, as well as her property, came into his charge. Or why his stewardship was so narrowly defined: only here, on the Ridge, not anywhere else, and only to prevent her outright killing herself while laid up with a bottle.

It was a game she played with him, and like many another of the alcoholics he had known, she was endlessly inventive in her self-destruction. She never called to say she was coming. The game required he discover her, like a fateful secret, while on his rounds. Or by word of mouth from some local who had seen her pass. It was helpful of her to have bashed hell out of George Fogg's Jeep Friday evening, or he might not have known she was at the house until he found her frozen stiff or near to it, crouched over one of her jigsaw puzzles or curled up on her bed.

He had his rules too. He had forbidden her to light the fires, knowing she would be too far gone most of the time to remember to turn up the thermostats for the electric heat. It was a calculated risk that she would die of exposure or pick up a pneumonia bug while run down from a diet of Wild Turkey. By keeping an eye out for her and then nursing her through the weekend, he was pretty sure to prevent that. If she lit the house up, there would be no saving her; in that empty, isolated place, by the time the fire was reported, it would be too late for her.

That was not something he wanted ever to go through again.

SUMMER OF '56 was dry as a dust pussy under the bed.
Aside from supervising grass fires, the members of the
Nodd's Ridge Volunteer Fire Department had done
little besides organize the annual chicken barbecue at
the Community Church and speculate about the danger of forest fire come fall. The fires of '47 were branded
in the memories of most of the volunteers; it would be
a long time yet before the destruction of Mount Desert
Island on the coast, and most of York County, which
bordered Sabbatos County only forty miles south of
Nodd's Ridge, would fade to the stuff of legend. Such
nervous talk was thoroughly dampened when fall
brought hurricanes to the coast, felt inland as heavy
rain and violent wind that soaked the woods to a
nicety.

When the alarm was rung at 3:40 of a Saturday
morning in November, Joe Nevers was probably the
only volunteer awake. Newly divorced, he had fallen
into the habit of reading into the small hours as an
excuse not to go to bed. But *Peyton Place,* circulating
discreetly among the adult patrons of the public library,
was more disturbing than distracting. He was relieved
to throw it down and go for his mackinaw and cap.

He had exchanged those for a steel fireman's helmet
and one of the yellow rubberized canvas coats the
company had picked up secondhand from the Lewis-

ton Fire Department in '48, the year the voters suddenly got generous on the subject of fire fighting, and
was backing the hook and ladder out of the fire barn
when Pete Buck's pickup squealed up in a cloud of
dust. Because Pete was chief that year, he had taken
the call from the forest ranger at the Thugless Mountain lookout. Pete was still trying to button his beer
belly into his shirt when he heaved himself out of the
pickup's cab.

"Christafa place," he shouted at Joe Nevers, and
headed for the pumper, in the fire barn, at a trot.

The volunteers had trucked down that miserable
dirt road within seven minutes, hardly a quarter of an
hour from the time Pete took the ranger's call and
raised the alarm, but all their haste was to no good,
nothing new. The old Christopher place was in flames
to its turrets. Any fool could see it was a goner, and so
was anyone unlucky enough to be inside it. This time
of year, it should have been empty. But there was a fat
shiny new Lincoln Continental squatting in the driveway that didn't get there by itself.

Joe Nevers was off the truck before it stopped moving,
rushing the back door though the back porch roof over
it was burning merry hell. As he reached for the handle of the storm door, a sudden flurry of fragments like
fiery snowflakes whirled down from the porch ceiling
to singe his eyebrows and blister his face. Instinctively
fending them off, he faltered just long enough to give
Pete Buck's brother Freeman a chance to haul him
back. Freeman locked his arms around Joe Nevers from
behind and hauled him with all his might toward the
steps. Completely overpowered by the larger man, Joe
Nevers lost his balance and fell backwards onto
Freeman. The two men sprawled "arse over teakettle,"
as Freeman put it later, down the steps. No sooner had
Joe Nevers arrived nose first at the bottom step with

Freeman, who weighed two-fifty and stood six-five in his home-knitted woollen socks, on top of him than the porch roof gave way with a frightening roar. He and Freeman had to roll like a couple of logs down a muddy riverbank to get out of its way.

Hours later, and not so drunk as he needed to be, Joe Nevers told Pete Buck he didn't know what had possessed him. It was entirely his own fault that he almost got Freeman and himself killed.

Pete, far drunker than he needed to be but not so drunk as he wanted to be, solemnly drowned the stub of his Camel in the dregs at the bottom of his bottle of Narragansett, stared at Joe Nevers with red-rimmed, watery eyes, and observed sagely, "You was shitass lucky, Joe. Shitass lucky."

Joe Nevers gave consent to Pete's verdict with his silence. He would suffer the pain of his blisters and the heavy-handed wit of the town in the same way, keeping in mind the jokes might just as easily have been told with less amiability at Freeman's funeral, or his own. So ashamed was Joe Nevers of having caused another man to risk his life for him on a fool's errand, he volunteered for the grisly task of helping Doc McAvoy wrap the charred body of the victim so it could be taken from the scene for autopsy. It was not the first corpse Joe Nevers had to do with, nor the last, but it was assuredly the worst.

It seemed likely to him that it was the price of his folly, the memory that was like a rotting chicken hung round the neck of a chicken-killing dog to cure it of the vice. As well as he remembered his mother and how it felt to be choking to death on the front porch of the old house whenever he stood on the deck that had replaced it, so he was cursed whenever he laid his hand to the handle of the back door of the new house to remember the fire and the awful corpse that had been in life the man he knew as Dana Bartlett.

The face came to him always both living and dead, like the two-faced dolls the grandmothers of Nodd's Ridge made for their granddaughters, that showed on one side the innocent face of Red Riding Hood and on the other, hidden in her red hood, the face of the wolf in Grandmother's lace-trimmed night cap. It was smoke inhalation that killed Dana Bartlett, but the fire had destroyed his handsome face and reduced him to a sexless effigy, curled like some monstrous fetus in mockery of life's beginning.

It was not the wretchedness of the man's death that made a nine-day wonder on the Ridge, but the mystery that surrounded it like acrid smoke. The first and natural assumption of the volunteer firemen was that the remains were Guy or his wife Torie. But when Joe Nevers insisted to Pete Buck that the papers in the glove box of the Connie in the driveway be examined, Pete was astonished to find them in the name of Dana Bartlett.

Pete scratched his flattop with one ash-smeared thumb. "Here I was, just thinking it was a friggin' shame Guy wasn't going to be driving this nice new car nowheres, and it looks like Dana's the poor son of a bitch went to hell in it. What t'hell do you s'pose he was doin' here?"

The question was no more than a straight line on Pete's part, and crude suggestions followed it at once. Everyone knew Dana liked the ladies and they liked him. It was rumored he found his father's summer house, not half a mile away, handy in the off-season. That didn't exactly explain why it was the Christophers' place he burned down, instead of his father's, but it pointed the way. Right there among the unshaven, red-eyed firemen sifting through the ashes the first nudging elbow accompanied the first low-voiced witticism about how old Dana had finally gotten hot enough to set his pants afire. It was repeated to Roscoe Needham by the first fireman through the door when Roscoe opened the diner at six o'clock, and Roscoe repeated it to everyone who came in, all the livelong day, until closing time. By then, everyone in town had heard it and repeated it to someone else.

A phone call to the Christophers' number in Falmouth by Joe Nevers quickly established that it was indeed Dana who had parked his new car at the old summer house.

Guy Christopher took on the task of notifying Dana's widow, Jeannie, who thought he was out hunting with Guy. And Guy identified the body, which might be why it was he and not Jeannie who cried at Dana's funeral.

It was taken for granted, before Joe Nevers said so at the coroner's hearing, that Dana Bartlett, a lifelong friend and near neighbor of the Christophers, knew where the spare keys to the summer house were hidden. But Joe Nevers could not say, nor could anyone else, what Dana Bartlett was doing drunk and smoking, then passed out, and finally deader than Moses and all the Israelites and Pharoahs, in the master bedroom of the Christophers' summer house. Who the woman was— and that there was a woman was also taken for granted— and why she didn't stick around to die with Dana remained a mystery, though there was plenty of libelous speculation around the bullshit table where the old farts gathered in Roscoe Needham's diner. So Dana Bartlett's life and death were reduced to a snicker in the memory of Nodd's Ridge, soon all but forgotten, with the memory of the Victorian gingerbread of the Christophers' summer house that died with him.

Dana Bartlett came to mind more than Joe Nevers

liked. It might be that he was the last, or nearly the last person, to still remember there ever had been a Dana Bartlett. Lately, though, when he took out his memories of Dana, he did not think about those memories so much as hold them there in his mind like an old dish on an oilcloth covered table in a morning sunbeam. He thought instead: *Well, he would be as old as I am now, no, a few years less, he would be close to seventy*. There was no need to think beyond that; it was a given that if Dana Bartlett had lived out his natural span, he might be close to dead now anyway.

If anyone had troubled to ask him, Joe Nevers would have said, "Ghosts? 'Course I believe in ghosts. I am one." And laughed.

Not just because everything was okay, but because it was more than a joke to him. He often felt more ghost than not, for the people and things and very often places most real to him were more and more ghosts.

"*Ayuh*," he might have said. "*Even houses have ghosts*."

When he stood on Torie's deck that looked over the water to the hills, he stood on the ghost of Fanny's front porch, and felt the arms of his mother snatching him back from the choking vise of death. When he knocked, gently and politely, at Torie's back door, he reached again for the black iron handle of the old mansion's back storm door, though it was ashes within an hour of his reaching for it, and the ashes windstrewn across the lake decades ago. All because, he supposed, he had grown old in the place where he was born.

There were in his basket several packets of loose tea that he did up for himself out of small brown paper bags of the size he had filled years ago in his father's store with penny candy. All he had to do was rip the corner off, to funnel the tea leaves neatly into a fresh-rinsed pot, just enough for one good-sized pot with not a leaf of waste, once he had added the boiling water from the kettle.

While the tea brewed he stood behind Torie, watching her hands move with disturbing surety over the pieces of the puzzle. They sought and found and sought and found again, though slowly, and so mechanically they might have been manipulated by some unseen, heartless puppeteer. Joe Nevers could not help watching. At last he forced himself to break her concentration.

"How 'bout a cup of tea to warm your hands, Missus?"

Torie started, a little more than he believed. As she rolled her eyes in exaggerated fright, her right hand wavered once and struck the bottle on the table. It tipped delicately as if it too were slowed by the cold, and pitched to the floor where it shattered and spattered in as great a mess as it could make.

She did not flinch from it any more than he did. There was nothing new about broken bottles for either of them. She stared at it blindly.

"Shit," she said.

Joe Nevers sighed. "Don't touch it. I'll clean it up." No sooner had he turned his back on her to fetch what he needed from the kitchen than she began to move, slowly and carefully, as if she too might fall and break. The wooden legs of her chair, squeaking over the waxed wood of the floor, betrayed her and she pushed away from the table.

Joe Nevers did not look back but repeated his order. "Don't touch it now. Let me clean it up."

As if she had not heard a word he said, she hunkered down at the edge of the mess and began to pick up the pieces of the bourbon bottle with the same blind certainty with which she puzzled, as if she had in mind to put the bottle back together, and then perhaps its contents, drop by golden drop, molecule by molecule. The hem of the blue mink coat dipped into the puddle and darkened. Though her wool trousers were buttoned around her boots at the ankle, there was so much slack in them that the cloth ballooned and dipped also into liquor, along with the fringe of the cashmere scarf wound round her throat.

Joe Nevers returned from his rummage in the broom closet armed with mop, pail, and sponge.

"God bless it, Missus," he said without anger, standing over her, "I said I'd clean it up."

Torie looked up at him, her wide eyes narrowing, full lower lip pouting. As she glared at him, her hands still moved restlessly over the shards. All at once she flinched and cried out, clutching the one hand with the other. Blood leaked between her fingers. A few drops dappled the surface of the glistening alcoholic puddle on the floor, but their essential redness was instantly absorbed and lost.

Stooping slightly, as if to bow, Joe Nevers snatched a handkerchief from his breast pocket and wrapped it with a single economic gesture around both her hands at once. The force of his tightening it brought her uncertainly to her feet. The fringe of her scarf dripped golden drops of bourbon, spotting the already creased and wrinkled legs of her trousers.

Without a word, he began to pry her hands apart. She resisted as perversely as she had resisted his binding them. When he had separated them, to see how deeply slashed was the thumb mount of her left palm, he shook his head. He led her, dragging her feet, to the kitchen, where he took a first aid kit down from the cupboard. With boiled water from the kettle he washed the cut, disinfected it and then bandaged it with a severe care. She suffered his attentions in unfocused silence, staring at him occasionally as if she were trying to remember who he was.

Done, Joe Nevers grunted his satisfaction with the job and told her, "Go sit by the fire now and warm up. Your hands are like ice."

Instead she went directly to another of the kitchen cupboards to take down, one-handed, a new bottle of Wild Turkey. Clenching the hurt hand against her chest, she curled up on the sofa in front of the stove. To keep even an unreliable grip on the bottle, she had to prop it against the damaged, fisted hand, in the lap folds of her inside-out fur coat. After loosening the cap with her unhurt shaky right, she pulled out the plastic-capped cork with her teeth and spat it away. She rewarded herself with a single sip, and then, worn out with the struggle, closed her eyes and relaxed into the pillows of the sofa.

To Joe Nevers, peeking at her as he cleaned up the spill, she seemed too fragile for everyday existence. She rested in her layered clothing as lightly as a Christmas ornament in tissue. Her face was partially hidden from him in the hood formed by the huge cowl neck of her sweater, under her coat. One hand, as transparent as a grease spot on a piece of white paper, was tight around the bottle. Her scarf had slipped over the slippery shoulders of the satin lining of the coat to her elbows, where it seemed to bind her. The toes of her red leather boots peeped out from under the draped folds of the voluminous gray trousers and the fur-trimmed, silvery lining of the coat. It was easy to imagine her as made of ice, melting away so near to the fire, so soon there would be only the untidy heap of clothing upon the sofa pillows.

It was an instant of fancy that made him shake his head at himself. Such fancies were for women and children. A man's thoughts had ought to be useful ones.

Now Torie Christopher was full of fancies, and a lot of good they had done her. He could not help but think his neighbors on the Ridge were mostly right to suspect these flighty women with too much money, too much book-learning, and too little sense. A woman best cultivate strength of body and mind, and a sense of her honor.

No one much held it against Torie, though; her sins, it was conceded, were bought and paid for. More to the point, she was not one of them, and the Ridge dwellers never treated outsiders with any great degree of seriousness. It was not entirely cut and dried, of course. It counted with the Ridge folk that the Christophers had spent their summers thereabouts for generations. Torie was not quite a Christopher, not a real one, having married into the family, but she was granted a certain significance and latitude not given the newcomers or daytrippers. It could not be expected that anyone would ever really forget she was from away, and it did not matter that away was only one hundred and fifty miles northeast in the same state. It was far enough.

But when her husband Guy died, the obituaries in the Portland papers, and the Boston papers too, and a cutting from the *New York Times* that Joe Nevers' sister Gussie sent him from Florida, all called the dead man Victoria Christopher's husband, right at the top, instead of just he was survived by, somewhere in the text of the piece. Joe Nevers thought he might be the only one on the Ridge to notice, and had clipped the obituaries and tucked them away in his album, like clues to some mystery he had not yet deciphered.

Whoever would have thought she might be Somebody?

AT FIRST GLANCE, he took the kid on the other side of the
screen door for a connection of Fanny Christopher's
live-in cook, Beulah Clark. Beulah was a rangy harri-
dan in her sixties who traded on her notable skills as a
cook to terrorize the local girls hired for the season.
Beulah presumed much and got away with it; she
frequently exercised what she considered to be her
privilege as a family retainer to inject her lurid opinions into the Christophers' family conversations, where
they were always received with great courtesy and just
as reliably discounted in a genteel way by Fanny.
Though Beulah counted herself a cosmopolite on the
strength of the twice-yearly migrations from one Christopher house to the other, she came from an isolated,
inbred little settlement on the vast upcountry wilderness. Over the seventeen years she had ruled Fanny
Christopher's kitchens, she had entertained an endless
parade of female relations, who typically arrived unannounced and uninvited, to stay a week or two underfoot and eat prodigiously, bunking with Beulah in her
two-room apartment over the garage. Though the faces
bore the unmistakable stamp of family likeness, the
exact degree and nature of kinship to Beulah was
invariably too complex to grasp. At any rate, none of
the visiting Clark females was worth a damn, being
neither competent nor decorative, but settled their

skinny hams upon kitchen stools and did the heavy looking on, smoking like forest fires and nodding wisely in agreement with Beulah's nonstop rants, perhaps because their mouths were usually full.

So it was natural when he did not recognize the girl who answered his knock, the screen veiling her face, as local, he took her for one of Beulah's cousins or nieces. In the instant it took her to shift awkwardly from one foot to the other, as she stared at him as boldly as a little child, he changed his mind.

"Name's Joe Nevers," he said, taking off his cap. "Is Missus Christopher in?"

She flashed him a smile as quick as light on the water and pushed open the door to admit him.

Beulah peered over her bifocals at him, and interrupted her bawling a grocery order into the speaker of the old crank phone long enough to catch her breath and berate him.

"Joe Nevers! It's about gee dee time! We've been waiting on you all the livelong morning."

No doubt Beulah rose with the sun, being advanced in years and a country woman to boot, and her day was as long as his, but it was still barely nine in the morning, and the breakfast dishes only just cleared away. He had no doubt if he had presented himself any sooner, she'd have faulted him for lack of consideration. And it was Fanny who had sent for him, regardless of Beulah's royal We. Clearly he had timed his arrival inopportunely, when Beulah could not bear to tear herself away from the hard time she was giving the grocer's boy.

"Morning, Beulah," Joe Nevers said.

She shook her head at him in disgust. It was a principal tenet of her life that all men were useless, but one with a grin on his face drove her into a frenzy. She took a hasty suck at a cigarette that was mostly attenuated ash and dropped it into a lard can. Cheated of the chance to put Joe Nevers in his place, she settled for being rude. She turned her back on him to address the phone.

"Speak up, you gee dee fool!" she shouted into the handset, and glared all around by way of warning not to interrupt her again with minor matters.

Joe Nevers took another look at the girl. She stood beside him, hands clasped behind her, still as a cat on a railing. Not hungry, but keeping a sharp eye on things.

She was no Clark; she was about as different from Beulah and her clan as could be. The Clarks ran to height and stringiness, sallow complexions and pitch-black hair that hinted an Indian in the woodpile. This girl was small, shorter than Beulah by at least a foot, and as pale as a ghost in a blizzard. Her hair was a glory, the color of sherry wine, and wild to escape her ponytail. Her eyes were that hazel that suits itself; in Beulah's cigarette-smoky kitchen, they had gone squirrel gray. Her face was round with baby fat; she wore a man's shirt, too large, with the sleeves rolled to the elbows, and shirttails out, to disguise adolescent plumpness, over blue jeans rolled at the cuff. And she was barefoot.

Suddenly she moved toward the door that led to the parlor. He saw his mistake then. She moved too lightly to be a chubby teenager, and too regally to be anything but pregnant.

He followed her through the parlor, where the curtains were drawn to keep the morning sun from fading the furnishings, to the sun porch where Fanny customarily spent her summer mornings. He wondered if Fanny were now taking in unwed teenage mothers. It was the sort of thing she might do. There was a lot of talk since the war about the problem of unmarried pregnant teenagers. But this girl went barefoot as if she owned the place. Even the tangle of red hair caught in an elastic band seemed, in its absurd vulnerability, to assert her right to be in this place.

Fanny looked up expectantly from her place in a wicker rocking chair. She must have heard Beulah take his name.

The girl hung her toes over the step down into the porch and leaned into the room like a figurehead on a clipper ship.

"Name's Joe Nevahs," she recited, mocking him.

"Well, of course it is," Fanny said, and laid aside her needlework to take his hand in both of hers and squeeze it. "How are you, Joe Nevers, and how is Marion?"

"Can't complain," he said, "and Marion's fine."

Just, he did not say, not so fine as she'd like to be.

"Yourself?" he asked.

Fanny shook her head and sighed. "The same, the same, Joe. Still old and useless. But never mind. Come sit with me and tell me, what are we going to do about that old dock? Mend it again, or build anew?"

"Well," Joe Nevers said, sitting down as bid. Leaning forward, his cap clutched in one hand, he paused to give due consideration to Fanny's options.

"Mother," the girl said, "would you like me to ask Beulah for some tea for you and Joe Nevers?"

Fanny raised her eyebrows at him. He nodded yes. She smiled at him as if he were a very small boy again and had just done something clever.

"Oh, do that, Torie dear. And then sit down. You make me tired, flitting about."

The girl smiled at Fanny, and then, damned if she didn't flit away, though how she managed to be so light of foot when her belly was so swole up, he did not know. It came to him as he looked at the doorway she had been standing in, that she was one of those people whose absence amounted to an actual emptiness, a place abandoned.

Fanny fixed a severe look on her grandmotherly features. "That baby'll slow her down," she remarked sagely.

He agreed; he supposed it would.

The girl had called Fanny mother. She must be Guy's wife, whose name had long since escaped him. Victoria. "Torie," Fanny called her. Not a diminutive form he had ever heard before.

Joe Nevers and his wife had missed the wedding. Marion had been fit to be tied. His father had taken such a long time dying. Already last fall.

Though Guy had come to the lake once or twice the previous summer to see his mother, he had not brought his fiancée. Off gallivanting, Joe Nevers had heard. Girl had gone off to New Mexico or some such place to look at Indian relics. Funny sort of engagement. Then the young people had married in September and honeymooned a month in the Mediterranean. That at least was a success, if the girl's belly was any evidence. That was the way it went, old man dying, young folks marrying, a new baby. He felt something like gratitude toward the girl and young Guy for continuing the natural cycle.

He tried to remember what he knew of the girl, precious little. From upcountry, though the civilized part. Father a prodigiously successful contractor. But Joe Nevers had an idea she was supposed to be a bit long in the tooth. This girl had been snatched from the cradle. Guy was thirty-five if he was a day, even if Joe Nevers still thought of him as barely out of short pants. Fanny had been relieved to marry him off, and said so.

"That young lady," Joe Nevers asked Fanny, "she your daughter-in-law?"

"Why, 'course she is!" Fanny exclaimed. She leaned over to slap his knee playfully. "You must think I've gone soft in the head. I clean forgot you couldn't come to the wedding. Dear Will. So you've never met her. Well, I'll remedy that. I tell you, I can't remember what I had for breakfast anymore. This business of getting old is hard, Joe Nevers." The old lady shook her head. "Mind you, I'm glad to be having a grand-child."

Be glad to have a child a'tall. But Joe Nevers would never say that aloud, not to Fanny, who fretted over him as if he were a son of hers, and certainly not to Marion.

Fanny rambled on: about the winter past, the people on the Ridge, the summer residents arriving daily, telling stories he had heard a dozen times.

He ought to have been working. There was more than enough to do, more than hours in the day to do in, even in the long, long days of summer. But he sat a full hour with Fanny Christopher, mostly listening and sipping the tea the girl brought back. That was really why Fanny had sent for him. She was just back on the Ridge and wanted a winter's gossip from him. The ice-damaged dock was just an excuse; it was his business and she would go along with whatever he wanted to do about it.

After Fanny put them through introductions, the girl curled up on the porch swing. She was sewing small bright-colored scraps of cloth in patterns for a crazy quilt, and paid it strict attention. Fanny included her in the conversation, explaining who was who, and a good bit of why, what, and how. Joe Nevers peeked at Torie when he dared. She still looked too young to have a baby. And once when he looked, he caught her looking back. For an instant, her needle stilled, while she smiled a secret smile at him, and then she returned to her sewing.

His ears burnt. She had her ears open, that girl, and was gleaning information about the Ridge, stitching it all together in patterns, like the little scraps of cloth. He might's well be another rag to her to be placed where she pleased in her design. But he wasn't insulted, just a little embarrassed, as if she could see right through him. Sharp as her own needle, the way his sister Gussie had been as a girl.

The baby was born at the end of July, a boy named Thomas after Torie's brother. Joe Nevers replaced the old dock, which was still there when the old house burned five years later. Summer of '51 passed.

At Christmastide, Fanny fell victim to a stroke that left her dependent on a walker or a wheelchair, and childish. She came to confuse her son Guy with her late husband, and the baby Tommy with the infant Guy. That was understandable. More curiously, she often took Torie for Joe Nevers' mother Josephine, dead three decades, long enough to be forgotten by all but a few. But Fanny knew Beulah Clark, and Joe Nevers' sister Gussie, and Joe Nevers himself, when they visited her both in the hospital in Portland and at the summer house, for the remaining seasons of her life, which were, God giving as well as taking away, many.

He delved into his basket. A quart mason jar of his own beef stew went into a pot on the back of the stove to warm slowly. The bread he unbagged and wrapped in foil to stow in the warming oven. There were several small plastic bags of salad materials, enough for two meals, and a small jar of vinegar and oil that he set aside for the moment when he was ready to dish up.

Joe Nevers liked what he called a pretty dish of salad but which was really anything remotely vegetable that he found in his root cellar or his refrigerator plus anything that could stand a dash of vinegar and still be edible. With his nightly glass of tepid water and lemon juice, he believed as much as he believed anything that a daily dose of salad kept him regular. He was the only man of his age or near on the whole of Nodd's Ridge who lived on his lonesome, either divorced, widowed, or inveterate bachelor, who could make such a claim. It wasn't in him to be actually smug about anything much, especially since it could be argued (and had) that heredity had merely blessed him with superior works, but the maintenance of what he thought of as his regular habit was one of the few things about which he would allow, at age seventy-three, he had learned something worth knowing.

Leaving out packets of salt, pepper, and butter, and a can of sardines the mice might chew until they needed dentures and still go away hungry, he emptied the rest of his basket into the small refrigerator that was keeping cold only some desiccated ice, another half gallon of bottled water, and a plastic polar bear full of baking soda that didn't stop it from smelling stale. When he had tucked in half a dozen fresh eggs from his own hens, a can of frozen orange juice to reconstitute, a package of Parker House rolls from his freezer, a small jar of blueberry jam, a half pound of bacon, a large ruby grapefruit, three late McIntosh apples from his own trees, half a pound of Vermont cheddar, a pint jar of home-baked beans, a half dozen sausages, and a packet of dried milk, there was no room for anything else.

When there was no more to fuss about in the kitchen, he glanced curiously into the cupboard where Torie stashed her booze. What he saw, or rather didn't see there, gave him pause. It was her habit to stock three bottles for a weekend, double what she would need, small as she was, to stay soused from Friday afternoon to early Sunday morning. Of that brace of Wild Turkey, one full bottle remained, its seal unbroken. The one she cradled against her, as a kid might cling to a dolly or a teddy bear, as she dozed by the fire, was just begun, less a single sip. The one he had cleaned up was nearly full too, and if he hadn't just mopped a good half the floor to account for it, he might have doubted his own eyes, which he did not. He still wore glasses only for reading. He checked the trash cans in all the rooms on the first floor for empties and found none. There was no need to go further; that was it.

Torie never went above the first floor; hadn't in donkey's years. He might have hidden a still, or a greenhouse full of marijuana, a ton of opium or ten small boys to torture in the upper rooms, and she'd never have known. Ruby Parks would though, for she came in once a month or after Torie's visits to dust and change the linen whether it needed it or not. To be sure, none of the beds except Torie's had been slept in in years. He wondered if Ruby ever felt any of what he felt when he went upstairs. He dared not ask for fear that Ruby might then wonder, as he did, if Joe Nevers was going soft in the head. The upstairs was his secret.

Downstairs was very different. The rooms were full of Torie's other life as an archaeologist, decorated with the exotica of her travels and studies, which reminded him constantly how far away she had been and he had not. Ruby called it "Torie's junk," but treated it with the awe appropriate to the relics of saints: shards of ancient pottery, shining bits of gold and glass and bone, mysterious stones, and fragments of cloth framed under glass, the evidence of lives lived long ago and far away. Joe Nevers thought none the less of Ruby for that superstitious reverence; he understood the power of years to render ordinary objects holy. He willingly granted "Torie's junk" the honor of its accumulated years but chose not to examine any of it too closely, for if it was true that the years might give, it was also true they might take away, and truer still that there are things best left undisturbed.

He wandered restless through the downstairs, turning off unnecessary lights. The shallow glass boxes that displayed Torie's discoveries were lit from within, and he left them so, for the effect. In the dark, the boxes seemed made of light, and their contents—what he knew to be the rubbish of civilizations he could hardly imagine—seemed so solid and indestructible that for the first time ever he felt an urge to touch them: to judge their density with his own ephemeral flesh. But the glass kept them and their revelations from him as surely as the layers of volcanic mud or ash or peat bog or desiccating desert sand that had heretofore preserved them from decay.

Joe Nevers had never been afraid of empty houses, had in fact a certain sympathy with them. But things had happened to him in this one that he did not fully understand and suspected he never would. Most recently, he had stopped there more often than he strictly needed. The thought occurred to him then, and he embraced it with a tremor of relief, that he had unconsciously been aware of Torie's long absence, and it was this that had drawn him to the house, as if he could make her return by being there.

But the thing of it was, he rarely needed to enter the house. Every other day or three, he rattled the doors to make sure they were still locked, and walked around the house looking for cracked or broken windows. If he found none, and the light that was rigged to warn him the temperature inside had fallen below freezing did not show, well then, he could be on his way in good conscience. Periodically he paid a longer visit, to replace a burnt-out light bulb in the porch fixture that was always on, in case he happened by after dark, or to reset the mouse traps, or just to walk through with one eye peeled for mouse droppings, water stain on wall or ceiling, furniture too close to the electric radiators, or anything out of place, but really showing himself to the house as if to say *I'm here, you know me. For these few moments you are not empty or abandoned.*

Once, only weeks ago, he had paid just such a visit to the house. At first it seemed an ordinary walk-through. Then he noticed an odd smell and let his nose lead him to one of the glass boxes, this one in the bedroom. Inside, a fragment of bone, its convex curve unmistakably that of a human skull, rested on a piece of black velvet. He stared at it a long time. That was all that was in that box and nothing else, and no way for anything to get into it. He had found more than one dead mouse in a drained toilet bowl, or a deep laundry sink, and in other unintended traps, and thought at first it was one of those he smelled. Then he knew what he smelled, not decaying mouse, but more awfully, burned human flesh. As he realized it, it made him faint to know it.

Suddenly his heart thudded and his nostrils flared after extra oxygen; that stench came with it in a flood and he cringed from the very consciousness his body fought for. Raising his hands to fight it off, he backed out of the room.

The smell pursued him. It seemed to come from every one of the glass boxes, on every wall, in every downstairs room, and with it the smell of the house itself, stale and cold and empty as a robbed pyramid or the tomb of Jesus Christ.

He knew himself alone in this empty house. So far away from everyone else that if his heart, pounding so hard it felt like it was trying to escape the bony cage of his ribs, burst with the effort, no one would hear him cry out with the pain or fall upon the polished wooden floor. He might scratch the floor with his nails, trying to hold onto life, or drum his boots upon it in the last convulsion, but no one would hear him dying, and then it might be hours or days before his corpse was found. He knew just what that looked like and smelled like, for in his time and in the course of his duty he had found old men and middle-aged men, and young ones too, surprised by death in empty places.

His one thought was of escape. He stumbled upstairs to where he knew the sun still shone. And panting, fearful that he might be having a heart attack, laid himself down on the quilted spread of a child's bed. His hands fell upon the silken fur of the stuffed animals that waited open-eyed for children who did not come here anymore, and found their glassy eyes kindly, unjudging, forgiving. Teddy bears, Raggedy Anns, cats and dogs and baby dragons, they were evidence, on bright-colored scraps of cloth that Torie had long ago crafted into quilts, of other lives beyond recall. The sun fell on him as he lay there, warming his bones, blood and brain. His heart quieted; his lungs took the thick air evenly and calmly. He had no memory of falling asleep. Dreams germinated in the heat and flowered gorgeously.

Thirsty. Thirsty was the name of that summer. Joe Nevers was thirsty again. He mopped his forehead and his chest with a big old bandanna. Electing to go shirtless in the heat, he was soon patched stickily with pine resin from heaving branches, pruned the day before, into the back of the truck.

He sauntered to the lake and squatted on a rock to pull a can from the six he had stashed in the water between a couple of rocks. The beer was lovely and cold. He thought about sinking another six.

"Jesus, David!" Tommy yelled. He threw down his bat. And sneaked a glance at Joe Nevers to see how he was taking the swear.

Joe Nevers had seen the problem building, out of the corner of his eye.

On the lawn near the shore, where the ground levelled out, David was trying to pitch to Tommy. The technical problems were unsurmountable. David was too short in the arm and leg, and the ball was too big for his hand. He wasn't much more than five, coordinated enough to walk and ride a tricycle, and that was about it. But he was trying.

And Tommy, desperate for a pitcher, knowing how much David wanted to pitch for him, had tried too, but his patience was exhausted, as the ball sailed off into the lake. Again.

David's lower lip trembled, but he trotted stolidly to the water, kicked off his sneakers, and retrieved the ball.

"Forget it," Tommy said. "It just isn't gonna work."

"Maybe I can help," Joe Nevers said. "Toss me that ball, David."

The two boys looked at him. They looked at each other and broke into grins. David tossed him the ball.

Joe Nevers caught it one-handed. "You catch, David, then it'll be your bat."

Carrying his sneakers by the laces, David backed, looking over his shoulder, one step at a time, some distance behind Tommy. Then he stuffed his bare feet back into his sneakers without bothering with the complications of laces.

Tommy grinned at Joe Nevers. "Thanks, Joe."

In between pulls at the can of beer, then another, Joe Nevers pitched to one boy and then the other. He did it for the sight of Tommy's face looking for that ball. Tommy was good. He didn't miss many. David wore his short legs out running after the ones he did miss. And David even managed to hit a couple when it was his turn but what really made him grin was Joe Nevers ruffling his hair when they were done, and offering him a sip of beer.

Joe Nevers felt himself growing looser. The boys didn't seem to care. They took his cheerfulness for granted. Probably used to it, around their mom. He began to feel he could go on pitching balls to Tommy for eternity. The boy's face lifted to him, watching the ball coming to him. Crack!

When he wakened, sodden and muzzy, the day's shadow was upon him, the light thickening over the mountains.

The smell of disturbed graves was still there; he had grown used to it. He still shivered passing through it. More frightening now was how the upper rooms drew him, however much he resisted and promised himself he would not go. He whiled away many more afternoons there, dreaming, than he cared to account for. The upstairs ghosts were the ghosts of children, children he had known, who wanted only that he come and play with them as he once had. He told no one and looked in the mirror no more than was necessary to shave properly.

He could face the fear that all this meant he was failing in his mind; that was a dry fear, like the rattle of old leaves. But even the fear that the smell of death in the house triggered in him, skin-crawling, cold-sweat fear, could not keep him from the upper rooms. Mostly it was being addicted that worried him; he believed that a man whose wants have become needs must know himself to be lost. That all his ghosts were children kept the dreams themselves from being frightening. The dreams were old bones that must lie where they fell; their meaning waited on revelation.

Easier to work on the riddle of why Torie had drunk so little and yet seemed as drunken as ever he had seen her, short of passed out. He went to look at her; she had slipped into uneasy sleep. Despite the heavy clothing she was swaddled in and her proximity to the heat, there was no color in her face. A curl of hair had slipped out from under the cowl and he tucked it back, unthinking. Then he realized it was white, white as the snow piling up on the deck, and the cold crystal-lized under his collar bone in a hard, jagged lump like a snowball. Not wanting to wake her and have her cross with him for touching her, he pushed the cowl back a little way. The hair he exposed was as white as the first curl, as white as his own, though she was fourteen years younger. It was all quite short, not much longer than his own. When last he had seen her, nine months ago, her hair had been as long as ever it was, though it was true that silvery gray predominated over the warm glowing red of her youth. Now her hair was all but gone, and gone all white, and wispy as a dande-lion seedhead.

The shock of it took his breath away; he felt bruised as if he had taken a hard-driven snowball over his heart. A sudden rush of fear and panic coalesced into the irrational conviction that she was waking and would discover him there, looking at her, naked in some secret way as Susannah in the eyes of the evil-minded elders. Shamed, he covered his eyes so that he could not look upon her anymore or she see him, and stumbled away to the bedroom. Once there he could only look all around him in confusion, as if he did not know where he was or why he was there, a flood of questions breaking in his brain.

Had age played another nasty trick on him, causing him to misplace a whole great chunk of time, the way he sometimes forgot where last he had left his reading glasses or the book he was reading or his smokes? He groped his way to the bathroom to confront himself in the mirror.

Old he still was, no older than he had ever looked. It was a comfort to discover the same face, time-battered as it might be, that he had worn all his life. True enough that pink scalp showed through the thinness of his white hair, and that his skin had aged to a fine shade of parchment, much crumpled about the eyes and on the neck, but all his own good teeth were bared at him, skull-like where the gums had shrunken away, when he grinned at the glass. If the blue of his eyes had faded and the whites yellowed, there was still a twinkle in them. None of that mattered to him; as far as he was concerned, to be well preserved was a fate more suited to a pickle than a man. What mattered was that if he was no older, well then, she couldn't be either. He had not after all dropped a decade or two in the bog of failing memory.

It seemed now that the trouble must be with her. It was no less alarming. How could Torie have passed, in the space of ten months, from late middle age to old, nearly past him?

Perhaps she had had one of those fits women have, both young and old. Hadn't both his wives and his sister Gussie and every other woman he had ever known torn off on occasion to have their hair sheared off, kinked all over, colored or bleached, according to those

mass whimsies women called fashion? He had seen
more than one woman, growing older, who had decided to seize control of the process, denying or ad-
vancing it to suit herself. Likely that was it. Torie had
decided to have her hair all white and be done with it.

But other explanations insisted on being thought.
He could no longer run fast enough to outdistance
such uncomfortable thoughts.

Forgetting himself even as he turned away from the
mirror, he went directly to the bed where Torie had
left her pocketbook. It was a leather bag of some years
and only moderate size. So many women carried their
whole blessed lives about with them in one enormous
handbag, for reasons—fear of thieves breaking in and
stealing the whole motley assortment of things females
valued, or as if they were charged, the mothers of the
race, to be prepared for every conceivable emergency
and then some, from earthquake and blizzard to flu
epidemic, sudden attacks of lust or the possible consequences of same in childbirth, or a worldwide dearth
of lipstick and powder—that he could only speculate
and wonder. So much to the heart of the mystery of
females did the purpose and contents of a woman's
handbag speak that Joe Nevers could only tip his cap
and back away, forever a pagan in the presence of an
impenetrable liturgy.

Now he did what he had never done in years looking after the woman in her alcoholic binges. Without
hesitation he picked up her purse and looked into it.
He could not stop his face from heating rapidly in
shame.

Only once had he entered a house of hers without
knocking, excepting the old one when it was afire.
That was at the other place, the one by the sea, the day
when he and Marion had paid their uninvited call. To
look into Torie's purse went against the whole stan-

dard of civility his parents had raised him by. But this, he was sure in his heart, was akin to rushing the back door of the burning house. There might be a life to be saved within, even if it cost a life.

It was as much a mess as any other woman's purse, and so he spilled it with trembling hands upon the bed. Out poured a flood of coins, crumpled bills of all denominations like wilted flowers, a wallet bursting its seams with charge cards, its change purse opened by the weight of coins, a watch with a badly scratched crystal, a cloth sack whose odd bulges and corners suggested it held makeup of one kind or another, a ChapStick, a flask of perfume with its cap off, an unopened packet of tissues, a nail file and an emery board, the cap of the perfume atomizer, three bunches of keys, five pens, one of them leaky, a checkbook, and an ordinary lined notebook. And on top of that miscellany, four, no five, plastic bottles of pills. Prescription bottles, labelled as to source, usage, and doctor, and capped with easy-opening lids. The brown plastic was discreetly semi-opaque, but he could see each bottle contained many more than one kind of pill. Opening one, he spilled an assortment as colorful as an Easter basket of jelly beans into his calloused palm. In the five containers there were more than a dozen kinds of pills and capsules.

The drug names on the pharmacy stickers were familiars, if not old friends, oft encountered at the bedsides of the sick and dying. Three—Darvocet, Darvon, and Demerol—were the kind of heavy-duty painkiller Cora, his second wife, had taken in the last few months of her life. These were present in quantity in the parti-colored mix, big fat shiny capsules, red, pink and gray, and black; he imagined if they had been jelly beans their flavors would be both exotic and bitter. One of the bottles was labelled Thorazine; he had never heard of it and didn't know which it was, mixed up with three or four other kinds. And the name on the last bottle he had learned simply by looking at it for hours, while Cora slept and sometimes while she waked, just for something to do. Or perhaps it had seemed more important than the others.

Don McAvoy had referred Cora to a specialist, Dr. Bickel, in Lewiston. Once Dr. Bickel had diagnosed the terminal nature of her illness, she ceased to be a responsible adult in his eyes; he began to treat her as if she were feebleminded as well as sick. He charged Joe Nevers with seeing Cora took her medicine.

"Now this one," the specialist remarked, tapping the prescription form with a massive forefinger, "hasn't any street value." He laughed in an embarrassed way as if he had just told an off-color joke in mixed company. "It takes a longish time to go to work. Normally, the patient is weaned from the stuff over several weeks." Dr. Bickel cleared his throat. "She won't have to give it up, of course. It should help with the depression in the time she has left. Let me know how it goes, will you? It's new; we want to know about unusual reactions."

Joe Nevers nodded and took Cora and her medicine home. He was grateful for the painkillers, almost as grateful as Cora. She suffered unimaginably even with them, even after the last operation that severed the spinal cord to kill the pain for good and all. But the name of the antidepressant stuck in his mind so that even now, when he thought of Cora, he found that word filling his mouth.

"Amitriptyline," he muttered, turning the bottle from one hand to the other.

A wonder drug, the specialist had called it, what they used to call penicillin and the polio vaccines, except this one didn't kill bugs and prevent death and disease. It cured despair.

He opened the bottle again and looked at the pills. Among the other ones he could not tell from aspirin or antacids or over-the-counter cold capsules, he recognized the pale pink pills that looked like anemic M&M's and small purple or yellow ones that looked even more like penny candy, the dots that had to be pried off strips of waxed paper. Though his hands still shook, he restored all but that bottle to Torie's handbag. He sat on the edge of the bed, still holding it. *Take as directed. Amitriptyline.*

His vision blurred abruptly so he could no longer read the words. He found himself weeping as he had not wept since the year after Cora died, when it was a nightly thing with him.

After a time he drew a shaky breath and pinched the thin bridge of his nose between one splayed thumb and calloused pointer. From there he spread the digits like plow blades and his tears before them from the inside of his eyes to the corners of his cheekbones. With the left hand he fumbled for his handkerchief, Torie's blood dried maroon on it, in which to blow his nose with all the vigor he could muster.

He concentrated on reading the label again, over and over, pushing everything out of mind except the round, smooth syllables of the drug's name. The incantation worked as magically as if he had taken the pill itself, floating him gently into the lee of the flash flood of his emotions. With a sigh, he dropped the bottle back into her handbag with the others.

There were chores to do and only himself to do them. He opened the door to the deck to scoop up a handful of snow to wash his face. He loaded wood into the Jötel and adjusted its dampers. He smoothed the quilted spread over the bed so his presence there could no longer be detected. And all of it he did slowly and reluctantly, not wanting to go back to the living room and see Torie again. He could not trust himself not to break down again. And she would know just by looking at him that he knew.

Knew what? All he knew for sure was that her hair was white and that she had a lot of pills. What about the booze? Little or none of it drunk, to be sure. But she had seemed dazed when he came in, if not on the booze, perhaps it was the pills. Not all at once, but some of them anyway. And why? Why such a pharmacopia and why mostly painkillers? Except the amitriptyline. Why that? Was it given only to the dying, for whom even the doctors despaired? He didn't know. He wished Glen McAvoy were still alive; Glen would know. He didn't even know if the pills were something new with Torie, though surely he would have noticed if she had been into them for very long.

He had counted on her to outlive him. She had the advantage of her years, for one; she was not yet sixty, to his seventy-three. And him looking after her as much as she allowed. He subscribed with reservations to the old saying that God looks out for children and drunks. He suspected God kept a closer eye on the drunks. In his considerable span he had witnessed drunks surviving hellacious accidents, appalling living conditions, and Maine winters that claimed the young and strong with brutal ease. If alcohol was a preservative, Torie Christopher should live forever.

Contrary as she was, it was just like her to die before him, to spite him. She must have sensed in him the conviction he kept secret even from himself, that one day when he was gone, she would be grateful to him. He wanted to believe she needed him, to lean on, abuse, and keep her secrets. All her strength had seemed no more than the single-minded fury of his baby sister, sixty years ago, climbing the sheer face of his mother's kitchen cupboards in search of some forbidden thing. Why else did she come roaring back to the Ridge in her ridiculous big cars?

Alone on the Ridge, Joe Nevers knew who she was. Hadn't she been everywhere in the world and back again, seen wonders and learned things no one else on the Ridge ever dreamed? It seemed obvious that a life that demanding, that perilous, would need a refuge, a Ridge to come home to.

Now it seemed he was mistaken. Had believed what he wanted to believe. Some doctor had given her those pills because she was dying. He had not taken good enough care of her after all.

When she was dead, he would be just another useless old man waiting to die, as good as dead. His steps returning to her were slowed with dread, not of facing Torie anymore, but simply of seeing her even as she slept. He hoped she was sleeping, to spare them both.

Fall, 1953

AFTER LABOR DAY, the locals met each other with a geniality that at its source was fat and smug. The summer people were gone. Like the field mice moving back into the summer cottages and houses, the villagers had the leavings. Not just the greenbacks the summer people left behind, but the bright flawless days of September and October. Those were days the summer folk could not afford, or of which they never realized the worth. They were harvest days, not just in field and garden, but of the fullness of summer itself: warmth, ease, plenty, stored up against the winter cold. In the change of seasons, the leaves were ripened like the root crops by the first mild frosts, and harvested by wind, to mulch and feed the soil and seed of coming years. The promise was kept; the order of the seasons justified.

That year Indian summer was a glory. No one could remember when it had lasted so long or been so fine. Dark-tasselled corn still stood in the gardens and tomatoes ripened on the vines two weeks past expected killing frost. The tall windows of the old schoolhouse on the village green had to be opened with the aid of the great long hook the janitor kept in his closet, so that air could circulate in the hot afternoons and keep the scholars from dozing off over their books.

The heat brought a storm at last, and lightning struck

the schoolhouse in the night. It burnt out the fuse box and set off the fire alarm, which brought out all the village within hearing at a run—bare-chested men still zipping their pants as they ran, old men in long johns, old women in nightgowns and braids, mothers with their hair in pink curlers and children in pajamas, most of them barefoot, through the wet grass and steady rain. The women and children sheltered on porches to talk with each other and watch the fire fighters, what could be seen of them in pitch dark illuminated with an occasional flash of lightning and the smoky flames erupting from the back door of the schoolhouse. The fire was put out with extinguishers before anyone thought to call the fire chief; most of the volunteers were there anyway. The rain, everyone agreed, would have put the fire out before it got very far, yet one couldn't be certain sure, and it was a great thing to bring the village together to save the schoolhouse, and made everyone exceedingly cheerful, especially after the old women started passing out coffee and fresh doughnuts, which they must have gone to work on before the alarm stopped ringing.

The damage was not great—the janitor's closet charred and smoked because of the cleaning fluids, and the electrical system burnt out. But the electrical system was a simple one, a matter of lights and a water pump for the fountain, the basins and the toilets, and one outlet in each of the four classrooms for the occasional projector or record player—Roberta Huffy showed the seventh and eighth graders slides of her missionary years in Africa, and Joe Nevers' wife, Marion, liked to play *Peter and the Wolf* for her subprimary and first graders. Ronnie Linscott proposed to rewire the building in one straight-out day, with the help of Pete and Freeman Buck, neither of them electricians as Ronnie was, but handy. The kids and probably the teachers, in their heart of hearts, hoped the work would stretch into a second day's holiday.

Marion was as much a kid about the unscheduled holiday as her students; she had been cooped up with them through the best of the fall weather. She wanted to go to Portland, so Joe Nevers made a list of errands he had put off, and they set out, though he had things he would rather have been doing. Still, it was pleasant enough, sight-seeing on the long drive. The first color was in the trees along their route, just edges and trimmings, and the route was a scenic one, twisting around and over ponds and lakes, away from the mountains to the sea, to Casco Bay.

When Joe Nevers' errands were run, and Marion had window-shopped on Congress Street, they went into a Deering Ice Cream restaurant and had a lunch of fish chowder and grilled cheese sandwiches. Outside again, they strolled on sunny Congress Street, in complete idleness, staring at the multistoried buildings, some of them more populated in the business day than all of Nodd's Ridge in winter. They stared at the city people, so busy at business that did not seem much like real work to Joe Nevers, or at pleasures that were like his own business in the town.

"Smell the sea!" Marion exclaimed.

Joe Nevers did, and nodded. It was a fecund, female smell, miles different from the crystalline sweetness of the lake.

"Whenever I smell the sea," Marion went on slowly, as if Joe Nevers were one of her kindergartners, "I think I could live here."

Joe Nevers, now unable to smell anything but the overpowering sea smell, walked beside her in silence.

Marion looked at him. "Joe, don't you ever think about living someplace else?"

Joe Nevers shook his head. There wasn't even any need to think about it.

"Well, I do," she said.

She put her left hand on his arm, halting him, and looked at him intensely, determined that he would take the lesson.

"I could."

He shook his head again. He tried to laugh but it came out weak and embarrassed: *You know me, I can't change.*

She sighed and started to pull away from him, but he clamped his hand over hers, refusing to let her go. He led her back to the truck. She went arm in arm with him, but he felt the distance between them ever widening.

A little while later, as they waited in traffic for a light to change, Marion stared at town houses and into Deering Oaks Park, where big old trees shaded pleasant walks and ducks swam in a pond. She had a fine, striking profile, of which she was vain, though now she was within spitting distance of forty there was a hint of weakening along the jawline, under the chin.

"Where does Torie Christopher live?" she asked, much as if she were asking if that were Longfellow's statue over there.

"Falmouth Foreside," he said. "Twenty miles if it's an inch."

"Tell me about it."

After a little silence, he said, "Not much to tell. Great big stone house. Must be a fortune to heat."

Marion showed him her profile again. She still held it against him that she had been unable to go to Guy and Torie's wedding. It seemed as if her father-in-law had taken that moment to stage his prolonged death to inconvenience her; she believed the old man held her childlessness against her.

"Don't know if I could find it," Joe Nevers said, close to a lie.

She knew it, too. Joe Nevers had never been lost in his life; his sense of direction was uncanny. She was sure he was spiting her. He just didn't want her to see the place, say hello to the Christophers as if they were friends and neighbors instead of people he worked for.

"We could ask at a gas station," she suggested.

Now the rows of ordinary frame houses they were passing held her interest as if she were looking for a house number, a street sign. She was not going to meet his eye or his anger.

He did not respond. The day he asked directions at a gas station, he would ask Pete Buck to take him to the men's room to help him unbutton his fly, since his daddy wasn't there to take him anymore.

"Let's go see it," Marion said. "Maybe they're not there."

"Maybe they are," he said. "That'd be nice, wouldn't it? Gawking at the Christophers' house like a couple of tourists."

"No, we'd better not go," Marion said, after a tight pause. "Your hands aren't clean enough."

They were as close to fighting as they ever got. When Marion treated him like a subprimary kid, she was enraged. But he ignored her sniping, and after a while she would cool down.

Since Guy had brought Torie back to the lake, Marion had developed what Joe Nevers considered to be an unhealthy interest in her. Marion had decided that there but for Joe Nevers, she might be. Excepting Torie's baby; Marion wasn't about to take up babies just because Torie had.

In the first years of their marriage, he had believed her when she said she wanted time to get used to being married. He put her reluctance down to the

shock of the early miscarriage she had suffered that
first Christmas together. They were very young yet, he
thought, and couldn't blame her for shying. In time he
realized she didn't want a child and that was that. He
went on buying and using condoms, as if it were his
choice, but it was hers; she wouldn't have him otherwise. Gradually there was less occasion for prophylac-
tics, which Marion at first interpreted to mean a lessen-
ing of his drive. That wasn't so. She came to suspect
him, and then to feel contempt for him. Cheating went
against his grain, so much so he refused to lie to
Marion about it, but he couldn't seem to stop either.
The women were always there, wanting a tumble. He
told himself that was the way it was with all men; it
was unnatural to be one hundred percent faithful.

Marion wanted to be rich, to be somebody, and he
had disappointed her. Perhaps if he had made her rich
and somebody, she would have given him the child he
wanted. But he wasn't ever going to be rich, and he
already felt himself to be somebody. He kept on trying
to please her. More and more, he saw his efforts rewarded with the appalled look she gave the cat's hunting trophies left all bloody and mangled on the back
porch.

So he held his tongue and drove on, until he turned
into the avenue that ran between brilliant crimson
maples, as yet untouched by frost. The garages were
closed, the circular driveway empty, the big stone
house silent and bleak, monumental, the farthest thing
from cozy he could imagine. Marion was silent too,
perhaps surprised by the reality of it, which looked
less palatial than dangerous, a hard place, unforgiving
of small stumbles, gracelessness, slips. A fall on the
stairs might crack one's head, or break a leg or a neck,
and every day take a tithe of skin from scraped knuckles,

a tithe of bruises on elbows and knees. A grand place
to brick up a jealous spouse.

He stopped the truck in front of the door and said,
"I'll just knock. Most likely they're out." He spoke
softly, as if near a sickroom, a deathbed or a church.

His first firm knock at the old-fashioned double door
pushed it open, for it was not only unlocked but
unlatched. He found himself looking down the stone-
flagged hallway that split the house front to back,
driveway to seaside. When he looked back at Marion,
her face behind the windshield of the truck was an
unreadable blur, but she stayed put.

Taking off his cap, Joe Nevers stepped into the
hallway, onto the Oriental carpet, and felt and smelled
the sea breeze coming through the open French doors
at the other end. Most astonishingly, there was not
only the thick smell of salt water, tidal flats, and
seaweed, but also the undeniable scent of sun-warmed
tomatoes on the vine. As quietly as he could manage
in his work boots, he walked down the hall and stopped
in shadow, just inside the doors.

Outside, broad granite steps made a patio. Fanny,
asleep and open-mouthed, sat like a sack of potatoes
in her wheelchair, her head protected from the sun by
an old straw boater. Her hands lay over her belly, pale
and spotted skin tightened to a waxy shininess by
bloat.

Tommy, a sturdy red-haired toddler in short pants
and a sweater, crouched on the middle step, arranging
a dozen or more bright-colored matchbox cars in ranks,
with muttered vrooms and engine growls.

At the bottom of the steps was a garden. It was more
an exotic jungle than a proper garden. Flowers, herbs,
and vegetables had escaped the beds and gone wild.
Directly in line with him was a thicket of tomato
plants, burdened with an extravagance of fruit. In the

middle of them, having found some small patch to stand her ground against the untamed plants, Torie stooped over the green and musky mass. She had gathered her skirt in one hand, the way Joe Nevers remembered his mother gathering her apron, to form a catchall. She was filling it with tomatoes. The sun behind her shone through her hair in a red corona, and through the slip she had exposed in lifting her skirt. She was luminously happy.

He watched a few seconds, twisting his cap in his hands in a frenzy of shyness. His greatest wish was to creep away unnoticed. He stepped backward and nearly fell over a big marmalade tom that must have come from somewhere in the house to investigate his entry. Joe Nevers caught his balance against the French door; the cat yowled and jumped, seemingly between his feet, and flashed out the door, disappearing into the greenery.

Torie looked up at him. Her face stilled and closed.

Tommy looked up and dimpled hugely. "Joe!"

Joe Nevers forced a smile for the boy. "How-do, Tom? Torie," he tried to say, the commencement of a cheerful greeting, but he choked on it, as if her name were all sharp edges tearing his inside, like shards of glass going down.

She smiled warily. Then she realized her skirt was full of tomatoes, and her slip was exposed to him. She stared at the tomatoes wide-eyed, then up at him. If she let go her skirt, the tomatoes would fall and be bruised. She stood a litle straighter, and brushed a wisp of hair from her forehead, as if daring him to find something come-hither about her.

If he had not been so embarrassed, he might have told her he was proud of her not wasting the fruit to save her modesty. But he couldn't. He began to back away, with one quick glance for the cat, back into the obscuring shadow of the cool stone hallway.

"Just passing by," he stammered.

"Yes," she said.

The little boy between them looked from one to the other, excited by the unexpected appearance of his friend Joe Nevers, the caretaker, in the wrong place at the wrong time. Torie's quick smile, just for him, reassured him that there was nothing to be alarmed about in this.

Torie looked down at the tomatoes. She bent a little, reaching for another.

"Bye," Joe Nevers muttered, and fled.

Tommy stared after him, then shrugged, and picked up where he'd left off, moving cars along the step.

"No one home," Joe Nevers told Marion. "Just the housekeeper."

Marion stared at him, crossed her arms and peered out at the house as they drove away, as if she were trying to peek through the windows so she could call him a liar.

He watched the road, grateful to have it to watch. Marion's contempt stood between them like an invisible wall. He didn't care anymore about that; he was grateful for the wall too. It meant she couldn't reach him or read him either.

He had intruded on Torie and was sorry for it. Marion's social climbing was a thoroughly unworthy excuse. More than that he was so frustrated he wanted to pound the steering wheel with his fists.

He knew a head of steam when he saw one. Did the girl think he wanted a good scalding? They had looked at each other but once and recognized it. It had happened to him before if it had never happened to her. A body needn't give in to it.

Perhaps that was all that was wrong; she was hardly

more than a girl. All he wanted was for her to understand how it was with him. He was getting on for
middle-aged. He worked for her husband, had known
Guy's family all his life, and Guy all of Guy's life, seen
Guy in his bassinet and at Fanny's tit too. Did she
think he would make a move in the face of that? A
weak man he might on occasion be, but a fool he was
not. All he wanted was that they be friends, for he was
certain if they did not become friends soon, they would
be enemies; there was nowhere else for that heat to go.
He was almost as scared as she was. He had to find a
way to show her, tell her, he wasn't about to hurt her.
Now there was another thing between them, an un-
guarded moment. She would not forgive him seeing
her with her dress up and her guard down; that was
how much she feared him, and herself.

On her side of the truck, Marion was weeping into
an embroidered hanky in a very ladylike way. He felt a
sudden urge to pop her one, slam her against the
window.

Damn the both of them; whatever it was they wanted,
he didn't have it to give. Bewildered by his own rage,
he fled homeward to the Ridge, taking with him, like a
seed, the dream of Torie illumined by a red sun, that
recurred over and over, nights without number, through
a quarter century of his life and hers.

"Well, old man, you look like hell," Torie said, and
laughed. Her low-pitched voice crackled as if it were
being transmitted through the atmosphere by short-
wave radio, but her laugh was the sound of a dead
branch breaking overhead. It raised goose bumps on
his arms.

"What is it?" she demanded to know. "Constipation?
Or did your best friend just die?"

"Amitriptyline," he said. Even as he forced himself

to say it, he knew he was striking at her weakness to cover his own panic, and was ashamed, which made him savage.

"What?" She sat straight up, straining to catch what he had said. Her eyes widened; her lips twitched. Another harsh chortle escaped her. She hauled the bottle of bourbon upward by the neck with both translucent hands to make a toast.

"I'm relieved to know you're still regular as the heartbeat of the universe," she said.

A last ragged spasm of laughter faded to a sigh as she folded back into the sofa pillows. When she had caught a little breath, she swore at him.

"Goddamn it, you beat me to my punch line, you old spoilsport. I was going to tell, you were wrong as usual. I'm not your best friend, and I'm not dead. Yet." She winked at him. "You can hope though." She admired the bottle, glinting with its own fiery light. "And so can I."

Her ragging comforted him. Nothing much had changed. This was how it always was, give or take for the degrees of her sottedness or hangover.

He shook his head in exaggerated rue. "One thing I like about you when you're drunk," he said.

"Oh, boy," she interrupted. "I can't wait to know."

"Leastways then both of us know you're talking bullshit."

"My word. You ought to be glad I'm too tired to wash out your mouth for you."

"That's not half-fair. Why, all those bad words, I learned from you."

"That's a goddamn lie," she rasped. "You were out behind the barn, peeking under Hetty Linscott's skirt before my mother was morning-sick with me."

"Everybody peeked under Hetty's skirts," he said. "One thing's not the same as t'other, anyway. My dad would have waled me for so much as a goshdarn right up until I could vote."

One fragile hand left the bottle long enough to wave a dismissal of his defense. She peeked at him from under her lashes.

"I look that bad, do I? You went peeking in my handbag?"

He blushed. If he'd had his cap in his hands he'd have twisted it. He was totally tongue-tied.

"When I get to hell, want me to say hello to Cora?" Torie asked slyly.

"Now, Missus," he managed.

She sat up again, to clunk the bottle decisively onto the end table between the sofa and a rocking chair.

"Do you suppose she's been holding her breath all these years, waiting for you?" she asked him.

Knowing she didn't want an answer, only his attention, Joe Nevers said nothing, but wandered into the kitchen.

"Must be what keeps you alive," Torie continued. "The thought of Cora waiting, down in the bad place, to stuff all the slick little gobbets of her sick fantasies down your throat. No wonder you don't have the decency to die before you start to rot."

He lifted the lid on the teapot. "State road crew could use this to patch potholes."

"Give it to me anyway," Torie said. "Maybe it'll patch the holes in my intestines."

He spilled the too-strong tea into the sink. It made a wet plopping sound and filled the air with a tannic perfume.

"Should think," he said slowly, picking up where he had left off, "you would speak better of the departed, seeing as you'll be joining 'em so soon."

"Is that why you built this fire so goddamned hot? Foretaste of the fire down below?" She laughed. "Think of all the pious souls who'll have a chance to piss on me when I'm gone. I'm just getting my own back while I can."

He had to laugh too; it was all perfectly right and true.

Torie began to struggle out of the fur coat, while he rinsed the teapot and began again to make tea.

"There," she said, and flung it aside weakly. She began to pull off the red boots.

"Well, the hell with all of them."

She kicked off one boot, without any apparent interest in where it fell. The second one went just as carelessly in a different direction. She propped herself on the pillows to watch him over the back of the sofa.

"Are you disappointed in me, old man?" she asked, seeming pleased at the possibility.

The tea kettle began to whistle shrilly. He set about making the tea with a flurry so as to delay answering her.

He could say yes; *I never expected to have to bear your passing. I meant you to suffer mine.*

He could say yes; *I wanted you to be a mystery I could go on puzzling until my own time ran out. Now you have made me see you are no more a mystery than myself, solved easily by such an idiot savant as death.*

He could say yes; *you would not be kept from it. You lay down eager in the grave's embrace.*

But what he said was "Naw," as he ripped open the second packet of tea. His hands shook momentarily over the pot, spilling the tea leaves along the counter top like a trail of breadcrumbs.

If he said what he could have said, there was no telling what might happen. What more might be said.

When he was a lad, his mother had read him the Scripture. He remained a pagan, the grace of salvation denied him. But it was her voice that enjoined him to forgive seven times seven, even to this, his seventh decade. As a boy he had been concerned, what terrible sin could one commit against another to require such forgiveness? Could an ordinary man, such as he knew himself to be, ever find a well of forgiveness that deep within his soul?

As a man he came to wonder if there was a corollary to the biblical injunction he had had from his mother, requiring him not to forgive, but to give seven times seven. He was afraid such giving might be more than he could manage, and worse, more than he wanted to know he could give. He thought he had mapped his own limits as far as he wanted to go. If the world held anything new and wonderful to be discovered, he must find it outside himself.

He had to stop setting the tea on a tray to plow a sudden angry tearing from his eyes, turning his back so she would not see it.

"Jesus," she said, stretching her toes luxuriously.

He picked up the tray. "Name's Joe Nevers," he said.

She snorted and she looked at him. "Jeez-us," she said. "I was going to tell you, you ought to be relieved."

Navigating between her layabout boots, he placed the tray on the end table.

"Oh, God that smells good," Torie said.

"Name's Joe," he began.

She snatched a wedge of lemon from the tray and threatened him with it.

"Nevers," he insisted.

She threw the wedge. He caught it easily and dropped it back onto the tray.

"Thanks, old man," she said. "You're still good for something."

He picked up her boots and paired them neatly out

of the way, then dropped into a rocking chair. "You're welcome, Missus."

Torie reached for the bottle and struggled to uncork it. Meaning to lend her a hand, he reached for it, but she drew back, holding it tight.

"I'll do it, goddamn it," she said.

And she did, spilling a little on her sweater and trousers, sprinkling the sofa as well, as she slopped a small quantity into one of the tea mugs.

"That won't do you any good, will it?" he asked.

She snorted. "Nothing does me any good. It's a question of what does me the least damage." She dropped a lemon wedge ceremoniously into the mug.

He leaned over to top it with hot water. She did not stop him until the mug was nearly full. Then he poured tea for himself and sat back to feel its heat in his hands and to breathe its savory steam. Their moods coincided; she too sat back to savor what she held in her hands.

"You've changed," he said.

BEYOND THE BARE EXCHANGE of information—"I've a church meeting at seven, there's a casserole in the oven," or "Cow's quarter's tore so bad I'm putting her down," and the like—Cora and Joe Nevers had nothing to say to each other. But Cora's silences spread like the black reflection of storm clouds on the lake. Sometimes her response was as much as ten minutes after a question was asked her. There were terse notes in her tiny, upright hand to impart what he might need to know, pinned to the kitchen table by the salt shaker. Joe Nevers began to come upon her, quite still, as if under a spell, in the midst of her work, her mind clearly elsewhere. And she was a woman who claimed never to dream, who dismissed novels, movies, and the soap operas on TV as "piffle," who thought in black and white. Surely she was not daydreaming.

And then, looking for the leak that was swelling the floorboards in the bathroom, he unlatched the small panelled door that covered the crawlspace, giving access to the pipes, and found a large box of sanitary napkins wedged there. When he extracted it, the wet bottom of the cardboard box let go, and napkins spilled out into the crawlspace and out onto the bathroom floor. They were all either damp or dirtied by their contact with the floor, so he picked them up and

placed them in the wastebasket. Then he took it to
Cora, paring apples at the kitchen table.

"What's this?" he asked, showing it.

She started, then blushed.

"They're all no good," he said. "The box was wet,
and they spilled all over. I'm sorry."

Cora stared at the contents of the wastebasket, then
at him. She was past menopause then, had not men-
struated since their marriage.

"I been spotting," she whispered. "Nothing to worry
about."

"Spotting? Ain't these the big ones?" He was blushing as furiously as she.

Marion had always been exceedingly discreet about
her menstruation but she had not thought it necessary
to hide her supplies in the crawlspace. To be sure,
Cora was the epitome of modesty and fastidiousness,
but this degree of secrecy seemed extreme.

"It's nothing to worry about," Cora insisted.

"That why you hid 'em?"

The question only seemed to confuse Cora. She stared
fixedly at the paring knife and the half-peeled apple in
her hand.

"How long?" he asked.

She shrugged stiffly. She was taking pains to peel
the apple in one long continuous strip. "Not long.
Nothing to worry about."

Joe Nevers took the wastebasket to the shed and
emptied it into a trash barrel. Then he carried it back
to the kitchen, set it down, and picked up the phone.

Cora looked up at him, her face tight with anxiety.
But she could not bring herself to ask him who he was
calling.

" 'Lo, Hope," he said into the receiver, when he had
an answer. "Like to talk to Glen if he's able."

There was a pause, during which Cora stared at Joe

Nevers, and he stared back, until she resumed peeling the apples. But she stopped to listen when he spoke again.

" 'Lo, Glen," he said. "Cora's been bleeding awhile. She won't say how long or how much to me, but she will to you."

Now Doc knew. He'd have it out of her.

"Thanks Glen, eight-thirty it'll be."

Cora took up another apple and cut into it. Her hands were unsteadied; the peel broke into segments as it fell away from the apple. Bad luck.

"I'm taking you over there, first thing in the morning," Joe Nevers said, hanging up the phone.

Cora took a deep breath. "It's nothing to worry about."

Joe Nevers nodded. He had done what he could. He had a leaking pipe still to find. But when he looked back over his shoulder, going out of the room, he saw Cora lay the knife and apple down with enormous care, and bury her head in her hands. He hesitated, thinking he ought to go back to her, to give her what comfort he could. But of course she would not want it, not from him.

When he took her home again after the long siege of tests, the carton of pills and nostrums from the hospital pharmacy on the floor of the pickup between them, he broke in upon her silence.

"Cora," he said.

She stared straight ahead at the road running home to the Ridge.

"You know what ails you, don't you?"

She jerked her head roughly; she might have been hit, she might have been indicating she did know.

Joe Nevers gripped the wheel tightly. "Doctor says you needn't be in any misery. There ain't no reason to spare the pills."

She sat straighter, drawing quick little breaths. "I ain't afraid," she said, but she hugged herself tight.

A quick glance at her made him purse his mouth. It was a troublesome time. The young folks, even on the Ridge, were all of a sudden speaking their own tongue. But they had one word he had understood at once, without translation, if he could not bring himself to speak it. It was a word that made you grit your teeth. Uptight. Cora was uptight, all right.

Sparing another glance from the road, he reached out and patted her arm. She flinched from his touch, eyes gone starey and wild.

Sunk into her skull, hooded with fragile blue veins, her eyes bulged and showed watery and yellowed white, behind the lenses of her glasses. Her thin nostrils flared in panic. Her mouth hung open, working. Saliva webbed from the glare white of her false front teeth, back to her own yellowed molars. Her tongue twisted and convulsed in the veiny, glistening gawp of her mouth, that was so like an internal organ exposed unknowingly, immodestly, that he was embarrassed to see it. Her scalp showed through the colorless threads of her hair, thinned so much in recent months that she refused to go out of the house, even to Sunday mass. Her collarbone tented the cloth of her shirtwaist like a pail buried in the sand.

"Goddamn you," she said, gasping for the breath to curse him. "Why ain't it you?"

He took his hand back, laid it gently on the steering wheel. "I don't know, Cora. But I ain't going to leave you. I'll see you through it."

She laughed bitterly. "You won't get no credit from me. It's your bounden duty."

"I know," Joe Nevers said. "I know my duty."

She snorted. "You got the damndest sense of it." Her gaze drifted to the windows again. They were nearing the Ridge. Her hands in her lap went slack with relief. "You want to wait on a dying woman but you never had no time for the living one."

He had no answer to that.

"Promise me," she said, "you won't never put me back in the hospital."

"I promise," he said.

Doc McAvoy's wife Hope, long Cora's confidante, found a vocation nursing her. Cora was a good patient. It might be that Cora found her vocation too.

Hope could not forgive Joe Nevers his trespasses against Cora but she did mellow toward him. She was being paid for her work, deservedly so, and out of his pocket. He met the mounting expenses of Cora's care without complaint and in cash. Cora, not the breadwinner in the house, was uninsured. Perhaps it was as good an excuse as any for Joe Nevers to work overtime.

By day the house stood open to Cora's friends. Visiting the sick had always been a favorite duty of the village women; the additional bad luck of having her natural span cut short, on top of recent marital troubles, drew the women in flocks. Cora seemed to thrive on their attentions, but in time even Hope, who loved the drama of it as well as the company, noticed how weakened Cora was after the women departed. Hope fell on this as only another example of Cora's abundant courage.

"Horseshit," Cora's daughter Jane told Hope baldly. "She's playing martyr. Practiced all her life for this role."

Hope was shocked. Just as she had begun to think better of Jane for trekking north from Boston every weekend to see her mother. Cora still refused a rapprochement, which had troubled Hope as seeming stiff-necked, but no more. Jane was unnatural, condemned by her own filthy mouth, and that was that.

On an evening near Halloween, Joe Nevers came in from his work and looked in on Cora. She was sleeping, as usual for the time of day. He had an accounting of Cora's day from Hope, and was then left alone to eat the supper Hope had prepared for him. That cleared away, he checked to see that Cora was still asleep, and then went out to see to his animals.

About eight o'clock he came in again. She was stirring. Cora generally had a waking period in the middle of the evening, and it was then he most often sat with her.

After showering and changing to the clean work clothes he would wear again on the morrow, he made up a tray of bouillon and dry toast for her. He fussed over her a bit, giving her glasses, changing her drinking water for fresh, neatening her bed linen, plumping her pillows and arranging a large linen napkin to catch crumbs and drips from her supper, Then he fed her, and she often ate quite eagerly. Afterwards she lay back and closed her eyes while he took away the tray.

"I was awful hungry," she said when he came back in.

When he had sat down, she asked, "Raise the shade, will you, so I can see the moon rising."

He ought to have thought of it, so he was not really irritated with her, but she did always manage to find one of a dozen reasons to have him up again when he had his sitting britches on. In particular, the window shade always seemed to be in the wrong position.

"That's better," she said.

She looked around the parlor where her hospital bed had replaced the sofa against the wall, and the paraphernalia of her illness was now the dominant motif. Her expression was pained. Cora was nothing if she was not house-proud. She hated seeing the neat, old-fashioned parlor with its climbing-rose wallpaper and chintz-upholstered overstuffed furniture cluttered and disrupted into a sickroom. But it was next to the bathroom and on the first floor.

"I can't think why Jane keeps coming. I wish you would tell her to stay away," Cora complained. "She only distresses me."

It was the very same phrase he had heard from Hope McAvoy as he washed his hands at the kitchen sink before his supper.

"It's a long trip for Jane," he pointed out. "Nobody's making her do it. Some people might think she was just trying to do what's right and proper by her mother."

Cora did not argue the point. Appearances, particularly of what was right and proper, still meant too much to her. Let the village think Jane was humbling herself at her mother's deathbed. Jane owed it to her, God knows. Nobody need know that Cora did not intend to forgive Jane, not ever. And she was confident if they all knew what Jane had said to her, they wouldn't forgive her either.

"Well," Cora said, "it's not as if I don't have enough to suffer."

And she did. There was so much truth in that, it could swallow a lie as easily as the lake could swallow a bag of kittens.

Joe Nevers took out his cheroots. "I should think you would want to put things right between you, while you can."

Cora sighed and reached weakly for her water.

He got up and gave it to her.

"Some things can't be fixed, you know that," she said, straining to see out the windows, looking for the moon. She meant between them, as well.

He had not the heart to tell her that the clouds had thickened in the sky while she slept so neither stars nor moon was likely to be visible that night.

Her eyes behind her glasses were owlish and unfocused. The old prescription was not much good to
her but she refused to have a new one. "What's the
point?" she would say sharply, after complaining at
length about the uselessness of the old glasses.

Then, in one of the sharp jags in her conversation he
was sure were provoked by the conglomeration of medi-
cations she took, "My father never forgave me, no
matter I must have asked him a thousand times."

Joe Nevers sat up and took notice. He reached for an
ashtray and dropped a spatter of cigar ash into it.

"I never knowed he had anything to forgive you."

Cora smiled. "I ain't never been in the habit of
spilling my guts."

Joe Nevers nodded. "Weren't you his favorite? Your
brother says you were."

"Oh, yes," she admitted. "That's just it. I let him
down. I betrayed his trust." Her eyes filled with tears.

Joe Nevers was sure she was speaking her father's
words to him. He tapped his cigar against the ashtray
in his palm. "Jane?"

" 'Course," Cora said. "He never forgave me getting
myself pregnant nor marrying Church. He had his
chance to say I told you so too, when Church killed
himself. Said it proved he was right and I was wrong
and I deserved to be left a widow with my bastard
whelp."

"Jesus Christ!" Joe Nevers got up and stamped around
his chair. "Cora, how the hell could you want forgiveness from a son of a bitch like that? What kind of
father says something ugly as that to a woman who's
just lost her husband by his own hand? Christ, I'm
glad I never knew the old bastard."

Cora was quiet, whether she was offended by his
uncustomary roughness of language or was merely considering his opinions he could not tell.

"He was right," she said at last. "I tricked Church into marrying me, into making me pregnant."

"So what if you did?" Joe Nevers said. "You wasn't the first. And Church had his fun out of it. If that was the biggest sin a person could confess, half the Ridge has already paid for their own pew in hell. Most folks that happens to make do. I'd be surprised as hell if Church killed himself over that, Cora. You told me, and I heard it around too, before I ever met you, that he was a bad-tempered, moody bastard, and a drunk, too, before he married you. He had an uncle and a brother done away with themselves too. They didn't do it 'cause you rolled in the hay with Church and made him marry you when the bread rose."

They were the most words Cora had ever heard at one time out of Joe Nevers. But she did not expect much moral sense from Joe Nevers, not after all this time. He was an honest enough man, but still a womanizer who let his cock lead him around. She wasn't even angry with him anymore. It was just hard to admit she had been made a fool of again; that Joe Nevers was just another man.

"Everybody doing a thing don't make it right," Cora chided. "I just wanted to get out of his house. I was wild to get out. All I did was work. Raise the kids, housekeep, never a moment to myself or with the other young folks, after Ma died. I don't know what made me think getting married was going to change that. I might's well have stayed home and kep on looking after Dad."

"I don't know why you want to go on beating yourself with his stick," Joe Nevers said. "It's only natural for a young girl to want herself a baby and her own man and her own home. There's plenty girls, and you know it, who wouldn't never get out of their parents' house if they didn't shame 'em into letting 'em go."

"But he needed me."

"He needed a wife, he should a gone out and married one. He did, now didn't he, as soon as you was gone?"

Cora wrung her hands. "She wasn't no good. She was a slut."

"That wasn't your fault." Joe Nevers poured water for her, "Time for your pills."

Cora smiled. "You want to shut me up."

Anybody could see she was all wrought up, never mind, it was time for her pills. When she got excited like this, it meant the painkillers were wearing off.

She swallowed her pills and lay back. He sat down to smoke another cheroot, one more than he usually allowed himself, but he had to admit he was a little upset by Cora's talk. It was all so much of a contrast with the proper, prim woman he had married.

When Cora spoke again, half an hour later, he had no doubt at all that she was under the influence of the narcotics.

"She was no good," Cora said. She balled her fists on the quilt and stared wild-eyed into the night framed by the window. "He told me so. She never treated him right. He said I was a better wife, he said that to me. One night when Church was out drinking, and I was home with the baby, he came around." She giggled. "He kept kissing me. Calling me his Corrie, his dolly." Cora sighed happily. "He wanted it awful bad. But I was married to Church and I knowed right from wrong by then. He couldn't fool me no more. I let him kiss me until he was just as hard as a poker, standing right up in his pants, and my Daddy he was big, you know, yes he was, bigger than Church. Bigger than you, Joe Nevers, with all the women acting like you had something special. They should a seen my Daddy's. But it was terrible ugly. They all is, but his was the ugliest I ever saw. He thought I'd do anything for it. I give him a surprise. I let him get hard enough to hurt, then I give him a good kick in the basket. When he stopped screaming I'd killed him, he set out to beat me, but I dared him to, and said I'd tell Church." She sounded more than a little disappointed that her father had not beaten her. "That set him on his way, and he never bothered me again. No, sir."

Joe Nevers sat still, the cigar stub dying aromatically between his fingers.

"He was the best, though," Cora said dreamily. She touched her shrunken breasts in her flannel gown delicately, with the tips of her fingers. It was the only time in their married life that Joe Nevers had ever witnessed her giving in to a spontaneous erotic urge. Grotesque as it was in the context of her ravaged body and the squalid tale she had told, he felt an answering spark within himself that died at once, like some distant shooting star on an August night. Slowly, he lowered his head into his big hands.

"Yes," he said, "you've changed."

Torie studied him, turning over what she might say.

He sensed she had reached some point beyond which she was not sure she wanted to go.

"That," she said finally, "is the nature of things, isn't it?"

He nodded. Right and true, for sure.

Torie sipped absently at the hot toddy, then made a face. "What a waste of good booze." She put the glass down. "Shit," she said. "I can't drink this. Doctor told me not to. This and the dope together'll half-kill me. I don't know why I even brought it with me. Habit, I guess." She stared at it desconsolately. "Don't know why I came at all."

Now Joe Nevers felt she was talking to herself; he

felt like an eavesdropper. Worriedly, he cleared his throat. Sometimes, he knew, the speaking aloud of what a body most fears will rob the fear of its power. So it was Joe Nevers, trying hard to say it light and having it come out tentative and atremble, said to her, "Unfinished business?"

That brought her eyes to focus on him again, but there was no comfort in that. She saw too much when she cared to look.

"Have to put the coup de grace," he said, pronouncing the French phrase as it was said locally—coop de grass—"to that oak," and laughed nervously.

She looked past him to where the snow was piling up against the glass of the window wall. "Good fucking riddance," she said.

Joe Nevers felt as if he had lost his footing and was slipping, at a terrifying rate, down a hill of glass. He could not stop himself from blundering on.

"Don't know if I can get that car out of the ditch without giving myself a coronary," he said, shaking his head.

She bared her teeth at him. "That's it," she exclaimed. "That's what I came for. To make sure you had that goddamn heart attack of yours, you been looking for the last thirty years. Why don't you go ahead and have the fucking thing right now. I'll unditch my goddamn car."

He shook his head again. "I guess maybe I'll stay alive long enough to see that. Ought to be funnier than pants on a horse. You can start a car with a dead batt'ry, you probably can bring an old man back from the dead, too. You do that, you can change your name to Jesus and mine to Lazarus."

"Your name's Joe Nevahs," she said, dry as the sand in an hourglass, "and if I were Jesus, I'd take Martha's advice and leave you stinking."

"You know," he said, "I don't think you're half so bad as you make out."

"I don't give a shit if you ever get that car unditched. I'd just as soon die here as somewhere else. It's all the same to me," she said.

"Can't have you dying here," Joe Nevers told her. "Ruby'd have my ass. She finds a mouse turd in here, she reams me out good and proper. I don't even want to think what she'd say if I let you leave your carcass here. Draw all kinds of bugs and vermin. 'Sides, what's your hurry? I seen quite a few folks looked a lot worse than you do right now by a country mile stretch out dying into a regular holiday. See'n' as a body has got to do it, seems to me to be a lot smarter to get what you can out of it."

"Shit," she said.

"You talking to yourself again?" he asked innocently.

She sat up and pitched a small sofa pillow at him. He caught it casually, one-handed, and leaned over to drop it back into place on the sofa.

"Goddamn it," Torie said. "We need a new routine."

"I'm too old," he said. "Can't teach an old dog, you know."

"That's your excuse," she said. "You've been too old since the *Chicago Tribune* thought Dewey was elected. Well, now I'm too sick, and too goddamned tired. What a pair we make."

He stretched extravagantly, with an audible cracking of joints. That made her laugh, and he grinned, delighted to have navigated dangerous waters once more and somehow improved her spirits. Suddenly he was ravenous. It had been a long day, and he wanted his supper.

Outside, the wind had risen to a steady shriek. It bent and twisted the trees around the house, which scratched and scraped at shingle, glass and clapboard where they could. The house was alive with its own sounds, creaking like Joe Nevers' joints, contracting, resisting the wind and the cold. In the stoves, the fires snapped and crackled and popped like breakfast cereal. The house was finally habitable, warmed enough to melt even the frost that had formed at the edges of the window wall, so that it was no more than a chilly sweat.

The snow blowing out of the dark against the glass melted and froze again almost instantly, in trickles like low-relief icicles.

For Joe Nevers the storm around him was spice and relish to his supper. So it had always been and should be, as far as he could know.

"Awful good, missus," he commented to Torie after his first mouthful of stew.

To his surprise she shook her head most reluctantly.

"Pardon me for a rude son of a bitch," he said, laying down his spoon. "Bless me, missus, I'll feed you if you want."

"Don't you dare jump and let your supper get cold, waiting on me. Why should you expect me to eat when I haven't wanted a decent meal in years?"

That was right and true, of course, and he picked up his spoon but did not use it again.

She sat up with her hands around her knees, resting her head on them while she watched him.

"Funny how good that smells," she said. "You know, I don't remember the last time, before this, I was actually hungry?"

That made him smile sadly; it had been years since he had seen her eat like a healthy body ought.

"Not drinking," she speculated. "See what trouble I've gotten into, staying sober. If I do eat something, it'll probably half-kill me."

"What about a poached egg on a slice of toast?" he

proposed. "I'd a brought crackers and milk or a little oxtail broth if I'd a known you was sick."

"God, that sounds good," Torie said fervently.

"Name's Joe Nevers," he said, "but thanks for the compliment."

"You're a ticket, old man," she said. "You'll never change."

He didn't stop to challenge her. This was an opportunity he wasn't about to let go by.

When he put the plate on the coffee table for her, she caught her breath in a little gasp of anticipation. He sat down in the rocking chair with his bowl of stew in hand, to watch her eat. She closed her eyes at the taste of the first bit of poached egg. When she opened them, they brimmed with tears.

"Missus," he murmured, and produced his much overworked handkerchief.

Her fork rattled on the glass top of the coffee table as she put it down, and reached with the other to accept the bandanna. She hid her face in it and blew her nose. "Never mind," she said, through the cloth. Then she reached defiantly for the fork, but her mouth twitched with the effort of not crying. "I'm just mad at myself," she said. "Can't even eat a goddam egg without getting emotional about it." She took another bite, and it seemed to buck her up.

It came to him that there was a time when she would have thrown the dish or the fork at him, or at the wall. It seemed that time was past, gone for good and all, and wasn't he the fool to sit here regretting it? If she would only toss that plate at him, then he could dismiss the pharmacopia in her handbag, the change of her hair, her frailness and sobriety.

MAY OF '57. The ice just out, Joe Nevers dropped his canoe in the lake nearly every fair morning, an hour or so before dawn. Out in deep water, he fished for trout and perch, bass and land-locked salmon. Often he made his breakfast of fresh-caught fish over a small fire on a deserted beach, or sometimes on some summer resident's abandoned barbecue grill.

One day late in the month, he fished the north end of the lake where there were few cottages or summer homes, and the woods were wildest. Intending to beach just beyond the Christophers' at a secluded clearing he knew, he passed within sight of the old house's remains. The blackened skeleton was visible from far out on the lake. No sooner had he seen it than its ugly stink assulted him. It shook him, fair killing his appetite for the string of fish in the bottom of his canoe.

Then he saw the thread of smoke hanging in the air, evidence of a campfire. The stink clarified itself into woodsmoke enhanced with a thick, burnt coffee smell. He could make out a tent, and beyond it, a mud-spattered behemoth of a Cadillac. He could guess who owned that.

It was his job to know who was there and why. Even before he decided he would, he had begun to turn the canoe. Then he saw her.

Torie. Barefoot and dancing. Dancing across the newly

greened lawn between the lake and the burnt-out house. Her white trousers were rolled in cuffs above her ankles and her hair flew around her head, bright as a burning bush in the wilderness.

Nothing in his experience could help him imagine what she was up to, dancing like a Druid priestess before the ruins of her husband's family house. Practicality undamped, he wondered that the cold wet ground did not afflict her on the instant with paralyzing chillblains.

His instinct was to pass by, as quickly and silently as he could. Whether he did so merely out of courtesy or out of fear accounted for nothing in the end, for she turned around in her dance and saw him. At once she ceased the dance, which unexpectedly produced in Joe Nevers a pang of regret. She waved both arms at him, like a signalman.

Obedient, he came ashore, tying up at the dock he had replaced for Fanny the summer before she had her stroke and became childish.

"Joe Nevahs!" Torie shouted.

She jumped up and down, as if she were his excited child, welcoming Daddy home. She bounded to the dock, came up short, and breathless.

" 'Morning, missus," he said.

"Come have some breakfast with me," she commanded, and took off toward her campfire at the same speed at which she had come to meet him.

He shook his head in wonder at her energy. Fish in hand, he followed her across the lawn, not even trying to keep up.

She squealed when she saw the fish.

"My contribution to breakfast," he said, handing them over to her as solemn as an Indian chief might present a gift to a Great White Mother.

She examined them reverently. "Thank God and Sonny Jesus I brought bacon with me."

"Want me to clean 'em?"

She shook her head. "Give me your knife."

He handed it over and looked around her campsite. "If you're gonna do the work," he said, "I'll just pull up a rock."

"Coffee in the pot," she said briskly, all her attention on the fish in hand.

"I know. Smelt it way out on the lake, above the smell of the fish."

He found a tin cup and helped himself from the blue-enameled pot, and sat down on a comfortable-looking slab of granite to watch. It was as pretty a job of fish-gutting as ever he had seen. Her fingers used the evilly sharp filleting blade as deftly as once they had used a needle.

"How'd you know I would a killed for a trout this morning?" she demanded.

"Didn't," he confessed.

The laugh that exploded out of her was not at him, or with him, he thought. It came from her belly, as he had sometimes heard women laugh after lovemaking. He did not know whether she was intensely pleased with his offering, or so enjoyed the gutting. Perhaps it was only an innocent anticipation of the taste.

Sometime earlier she had hauled a bucket of water from the lake. There was enough left after her coffee-making to rinse the fish of the blood and scales that remained.

"Put that skillet in the fire," she ordered.

By the time she had the fish wrapped in bacon from her own cache of food in a cooler, the iron skillet was hot enough to make water dance in beads across it.

"You could make a meal on the smell alone," she said, squatting near the fire.

He nodded.

"How's the coffee?"

"Terrible."

She fell over backwards on the wet grass, hugging herself. "An honest man," she gasped.

They ate the fish in amiable silence broken only by grunts of pleasure. The fish was reduced to a pile of bones when Torie spoke to him.

"Thanks."

"And thank you back, missus," he said. "That bacon set that fish up just right."

"Amen." She poured coffee onto the fire, extinguishing it. "The hell with that swill."

"Amen," he said.

She grinned and tossed him a damp towel to wipe his hands.

"Help you clean up?"

"I was hoping you'd ask. You get the skillet."

While he scoured the skillet with sand and rinsed it in the lake, Torie packed her gear. He noticed a long cardboard tube sticking up out of the heap. House plans were his first thought.

"You're brave to take on the bugs this time of year," he said.

"Never bite me," Torie said. "Can't take any credit for it." She tossed her head at the lake. "Bother you?"

"No, not much. I ain't their cup of tea either."

Torie sat down cross-legged on the grass and hugged herself. "You getting used to being divorced?"

He didn't mind her asking, somehow. "I guess so."

"Bugs bite Marion?" she asked.

"Something wicked," he said, and they both laughed.

"Well, Jesus'll give her an extra crown when she gets to heaven, won't he?" Torie said.

"Maybe."

"I hear you damned near got yourself killed in the fire," she said. "Freeman Buck too."

He nodded; she had the right of it.

She looked up at him, standing loose with one hand fumbling in his jacket pocket for his cheroots. "I don't know what you were trying to save. There wasn't a thing in that house worth a good goddamn, let alone a life."

He shook his head no, as if he were still puzzling on that one himself. It was what he said to everyone else who had asked.

She would not be put off. "Who the hell were you trying to save?"

She met his eye without flinching.

"Dana."

"You knew he was there." She wasn't asking, just saying.

He lit his cheroot carefully, shook the match out. "Had an idea," he said.

"You got any others?" she asked calmly.

He grinned around his cheroot and shook his head. "Not a one."

She grinned back. They took a good long look at each other, acknowledging that at this moment they had entered an unspoken agreement. He was as relieved as she, wanting to believe as much as she did that she had not been to blame, that the man had died by accident and his own careless hand.

She jumped up, pulled the long cardboard tube out of her gear and thumped the ground with it. "We'll be building as soon as this frigging mess is cleared away. Will you have somebody clear the site?" She tossed the tube into the air, caught it, balanced it on the palms of her hand. "Doubt you'll care much for the new place."

He shrugged. Work was work; he wasn't paid to like it.

"Have to dump some gravel on that boggy stretch to get a truck in here this early but I'll do it myself, today. Call you when everything's cleared away."

"Hunky-dory," she said.

"Be done in a week, the weather holds," he said.

He walked away from her, around the ruins of the house, taking a good look at them. He needed to know what was where, what he might be dealing with. Then he went back to her.

She was sitting on the ground again, cross-legged, eyes closed, showing her face to the rising sun.

"Need any help?" he asked, out of the corner of his mouth, around the cheroot.

She opened her eyes on him. Her lips curled in a slow smile.

He would convince himself later that it was a fluke, the result of the long self-imposed celibacy following the divorce from Marion. Much later still, it came to him that even then he was too old.

She held up her hands to him. He took them, and she stood up in one slow inevitable movement. She plucked the cheroot, nearly a stub, from between his lips.

"You're a liar, Joe Nevahs," she whispered, as he placed one hand at the base of her spine, pushing her toward him. "You do too have ideas."

"Oh, missus," he said, "you don't know the half of it," and covered her mouth with his.

She only moaned into his mouth.

So it was in his dream, when he spilled the fruit from her skirt. Her whisky-colored hair was sun-warm, as if it had its own, touchable fire, and her lips were cool and silky as the lake water over his hands. He was surprised then by his own ejaculation, though he was not entirely tumescent. He could not help driving himself into the softness of her belly, holding her so tight she had to struggle for breath.

At once he was afraid. She had done this to him effortlessly. She had started this. Only yards from where they stood, a man had died for her. It excited him; he was ashamed, and then panicked. Anything might happen to them now.

He had let go of her, or she had struggled free; he did not know. Only she stood breathless, wiping her mouth with the back of her hand, tears in her eyes. He could not bear to look at her. He made himself walk away, though he wanted to run, knowing he was abandoning her to save himself.

He took the canoe to the deepest water of the lake, vowing he would not look back. But he did, couldn't help it, just the one time.

She was not there, frozen, watching him leave her. She had turned her back on him, and entered the ruins of the house that he had seen for himself was a dangerous heap of ashy refuse. Carefully, as though she were looking for something, she was picking through it.

He paddled harder. Out of sight of her, he laid his paddle across his knees, twisted himself over the stern of the canoe, and vomited his breakfast into the lake.

Already deathly white, there was no color left in her skin to pale any more, but it was damp with perspiration. Torie held herself very still among the sofa pillows, her eyes shut tight, biting her lower lip. She could not control her breathing; mostly she held it, and once in a while gasped for air.

Silently Joe Nevers left her to fetch a dishpan from the kitchen. He propped it on her knees, guiding her hand to it. She sat up convulsively, hands grasping the rim of the pail as if she would drown if she let go, and then curled over it. He held her shoulders as she very neatly vomited the few mouthfuls she had eaten and then bile into the dishpan. She shook like a dry leaf afterwards, and he pulled her fur coat over her before he went to empty the pan.

He came back with a face cloth dampened with warm water from the kettle and a glass of water. He washed her face gently, then helped her drink the water, to spit some into the cleaned pail to clear her mouth. She lay back and turned her head on the pillow; her skin was shadowed blue.

"My handbag," she whispered to him, between gritted teeth. Joe Nevers hurried to fetch it, cursing himself for forgetting the pills. She had not brought them with her for the pleasure of their company.

When the bag was on her knees, she extracted the pill bottles with quick, desperate fingers, and downed several—all painkillers he recognized—dry. He offered her the glass of water, which she took with a sardonic twist to her mouth.

Torie raised the glass to him. "Long life," she said and tried to laugh.

He held her while she coughed, and got a little of the water into her.

When she relaxed a little and the pills seemed to be working he left her long enough to make a fresh pot of tea for himself. He found her quiet when he returned, her movements slowed and languorous. She was arranging the pill bottles in a little Stonehenge on the coffee table.

"I used to think I was tough," she said. "Then I had a little pain and I found out how fast I could go for a pill."

"In a hundred years," Joe Nevers said, "who'll care if you ate 'em like peanuts?"

She smiled at him. "Thanks."

"That's quite a collection of dope you got there," he said.

"It is, isn't it? Expensive too. Some of these goddamn things cost four or five bucks a piece." She propped herself up on the pillows. "I'd rather be out collecting old bones." She looked around the room at the glass boxes lining the walls. "My life's here. Did you know that?"

He shook his head.

"There's a lot you don't know, old man." She drew the fur coat up to her chin. "The house in Falmouth, that's Guy's house. Fanny's. The Christophers'. This is the house I built." Her pupils were large with the painkillers, and bright, at least partly with amusement, as she looked at him. "And you still don't like it, do you?"

He shrugged. "It's got its points," he said.

"Like what?" She was teasing him, but he didn't mind. It meant she felt a little better.

He ruminated a minute. "Upstairs," he said. "It's warm, holds the sun. And the view's real pretty."

He thought that might provoke a laugh, but he laughed alone. Had she forgotten making him trim the old pine, branch by branch, twig by twig, needle by needle, to get the view just right?

The eyes she turned toward the loft were as clear and unfathomable as the lake. "I haven't been up there," she said slowly, "since India was murdered."

To his knowledge she never had, nor had he ever heard her speak of India's death, not to him, not to anyone in his hearing. If he had not given her enough reason otherwise not to trust him with her grief, he had had the ill luck to be present when it happened, and must be a constant reminder to her of that terrible loss.

Fall, 1966

THE FIRST FEW DAYS of November were clear and dry. Good hunting weather, only to be improved on by a light fall of dry snow, followed by a sunny day or two. Reuben Styles would have like to be in the woods. He couldn't hit a moose if he had an atom bomb to drop on it, but he dearly loved the tramping around in the woods of a crisp fall day.

Joe Nevers never cared overmuch for hunting since he was a young man. He had been a damn fine hunter, still had his rifle at the back of the closet, but had not touched it in years except to clean it. He listened patiently, as he always listened, to the hunters and their exploits, in the general store, or at the bullshit table in Roscoe's, or at the post office. Every kill was legendary, and the dressed and butchered meat all that stood between the hunter's kids and starvation that winter. What he had always thought was that if any of the mighty hunters had ever worked as hard at a job of work as they worked at their bragging and bullshitting, they would surely be able to dine on steak and rib roast all winter. If any of them had just said outright, as Reuben Styles did, that they couldn't shoot off their own toes without help, or that what they really liked about hunting was getting out into the woods with a bunch of buddies to drink and play cards and tell dirty jokes and piss out-of-doors, he might at least have respected their honesty.

Indeed, he did sympathize with whatever it is in the human animal that summons us into the forest of a fine day in autumn. He was not too old at fifty-seven to feel that pull. But this glorious November day, he and Reuben Styles were going to have to be satisfied with the invigorating air and superior view of the woods available on the roof of the new Christopher house. Wind and rain after Labor Day had done some damage, torn away enough shingles to make work for two men, and if the day happened to be the first Saturday of hunting season, it was just bad luck.

Reuben was a big, strong lad who had worked for Joe Nevers whenever Joe Nevers had a job that required an extra man, off and on for the past three years. There was an openness in Reuben's face that made him seem younger than he really was. That innocence, with a sweet temper and slow speech, caused hasty folks to assume the boy was slow-witted as well. That he was not, nor did Joe Nevers ever have a better man work for him.

Reuben worked like the devil without complaint, doing as he was told as hard as he could, always giving a dollar's work and then some for a dollar's pay. He talked little, but always to the point, so that the two men invariably told each other more in their taciturn exchanges than all the garrulous Yankees on the Ridge. It seemed sometimes in the last few years to Joe Nevers that his neighbors' main industry was gossip, which went on the livelong day from six-thirty in the morning when Roscoe poured the first coffee and tea for the truckers and loggers at his diner, to nine in the evening when he threw out the last soaks. And the folks that didn't get into Roscoe's regular could make it up at the general store or the post office, excepting, of course, from twelve to one in the afternoon, when Adelina Porter locked up the post office and went home for dinner.

Something—he did not know what but perhaps it was that same aboriginal urge to go into the forest— brought Torie Christopher and her surviving children to the new house, nearly ten years old then, that same weekend.

He discovered her presence when he drove in at seven-thirty to find her car parked in the drive and woodsmoke curling lazily from the chimney. It was only polite to knock on the door to say how-do, and ask if some pounding and stomping on the roof would be a bother.

It was David who answered the door, fully dressed and alert, more than alert, possessed of an excitement that was just under control.

Joe Nevers was relieved to see the boy up and about, and to smell sausage and toast, confirming that breakfast was under way. He and Reuben had not inadvertently rousted the little tribe of Christophers from their beds.

"Hell, no," David assured him. "We're late getting started anyway. We're going fishing."

Reuben elbowed Joe Nevers, grinning; he was enchanted with the loose way Torie allowed her children to talk.

Behind David, India was creeping down the stairs, still dressed in flannel pajamas printed all over with calico cats and gingham dogs. She rubbed sleep from her eyes and then curled up on the bottom step, staring at them with wide-open, still sleep-glazed eyes.

"Hi, Joe Nevers," India said. " 'Morning, Reuben," to his helper.

"We're going fishing," David said, suddenly irritable, "if India ever gets dressed."

Torie, dressed like David in jeans and a plaid shirt, but barefoot, stuck her head out of the kitchen to say, " 'Morning, Joe Nevers. Reuben."

"Missus," Joe Nevers said.

Reuben grinned rather foolishly over Joe Nevers' shoulder. "Missus," he said, and blushed Torie had that effect on him.

She pointed a spatula at India. "You, get a move on."

India sighed, then scooted up the stairs. She stopped at the top to ask, "Reuben, will you play checkers with me later?"

"Sure," Reuben said, shuffling his big feet on the mat. He liked playing checkers with India. At the time they were almost matched, though she might soon have the edge on him.

"Reuben has to work," Joe Nevers said. "Maybe dinnertime if you're back from fishing."

India grinned and pointed her finger at Reuben and Joe Nevers. "Gotcha," she said, "bang," and disappeared into her bedroom.

"Do what you will," Torie said to Joe Nevers. "It won't bother us a bit."

So he and Reuben climbed up onto the roof to do what they had come to do.

Joe Nevers could not remember the last time he had seen Torie without her children. He supposed not since Tommy's death, which seemed such an important marker now, for them all.

Guy never lost the stunned look in his eyes that the boy's death had put there. He might well have died with Tommy, instead of two years later. Even when the family was together, it was clear Guy was not really with them. He had withdrawn from David and India and Torie into some private, perhaps kinder world, and lived the last two years of his life slightly out of phase with the real one. He spoke vaguely, spent much of his time staring at nothing, and showed little or no emotion, beyond a terrible puzzlement. Joe Nevers had hated to see Guy that way; it was too much like Fanny's condition. The massive coronary that took him off was nothing more than a definition, Joe Nevers thought, of what had happened to him; his heart had been broken, and that had killed him.

From the time of Tommy's death, Torie and David and India had formed a new family, intense, protective of each other, defiantly alive together. The intensity of Torie's relationship with David and India underlined Guy's increasing isolation. Now they were truly just three and stuck together like burrs.

From the roof beam, Joe Nevers paused in his work to watch them. They put the larger of the Christophers' two canoes, the red one, into the water; David at one end, Torie at the other, and India in the center, with the fishing gear at her feet. It was cold enough for the turtlenecks under plaid shirts under orange life vests, and the knitted wool caps they all wore. David's was green and his red hair curling out from under the cap's rolled brim glinted in the sun, as did Torie's hair, even now not showing silver or white, though she was forty-one, under her black one. India's towhead blended with the creamy white cap she wore.

At ten, David was wiry, stronger than he looked. He was still androgynous, but gave promise of being one of those men whose feminine qualities would be a complement, a grace note, to an unquestioned, never overbearing masculinity. He was distinctly Torie's child. Like her, he never merely moved; he roamed, stalked, darted, and pranced, as if something or someone were after him, just a reach from his shirttail. At times it seemed as if the boy might explode if he had to be still.

In David, impatience was always barely controlled, except toward his mother. With India he made the least attempt to control his natural bent, as if he were afraid of her challenging his authority. Still, he was protective of her, as he was of Torie. Joe Nevers felt sure David would willingly die for India, no matter how he teased and ragged her. She seemed to know that love he disguised with his chiding, for India never sparked against him, or defied him beyond mild irritation, but did as he ordered.

Of the three children Torie Christopher had borne, Joe Nevers was most taken with India. She was tall for her age, and stronger built than her mother. Towheaded, she had her mother's creamy skin that never burnt and never tanned, either. India's eyes were blue, the left one flawed with a patch of brown at nine o'clock on the iris.

Perhaps affected by the near-constant grief that assailed the Christophers since Tommy's death, she was a sober child, and had a self-possession that was rare in those days, though such sophistication became common with the epidemic of divorce that began in the sixties. Torie was as cavalier about her children's formal education as she was about their language; even before Guy died, she had begun traipsing all over the world, dragging them with her. As a consequence, India spoke American English heavily laced with Greek and Arabic, but had not been able to make change in American coinage until Joe Nevers taught her.

He spent half one afternoon, the previous summer, when he should have been painting the boathouse, emptying his pockets of loose change and laying out the coins on a flat rock in the sun, teaching India what she did not know. She was quick, which had pleased him enormously. He had always been quick with numbers himself, though he had the benefit of being a storekeeper's son, and had learned to do his sums on brown paper bags, on the silk-skin-smooth oaken counter in his father's store.

He wondered how much of the lesson India retained. If she had not used it since then, she might have forgotten it; nothing, he thought, particularly numbers, was ever really learned unless it was relearned, over and over again, in daily practice. Perhaps when the fishing expedition was done, he would have a chance to find out what India remembered of dimes and nickels and quarters. He was surprised at how pleased he was at the prospect.

So he watched for them returning, glancing frequently at the lake. It was no hardship; the lake was at its most beautiful, like a sheet of smoked glass from one end to the other. The sun fell beneficently on Joe Nevers and Reuben Styles alike, warming them to a wonderful degree considering that it was November. Soon they had stripped off their wool shirts and worked in their undershirts, Joe Nevers' the old-fashioned sleeveless strappy sort, Reuben's a plain cotton T-shirt.

Near onto one, just after the two men had scrambled back to the roof after eating their dinners, the canoe came round the bulge in the shoreline that obscured the northern end of the lake from the southern, where the narrows were. Torie and David had swapped places; her back was to Joe Nevers, and David faced him.

India looked homeward. He was pleased when she picked him out and sat up very straight on the middle seat to wave at him. Her mouth opened in a joyous shout.

Torie turned a little in her seat, looked over her shoulder at him, and waved.

David tossed his head in greeting, his hands busy with swinging his paddle from one side to the other.

Joe Nevers, riding the roof beam, stopped, his hammer held high, a smile spreading across his face.

Reuben Styles, squatting on the slope like a spider, looked up from the box of shingles, glimpsed the canoe and its passengers and grinned, all right in his world.

A crashing noise erupted from the woods, something moving, panicked, through the brush, which carried over the water, blending with India's high clear shout of greeting.

Torie, David, India, the two men on the roof beam, all looked after the sound, startled.

A deer, a young doe, exploded from the woods, headed for the lake.

There was a crack, the doe jumped and fell, as a second crack broke like a thunderclap over the water.

Gunfire, thought Joe Nevers. Startled as the others, he registered the doe. But his mind was still on India; he still wanted to know if the little girl remembered how to make twenty-five cents from nickels and dimes. His eyes went back to her.

He saw her eyes widen.

Her mouth lost its shape, the lovely oval of her lips as she formed his name, "Joe," crumpling like an inflated paper bag being ruptured between a child's hands.

There was a dark place, at the first instant merely a dot, then like a camera flash, a widening circle on the white knitted cap.

She fell backward and to the port side of the boat, as if she had been pushed. Her arms flew up and open. Torie threw herself at India, but her hands seized empty air. India's body flipped over the side and into the water and was gone.

The two men watched, stunned. "What the hell?" Reuben muttered.

Then Torie's wail was carried over the water to them, the sound of a veil being rent. The sudden shift of her weight to one side of the canoe, the loss of India in the middle, caused the boat to tip. David was unbalanced, threw up his arms to compensate, and an instant after India's body disappeared into the lake forever, the boy and his mother went under the canoe as it turned turtle.

On the roof, Joe Nevers felt the world darken before his eyes; it seemed as if the roof beam under him moved.

Already, Reuben had started down, devil take the hindmost. Joe Nevers steadied himself, drew breath frantically, and followed, though he knew it was too late.

Whenever he stopped to assure his footing as he climbed down, he looked to the lake again. Two heads were visible above the level of the water. The red canoe bobbed serenely like the pointer of a compass.

Joe Nevers' memories of the mad scramble off the roof, during which he lost two fingernails, torn from their roots, and never noticed until he huddled exhausted on the shore some hours later, were still as crystal clear as the waters of the lake. He remembered because he could not forget: Reuben not dropping but throwing the other canoe into the water, not waiting for Joe Nevers, but pulling at once for the red canoe, where he fished the boy, who fought wild as the oldest wily bass or salmon ever taken from the lake, from the water, and held him there to keep him from going back in. Anymore than he could forget a single stroke of his own race through the water, fully clothed except for the high-laced boots that kept him cursing on the shore while he tore them off.

The water was as cold as the devil's heart; he thought when he first entered it, it might kill him, the shock of it might trigger a fatal heart attack and there would be two bodies to drag from the lake. He half wished it would happen; why would he want to go on living in such a world?

He and Torie dove and dove. Somehow Reuben broke through David's hysteria and convinced the boy they could best help by summoning more help. After righting the red canoe, so that Torie or Joe Nevers could cling to it for a few seconds' rest when they needed, Reuben and David made for the shore; the frantic pull gave the boy an immediate remedy for his shock and frustration.

It took three men, the volunteer firemen summoned because that was all Reuben could think to do, to haul Torie from the water, wrap her in blankets like a straitjacket, and bring her to shore. The powerful sedatives Glen McAvoy pumped into her calmed her but did not put her out; she would not leave the scene but sat on the shore, watching the dragging that went on until dark fell. He sat with her until Glen McAvoy forced him to come inside and change his clothes for dry, old things of Guy's still in the house; he and Doc had gotten Torie to do so earlier only by threatening to change her clothes for her, right there on the beach, if she did not. And he was sure that it was their modesty she conceded to, not hers, in the end.

The Sabbatos County coroner called India's death a "misadventure." No hunter ever came forward to claim the bullet, or the doe that died on the shore, her feet already in the water. The town kept its own tight silence. If it were not for the eyewitness of Reuben Styles (who was, perhaps, a little simple) and Joe Nevers (whose connection with the Christophers was lifelong, thus suspect, and there were other, more scandalous rumors), and the evidence of the doe, the whole business was hardly to be believed. As it was, there was no body and no bullet. As always there were those who believed what they wanted to believe. Everyone knew that if the child's death was an accident, the cowardice of the killer was not. Whoever fired that bullet knew they had done it, whether they meant to kill India Christopher or not. But who would have reason to murder a child? The doe was a powerful argument against that word being spoken too loudly.

David refused to come back to the lake. Torie came, as if she could not leave it alone, but she drank, she seemed to have given up trying not to, and she did not go upstairs to her children's rooms.

The very next dry day, Joe Nevers and Reuben Styles climbed to the roof again and finished their repairs. They had nothing at all to say to one another, and if one or the other stopped of a sudden to cover his eyes or blow his nose with suspicious hardiness, the other politely looked away. At the lake, always at the lake. It was smooth as glass, a pale blue aquamarine, and in the depths there were shadows, only shadows, that could be seen from the roof beam.

"I know," Joe Nevers said.

"What?"

"What you said." He took out his cheroots, examined the wrapper, and put them down. "You haven't been upstairs since India . . . died."

Torie leaned over the pill bottles on the coffee table, rearranging them in a new pattern. Her silence made him uneasy.

"I have," he blurted.

Her hand, hovering over the bottles, stilled. She did not look up at him. After a few seconds, she said, "Of course you have."

"Had to," he said. "Might be a leak in the roof, anything. Can't look after just one floor of a house."

She nodded, still keeping her face from him. " 'Course." She pounced on a pill bottle, then tossed it to him.

Surprised again, he made a clumsy catch.

"Tell you why I'm here," she said.

He replaced the container carefully on the table next to its mates. He picked up his tea cup and sipped at it. It had cooled a mite but was still palatable. "I'd like to know that, if you've made up your mind."

Earlier she had said she didn't know why she had come. Most likely she had come without thinking one out, but that didn't mean there wasn't a reason, back of her mind. He could only guess. It might even be she was guessing too.

She was quiet a moment, then with one violent motion swept the neat arrangements of pill bottles aside. They rolled as they pleased over the table top, coming to rest against the lip of the table's edge.

"I came here to die," she said. There was no melodramatic or rhetorical quality in her voice. She was stating a fact.

He believed her at once. That explained the jumble of pills. It was almost a relief to have his suspicions confirmed, that she did indeed mean to spite him. He thought about what he might say for a long time. In the end, he asked the first question that entered his mind. "Why now?"

She marshaled her reasons. "I'm going to die anyway, in six or seven months. Might stretch it out a little, with more radiation, or more medication. I'm useless the way I am now. Can't work, can't even read. I hurt like hell. I might be able to stand it if I thought there was any point. I'm satisfied there isn't. And I don't believe I'm being punished for my sins. If I am, it's too goddamn late to do any good. And I'm afraid if I wait too long, I'll be too weak to do what I should. I can't stand the thought of tubes and drips and beeping machines."

He nodded, remembering how Cora had suffered every pang for the sake of virtue. There were other deaths he could recall, quick and slow, hard and harder. Mostly, death was a mercy, when it put an end to dying. He had had occasion to put animals out of their misery. Simple compassion argued powerfully for her resolution. But it troubled him that he could summon no argument, or authority, to stop her. After all these years, it was hard to disengage himself from what had been his duty—to keep her alive.

"If you'll go away, I'll be about my business," she said, and buried her face wearily in the fur of her coat.

"Pardon me, missus," Joe Nevers said gently. "I can't go. I'm not fool enough to go into this storm again." It was as good a reason as any.

"Shit," she muttered, glaring at him, daring him to respond facetiously.

But he was sober. "Yes, it is. Shit."

"Well, thanks," she said, resigned. "For sparing me the lecture on waiting on God's plans. I'm a hell of a lot more scared of God's plans than I am of dying."

Joe Nevers shook his head, amused.

"I'm used to it, you know," she went on, smoothing the coat over her knees. "Been handling human remains most of my adult life. Leave mine in the ground long enough, some other human being with the same kind of curiosity in his bones will dig mine up and try to figure me out." She laughed. "Good luck to 'em. I never saw curiosity in any old bones, but I saw a lot of other things. Love and murder, once or twice. Christ, I'm tired."

She sounded it. The old man rubbed the arms of the rocking chair nervously. He didn't much care for those dark blue circles under her eyes or the way her speech had slowed. But he was glad she had gotten away from the subject of suicide.

"David's the only person in the whole world I give a shit about anymore, and all I've got left to give him is my property and the spectacle of my deathbed."

Now she looked at Joe Nevers, and he was surprised to see a flicker of apprehension in her eyes. She was worried about him. Getting ready to tell him the bad news, but he could guess it.

"You know what that means, don't you?"

He nodded.

"David will sell this place, if he doesn't burn it down," Torie said, her voice suddenly tremulous. "Maybe he's right." She put her head on her knees and shivered.

"Might be. Should think you'd want to turn in, missus." Joe Nevers gripped the arms of the rocking chair, the first move in heaving himself out of it, to help her to bed.

There was an enormous cracking noise, some great tree sundered, followed at once by glass shattering. The house shuddered on its foundation. The lights went out.

In near-total darkness, the house settled itself with a cacophony of small noises. The wind outside absorbed them into itself. The light of the fire behind the isinglass window of the old stove showed them each other's shadowy shape, before their eyes adjusted to the dark. Knowing she could not see it, Joe Nevers ventured a smile. Torie Christopher was the one woman he knew who would not scream if a tree fell on her house while she was in it. She had no more than jumped and exclaimed, as he had himself.

Her laugh pealed richly in the dark. "Is that God answering me, Joe Nevers?" she asked. "I do believe we have been cast into the outer darkness. And look, our fire still sheds a little light. Perhaps hellfire does too."

"Might," he agreed. "Stay put, now. I'm going to find a flashlight and have a look-see at the damage. Sounded like your bedroom to me."

Had his eyes not made a quick adjustment to the dark, or the stove's fire not lent faint assistance, he could still have located the flashlight in the kitchen cupboard by memory alone. He laid his hands on its cool metal shaft and was surprised again, nearly overwhelmed by mourning for this house he never thought he liked. David *would* burn it, he was sure of it. Even now it was wounded, and he was full of concern for it.

Quickly he confirmed his guess: The huge old oak that Torie had battered with her bulldozer Cadillacs had been torn loose from its moorings. It had fallen toward the house, its topmost branches smashing through the bedroom window.

He returned to the kitchen to find and light a pair of hurricane lamps. "Your friend the oak has had its revenge," he reported to Torie.

She laughed, and wave done hand dismissively. "I might have guessed it."

On his way to the cellar, he checked the phone and found it out, just as he expected. Downstairs, he flicked all the circuit breakers to off. Sometimes when the power was restored after a period of outage, the sudden surge of electricity would blow circuits. If the line outside was still live, there was little he could do about it, but he could at least minimize the damage inside.

He kept a few stray pieces of plywood in the cellar against exactly this event, a broken window so that the weather could be kept outside while he had new glass cut or the frame repaired if it was broken too. These he collected, with a handsaw, and carried upstairs.

It was half an hour before he had severed the branches that intruded into the room, cleared the shards of glass still standing in the window frame, and nailed the plywood over the hole. The broken glass, wrapped in newspaper, and the smaller bits and pieces of the branches went into a trash bin on the back porch. He had to drag the larger pieces out and heave them into the snow to one side of the porch, and came in chilled and damp, with snow down the back of his neck and melting in his eyebrows. After taking off his boots again and hanging his mack up, he mopped the floor and stoked the fire in the small stove.

All heat in the bedroom had fled out the broken window. The fire would at least keep the pipes in the bathroom from freezing but that was only a holding action. The room would not hold enough heat to make it comfortable or even safe to sleep in. After stapling old blankets over the plywood, for whatever good they might do, he went back to the living room, shutting the bedroom door firmly behind him.

For once Torie had stayed put on his instruction. She was half-asleep under her fur. The old man crouched beside her and touched her hands gently. He was struck by how cold her flesh was, though the stove was only three feet away.

"Missus," he said, "that room won't be fit to sleep in tonight."

"Don't care," she whispered. "Sleep here."

"No, you won't," he said. "You're going upstairs, where it'll stay warm. I'll sleep here to keep this fire going."

He waited patiently for her assent, though his knee and hip joints made it a torture.

Her voice was shaky. "I don't think I can."

" 'Course you can," he assured her roughly. "Why I've slept there and it's as pleasant as can be."

Now it was out. Oh, how his joints hurt just then; they wanted to shake and shiver as if he were palsied. Old fool, he cursed himself. Old fool.

"You have?" She seemed less shocked than surprised, wondering.

"Told you I been up there. You know how it is, all warm and cozy. Catches the heat. Way you had it built, you know." He studied his big gnarled hands in the soft light of the kerosene lamp. He swallowed hard. "S'pose I'm getting old. I . . . got sleepy onct or twict of an afternoon."

"Oh," she said.

And that was that.

Drawing a deep breath of relief, he tucked the fur coat around her and picked her up. She made no resistance. He was startled at how little there was of her, how light she was. The word *remains* forced itself into his thoughts. She was weak too, slack, as if she were already dead.

He climbed the stairs. More of her glass boxes of relics lined the way up. Though the lights within them had been extinguished with the rest, he could still see them, reflecting the light from the fire and the kerosene lamps. He was reminded of the Catholic church in which he and Cora had married. The ceremony, austere and a little furtive, had occurred in a side chapel because he was not converting to Cora's religion, only consenting to its blessing on their union. He had not had to promise, as Cora told him the non-Catholic spouse was usually required, to raise the issue of the marriage as Catholic, because Cora was even then in the midst of change. There would be no babies from their union. He had told himself he was too old too to have young ones about but now he wondered if it had merely been cowardice on his part. But he remembered clearly the one thing that had seemed most foreign to him: the markers on the wall, shallow relief pictures of the Passion and Crucifixion of Jesus Christ. Cora had called them the Stations of the Cross.

In size and depth they had been the spit of Torie's display boxes that housed the prizes of her life's work. To Joe Nevers, her treasures were as mysterious as those Stations of the Cross. In the near-dark, they were hollows in the night itself, blank and glinting like the metal skin of the black Cadillac outside, their contents suggested rather than seen. Joe Nevers wondered if Torie ever felt their strangeness, if they still had power over her, who had garnered their secrets.

The second story actually opened to the third, reaching above part of the length of the roof beam of the living room. Besides the children's bathroom tucked under the eaves, there were two bedrooms, the boys' and India's, separated on the first level, corresponding to the second floor, by bookcase partitions that afforded privacy in a clever way. The rooms were also divided horizontally, each furnished with a play area below and a sleeping loft above reached by ramps, where the third floor would be if there were a conventional third story. The rooms looked in different directions, the boys' north toward the end of the lake and the woods, and India's directly across the water to the west and the mountains.

At the top of the stairs Joe Nevers hesitated, then turned to India's bedroom and climbed the ramp to the little girl's sleeping loft. He settled Torie in India's child-size rocking chair so that he could turn down the sheets. She fit too well, like Goldilocks on the Little Bear's chair. Torie had not ever been a big person, but she had been vital, her substance somehow more dense and alive than others'. In pregnancy, she had glowed, drawing people like a good fire in the depths of winter. He had not been surprised to learn she was in the early months of her pregnancy with David when he saw her in the garden in Falmouth, that fall of '53.

Now she hardly noticed him, as she looked around India's loft, her lips quivering, eyes blinking against tears.

He picked her up again; she seemed no heavier than the big Raggedy Ann doll he had pushed to the other side of India's bed to make room for her. He rolled her between the sheets, as he had learned to do for Cora. At that instant, as a blind person reads Braille, he read the ravaged geography of Torie's body: She was as breastless as India had been on the day of her death.

She flinched against his arm.

He swore at himself. "Jesus Christ, I'm sorry."

"Not me," she rasped weakly. "I'm just Torie, is all."

"Pardon me, missus. I didn't mean to be so clumsy."

"Goddamn doctor," Torie said. "Liked my tits so much he cut them off. I think he's cutting me up for a crazy quilt."

"Now missus," he said, and could say no more, paralyzed with his own helplessness.

Instead he spread the fur coat, fur side down again, over her and tucked it in. It might make up for the scantiness of her own flesh a bit.

"Don't fuss," he told her. "This is the warmest place in the house. And I never dreamt any but good dreams here."

She smiled vaguely at him, already floating away on the narcotics. He counted only seconds, as he sat on the edge of the bed by her, before she slept. Then he left, feeling the intruder. All his fears on that score had come to naught, as they so often did. She had accepted his invasion of her dead child's space as easily as she now slept, and perhaps for the same reason. Perhaps she was merely anesthetized or too exhausted to summon any emotion other than resignation. It occurred to him then that there was another perhaps: Had he only prepared the way? For her? He wished her good dreams.

He made his way slowly down the stairs, careful in the pathetic light of the fire and the lamps. Old man, he reminded himself, at the end of a long, trying day, afraid of falling and breaking brittle bones. He was suddenly very tired too.

Ordinarily he would have banked his fires and gone to bed, trusting they would last the night. The house would cool, of course, but he never minded that. Had slept all his life in unheated bedrooms. In the morning he needed only rekindle the fires from the coals and soon the cold would be driven from the house.

This night, though, the entire house depended on the fires just to keep the cold at bay. The electrical radiators were no longer working to assist them. Torie needed that precious warmth. He must keep them burning at their fiercest. He could no more than doze, which was no hardship. An active life afforded him better sleep than many older folks, but he had always slept little and light, and risen early. Age had only made habit natural.

Picking up Torie's castaway bourbon he poured himself a shot, thinking she would rag him in the morning for it. At least he could tell her it had not gone to waste.

It tasted surprisingly good to him, a lesson no doubt in the benefits of abstinence, which allowed the rediscovery of a pleasure he had nearly forgotten. There were many of his peers on Nodd's Ridge who were alcoholics, and more who looked with horror on drink, styling it the devil's chief agent. He had observed that there were some who shouldn't drink, and some who could, and no doubt some who should and didn't. He fell, he thought, into the second class, having abused drink chiefly during the low of his marriage to Cora. He had put it out of his life after her death. A penance, she would likely have called it, for all the sins he had committed against her, and so some in the village thought, he knew. But that was not it at all. In fact her death had relieved him of the need to drink, to anesthetize him to her needs. He could bear the guilt of surviving her; it was the guilt of his constant failure to be whatever it was she wanted that had made him drink.

Outside the storm continued, fanning his innocent pleasure in the bourbon, which kindled an interior warmth to match the fire in the stove. He listened carefully, trying to guess what the storm might come to, and to the shallow, labored breathing from India's room. He smoked a cheroot. Now and again he stirred to tend the fires.

He would put the story of this weekend down in a letter to his sister Gussie. Now that she lived in Florida with her second husband, they wrote each other once a week, nice long gossipy letters, cheaper than the telephone that reduced the both of them to terse, shy, caricature Yankees. The letters made up some of the loss of decades of nearly daily conversation. Astonishingly to Joe Nevers, he had become Gussie's link with the Ridge, the main one anyway. It made him feel a little less guilt about staying behind. There was surprising activity from Gussie's end; it seemed sometimes as if half the population of the Ridge had retired to Florida, and Gussie kept tabs on them all. He had never expected his sister to join the migrating flocks of elderly, but he knew she did it out of her love for Peter Finney, not because the Ridge had defeated her.

It must have been the bourbon that slipped him slyly into a sound sleep. The storm spent itself in the

wee hours, degenerating into sleet and rain. The fires
burned down to coals.

Joe Nevers started from his sleep, drawn to waking
by the falling temperature of the room. Panic closed
his throat as still twitching off sleep he felt the change.

"Shitagoddamn," he muttered, vexed with himself
for falling so deeply asleep and letting the fires go.

He clambered to his feet, stretched, and shook his
head free of the cobwebs of dreams and memories.
The damp cold made him shiver. It came to him then
that it was not as cold as it should be. He sniffed the
air. He could smell the water in it. And over the
diminished breath of the wind, the eaves dripped a
steady drumroll on the deck. Here was a wonder or
nothing: the snow gone to sleet and icy rain. The
danger of freezing to death, or the pipes freezing, which
was almost an equal horror, was past at least for the
day. Relief was only momentary; the change brought
its own discomforts and troubles.

The coals were too feeble to kindle a kitchen match,
or warm his fingers sufficiently to ease the early morning arthritic ache. Painfully, he built new fires in each
stove. It did not take a long time to do, but the cold
made it seem longer. He tucked up close to the living
room stove, fanning his hands before the flames before
closing the firebox for a little relief. He rubbed his
hands vigorously until they had absorbed some warmth
and the joints moved a little easier.

The night was giving way outside. He made himself
a cup of tea as soon as the fire brought the kettle to a
boil, and wrapped himself in a blanket on the sofa to
watch the dawn lightening the sky while the fires
warmed the house to something livable. On the deck,
gaps between the floor slats showed where the wetter,
heavier precipitation had driven the accumulated snow
through to the ground below. The snow that remained

was rowed neatly as a patch of corduroy, and glazed with sleet. The glass of the window wall was still cold enough to his touch to make him shiver. He misted it with his breath. Slowly, Joe Nevers drew his finger through the condensation in the shapes of his own name.

GUSSIE BLEW ON THE PARLOR WINDOW, which looked down on Main Street over the sign that read WILL NEVERS & SON. Her breath made a little cloud on the glass.

The boy kneeling next to her on the sofa reached over her head and drew the letter G in the mist. The water his finger plowed out to form the letter trickled slowly from the bottom of the G to the windowsill.

"What's that?" he asked.

Gussie, five, giggled. "Gee, gee!"

The boy blew another cloud on the glass, and drew another letter. Gussie was entranced, still for once.

"What's that now?" the boy asked.

Her brow wrinkled in serious thought. "Double U?" she ventured.

"Silly," the boy said. "It's U."

"Well, how'm I s'posed to know?" Gussie demanded hotly.

This time it was her turn to make the cloud. She blew from the tips of her toes, as if she were trying to extinguish candles on a birthday cake.

The boy squiggled two S's, side by side.

"I know that," she told him. "That's sssss," she hissed.

"Well, that's how you say it, but the letters are called S's," the boy lectured, in almost perfect imitation of his first-grade teacher, Miss Esther Linscott, from the safety of the second grade.

On a new patch of cloud, he drew an *I.*

"I, I," Gussie shrieked.

The next one was more difficult for her. At last the boy prompted her. "Guss-ee. What it sounds like."

"E?"

"Right. Now put it all together."

They wiped the windowpane with a dish towel and then, on the count of three, blew a huge cloud of mist onto the glass. The boy took Gussie by the finger, and guided her through the forms.

"G," he said, "*USSIE.* Who's that?"

"Me," Gussie said, and planted her lips on the condensation under her name.

The boy laughed. "Don't let Ma catch you doing that," he warned. "She'll be proud you know how to write your own name, but she won't like you kissing the window. She swotted me once when she caught me licking the water off the window. When you were too small to remember."

"Why? What's so bad about that?"

"Well, wait until spring and you'll see how much dirt there is on this window that's invisible."

"Yuck," said Gussie. "Why didn't you tell me 'for I kissed it?"

The boy ruffled her hair with one big hand. "Didn't know you had any of my bad habits."

"I don't," she told him. "So there. Onct doesn't make a habit."

But she had a new one of her own, learned from him. He thought of it as proof of the old adage: A little learning is a dangerous thing. Not necessarily dangerous, but pesty. For weeks after, Gussie scrawled her name on the walls, the floors, the sides of dressers and inside the drawers, as well as on the windows. Years later, he would open a drawer in a dresser inherited from his parents and find her autograph chiseled by her pencil stub into the wood.

The old man shrugged on his mackinaw, pulled on his packs, and stepped outside, bareheaded, to pee off the back porch. His urine in the clean wet morning air was sharp and hot. He did not much care if it came blue and red like the French flag, so long as it came.

In the light of early morning, the driveway was a slick of wet, untrammelled, and drifted snow. The wind had made the drifts into glossy white dunes, arranged in a herringbone pattern. It made him glad, of a sudden, to be alive to see it.

Part of his view was the oak, fallen heavily over the hood of the black Cadillac. He would need the chain saw in the back of his truck to cut the trunk of the oak into movable pieces. The downed powerline was out of the way, a black line torn from its junction box at the top of the driveway and buried under the snow. Slack as an old clothesline, it emerged from under the top branches of the sleet-glazed tree to high on the corner of the house. The oak's branches could be severed near the trunk of the tree without danger from the dead line.

Suddenly feeling frisky, he ducked back into the house long enough to grab his muffler, gloves, and the cap that flapped down over his ears. After shovelling a hasty path through the snow on the porch and clearing the steps, he shouldered the shovel and set off up the driveway. Slogging through crusted snow in some places well above his knees took the starch out of him quickly. It was a lot like wading through mud, only colder and deeper and more slippery. He was not much cheered to think that if he lost his footing, which seemed likely since he was unbalanced every time he dragged one boot out of the snow and stepped up to break the crust before sinking to his knees again, he might sustain abrasions from the sharp-edged crust, but the snow at least would provide enough of a cushion to prevent broken bones.

The air might be warm enough to smell fresh and good and make him hungry as a bear in March, but it was also just right to slick every surface with a treacherous scum of freezing cold water. He upended the shovel to use as a walking stick until he reached the car, where he planted it handy for digging. He was glad to be rid of it; it felt altogether too much like a cane. By the time he reached the truck, he had worked up a respectable sweat. His nose was red and runny with the cold damp that lurked in the air's deceptive crispness.

When he fumbled in his pockets for his handkerchief he discovered he no longer had one. His had done duty as a bandage for Torie, and then she had used it for what it was made and still had possession. He wiped his nose on the sleeve of his jacket, something he hadn't done since he was a boy. He had a clear memory of his mother's pinching his cheek when she caught him in a surreptitious nose-wipe during Meeting one Sunday. He knew very well it was wrong, even at five or six, he had forgotten just what age he was. His mother was always rolling her eyes at grandfather Will, who chewed tobacco and spit it on the ground or sometimes at the side of the potbellied stove in winter, where it sizzled and stank, and who would sometimes blow his nose by pinching the base of his nostrils above the dimple of the upper lip and blowing the mucus onto his fingers, which he then flicked toward the floor or ground. The boy that was Joe Nevers had understood that allowances had to be made; Old Will was slipping. He pinched his own nose to remind himself to daub the sleeve clean. He didn't want people saying Joe Nevers was getting to be dirty in his old age, slipping.

The air coming into his lungs had begun to hurt. His sweat was giving way to goose bumps.

It took heating the key with his pocket lighter to open the door. He retrieved the chain saw and the can of gasoline to run it on and wished his snowshoes were still there with all the rest of his store of emergency gear (Whoever heard of an Easter blizzard? And why was he so cussed neat; the snowshoes went up on the garage wall on April Fool's Day every year, and who was the April fool this year?). He relocked the door, more by habit than for fear of thieves. Climbing into his own boot tracks, he started downhill at an even slower rate than the climb up. He felt like a small boy trying to walk down the steep stairs from the attic or into the cellar, wearing Dad's enormous boots. The gas can and the chain saw worsened the problem of keeping his balance and banged his legs repeatedly.

It was a relief to leave his burdens near the shovel he had planted like a flagpole in the drifts. By the time he reached the back door, he was shaking and shivering. All he could smell was his own acrid sweat, and his head buzzed. He was nearer panting than he liked to admit. That was what he got for haring off without a decent breakfast on his stomach. Patting his pockets for a smoke, he let himself in.

He lit the cheroot in the hallway, dripping onto the runner. The striking of his match, the sound of his initial suck on the smoke, were loud in the stillness. He listened for the sound of Torie's breathing, faint and far away. Wood in the woodstove crackled and burst; otherwise the house might as well have been empty.

A tinny slosh when he shook the kettle confirmed

that it was nearly empty. He refilled it with bottled water and set it to boil again. Taking a stock pot and a floor bucket from the kitchen, he stepped outside long enough to fill them with clean snow. He left the floor pail of snow in the hall to do a slow melt at room temperature; it would be handy for washing up and flushing the toilet. The stock pot he put on the stove to boil hot water for the dishes.

All that carting and hauling, besides the struggle up hill and down, set up a fearful racket in his stomach. Satisfied that the day was off to a proper start, he turned his attention to breakfast. He heard the faint sounds of Torie stirring upstairs. He made a fresh pot of tea and carried it up to her.

She had propped herself on the pillows to take in the view of the lake and mountains through the window. She looked the worse for wear: her hair matted with night sweat, her color ashen. Her face seemed thinner, the bones indecently prominent, great wells of bruised shadows in which her eyes had grown bigger, as if they were the catch basin for the vitality that her flesh had lost. Had he not known otherwise, he would have thought she had not slept at all. She seemed neither refreshed nor healed, but quieter, more at peace with herself. He wondered what she had dreamt.

"Dear God," she said, as if she disbelieved he was still underfoot, when she noticed him.

"Just Joe Nevers," he said.

"Are you sure? I thought only God got up this early."

"Don't know," the old man said. "Never run into Him this hour a the day."

"What about the Easter bunny, then? See him this morning?"

He had forgotten. To a childless old pagan like himself, Easter was no more than a day that marked

the change of seasons, when he would eat ham, sometimes in company, and talk to Gussie on the phone.

"Think he missed us. Good weather for him, though.
Crust on the snow; he'd go right along on his big flat
feet."

She studied him, noticed his cold-ripened apple
cheeks.

"Been outside already? You know you always carried this early to rise shit too far. When's the last time
you slept until ten?" she said

He thought about it. "Never have. Anyway, a man
has to pee."

She laughed. "Off the back porch, I suppose. No
wonder the Easter bunny passed us by."

"Is that breakfast I smell?" She sat up straighter and
punched feebly at the pillows behind her.

"All I need is a customer."

She settled back again. "What if I said just the smell
of it makes me want to puke?"

He shot the cuffs of his old work shirt for the effect.
"More for me," he said. "Like my own cooking, too.
But you might find a mouthful of food settle your
stomach."

She shrugged and took the tea cup when he handed
it to her. She drank it in short order, which surprised
and pleased him. It seemed to brighten her, or perhaps
it was wishful thinking on his part.

She gave the cup back to him and moved tentatively,
as if she had borrowed her body and had to try it to
see if it fit, or if it worked. Sweat beaded her upper lip
as she pushed the fur coat and the bedclothes aside
and struggled to her feet. She was decidedly rocky on
her feet, but waved away his arm.

"Worse hangover from the pills than I ever had from
booze," she said. "I'll be okay in a bit." The only thing
she allowed him to do was to drape the fur over her

shoulders. She sagged under its weight and then recovered.

He fretted in the bedroom at a discreet distance, while she used the bathroom. She was in there a long time. When she came out, he was surprised again: She had brushed and combed her hair. He wondered at the power of wishful thinking; sometimes it seemed as if it worked, or perhaps it was no more than the odds. He must not put too much significance in a woman's combing her hair.

Still, she used the bannister for a crutch going downstairs.

She went to the table instead of the sofa. The puzzle she had been working on was still at the nether end from the place settings. She looked it over, pushed a piece around idly, and sighed.

"Maybe I should finish it," she said.

"To be sure," he said. "Be a shame not to."

She let go the fur coat; he took it and draped it on the back of a chair. She sat down in the chair next to it, and patted it affectionately.

"What'll ya have?" he asked.

She grinned. "My pills, to start."

He fetched them willingly from the coffee table, and poured a glass of orange juice for her to wash them down with. She selected a few with great certainty; it was a relief to know that she knew one pill from another, and presumably was self-medicating whatever her pains and discomforts were and not just pilling to get high. And that she wasn't going to toss back the whole lot right then and there.

She caught the anxiety he was trying to hide from her and grinned.

"Eggs to follow?" she said. "What's Easter without eggs?"

"Dull," he said. "You want to have an egg roll? I'll

hard-boil the eggs and we'll roll 'em up the driveway and down again."

"With our noses," she said.

"Is there another way of doing it?" he asked.

"I think that's what the minister said to the chorus girl," Torie said, and then laughed. "You asked for it."

"So I did," he said. "So I did."

He left her smiling, looking over her puzzle, which was not quite in reach, more interested in it than she wanted to admit.

He waited while she took the first bite of soft-boiled egg.

"Okay?" he asked.

She nodded, and then, outrageously, winked lewdly.

He guffawed, and went back to the kitchen to finish assembling his own breakfast.

She looked at it, when he sat down, with a queasy eye, and shuddered. "Jesus. And don't you say a goddamn thing!"

"Fresh air stimulates the appetite," he said, spreading beans on toasted bread unfazed.

"You eat many of them," she said, flicking her hand in the direction of the beans, "we'll both need the fresh air."

"Ayuh," he said.

When he had taken the edge off his appetite, he sat back and reported to her.

"Took a look at that tree. The line's down between the house and the road but it's not in the way. Just got to get the tree off the car that's all. And dig it out—then jump it."

"You and who else?"

"Ain't the first tree I ever cut up," he said, breaking a sausage in two with the side of his fork. "Won't be the last."

She took a roll, well buttered and sticky with jam.

"Maybe I could help. I don't feel too bad. I mean, I'm not dead yet."

He covered his surprise. She was having a hell of a good time unbalancing him. "Whatever you think you can do," he said, meeting her eye levelly.

"You might be surprised."

He considered his plate, and was surprised. It was empty again.

"Goddam good cook," he observed. "You do away with yourself, you'll miss it."

She snorted. "Too far gone to get much relief from blueberry jam, old man."

"That's too bad," he said, and meant it.

She shrugged.

"You're awful cheery," he observed.

"Last day," she said. "Now, that's a relief."

"You're so contrary, cheese'd physic ya," he said.

She waved it away. "Wouldn't have done a goddamn thing of any value in my life if I hadn't had that," she paused to fix it clearly, "gnat of contrariness to goad me on." With that, she spread her hands palm down, fingers splayed, and pushed to her feet. One hand went casually to the hem of her sweater to roll it up in a catchall; the other plucked the pill bottles from the table and dropped them into it.

He felt, watching her do it, as if he had been hit in the chest with a hammer. He caught his breath.

She seemed not to notice his distress, but when the bottles were all neatly stowed, showed him her free hand, as steady as his own.

"Better living through chemistry," she cracked. "Well, better dyin'."

He swallowed hard, worked a semblance of a smile onto his face and admired her. "That's good, real good."

He watched her going back to the sofa. Her trousers were wrinkled from having done night duty as pajamas and were mottled where spots and splashes of bourbon stained the ash-colored wool. She still walked as if something might break. Chemistry, as she called the pills, had neither healed her nor entirely mitigated her pain. Nor had it for Cora. It was a hard go, no getting around it.

He cleared the table while snow-water boiled for dishwater.

"Got a schedule?" he asked her from the kitchen. "What time you planning on doing away with yourself?"

She put her stockinged feet up on the sofa, and looked over the back of it at him. "Thought I'd follow my instincts. My first instinct is a long, hot, soaking bath."

"Too bad for your instinct," he said over a clatter of dishes in the sink. "No hot water without power."

A look of total dismay swept over Torie's face.

" 'Course, you could boil some up on the stove. Coupla gallons to a time. Soak a piece of you at a time, while the next batch came up to a boil," he advised.

"Shit," she said. "Nothing ever goes right around here. Not one fucking thing."

"Best laid plans," he began.

"Jesus H. Christ!" she shouted. "Spare me another one of your village idiot clichés."

Hurt a little, he muttered, "Name's Joe Nevers."

"No wonder they crucified Jesus," Torie snapped. "He probably kept telling them his name was Joe Nevers."

She went back to playing with pill bottles on the coffee table, ignoring his injured silence.

He finished pouring boiling water into the sinkful of dishes. "Figured I'd cut up that tree. Get it out the way." He scrubbed the iron spider vigorously. "Then, dig the Caddie out. Can't move her until she's free of the snow."

"Ayuh," Torie said.

He looked at her sharp. There was no mistaking the mockery in her voice.

"What then?" she said.

"Get the truck down the hill, chain her to the car, and haul the bastard out of the ditch. Then jump her, if she'll take a charge."

"Good luck," Torie said. "You gonna rest on the seventh day?"

"Never have." Then, "What? Ain't you helping me?"

"Changed my mind," she said. "That kind of work'll kill me, if it doesn't kill you."

"Thought that's what you wanted."

"What? Croak while getting the car out of the ditch? Goddam it, you senile old fool, unless you plan on using that Cadillac for a hearse, I'm not ever getting into it again, not this side of hell. You think you have to haul my corpse to Falmouth so as not to upset Ruby, you do it." She sat up and slapped the pill bottles all over the coffee table.

"That ain't what I meant," he said, drying his hands on a dish towel. He patted his pockets and lit a cheroot. "I meant, I thought you wanted to die. You might's well do it helping me unditch the car."

She wouldn't look at him. "I'll be goddamned if I'll die helping you do anything as stupid as unditching that frigging car. You want to bury it, I'll help."

"Thanks," he said mildly.

"Anytime. You just go give yourself a fucking coronary. Maybe I'll pass you on the way to hell."

"Don't doubt," he agreed and held his tongue though his neck stiffened at the implication he was too old to do his job.

It was his own fault for reminding her she liked to be contrary. More fool him. It wasn't as if she hadn't sharpened her tongue on him a hundred times before.

"IF YOU CAN'T SEE straight through that bitch," Cora said, "I can. I ain't blind."

His supper curdled under his breastbone. He stared at the beer bottle sweating in his hand. She had been at him since he walked through the door at six-thirty, beat from the day's work. A summerday's work, at that, and not finished by a long sight. He had been looking forward to a decent supper and another two or three beers on the screened porch, feeling the first cool of the evening, if there was any. It was this time of day that he felt his age, before he got his second wind.

It seemed to him that Cora had been standing there in the porch door, strangling a dish towel, and chewing at him all day and headed for forever. The heat of the kitchen was behind her, fueling her, along with her crazy fixation on Torie Christopher. The underarms of her housedress were marked with the wet crescents of her sweat, which beaded along her hairline and trickled along the side of her nose to her lipline, where now and again she licked it away with hardly a pause in her ragging.

Feeling as if he were trying to shoulder the heat of all hell aside, he started to his feet, muttering he had work to do. He could drink his beers in the cool of the barn, among the mercifully dumb animals.

Cora stood in front of him, blocking the door to the

kitchen. Her hair was coming out of the neat twist she had done it in that morning. The colored light of the setting sun through the porch screens reflected off her glasses in a mad parody of X-ray vision.

"That's right," she said flatly. "That's goddamn right, Joe Nevers. Don't you think I know where you're going? I see right through you, you stupid bastard. You got all the time in the world for her, but not one solitary minute for me."

"I can't take this no more," he said, and punched her in the face. And into his other fist, hitting her so hard it jarred him.

She gagged, as if on her own poisonous words. The force of his blows knocked her backward into the kitchen. She blocked him with her arm as he raised his fist again, and staggered out of his way.

He stopped, staring in horror at the fist he had raised to her. There was blood on it.

Crouched in the corner between the door and the cat's litter box, she began to make a high mewling sound in her throat. Blood spurted from her nose. Her left eye was swelling shut. Her glasses hung on one ear by the bow.

He reached out for her.

She shrank from him, curling in upon herself like a frightened porcupine. It made him angry again, for her to act as if she had grounds to fear him. He grabbed her by the shoulders with harder hands than he meant to use. Her glasses dangled like a grotesque earring from her ear.

"Stop it," he said calmly.

The mewling kept on, higher and higher.

He shook her, trying to shake some sense into her. Her teeth chattered.

"Stop it," he repeated, a little more desperately.

And she did.

Then there was only his own hard, panicked breathing, and hers. She stared at him out of her glazed right eye. He set her down gently in a kitchen chair and began to back away, wiping his hands on his shirt. His throat closed up on him. It felt as if his mouth had been stopped with sand back to his gullet. He held out his hands helplessly.

She laughed at him, a paralyzing insane burble that must have hurt like hell through her shredded lips.

Lowering his head like a confused bull, he swayed on his feet.

Amazingly, she pursed her bleeding, swelling lips and spat at him.

He backed away, encountered the sink, and turned to it as a refuge, throwing the cool water drawn up from the icy depths of his well over his face, washing her bloody spittle away, and then the blood on his knuckles. He wiped his hands on a clean linen dish towel. Then he could look at her again.

Head in hands, she slumped at the kitchen table, where the remains of their supper was spoiling in the heat.

He brought ice from the icebox, wrapping it in the towel he had dried his hands on. He was afraid to touch her again, but made himself do it, a light tap on the shoulder.

Cora looked up at him but seemed not to see him. Her face was shattered. She grasped the edge of the table with both hands and tried to rise. He caught her as she pitched forward. Her glasses slipped at last from their precarious suspension from her ear and shattered on the floor. He picked her up and carried her out to the truck.

Doc McAvoy was just cutting into a rare steak when Joe Nevers knocked at the screen door. Across the kitchen table, his wife Hope was sitting down to hers. Doc looked up, unsurprised, indeed expectantly. He was used to having his meals interrupted. But the sight of Cora in Joe Nevers' arms brought him to his feet so quickly he knocked over the water tumbler at his right hand. The water splashed to the floor, spreading over the black-and-white linoleum tiles and under the table, disturbing Hoover, his old sheep dog, who had been sleeping there. Hope's mouth dropped open, her knife clattered on her plate.

"Lord" she said.

The smell of the char-broiled beef turned Joe Nevers' stomach as he stood on the stoop, waiting for Doc to throw open the screen door and admit them. He like to puke, but he couldn't, not with his hands full of Cora.

Doc peered at Cora anxiously, then sharp at Joe Nevers. His Cupid's bow mouth tightened to a seam in his Santa Clause face. He nodded toward the front of the house, where his office and examining rooms were located. Joe Nevers obediently crossed the kitchen, headed for the front hall.

Hope seized Doc's wrist. "Lord!" she said.

Doc patted her hand on his wrist absently. "We'll need some ice, dear," he said, and waddled down the hall after Joe Nevers.

Hope nodded and wrung her apron in her hands.

When Doc came into the examining room to find Cora on the narrow, leather-upholstered table, and Joe Nevers shamefaced at her side, he went directly to the sink to wash his hands. Then he took down a white coat from a hook on the wall and struggled into it, which was an effort. The buttons strangled in their buttonholes. He turned to Cora.

Joe Nevers did not want to watch Doc examining Cora's battered face. He drifted onto the front porch that Doc had enclosed to make a tiny waiting room, and stared across the Ridge. The lake pooled in its symbol of infinity at the foot of the bruised blue mountains. There was tension in the air that promised thunderstorms in the night.

He looked around again only when he heard Doc's hum. Doc always started to hum when he had reassured himself he was going to be able to do something useful for a patient. Joe Nevers watched him squirting a syringe full of some liquid to push out the air.

"You won't feel a thing, dear," Doc said in his high voice to Cora, still slack in semi-consciousness, but she jumped when the needle went in.

Joe Nevers felt sick again.

Hope came in with ice and began to make up ice packs for the swelling. She looked daggers at Joe Nevers, but when Doc dropped the syringe with a great sigh and looked up at her, she scuttled out of the room.

Doc frowned after his wife, then closed the door to the hall firmly. He pushed the bulky old X-ray unit toward Cora.

"Broke her nose," he said. "Going to need a picture, see what the damage is. Might have cracked some other facial bones. Must have been a hell of a crack you give her. I'll stitch up her mouth, what I can, but she's already swelled up bad. Might have to let it heal, then break it again to fix it."

Joe Nevers went back to the porch door to look out at the mountains.

Behind him, Doc added, "Christly mess, Joe."

Joe Nevers sat down, trying to concentrate on the lowered sun behind charred clouds. The buzz of the X-ray machine, the incidental sounds Doc made, his habitual hum, did not bother Joe Nevers. But smells assaulted him, antiseptic cleaners underlying every other odor, and the hot sickly smell of Doc's old sterilizer, the medicines in Doc's cupboards that were bitter, astringent, mysteriously herbal in their mingling, and the smell of sweat, his own, Cora's, Doc's, the smell of Doc's shaving lotion, the smell of blood. He staggered down the hall to the powder room Doc kept for his patients under the stairs, and vomited until there was nothing left to vomit but bile. Humiliated, he cleaned the porcelain fixtures with a paper towel from under the sink, rinsed his mouth repeatedly with water until the taste that remained was at least bearable, and sprayed the closet-sized, windowless room with the can of room deodorant that Hope kept on the tank. It was a nauseating smell, overwhelming, acrid pine, and he thought for a few seconds that he might vomit again just from that.

When he came out, he met Hope on her way from the kitchen with a glass of iced tea. She not only skirted him, she actually shrank from him, as if she thought he was going to punch her out too.

At that instant he wanted to keep right on going, right out of the Doc's house to his truck and as far away as half a tank of gas and the ten dollars in his pocket would take him. It was a powerful vision of himself, freed and on the road, that seized him, but he could not imagine an end to that road. The truth was he was afraid to leave the Ridge. He went around the newel post and sat down on the stairs.

Doc's house was very clean. The women all nodded when Hope said, *of course*, a body could eat off her floors. Nothing less was expected of a doctor's wife. It had given Hope a real purpose in life until the three McAvoy boys were grown up and gone away, and then it was not quite enough. She did a lot of church work, but since the lines were pretty clearly drawn between the saved and the sinning, there wasn't enough in bean suppers and church fairs to keep a woman of

Hope's energy occupied. Much to Doc's private distress, Hope had found a new career as the biggest gossip in town. Some people said Doc didn't know, that he was too busy; others said he didn't give a damn, as long as she left him alone about his weight, but Joe Nevers knew better. Everyone knew Doc had lost some of his practice but he was still the only doctor in town, he paid housecalls, he was cheap, and willing to take an occasional bushel of potatoes or a couple of capons from the cash-poor farmers. If his practice had fallen off some because of Hope's big mouth, there was still enough work in doctoring to keep him straight out.

Joe Nevers cursed Hope McAvoy heartily in his mind. He didn't doubt she would spread the whole sorry business all over town. She was one of Cora's connections on the telephone line that linked every family on the Ridge to every other. That Cora had confided, which made a joke of the word, in Hope, he was already certain. Hope McAvoy didn't suck in her stomach and glare at him every time he passed her at the general store, or in the church parking lot, for nothing. Almost as deep as the shame he felt for having laid rough hands upon a woman was the humiliation of knowing that a busybody like Hope now had the right to sit in judgment on him, and would.

She came out of the examining room again, looked at him as if he were something old Hoover had deposited on the step, and stalked by him. But she came back to hand him, none too graciously, a tall wet glass of iced tea.

He had no voice to thank her but he nodded stiffly, and then sipped on it, so she wouldn't think he didn't appreciate it. It wet his throat and sweetened his mouth and made him feel better.

She stood there staring at him, wringing her apron to remove the contamination of having touched something he had touched. Abruptly, too disgusted to bear the sight of him any longer, she hustled down the hall to her kitchen. Aluminum foil rattled and screeched as she ripped it from the roll to wrap the steaks for later.

Doc stuck his head out of the examining room and jerked it toward his office across the hall. Joe Nevers left his glass of iced tea on a stair tread.

Doc closed the door after him.

"Her nose is shattered. It's a job for a plastic surgeon. I'm afraid there's not much to be done until the swelling subsides. You want me to put Cora in the hospital for a couple of days? She don't need any special care but if you don't want to take care of her . . . if you think you can't take care of her, at home. . . ."

"I'll take her home," Joe Nevers said.

Doc nodded. "You did do it, didn't you?" he asked cautiously.

"Ayuh."

"You ever hit her up before?"

"No. No, I ain't."

Doc sighed. "I don't know what your troubles are, Joe, but it looks like maybe they've gotten ahead of you."

Joe Nevers nodded. It was all true.

"Been drinking?" Doc asked

"Tonight?"

"Tonight."

"Not that much, a few beers."

"Been talk around," Doc said. "Seems to me you been hitting it hard ever since you married Cora."

Joe Nevers stared at the floor.

"Cora been rough on you?" Doc asked.

"Some." Joe Nevers felt doubly low to lay it off on Cora after breaking her nose. But the mouth on that woman. . . .

Doc nodded sympathetically. "Cora's had a hard time with change, I know."

"Ayuh," Joe Nevers agreed.

Doc cleared his throat. "Anybody else involved?" He fiddled with the paperknife on his desk.

Joe Nevers looked at him sharp.

Doc went red with embarrassment. "Well, whatever the trouble is," he said brusquely, "it's gone far enough. If you two can't get along, you better go see a lawyer, get divorced. It ain't like you got children to raise."

Joe Nevers looked out Doc's picture window to the mountains, but they were blurred by a sudden welling of tears. His throat closed up.

Doc went on, more gently. "I mean what I say, Joe. This won't go to law unless Cora wants it, but if she charges you, you know I got to tell the truth. I won't say word one unless she forces me, believe me. But it can't happen again. You best get divorced, Joe."

Joe Nevers nodded. This was *his* medicine Doc was making him swallow.

Doc wrote on a tiny envelope, then shook pills from a bottle into it.

"You give these to Cora, one every four hours. Prop her up good so she can breathe through her mouth. I'll be by in the morning to look in on her. You want me to bring Hope to stay with her through the day?"

Joe Nevers most assuredly did not, but there was no one else to sit with Cora. He couldn't stay home and not work.

" 'Preciate that," he mumbled.

Doc pressed the envelope on him. "Try to keep an ice pack on the swelling. Call me if anything worries you. I'm handy." He hesitated. "What about you? You need anything?"

Joe Nevers shook his head no.

Doc fumbled in a cupboard. "Just in case," he said,

spilling a few pills into another envelope. "You have trouble sleeping, take one of these. Don't drink with 'em. Don't drink anything except water and tea," Doc warned. "Cora wants to file an assault charge, you don't want to have somebody say they saw you at the store getting beer, or hungover tomorrow."

Joe Nevers slipped the envelopes into his breast pocket next to his cheroots. "Thanks, Glen," he said awkwardly. "I'm real sorry this happened. I never laid a hand on her before tonight."

Doc put his hand on Joe Nevers' shoulder. "Joe," he said, "you been a friend of mine since we were both in short pants. I think we both lived long enough to know bad things happen, things go wrong. You don't want to blame yourself entirely."

Shocked, Joe Nevers stared at him. He never expected to hear Glen McAvoy making excuses for him punching out his wife. Doc had been known to give more than one hard-handed, bad-tempered farmer a hard time if he saw a kid or a wife too many times for unexplained bruises or bone breaks.

"Joe," Doc went on, "you're feeling bad about yourself. You should, I ain't excusing you. You did some bad damage to Cora. Did some to yourself, too, that don't show, and you'll be feeling it the rest of your life. But you remember, this ain't the end a the world. You ain't the first fella to punch his wife. It's happened before and it'll happen again."

Something let loose in Joe Nevers, and he had to fight tears again.

"Cora was a widow, wasn't she?" Doc asked. "When you married her."

Joe Nevers cleared his throat. "She was."

"Well," said Doc, "if I remember rightly, her first husband done away with himself? Shot himself?"

Joe Nevers stared at him.

" 'S'true, ain't it?"

Joe Nevers agreed, reluctantly, that it was.

"I seen a few cases a suicide, Joe. I don't like to make judgments on the survivors. But that ain't to say none of 'em was blameless. Maybe Cora didn't help the poor son of a bitch when it might a counted, maybe she helped him along to do what he did. I don't know. Maybe she didn't have nothing to do with it. But goddamn it, Joe, the woman's been married twict, and by all accounts, the first time wasn't no more successful than this time with you. And that daughter of hers is a lesbian," Doc said, implying, Joe Nevers thought, that that was somehow Cora's fault. "People figure," Doc went on, "someone who can't make marriage work twict in a row, maybe is doing something wrong, and they ain't entirely groundless."

"I been married before," Joe Nevers said slowly.

Doc turned red. "That ain't what I meant. Joe, I'm on your side. You know as well as I do that Marion left you, she was the one wanted out. You was a good husband, even she admitted that. It wasn't your fault, she didn't know what she had. Women like her are always convinced someone else's grass is greener."

"Thanks for trying to make me feel better," Joe Nevers said. In fact, he felt worse. Here an old friend was tying himself up in knots to excuse him. Doc had a good heart, but he had never had more than enough of the right kind of intelligence and shrewdness to make a good country GP. "You been a good friend. I know you're trying to help me."

Doc sighed with relief and mopped his face with a big white handkerchief. "I try," he said. "Now you take Cora home, and deal with all these trials and tribulations in the morning, when you've had a night's sleep.

*   *   *

The heat of the day had collected in the bedroom under the eaves. He threw open the windows and turned on the fan to supplement the weak breeze that stirred the curtains.

Cora's clothes were stained with blood and spittle. As gently as he could, he stripped her down to her underwear, then drew up the sheet to cover her. Even with the fan, she would not be comfortable in anything more. He took the bloodied clothing to the laundry hamper, and brought up a pitcher of iced water in case she should wake, thirsty, in the night, along with the ice packs Doc had prescribed. They had to be taped on just so. He made sure she could breathe through her mouth, then took the alarm clock that had been a wedding present and went downstairs. He set the clock for five, his normal waking hour. There were the animals still to be seen to, and the kitchen to clean up. He was not going to have Hope McAvoy come in first thing and see the place looking sluttish. It would be one more thing for her to spread all over the Ridge.

When the chores were done, he laid himself down on the daybed on the front porch. With the windows open, and just the screens to keep the bugs out between him and the night, it was like sleeping outdoors. The night was uneasy, waiting to be rent by thunder and lightning. After a while he took one of Doc's pills to release himself into sleep.

When the swelling subsided, Cora checked into the hospital in Greenspark to have her nose fixed. After the operation, the bruises seemed worse than the day after he did the damage. In time the bruises faded and the scars of the plastic surgery were only faint lines. Cora's mouth, her one point of real beauty, turned down at the left corner where a nerve had been damaged. She had never been much for smiling but now her smile was as rare as it was lopsided.

Everyone knew, without knowing the truth of it. Joe Nevers, accounted a good man if not a godly one, had struck his wife while drunk. It was agreed on the Ridge that Joe Nevers was in a bad season. But over the years, he and his father and grandfather before him had achieved a standing in the community that earned him the benefit of a lot of people's doubts. He would have to do something a lot worse than that to be entirely discredited. Joe Nevers worked harder, longer, and later than he ever had, so much so that he lost weight noticeably. Nor did his work seem to be affected by the awesome quantity of beer he was reliably reported to be putting away. Well, it was a damned hot summer; very likely he sweated it out. Plenty of men drank heavily and were still good men.

Cora seemed more Cora than ever before. When her husband came in from the barn at six in the morning, she had his breakfast on the table. To him, she looked as she always had, the picture of a churchgoing, self-respecting woman; the very woman priced above rubies, clothed in her strength and her honor. That was what he had married her for.

What vanity she had was in her clothes. The women admired them not just for her fine seam, which was very fine indeed, but because she did not dress above herself, but was content to be first among her equals with the needle and sewing machine.

Though she was a Catholic and had to go to Greenspark of a Sunday to attend mass, she had long supplied baked goods to the church suppers and fairs on the Ridge, and continued to do so. In a community in which every other old woman was counted saved on account of her heavenly pie crust, Cora's was judged the best among the "girls." Those were the women still in menopause. Any woman who had not experienced a hot flash had not had time to develop the expertise that a really good crust demanded.

Cora was judged a good woman as well as a good cook. It was possible to be a good woman and not a good cook but rare was the good cook who was not a good woman. Being a good cook was a virtue in itself.

Cora's friends took her part passionately, without being asked. Still, it was surprising the number of stable, reasonable folks who qualified the judgment with a shake of the head, meaning it was just possible Cora bore some of the blame. There was the business of her first husband doing away with himself. Of course that had not occurred on the Ridge but way to hell and gone in New Hampshire, twenty miles west. Despite her generosity to the church on the Ridge, which had long since become next door to nonsectarian, Cora's Catholicism was an undeniable eccentricity. And then there was Jane, Cora's daughter by the suicide, who had been divorced and lost the custody of her daughter to her ex-husband. Not Cora's fault to be sure; everyone had family difficulties from time to time. Still, there was a lot of smoke, and there was bound to be some clucking about fire among the hens.

Hope McAvoy was provoked to the offensive, scolding a number of fence-sitters for what she saw as favoritism to a native, but they would not be moved. It was the first time that thought had occurred to any of them, and the more they thought about it, the more they liked it. Cora was after all, a New Hampshirite.

Through all this, Cora never spoke of the matter. Her friends, particularly those such as Hope who counted themselves close at a time like this, could not pry a word from her. Hope McAvoy was forced to convert Cora's silence into heroic suffering.

The first frosts jewelled the Ridge. If Cora's closed

and twisted mouth accused him wordlessly, if Joe
Nevers drank more than was good for him, he rarely
showed it, and they were still living under the same
roof. A few folks ventured that the marriage might
survive. Worse had. And of course it was before folks
started divorcing over a cross word in the morning.

The day before Thanksgiving, Adelina Porter looked
up from sorting the mail to see Cora and her daughter
Jane coming through the door.

" 'Morning," Adelina piped cheerily, and shuffled
quickly through the remaining mail to see if there was
anything for Cora. She turned up an ad for a women's
magazine and a flyer from the church.

Cora waited patiently, the contents of the post office
box already stowed in her purse.

" 'Morning," Jane said.

Adelina handed the two pieces across the counter.

"Up for the holidays, Jane?" Adelina asked.

"Yup," Jane said. "Brought the turkey with me. Shot
it myself."

Cora smiled painfully.

"What?" Adelina wasn't sure she had heard it just
right.

"Turkey shoot. Bagged an eighteen-pounder," Jane
said.

"Well, good for you," Adelina said heartily.

"Thank you, Addie," Cora said. "Good day."

"To you too," Adelina said, but Cora was already at
the door. Jane, on her heels, grinned sheepishly over
her shoulder.

"You should a seen them," Adelina told Hope
McAvoy an hour later.

"No!" Hope said.

"Cora looked like always. Real neat. Had on her hat

with the autumn leaves on it. But that girl!" Adelina said.

"Lord," Hope shook her head in disbelief.

"Every stitch of her clothes came out of a men's store. Men's clothes, that's what they was all right. Fair give me a turn, I'll tell you. I thought for a minute she'd been in my brother Henry's closet. And her hair! Next door to a crewcut!"

"Cora upset?" Hope asked.

"I should say so," Adelina sniffed. "Bleached right out. Embarrassed to death. I never seen the like of it. I thought that girl was a college teacher. I guess I wouldn't send one of my kids no place where the teachers dressed like lumberjacks."

"What do you s'pose that girl's thinking of!" Hope exclaimed. "Poor Cora."

"Well, I don't know," said Adelina, airily, which meant she did know perfectly well but wouldn't dirty herself by saying the thing out loud.

That evening, Joe Nevers put on his jacket and took down his cap as soon as he had cleared his plate. He had not gained his truck when the screen door slammed behind him. He turned to find Jane at his heels.

"I forget something, girlie?" he asked, cracking as much of a smile as he had in him these days.

Jane planted her work boots firmly on the ground, shoved her hands into the back pockets of her jeans. "Joe," she said casually. "What the fuck is going on?"

He put one hand on the hood of the truck to steady himself, took off his cap and tucked it under one armpit.

Jane stamped one foot impatiently. "Goddamn it, Joe, there's something going on."

He licked his lips.

"My mother," Jane said, "hasn't spoken word one to you in the twenty-four hours I've been here. I know what that means. She used to do it to my father and me whenever one of us crossed her. So what the fuck did you do?"

Joe Nevers cleared his throat. "I hit her," he said

Jane's eyes widened.

"I hit her. Broke her nose. Broke her glasses too."

"She never said boo to me about it. When'd it happen?" Jane recovered quickly.

"Summer," he said. "July."

Jane nodded. "When I was camping the Gaspé with Marcie. When did she stop talking to you?"

"Since then."

"Shit," said Jane.

Joe Nevers groped for his cheroots, shook one out, and stuck it between his lips while he hunted up his matches. "We got to get divorced," he said around it. "I know it. We can't go on like this. We got to get divorced."

Jane sighed, and hooked a butane lighter from her breast pocket. He took it and lit his cheroot carefully behind cupped hands. He stared at the ground in shame.

"Look at me, Joe Nevers," Jane ordered.

Reluctantly, he met her eyes.

"She was at you, wasn't she? Chewing on you?"

He shook his head. "That ain't no excuse."

"Don't be so goddamn quick to take the blame," Jane said. "I've been chewed by Cora. It ain't no frigging picnic."

Joe Nevers hung his head. "Christ," he said, and shaded his eyes with one hand and sucked loudly on the cheroot.

"Christ all right," Jane said. She grabbed his arm and shook it. "Why do you think I married Gary? Anything to get away from her." She jerked one thumb toward the kitchen door. "He's a total asshole but even now, if I had a choice, I'd live with him over her."

His eyes met hers; it was his turn to be surprised. "Thought you married Gary Foster on account of you was pregnant."

Jane shrugged. "He had to have a reason to marry me. Yeah, I did it on purpose. Partly, I was trying real hard to convince myself I was a real woman." She snorted and shook her head. "Guess I found out."

"Jane," Joe Nevers said, switching his cheroot from one hand to the other so he could cover her hand on his arm with his. "I'm sorry. That's a sad story."

She shrugged. "You want me to talk to her?"

His cheekbones flared red. He thought about it. It seemed like something he and Cora ought to work out for themselves. He shook his head.

"Too bad," Jane said. "I'm going to talk to her anyway. You want to stick around and see which one of us goes to the hospital?"

"We got to get divorced," he said absently, not really hearing what Jane was saying.

"Smartest thing you could do," Jane said, "but first, I'm going to chew on Cora for a while. You can divorce her after I spit her out."

She put her hands back in her pockets and stalked to the house. She was one of those tall girls with small breasts and a big behind to make up for it. In the tight, faded jeans, her bottom had something of the formidable look of an aircraft carrier plowing through rough seas.

Throwing down his cheroot and grabbing his cap from under his armpit, Joe Nevers trotted after her.

Jane slammed into the kitchen. Cora was at the sink, up to her wrists in soapy water. Joe Nevers came in behind Jane and stood back against the screen door.

"You frigging bitch," Jane said.

Cora looked at her, apparently unsurprised. Then Cora slapped her.

Jane stood her ground, but the force of the blow knocked her head to one side. When she straightened, the print of Cora's hand was red on her cheek. A faint lace of foamy dishwater dripped across her jaw. She did not even touch the place she had been struck. She picked up a cup of cold tea from among the dirty dishes and threw it in Cora's face.

Cora flinched. Now she was breathing hard, staring at Jane.

"Now you know what it feels like," Jane said. "You use the edge of your tongue on somebody again, think about how it feels to be on the receiving end."

Cora looked past Jane to Joe Nevers. "You ain't got the right to talk," she said. "This ain't none of your business."

"I'm making it my business," Jane said. "It's high time you found out how it feels, what you been doing to other people all your life."

"Get out a my house," Cora said, and turned back to the sink.

Jane looked at Joe Nevers. "No," she said.

"You don't know one thing about what I've had to live with," Cora said. Her hands moved dreamily through the dishwater. "You ain't got the right."

"Shit," Jane said. "Your sainted cunt."

Cora sucked air as if she'd been punched. She was looking at Jane again, but her hands were still in the sink.

"Now Jane," Joe Nevers said.

"Shut up," Cora said to him.

She looked at Jane. "You are just like your father," she said, each word spoken as if she were throwing rocks at a glass window.

"No, I'm not," Jane said. "You'll never get me to blow my brains all over the bathroom floor."

"You always blamed me for that, you always took

your father's side. That's what you're doing now," Cora said.

"I know," Jane said. "I could forgive you that, he was a shit, too. I remember that, you know. But you liked it, that's what I think. That's what pisses me off. You like being martyred too much."

"Your cheap easy excuses don't interest me. When you straighten out your own life, then you'll have some grounds for criticizing me."

"Shit smells like shit," Jane said. "It doesn't take an expert to identify it."

"And you call yourself a professional woman," Cora said, wrinkling her nose with disdain. Her mouth twisted in a horrible parody of a smile.

Jane turned halfway to Joe Nevers.

"Leave your gun where she can find it, Joe. She's a good shot, you know. Hell of a shot. Daddy taught us both. Maybe she'll use it on herself. Then everybody'll say you drove her to it, you bastard you, and she'll be vindicated."

Joe Nevers was struck dumb. He had never suspected, behind the facade of politely kissed cheeks, there was so much spleen between the two women.

"You are no more child of mine," Cora hissed at Jane, "than you are a natural woman."

Jane laughed. "With you and Dad for examples, who'd want to be natural? Get fucked, Cora."

Cora dried her hands deliberately on her apron. "I told you onct before. Get out."

Jane shrugged. "Joe, you want me to go?"

He cleared his throat.

"What is it?" Jane asked. "Catching? She won't talk to you, now you can't talk either?" She shook her head. "Oh, Joe, you gonna stand there like a cigar-store Indian until she gets you to murder her?"

"No," he said. He looked at Cora. "We got to get divorced."

Jane heaved a sigh of relief. "Good. That's out."

Joe Nevers hung his cap on the hook by the door. "This is my house," he said to Cora.

Cora stared at him for a long moment. Then slowly, with shaking hands, she took off her apron. She folded it carefully and hung it over one arm. Then she stepped around Jane as delicately as a cat avoiding a puddle, and went slowly, with a deliberate tread, up the back stairs.

"Go to work," Jane said to Joe Nevers. "I'll do up the dishes for you. That big-mouthed friend of hers, Hope? She can get Hope to drive her to wherever the hell she thinks she's going."

Joe Nevers looked up the narrow back stairs. There was the sound of Cora dragging a suitcase from under the eaves.

"This ain't the end of it," he said.

Then he took down his cap and went out.

When he came home, Jane was sitting on the back stoop, smoking a cigarette.

"I took care of the animals," Jane said. "Want a beer?"

He allowed as how a beer would go down nice.

Jane went into the house. The screen door slapped gently behind her. The refrigerator door clicked and clunked. She came out again.

"Thanks," He said.

They sat down together in the light spilling from the kitchen.

"She's at McAvoy's," Jane told him.

He nodded.

"Look," Jane said. She dropped the butt of her cigarette onto the ground. Stretching out a long sturdy leg, she crushed it with the toe of her boot. "I've been thinking. I don't know I did you any favor, shooting my mouth off."

Joe Nevers shrugged. "Couldn't a made it any worse."

"Maybe," she said. "Got you off Go, though, didn't I?" She grinned at him.

He smiled shyly into the tab hole of the beer can.

"You want me to cook that bird just the same?" she asked.

"Sure."

"Good." She lit another cigarette. "Ask you one thing?"

He took out a cheroot. "Sure."

"What's she got on you?"

Joe Nevers sighed. He put down the beer can but held on to his cheroot. He showed her his hands. "I laid my hands on her."

Jane nodded. "I know that. What else? You aren't the kind of man puts bruises on his woman for the fun of it. She had to have been after you about something."

Joe Nevers lit his cheroot. "Working too much."

Jane snorted. "What's that mean? You aren't coming home when you're supposed to?"

"I guess."

"Drinking?"

"I guess."

"Why?"

"Hot," he said. He hooked one finger under his shirt collar and pulled at it. "Summer's hot. Work all day, get dry. That's all."

"Sure," said Jane. "I've seen you work. You sweat it out, do you?"

"I guess."

Jane sucked at her cigarette. "Who you balling, Joe?"

Joe Nevers looked at her. "Not Cora, for sure," he said, and grinned.

Jane laughed. "You sound dry. Want another beer?"

He looked at his can in surprise, shook it. It was empty. "My turn," he said. He stood up and stretched. "You want one?"

"I guess," said Jane.

He laughed.

When he was back, Jane said, "Sometimes I think I know what makes Cora crazy."

"What?" he asked

They popped their beer can tabs simultaneously.

"You can be pretty goddamn terse," said Jane. "You know that?"

"Sometimes," he admitted.

"You worried about a word shortage?"

He laughed again and shook his head no. "Just the way I was raised . . . I guess. We didn't talk about . . . some things. They was private."

"Well, I still haven't gotten an answer out of you," Jane said. "Who you balling, Joe?"

He laughed shortly and scratched behind his ear. "God the father, Sonny Jesus, and the Holy Ghost, where you young folks get your ideas? I'm fifty-three years old, girlie. You think I can work a fourteen, fifteen hour day and tomcat, too?"

"That's a mouthful," Jane said. "Yes, I do." She poked him. "You old bastard. Look at you. You know damn well you're stronger than most of the eighteen-year-olds in this town. Don't give me that old man shit."

Joe Nevers sighed. "Tell you, Jane."

She waited while he wet his throat.

"Tell you, Jane, I wisht I was getting it as much as all these goddamn old women on the Ridge say I do."

She laughed and threw her cigarette into the darkness. It shed a trail of sparks like a shooting star and then went out. "Never mind, I'll find out from Gussie."

"Cora's only got it half right," she said.

"How's that?"

"You hear what she said? Her saying I'm not a natural woman?" Her hand came to rest easily on Joe Nevers' forearm. "Sometimes I am. Let's go upstairs and be natural."

He patted her hand but tried to be stern. "Janie, you're like a daughter to me."

"Shit," she said cheerfully. "When you married Cora I was married myself and had a kid."

He thought about it. He was surprised how appealing the offer was. But he shook his head. "Wouldn't be right."

Jane shrugged. "Up to you," she said. She stood up, stretched and yawned. "Hard work, busting up a marriage. Guess I'll call it a day." Her hand on the screen door, she stopped. "Later on, if you feel like you'd just as soon be hung for a guilty man, I'll be pleased to be an accessory."

"Good night," he said.

But wishing didn't make it so, after he rapped gently at her bedroom door.

He wasn't surprised when Glen McAvoy drove into his yard next morning. He sank his ax into the chopping block and went to lean into the window of Doc's cavernous old Buick station wagon. Doc's dog Hoover was in the back, looking and smelling his age.

Joe Nevers thrust his hand in. "How-do?" he asked.

Doc wrung it. Doc's hand was slick with sweat. Hoover jumped up to slobber over Doc's shoulder. "Seen better," Doc said.

"How's Cora?" Joe Nevers asked.

"That's what I came for."

Joe Nevers nodded. "Thought so. Sit on the porch?"

Doc weighed the effort of heaving himself out of the

station wagon against the invitation. When he opened
the door, Hoover scrambled over him and fell out onto
the ground. Doc wriggled around until he had one foot
out and then delivered a light kick to Hoover's ribs.
Hoover yelped and staggered away.

"Sorry," Doc muttered to Hoover.

Doc lowered himself gingerly into a wide old wicker
chair. It was habit with him to treat all furniture as
fragile. He listened to the chair creaking as he settled
himself. It sounded up to him. He sighed with relief.

"Jane still here?" he asked, craning his neck to peek
through the screen door into the kitchen.

"If she ain't," Joe Nevers said, "that turkey's cooking itself."

Doc cleared his throat. "Cora's some put out."

Joe Nevers nodded.

"Put out with Jane, too."

Joe Nevers studied his woodpile.

Doc hauled out a handkerchief and mopped his face.
"Cora wants her out a here. Pronto."

Joe Nevers settled back into the porch swing and
took out his cheroots.

"Cora says she'll prosecute you for assault if Jane
ain't gone by noon," Doc said hurriedly.

Joe Nevers looked at him over the match he was
applying to his cheroot.

Glen McAvoy had hero-worshipped Joe Nevers when
he was the leader in all their childhood games, the
captain of all the teams, because Joe Nevers was not
only good, the best, but he was fair, and always made
a place for a clumsy fat boy. Just then he was very glad
he was not Cora. For that brief second, he wondered
how close Joe Nevers had come to killing the sad
bitch.

Joe Nevers shook out the match. "That Cora's hole
card?" he asked.

Doc nodded. "Won't give you a divorce, unless you give her the house. You try to divorce her on whatever grounds, she'll prosecute."

Joe Nevers studied the charred match. "I've lived in this house since I was first married." His voice was close to a whisper.

"I know," said Doc, as softly.

"We ain't been married long enough for her to have no rights to my house," Joe Nevers said. "She didn't bring nothing with her 'cept a used-up Ford, a treadle sewing machine, and the strop for her tongue."

Doc sighed heavily. "That don't matter, Joe. She takes you to court, I'll have to testify. You'll be fined, at least. Maybe see a weekend in the county hoosegow. You got to decide what's worst, that's all."

"I ain't got no name left," Joe Nevers said bitterly.

Glen McAvoy rubbed his nose. "Christ Amighty, Joe, I'm sorry. All I can say is nothing lasts forever. People forget."

"I don't," he said.

"Your friends ain't gonna stop being your friends," Doc said. "I'm still your friend, you know that, don't you?"

"I 'preciate that, Glen," Joe Nevers said. "I do."

"Cora don't come from here," Doc said.

"I know," Joe Nevers said dryly. "I brung her here."

"More's the sorrow," Doc said, and mopped his face again. Hoover had flopped onto the bottom step. He stank even from that distance. Doc was certain it was the smell of cancer. Hoover was dying. Doc had never felt so helpless in his life. He felt like crying.

"Glass a tea?" Joe Nevers asked, recalling his duty as a host.

"Why, that'd be real good," Doc allowed.

Joe Nevers left him suffering on the porch.

Jane was in the kitchen, humming over the hubbard

squash she was chunking. She looked up expectantly.
"When am I supposed to be gone?"

Joe nevers stopped, his hand on the refrigerator door.

"That's what Doc's here for, isn't it?" she asked.

Joe Nevers opened the refrigerator door, took out a pitcher of iced tea.

"Noon," he said. "She's gonna prosecute me for assault if you ain't."

With a particularly vicious chop, Jane whacked a large chunk of hubbard in two. "Bitch," she said. "I'm sorry, Joe."

"Wants the house, too, if I file for divorce."

"Shit," said Jane.

He poured a glass of tea.

"I'll be done with this in a minute. Then I'll make tracks," she said.

"I'm sorry, Janie," he murmured.

"Me too," she said. "I was looking forward to that bird."

Outside, Doc gulped half the glass at once. "What you gonna do?" he asked.

Joe Nevers examined the stub of his cheroot. He threw it into the yard. Hoover lifted his head to follow its trajectory, then resumed his stupor.

"Give her what she wants," Joe Nevers said.

"You sure that's wise?" Doc asked.

Joe Nevers didn't answer.

Doc finished his tea and struggled to his feet.

"Tell her Jane's leaving," Joe Nevers said. "Tell her I don't want no divorce. She comes back, we'll go on like before. That's what she wants."

Doc started to say something, thought better of it. He waited for Hoover to heave himself off the bottom step, then waddled toward the car. He opened the door. The dog heaved himself up and fell into a heap behind the wheel. Doc slapped his rump. Hoover moved over.

"Joe," Doc said. "Don't let her push you too far. You got to pay a price to get out of it, maybe that's better than doing hard time for something worse. Maybe you could let her charge you, plead guilty, pay your fine, or whatever. Then she ain't got nothing on you. You could dicker onct they was lawyers involved."

Joe Nevers shook his head. "Play it her way," he said. "Give her what she wants."

Cora got out of Doc's car at six that evening. Joe Nevers sat on the back porch, waiting for her.

Hope McAvoy was next. Then Hoover fell out and stood weaving on his feet. Doc heaved himself out from behind the wheel and hustled around the back of the wagon to retrieve Cora's suitcase. He stopped to pat Hoover's head. Hoover moaned, and slobbered over Doc's hand.

Hope stood and glared at Joe Nevers. Cora started up the porch steps, head high, ignoring him. He did the same to her, studying the McAvoys as if they were strangers who had wandered into his yard, their car marked with alien plates.

Hope mounted the steps behind Cora. She stopped to hiss at Joe Nevers. "You lay a hand on her again, I'll see you hung for it."

Joe Nevers raised an eyebrow at her. There hadn't been a death penalty in Maine for better than a century, since a case of mistaken identity had illustrated one of the drawbacks of the practice.

"Hope," Joe Nevers said. "You're a lucky woman."

Hope started. She had not expected a compliment, if it was one. She glanced nervously at her husband, who was puffing across the yard with Cora's suitcases and pretending to be deaf. She crossed her arms and stood her ground, ready for anything.

"Why?" she asked, and was immediately sorry she had.

"Glen and I been friends since we was in short pants. That's the only thing kept me from raping you the first time I saw you."

Hope gasped.

"You're disgusting," she managed to splutter, and stalked into the house, slamming the screen door behind her.

Glen McAvoy huffed up the steps.

"I'll take that," Joe Nevers said, getting up.

"Thanks," Doc said, and put it down on the top step. "Did I hear what I thought I heard?"

"Ayuh," Joe Nevers said, and grinned at him. "Hope you didn't take offense."

Glen McAvoy snickered, covering his mouth with his hand. "Shit, no. Hope and I gonna have a talk when we get home. I can see she ain't got enough to do. I'm the one owes you an apology. She ain't got no business sticking her nose in nobody else's affairs."

"Just don't knock her one," Joe Nevers said. "Christ knows what it'd cost you."

Doc's grin gave way to jiggling distress. He glanced around the yard for Hoover reflexively. Hoover stood stock still next to the car, just where Doc had left him, a blur in the gathering darkness.

"You don't know how sorry I am, Joe. You gonna be all right? The two of you?"

"Don't worry," Joe Nevers said, patting Doc's arm. "I'm just gonna give Cora everything she wants."

Torie had slipped into an uneasy doze. Must be the pills, he thought. He stood over her uncertainly for a time, trying to think of a way to make her more comfortable, something he could do for her. On the sofa pillow, her hand curled like a dry leaf, twitched and fisted and splayed. Baring her teeth, she growled, deep in her throat. Startled, he took an unconscious step backward.

He went out again, grateful to be out of the house. Outside, the storm had wrought a great tangible peace of snow and wind and empty woods. It was a marvel how a full belly in the aftermath of a good storm could make a man feel ten years younger. The shovel stood waiting at the bend, like a widow for the mailman, hugging herself against the cold. He set off slowly up the hill, pacing himself against the chores ahead.

When he touched the trunk of the Cadillac, it was so cold it telegraphed a shiver to his spine and back again, to the tips of his fingers. His nails chattered on the metal. The gloves he pulled from his back pocket restored only a surface warmth.

He freed the shovel from the snowdrift and groped his way alongside the car, pushing against the shovel to keep his balance. Rotten with rain, the snow would not support his weight and turned slick when it was packed down under his feet. At the crests of the drifts, his footsteps became holes to be climbed out of. Snow spilled into his boots. His feet chilled and began to ache with the cold.

The Cadillac was in worse straits than it first appeared. The oak had stopped its skid, which had happened before the snowfall on dry gravel, onto the grassy incline, as the same tree had done several times before, for this Cadillac and others Torie had owned. There was no telling the extent of the damage the tree might have done to the frame of the car, but the Cadillac's nose was as thoroughly smashed as Cora's had been the night he broke it for her.

The big automobile, in turn, had loosened the oak at

its roots and fractured its battered trunk, mortal injuries, never mind the storm. The wind had almost entirely uprooted it, as well as tearing it limb from limb and scattering the branches everywhere. Top-heavy, the oak had fallen in the direction it was already bent, toward the house, over the hood of the Cadillac. The weight of the tree trunk at the very front end of the automobile had weighed it down and lifted the rear end higher, as well as crushed the hood, already accordioned by the earlier impact. Windblown snow, under and over the rear wheels, fooled the eye into the impression the tail end rested on a bankment of packed snow. But it was drift, crusted with sleet, and rotten-hearted with rain.

When he broke the crust and scraped away the softened snow, he found the left rear tire barely in contact with the gravel underneath. The right rear, off the edge of the driveway the night before, had been lifted yet a little higher. If he could raise the dead engine to life, the rear wheels would quickly spin the snow off in icy gobbets. And then they could spin merrily in the air until hell froze over, for all good they would do. He needed them on the ground if he was going to get the bitch back on the driveway again. He decided to sever the trunk of the oak from its roots on the left side of the car, leaving the weight of it on the hood so as to prevent a sudden shift of balance. The snow could not be counted on if the Cadillac slipped from its precarious position. The slick crust might skate it any which way. If he sliced the trunk off the hood a piece at a time, he might be able to drop the car gently back onto all fours.

Behind him, the snow-shrouded and iced roots of the tree were a distracting snare. They looked a terribly easy place for a man to break an ankle. The space between them and the car, where he would have to work, seemed all too narrow. It was hard to turn his back on them. He nearly froze right there, afraid if he moved in any direction, even slightly, there would be a sudden constriction around the ankle, and he would tumble backward, screaming, into that female menace. And would never get out, for one of its hundred arms would coil around his throat and choke him.

The wind had strewn the Cadillac with broken branches and the sleet glued them where they fell. Leaves that had died on the tree the previous fall and not let go all the long winter had frozen with their twigs into the plaque of ice that coated the car. He made himself bend over enough to crackle one glazed leaf in his fist. Then he could breathe again.

Before he could do anything else, he must make himself room to work in. The first stroke of the shovel was an effort. With the snow this wet, it was going to be a long, slow, bitter-cold job. He began to trench along the left side of the car. For a moment, he regretted his own pigheadedness in insisting he was up to this chore.

He dug himself space to stand with the twisting nest of roots at his back, and sparked the chain saw. It screamed like a banshee, momentarily unnerving and deafening him. When he sank it into the trunk of the oak, its vibrations traveled the length of his arm, making his teeth ache. The oak was remarkably tough and not much easier to cut through than the skin of the Caddie might be. The way the teeth of the chain saw stuttered on the wood, Joe Nevers thought they might be aching about as bad as his did. He braced himself against the instant the saw bit through bark again, but still staggered when it happened and had all he could to to resist the downward pull of the saw, which once it was cutting air at such an invigorating rate seemed to want to keep right on going, say, right through one of his feet. He silenced it, and then there was only his own hard breathing to hear.

The great bulk of the tree, branch and limb, lay as it had fallen the night before, over the Cadillac and down the hill to the corner of the house and the bedroom window, now blinded with the makeshift panels of plywood. The top of the tree was bonded by the ice to every surface it touched, roof, shingle, wire, and snowdrift, by the rain and sleet that had fallen since. He would have to sever the trunk on the nether side of the automobile from that tangle.

He dug his way along the other side of the car, and rewarded himself with a break. Thrusting the shovel into the snow, he leaned against the slick cold metal shell of the automobile. He took off his cap and mopped his face as dry as he could of sweat and precipitation with his gloves. Glancing toward the house, he saw Torie in the door, watching. And him winded as an old plug. The sudden warmth of blood rushing to his face made a mask over the coldness that had penetrated to his core. He'd rather she see him naked than weak.

He turned his back on her and slogged around the car for the chain saw. For the first time, he was troubled with the disquieting thought that they might be in more trouble than he had imagined. A sick woman, an old man, in this empty place in savage weather. No phone, no power, no way out except the truck, and that depended on him. If something happened to him, she would have to drive his truck. His truck. And there were too many trees, and too many ups and downs all greased to a fare-thee-well.

He chided himself for a soft old fool. A body might live without electricity or phone, car or truck, millions in far places did. Just so his folks had lived the most of their lives, and never missed what they hadn't had. And there had been commons in their lives, clean air and clean water, that were threatened in his. If he was old, his age carried a weight of experience and was evidence of a talent for survival, if nothing else. If Torie was sick, in healthier days she had willingly lived in the most primitive corners of the world for the sake of a few old bones and some broken pots. A little snow, a little wet and cold, would hardly be the death of a pair of tough old birds like themselves.

Before he could set about separating the trunk of the oak from its branches on the left side of the Cadillac, he decided to make himself a little more space to work in. It was not going to be as neat a job as the other end. He was reminded, as he hoisted a few more shovels of snow over his shoulder, of the old superstitious rite of tossing a pinch of spilled salt over one's shoulder for luck. It seemed to him he had already tossed a goddam sight too much of spilled "salt" over his shoulder this Easter, and had a goddamn sight more to go.

The shriek of the chain saw deafening him, he did not hear Torie coming up the driveway, though she slipped and cursed several times. When she laid her hand, light as a leaf it was too, on his shoulder, he started and nearly cut his own hand off. Grimly, he killed the chain saw.

"Jesus!" he swore, over the fading mechanical scream.

"Sorry," she said. "I ain't Joe Nevers, either."

She had rigged herself out in layers of what must have been Guy's old hunting clothes, plus her fur, which had begun to look the worse for wear. She looked as outlandish as one of those scarecrow dummies kids make, in the fall, of ragbag clothes and dry leaves, except he had never seen one in mink, not even hard-used. When she laughed at him, atremble with the vibrations of the chain saw and the unexpected touch of her, he thought that's how it would sound if one of those Halloween effigies could laugh. Ragged. Abandoned.

"Didn't mean to scare you," she said. "You look like you seen a ghost."

Shaking his head, he hoisted the saw to the hood of the car.

"That goddamn saw'd wake the dead," she said.

With both hands, he struck the hood of the Cadillac as hard as he could. The ice crackled. The chain saw danced. Fastidiously, he began to pick the loosened debris of twigs and branches from the broken glaze.

"You'll catch your death," he said. "Go on back inside."

"Caught my death already," she said. She kicked one tire of the car. "Take your own advice, you old fart. Look at you. You're wet right through, aren't you?"

He shook his head no. Being childish, he knew. She meant no harm. Wanted to pass the time, or felt bad about cursing him out before and wanted to help if she could.

Torie reached for the shovel. "Let me do some of that. Don't worry. I'll leave you plenty. You go change. There's some of Guy's clothing in that dresser in the bedroom. Go on now."

Standing in an inch of icy water inside his boots, he shivered. He stuck his hands in his pockets. His pride crackled like the ice on the car.

"I'll change," he said. "But you needn't be out here. You come inside and stay warm."

"Get fucked," she said cheerfully. "You goddamned old woman."

He grinned at her. "Somebody should a smacked that mouth of yours one years ago."

She sank the shovel into the snow with a grunt and winced. Feeling that cut hand, he thought, noticing she had covered it with what looked like three pairs of mittens. "Too late now," she said, already a little breathless. "Don't you ever learn a goddamn thing? You tried that with Cora. Wisht I'd been a fly on the wall for that one. You'd ever tried that one on me, I'd a taken a butcher knife to you."

"Guess I'm glad I didn't, then," he said.

" 'Course you are," Torie said matter-of-factly. "Still got your balls." She moved the shovel shakily to one side to dump it. "Don't you?"

"Not so's you'd notice," he said. "The cold's chased 'em up alongside my tonsils."

He set off down the hill, and hoped she wasn't watching when he slipped and landed on his sit-upon. No favor for his old bones, and he'd see some bruises from it, but he was too old to borrow on tomorrow's aches and pains. He didn't look back at her.

The dresser looked like World War II had been fought in it, the way she had ransacked it. He turned out two pairs of long underwear, three pairs of heavy socks, a pair of wool hunting pants, and some heavy shirts the moths had only nibbled on. Guy had been longer of limb, but as wide of chest and slim of waist. A pair of Guy's old boots still stood in the back of the closet. He could fill them up with those thick old socks from L.L. Bean. And there was Guy's old plaid hunting jacket, hanging on its hook as if he had just taken it off. Looked as if it hadn't been touched in, what was it? Twenty years.

He scratched behind his ears. He hadn't had any idea she had kept all this gear. All this time. Hadn't expected it. Would a thought at least David would have taken some of 'em. India's things—toys and clothes alike—were just as the child had left them. And Tommy's, too. As if Torie expected them back any time. But he had not thought that was how things were between Torie and Guy. It made him hopeful to think they had had some good still between them, and then, surprisingly, sad, perhaps at what he had missed.

And as much as he had been in and out of this house, more than Torie since India died, he had never noticed this store of anachronisms. He supposed that wasn't in itself extraordinary. He intruded into the houses in his charge no more than was strictly necessary. They were all someone else's property; he respected that—after all, his life's work had come down to the protection of private property—and privacy was part and parcel of that. But over the years he built up a fair picture of what was where or should be or wasn't. He didn't like being surprised this way. Too much like finding out he didn't know his job or hadn't been doing it. Hadn't wanted to notice this stash.

After checking the fires, he went out. Torie had advanced the trench around the car to the far side. Head down, bracing herself against the shovel between efforts, she didn't notice him until he was all but on top of her. She tried to mask her relief by being brisk.

"You ain't gonna win a Miss America contest, but you'll do."

He took the shovel from her. "Get yourself inside now, missus."

"I like it out here," she said, propping herself against the car. Way to catch her breath without admitting she was winded, he thought, and admired her for it.

"If the tail of this bitch was any higher," she said, patting the Cadillac, "it would qualify for the Cadillac Ranch."

"What's that?" he asked, putting the shovel into the snow with renewed vigor.

"Sculpture," she said. "Believe it or not. Fellow in Texas has a whole line of 'em, buried nose down in the dirt. 'S'posed to be significant."

"Sounds like a waste to me," Joe Nevers said. "Don't nobody want the parts?"

"Guess not."

He grunted. "Never could make out Southerners. They got a lot of crazy ideas."

"Actually, I like it," Torie said. "I like to think they'll stay that way about five thousand years. And then some archaeologist will come along and find 'em and say, 'I'll be fucked. What's this all about?' "

Joe Nevers smiled. She liked to talk like that; he'd heard fantasies like that before. It *was* kind of funny to think about. He scratched behind his ear, then took out a cheroot. Might's well have a smoke, while she was keeping him from working. Catch his breath too.

"They'll think it's something religious," she said.

"Think so?"

"Well, it is, isn't it? The Great God Cadillac. I like that. Somewhere that Indian chief, old Cadillac himself, is laughing himself silly. In his own way, he's had his revenge on the white man, you know?"

"I guess," Joe Nevers said. He couldn't see, himself, just what it amounted to. Not much more than a Southerner's craziness, either.

"Why don't you just leave the damn thing, Joe Nevers?" she said. "Leave it for Reuben. Have him bring his boys and his tow truck and haul it out. We don't need it, you know."

"I'll get it out," he said. "Now you just take yourself inside, missus."

He took hold of the shovel handle firmly. The day he left Reuben and his boys do his job, he might's well curl up and die. He couldn't stop her calling him an old man but he wasn't going to let her turn him into one.

A minute later he lifted his head and there she was still, hugging herself and shivering.

"Ain't you got nothing else to do?" he asked crossly.

"No," she said. "I always like to watch someone else working their ass off."

"You and the rest a human race," he said. He leaned on the shovel. "What you waiting for?"

"Thought I'd watch you have your coronary," she said. "It's sort a fun, seeing an old fool working so hard at killing himself."

He pounded the car again and picked at the loosened plaque. He noticed, just then, he had not finished cutting the trunk from its branches on this side. She had come along and distracted him.

"Sauce for the goose is sauce for the gander," he said. "I got as much right to kill myself my way as you do yours."

"Right," she said. She turned on the heels of her red boots and clambered along the trench to the driveway.

He felt low. He clenched the shovel and drove it hard at an angle behind the right front tire, in frustration. As he did, he glanced under the car. He saw she had dug both the front and rear wheels on the other side free. He could see air underneath them. The Cadillac was rooted in position only by the weight of the tree trunk that stretched across the hood toward him, its top spreading over the snowcrust away past him, glued by a skin of ice to the snow.

The shovel slipped from his grasp, away under the car, like a paddle into the depths of the lake. He reached, convulsively, for the car door. Even as he did, the weight of the Cadillac shifted toward him, drawn by the weight of the tree trunk and its branches reaching for the house across the snow. The chain saw slid slowly across the hood toward him. He tried to brace himself.

His mouth went dry and slack. The drizzle fell coldly into the cracks in his lips and wet his teeth. He gasped once for air. It came into his lungs cold, and hurt as it expanded. He tried to push it back out, but his throat closed up, stopping the cold inside him. The chain saw crashed into his chest. He cried out, and the cold air escaped him. The Cadillac came down on him, black and heavy and slick. Surprised, and resigned, he slipped beneath it.

PART TWO

TORIE HEARD IT GO BEHIND HER, and the old man's single cry of surprise. She spun about too fast, slipping in the icy slush. On all fours she crawled a yard, regained her feet, and struggled toward the Cadillac. It was settling like a tombstone against the wall of the trench when she fell against it.

"Joe Nevahs," she wailed.

Trembling, she waited, but only the dripping eaves and a gentle susurration of rain answered her. She threw herself onto the surface of the snow and crawled across it, over a tangled nest of amputated branches of the oak, sharp with ice, that scratched her face and wrists. She circuited the hood toward the left. Here the trench had widened as the car had moved toward the other side. Dropping into it feet first, she sank upon her haunches, and then collapsed on her belly, dazed and gasping. In a moment she could discern the snow shovel, within her grasp, the ominous block of the chain saw, and the old man, a bundle of darker shadow in the obscurity under the car.

Head first, she squirmed through the soft wet snow halfway under the car. There was an instant of dizziness from the effort, and then her hands struck the chain saw. She pushed it weakly away from her and scrabbled at the old man's clothing. She curled up against him, crooning, trying to hold him. She found his hand, held her breath, and felt for his pulse. His flesh was clammy but the heartbeat was there, irregular and fading, but still there. A noisy breath wracked him. She cried out, frightened, and clung to him.

In a moment, the drilling of cold and damp into her bones sobered her. Her first panic passed, though not the fear. But now she was able to think and act on it. Her eyes, once adjusted to the half-dark, could see one of his legs was bent away from her, up under the side of the car. The weight of the car seemed to have pinned him from under the ribs of his right side over the groin and nearly to the right ankle, the foot being visible, with the knee, but hard to reach where the space beneath the underside of the car and the trench wall narrowed to a crack. At least he had not taken the weight of the car on his liver or spleen. The ribs might be broken, one or another lung punctured. His heart might have given way to the shock. There were too many possible disasters to consider.

He did not react to her hand on his brow. His eyes, when she pried them open, showed only white.

The cold shook her from deep inside. If she was cold, she realized, he must be too, perhaps dangerously so. She crawled out and pulled herself to her feet. A spasm of pain ripped through her vitals. She blanched, gritted her teeth, and waited it out. She had learned, unwillingly, that it wouldn't kill her, not right away.

The world around her had become huge and empty. A gauntlet of rotted snow and branches separated her from the driveway. When she could move again, she made her way to the house in a stupid daze.

Instinct took her to the phone in the hall. She heard only the dead sound of its silence mocking her, swore passionately at it, and threw the instrument angrily to the floor. She tore blankets from the bed, scrabbling and jerking them. Running back out, she tripped on the dangling corners, and left the door open behind her. The drizzle stinging her bloodless cheeks reminded her that the blankets were being dampened too. She bundled them frantically and struggled up the hill to the car. By the time she reached it, the pain was clawing at her. She fell against the trunk, clutching the blankets tighter as if they might save her.

"Jesus," she whispered.

At last she moved groggily into the trench and under the car. Covering the old man as best she could, she lay prone next to him and held his hand.

"I'll get you out," she promised. "Don't worry."

She wedged a corner of blanket between his head and the snow. His head was heavy, an awkward fruit on a weak stalk. His mouth was an open cave, and spittle glistened in it.

"There," she said. "There."

Lying next to him, she felt the wet seeping again through her layered clothing. Shivering made everything hurt worse. But she got her breath and for awhile held her own, listening to the sound of the weather, hard rain falling on punk snow.

She didn't know what to do next, except that she couldn't stay here with him and she had to get him out. She had said she would, though he had not heard her, she was sure. But she didn't know how. She was paralyzed by her own sense of helplessness.

Summer, 1961

UNDER THE BLUE DOME OF HIGH SUMMER, a light breeze stirred grasses below and leaves above. It cooled both players and spectators, moved the bugs along, and imparted, now and again, a nice quirk to the ball. It was a day for baseball.

And between the church and a fine gentle slope of hillside that made in winter a sliding place for the little ones and in summer a natural amphitheatre, the field had so obviously been made for baseball that no one could remember a time when boys had not brought their bats and balls to its dusty diamond. Over the years, a few traditions had grown up, the chief of them being the annual Labor Day game that marked the end of summer.

It was not yet Little League, just boys from nine to twelve, seasonal and year-round residents alike, who sorted themselves out into two teams by means of drawn straws, and played ball. Boys do not need uniforms, or coaches, or sponsors to do that; they do not even need to know each others' names. And because the teams were mayfly teams, existing only for the day, over the summer they came to know each other both as friend and foe. It was rare for enmity or resentment to grow up between the boys, who next game might be on the same team. Yet the competition was fierce, the games hard-battled all the same. Boys do not need to hate each other to play their hearts out, either.

Settled on the green incline as thick as wasps in their nests, more than the total winter population of Nodd's Ridge had gathered for the game. Kinship to a player was in the minority; they were all kin to each other at the Labor Day baseball game.

Torie shook out their old blanket and watched it settle gently over the mossy cushion of the hillside. Near her, David held tight to India's hand and stared at the boys clustered on the field. Like all the younger brothers, he wanted to be there, choosing up.

Torie followed David's gaze to Guy, just clapping Tommy on the shoulder and leaving the field to join them on the blanket, in a general exodus of fathers. It was time to start the game.

"David," she said.

Not afraid to let her see the rue in his eyes, he looked at her. He sank gracefully upon his corner of the blanket and pulled India down into his lap. She giggled, wrapped her arms around his neck, adoring him. If he had pulled her into tar or the open dump pit or off the end of the world, she would have giggled and clung to him just the same.

Torie reached for David, tousled his hair, and pulled his head between her breasts. She toppled gently backwards, David shrieking for joy with her, and India piled on top. People near them laughed to see them tangled in a heap on their ratty old blanket.

Guy plucked India from the top of the pile and piggybacked her on his shoulders. David sat up, brushed off his shirt, though it was not dirty, and blushed, embarrassed to be wrestling publicly with his mother.

Breathless, Torie lay still, staring at the improbable sky. Someday, she thought, there'll only be India to wrestle, and we'll be watching David play. And after that, no more wrestling on this old blanket, and we'll be watching India. She grinned. That would be a battle, when she and India made them take girls on the team.

Guy, cross-legged next to her with India still perched on his shoulders, reached for Torie's hand and squeezed it, but did not take his eyes from Tommy and the game below.

Shading her eyes with her hand, she studied Guy, profiled against the sky. His hair was thinning, losing its luster, his chin line softening, the blue of his eyes bleaching out. His hand in hers was heavy, dry with the callous of his tennis racket, and with constant cleaning with harsh soaps and antiseptics. By touch she found the wide gold band on his ring finger and picked at its edge with her nail. There was a ring of callous that marked the riding of the ring against his skin. He never took it off.

This day she was happier than she had any right to be.

"Joe Nevers!" Guy said.

Torie sat up and twisted around to see Joe Nevers and Cora making their way to the Christophers' nest. She reached for India, so Guy could get up to shake Joe Nevers' hand.

"Missus," Joe Nevers said to her, and took off his cap. It was an old Red Sox cap that he wore annually to this event.

Torie shaded her eyes again and held out the other hand to Cora.

The only thing she felt for Cora was a bloodless curiosity. What sort of woman had Joe Nevers taken it into his head to marry? What sort of woman would marry Joe Nevers?

Cora's hand was damp and nervous. She did not speak, only nodded politely and backed away.

Guy's hand reached for Cora's.

Core tore herself from Torie's level gaze to smile tentatively at Guy.

Guy invited the Neverses to sit on their blanket. Cora clearly didn't want to, but her husband accepted, and so she sat down, awkwardly, hugging her skirt over her knees, as if she were worried that someone lower on the hill might look up her skirt. Torie wondered why the woman hadn't worn slacks. Every other woman on the hillside had the sense to wear pants, including Torie.

Well, shorts. Until Cora stared pointedly at her legs, Torie forgot that she had opted for shorts. They were perfectly respectable shorts, too, tailored and pocketed and loose, the kind she wore on desert digs. The tightness of Cora's lips, Torie might have been wearing short shorts, or no pants at all. Torie closed her eyes and laid back on the blanket, stifling a giggle. Guy poked her in the ribs. She opened her eyes.

"Blanket hog," he teased.

She sat up to take less space.

Cora looked as if she had been inadvertently arrested with a wagonful of whores.

Torie was beginning to feel irritated. It was like the woman had not heard it was 1961. Curious, Torie looked at Joe Nevers.

He was looking at her legs. Ah, when he realized she was aware of him, he blushed, looked away a second, then met her eyes again.

Calmly, Torie assumed the lotus position. Joe Nevers glanced down, flicked a worried glance at her, and then stared at the baseball players changing sides.

Cora's back set in a rigid line to match her mouth.

Torie checked on Guy. He was watching the game, as she expected. Watching Tommy. So was most of the Ridge. Tommy had come to bat. The sun was in his hair. He brushed his hair out of his eyes, hefted the bat.

Christ, she thought, what a beautiful kid.

He smiled. There was a ragged cheer; Tommy was popular, not just because he was a respectable batter. People took to him, the way they had always taken to his grandmother Fanny.

"He's a corker," Joe Nevers remarked to Guy. Sounded like cockah. Made her want to giggle.

India crawled into the cradle Torie's legs made and reached under Torie's blouse to her breast. India's head followed, and Torie, with a little sigh that was only partly resignation, reached in to unsnap the cup of her bra. India found the nipple at once. The sound of her first suck was a loud slurp. Guy, Cora, and Joe Nevers all glanced her way. Cora's mouth tightened some more. Pretty soon it was going to come around and meet at the back of her head. Guy didn't react at all; everything was perfectly normal to him. Joe Nevers, looking quickly from Cora to Torie, suppressed a smile and politely turned his attention to the game.

Sometime soon, Torie thought, she was going to hear some woman say, "That child's two if she's a day, and still nursing . . . in public, too! Well. . . ."

India popped out from under Torie's blouse, grinned, and crawled away. Putting herself back together, Torie missed the rest of the play, but read Tommy's out in Guy's quick shake of his head. She was thankful baseball was a slow game, as she had to keep an eye on India, who had skipped her afternoon nap and was very active. The middle of the game found Torie feeding India potato salad and a sandwich from the picnic basket, washed down with lemonade from a paper cup. After that India settled down and shortly fell asleep against Torie's thigh.

Between innings the Neverses stood up and drifted

away, while others came by to sit or say hello. After
India dozed off, Torie once met Joe Nevers' eye, some
distance from her, and watching her. Later on, it was
clear he was watching India. In the eighth inning, he
turned up on his lonesome, and squatted silently next
to Torie. Guy was fixed on the game and didn't seem
to notice him.

"She's a looker," he said of India, in a low voice.

Torie didn't answer, only looked at him.

India stirred. Her bangs were damp with sweat. Torie's
hand automatically smoothed the fine tow hair over
her brow.

Joe Nevers hooked a finger through one of India's
curls and considered it dispassionately. "Don't often
see a true tow."

Torie sat still.

"Now my sister Gussie," Joe Nevers said. "She was
a true tow. In fact," he said slowly, "your India's the
spit of Gussie at that age."

Torie raised an incredulous eyebrow.

Joe Nevers looked beyond her.

When Torie twisted herself around to look where he
looked, she saw Cora, standing behind a tree, spying
on them.

Torie looked back at Joe Nevers, but he was gone.

Suddenly she wished the game over, the day done
with. Impatience made her watch the game more
closely.

A boy struck out, another made a run. Tommy was
up again. Torie sat a little straighter. He seemed a
little tired, a little hot and sweaty, but his grin was
hopeful and happy. He gripped the bat tightly with his
hands.

Freeman Buck's Gary was the pitcher. Gary had his
father's undertaker's face, and he was as slow and
careful. He exchanged signals with the catcher, glanced

hastily up the hillside to his folks and, turning on his heel, tried to surprise Tommy with the ball.

Tommy saw it coming. His grin faltered, the bat in his hands dropped slack. He flinched from the ball's path. But not enough. It took him in the face.

His mouth, thought Torie, already on her feet, India pushed unceremoniously aside. His nose.

"Tommy!" Guy and David cried out with one anguished voice.

The crowd groaned in collective disbelief.

Tommy was on the ground, his hands covering his face. They were already slicked red. Adults were on the field, moving toward him. The players moved in slow motion to form a circle around him. Except for Gary Buck, who was on his knees, his hands over his head.

People began to move in waves down the hill. Guy and David ran through the crowd, outstripping them. A woman sitting nearby grabbed Torie's arm.

"I'll take care of her," the woman said. "Go to your boy."

"Thanks," Torie whispered.

She stumbled down the hill after Guy and David, unable to think of anything but getting to Tommy. What she was going to do when she did never entered her mind.

She found herself in Glen McAvoy's wake. He was panting, and he jiggled as he ran.

Doc McAvoy and Guy between them quickly established that under the gore, the damage was limited to Tommy's mouth.

Doc stopped humming long enough to say, "Bet that hurts like hell," to Tommy so cheerfully Tommy tried to smile at him.

Blinking away tears, the boy shook his head in agreement from behind a bloody towel filled with ice chips from someone's picnic cooler.

Torie, crouched next to him and holding one hand, squeezed it. That was what she was able to do for him. It felt ludicrously insignificant. But Tommy turned his eyes to her and underneath his grotesque ice bag, she knew he was trying to smile at her, too.

Guy had a hand on the boy's shoulder, agreeing with Glen McAvoy.

"Big night for the tooth fairy, Tom," Guy joked.

David snickered, his eyes wide with hero-worship of his wounded brother's bravery and his father's gallant humor.

The crowd began to drift back to the blankets on the hillside to watch the remainder of the game, which would go on with a new pitcher as soon as the ambulance moved Tommy from the field. He didn't need to go to the hospital but the town's insurance required it.

Guy left Tommy long enough to speak a word of reassurance to Gary Buck, shaky and frightened, even though his own father's hand was steady on his shoulder.

Torie felt suddenly exhausted. Her neighbor could be seen threading her way down the hillside, India screaming in her arms. The woman's husband and children had gathered the Christophers' belongings and were bringing them to her. Torie went to meet them.

She saw no more of Joe Nevers or his wife that day, or thought of them either, until she saw him, alone, at Tommy's funeral.

It was at the church on the Ridge, only yards from the ball field. The church was filled with townspeople and such of the summer residents who had not already gone away. The boys who had played on Labor Day were Tommy's bearers, in relays.

Torie remembered little of the service, distracted as

she was by holding first David, and then Gary Buck. She tried to explain to Gary that he was not at fault. Bacteria had invaded Tommy's bloodstream through the open socket made by one of the three teeth knocked out by the baseball. Gary wasn't buying. When he came to see her in the summer of 1972, when he had his orders for Viet Nam, they got drunk together, and he cried as hard as ever he had at Tommy's funeral. Gary took the guilt with him to the jungle where he died.

Guy had known what killed Tommy from the moment he found him in his bed. The state had to force the autopsy on him. Like Glen McAvoy and every other doctor, Guy had to accept his own frequent helplessness. His mother's condition was a constant reproach, and he had never come to terms with it. The loss of Tommy was as terrible in its suddenness. He could not forgive himself, anymore than he could explain how he was supposed to diagnose a freak heart infection.

Torie understood his particular guilts. His was not the only heart cut out and buried with Tommy. But there was nothing she could do for Guy, anymore than she could do for Tommy. Because he could not let Tommy go, he lost David, and India, and her, what there was left of her to lose. And they lost him.

After the service, Glen McAvoy, assuming Guy would want to tell her himself, told Guy that the town wanted to name the ball field after Tommy. It was all the town would have of the boy; his body would be buried at the Christopher family plot in Falmouth, at least for the foreseeable future. After Guy's death, Torie had Tommy disinterred and reburied in a plot she had bought for herself and her children on the Ridge.

Guy never did tell her. Years later, leafing through the annual town report, Torie saw a black-and-white photograph of boys in baseball uniforms. Little League had come to Nodd's Ridge. But one tradition continued. The caption discribed the Labor Day game at Thomas Hayes Christopher Field. Torie looked at it a long time.

She longed for some warm dark oblivion. In the meantime though, reality was relentless cold and wet.

"Shit," she said, at last, and rolled out from under the car.

Hugging herself for the illusion of extra warmth, dancing clumsily from one foot to another, she took stock. Who would be looking for either of them before Monday morning? Maybe his sister Gussie, if she tried to call and became alarmed when Joe Nevers failed to answer. Except Gussie Finny was as unflappable as Joe Nevers himself; she couldn't be counted on to panic.

But sometime Monday, someone on the Ridge would miss Joe Nevers. One of the old farts. He was one of them. She often glimpsed them, at the bullshit table at Roscoe's, or outside the post office, or the store, or at the town office. There were four, five, perhaps six of them, the old men who were in a political, communal sense, Nodd's Ridge. Heavy boots on the selectman's desk, graceless, heavy-handed men, in green work pants and plaid jackets, propping themselves against the filing cabinets, smogging the room with cigar, cigarette, and pipe smoke, and filling the ashtrays with the detritus. She knew very well they mostly gossiped, but in their way, like a circle of Indian chiefs passing a pipe, they settled most things on the Ridge. And they noticed. Whose walk was pinched with arthritis, whose skin was gone gray, or weight too suddenly fallen off, who forgot things or wandered in their conversation, or was beginning to neglect their person. Who leaned on the bottle and when, who was not adjusting well to being widowed. Who was living on macaroni because the social security check was held up or had gone for doctors. Whose truck needed a new starter, whose septic tank was troublesome, whose roof was leaking. Whose kids were acting out, whose daughters going wild, whose sons hotrodding and tomcatting. The old farts would know, almost intuitively, that something was wrong. Joe Nevers: Haven't seen him this weekend, hasn't plowed his driveway, his cat Maggie's crying at the back door, his chimney's bare of woodsmoke, naught but the back porch light on, didn't stop at Pete Buck's for a doughnut Sunday morning, or for the Sunday newspaper at the store, like usual—that's odd. She envied him his belonging. Being part of an ordered, coherent world, all connected together, and not much different from the societies human beings had made for themselves for millennia. And the funny part was she who did not belong could see it, and he, who did, seemed not to know it.

But it wouldn't do any good, old farts notwithstanding, because by Monday morning he would be dead of exposure, never mind whatever the extent of his injuries might be, or how his ticker was faring, unless she got him out from under the car and inside.

Only yards away the house she had built on the ashes of the old loomed between the driveway and the lake, as empty as all outdoors around it. Still, it was a refuge. Fire inside to keep them warm, and beds and blankets, food and water, and her drugs. She could share them with the old man; ease his pains. In every other direction, there was nothing but woods and snow, the frigid lake, and the frozen mountains, except for Joe Nevers' four-wheel-drive pickup truck.

The thought of it arrested her. "The CB!" she exclaimed.

Only a hill away. A rush of adrenaline sent her scrambling over the embankment and up the drive. Within a few steps she was dizzy, and a stitch tightened in her right side. But this was her driveway, and she quite literally knew it blind drunk. Fueled with a raging contempt for her own weakness, she staggered onward, until she was within reach of the truck. She collapsed against it, gasping for breath that tore her lungs with icy jagged edges.

It was some moments before she could lift her head and breathe easier. Groping her way alongside the truck, she laid hands upon the door handle and yanked down on it triumphantly. Pain flared hot in her cut hand. And the handle did not move. The door was locked. She yanked it again anyway, this time in rage.

She screamed at it and pounded it until the side of her hand was an agony and she was fighting tears. When she had punished herself enough for her stupidity, she bowed her head against the window.

"Goddamn you, Joe Nevers," she whispered painfully, "for a goddam old maid."

He would just have to forgive her for needing someone to blame.

Her first impulse was to find a good-sized rock and smash the glass out, until she could reach inside and unlock the door. There was none to hand. Everything was blanketed with inches of snow and glazed with sleet, with only rocks that were too big and too rooted in the ground for her to dig out, left peeking out of the white.

Wearily, she shuffled around the hood of the truck and looked down at the house and the Cadillac. There was no sign that anything bad had ever happened here, beyond the crazy angle of the big black car. The drizzle smelled faintly of woodsmoke from the chimneys.

It was easier going down than up, and the thought made her laugh, or try to. The story of her life. By the time she reached the Cadillac again, she was all but crawling, and she was wet through from the armpits down. She crawled back under the car.

"You miserable old bastard," she said. "You think a fucking bear was going to come along and steal your fucking truck to go four-wheeling in?"

She embraced him, tight against his wet-wool, clean old man smell and scratchiness, listening to the faint trip-hammer of his heart, his ragged breathing, as she searched his pockets. Her fingertips found the jagged edges of the keys. She dug for them, and drew them out.

"You must want us both dead," she said. "This couldn't be worse if you planned it this way."

She passed a hand over his brow and fingered his pulse. By what margin he was still alive, she could only speculate. She held his wrist longer than she needed, letting go because she was shivering uncontrollably and dared not waste any more time.

Hand over hand, she dragged herself upright, until she could lean full against the car. It did not shift, either because it was now firmly planted in the nether snowbank, or because there wasn't enough of her to weigh on it.

She stared up at the truck. The hill looked higher than it had the first time. From her toes that she wriggled frantically to keep some kind of feeling in them, to her scalp, bristling with the cold, she shook all over. Her fingers had gone numb. She wondered thickly if they were frostbitten and decided she ought to look. Struggling to pull the mittens off one, she dropped the car keys into the snow.

"Shit a goddamn," she muttered crossly. "You fuck-ing idiot."

On the strength of a big, ragged sigh, she bent to pick them up. But her fingers refused to work. They only nudged the keys into a skitter across the surface of the snow. She put both hands to work then, though they felt like waldos in the lab, mechanical digits being worked from a distance, and cornered the little bastards, driving them into the snow to make them stay put. She lost her balance and fell like a mail sack on top of them. When she rolled over, the keys had disappeared into the snow. She tore off her other mitten and dug frantically into the snow, but the keys would not be found.

She sat up, nearly crying, and so tired that she thought it might really be possible to lie down next to the old man in his puddle under the car and go to sleep forever, never mind the cold and wet. But in a little while her bottom hurt badly with the cold, and she had to stand up. She stepped back and looked carefully where she had been. The snowbank held its mold of her skinny shanks, not like the wings of a snow angel made by a child but more like the anorexic wings of a starving moth. She stared at it until there was nothing else in the world. The keys were only pieces of a jigsaw, lost in a white ground. She would find them by their shapes if only she studied it a little longer. It was nothing she hadn't done drunk, for Christ's sake. At last she knelt, with a sigh, in the snowbank, broke the crust with the side of her unhurt hand, and wiggled her fingers down into the wet and jagged snow crystals. They met slick cold edges of keys, curled round the hard little bundle on its belt clip fob, and brought them up.

"Goddamn," she said, prayerfully.

She slipped them into the pocket of her coat, picked up her scattered, soaking wet mittens and laid them on the hood of the car. She thrust her hands into the cold, slick satin pockets with the keys, hoping the old man had left a spare pair of gloves in the cab of the truck.

This time she didn't try to hurry, but concentrated on putting one foot in front of the other, staying on her feet, breathing as calmly and deeply as she could bear. Her head thrummed steadily. Her bowels began to knot themselves in pain. Still she floated on a considerable calm, the knowledge of the keys in her pocket, that her fingers kept curling around, jingling, warming. Her hands hurt with the cold and the pounding she had given them on the door handle and the scrabbling and crawling about. The bandage Joe Nevers had put on the hurt one was loose and dirty and wet. The hand shook in the cold so she had to brace herself against the truck door to insert the key. It went in as slick as it felt, as if it were oiled instead of icy. But the strength had gone out of her hands, and she had to use both hands and her pathetic weight to open it. She crawled in behind the wheel, threw back her head, and closed her eyes. Her hands fell lightly on the steering wheel, quiet in their possession.

Summer, 1962

IN HER WHITE NURSE'S SHOES, Geneva Porter marched alongside the road toward the church. She was burdened
with a spray of multicolored gladioli, her handbag,
and her pie basket. Her handbag, which was white
straw because it was summertime, was stuffed with
her knitting, as well as her necessities: brush and
comb from Avon (her granddaughter Isabella sold Avon),
rouge, face powder in a compact, lipstick (the shade of
firehouse red she had been wearing since Avon stopped
making her old favorite, Truelove Scarlet), wallet and
coin purse, aspirin, antacid tablets, lemon cough drops,
digitalis, house keys (though she always left her house
unlocked), and the paperback-novel-sized photograph
album with its pictures of her great-grandchildren. Her
summer hat was a straw boater with a navy-blue gros-
grain ribbon band, to which an artificial white rose
was pinned. The hat shaded most of her face from the
fierce midday sun. She wore her second-best pantsuit,
a pale blue, with a sleeveless top of her own crocheting
under the jacket.

Torie was already slowing as she entered the twenty-
five-mile-an-hour zone that marked the residential bor-
ders of the village. She pulled off a few yards ahead of
Geneva. Torie got out and opened the door. Geneva
scuttled the last few steps so Torie would know she
didn't want to delay her.

"Oh, my," Geneva said breathlessly, sounding exactly like Judy Garland's Dorothy in The Wizard of Oz.

Torie relieved her of her glads and stowed them with exaggerated care that she hoped would pass for sobriety, on the floor in the back. Geneva clung firmly to her pie basket and handbag, though the basketwork must have pinched her considerable bosom as she wrapped her arms around the bag and basket in her lap.

"It's hot to be walking," Torie said. Too hot for an octogenarian trekking to the church fair, anyway.

The Cadillac's windows were all down, admitting the heat and the road dust, but also the exuberant smells of high summer. Torie hated feeling closed up with the air conditioning, and it was both wasteful and foolish to run it with the windows wide open, trying to cool all outdoors, so she didn't bother to use it. The weight of the air conditioning plant under the hood drove the gas mileage down and the cost of running the car up, but when she asked a mechanic to take it out, he just laughed like it was a huge drunken joke on her part. She laughed with him, because she could see the joke too, but also because she knew she wouldn't fight for it, and that made her the joke. It didn't seem worth the struggle to break the man out of his preconceptions about Cadillacs and their accessories. She was too goddamn tired.

"Oh, my," Geneva said, settling in. "Adelina was supposed to pick me up at quarter to twelve and it was noon when I left the house. My, the morning did fly, but I suppose she just forgot," she added querulously.

Torie peeked at the dashboard clock. "No," she said, "It's just after eleven now."

Geneva's withered cheeks burned as red as a potbellied stove in December under the bright artificial blotches of her rouge.

"Oh, my," she said. "Oh, dear."

"Well, you'll be there ahead of her," Torie told her, as if that were a highly desirable thing instead of no matter at all.

"I need bifocals," Geneva confessed, "but they're sixty-three dollars. Sixty-three! Imagine that! Well, I just told the doctor that's too dear!"

Torie tried to look properly shocked at the price of bifocals. She knew Geneva's husband's insurance had provided her with a comfortable annuity. Geneva had worked steadily as a nurse until she was seventy-five, when the doctors had forced her into retirement. She still baby-sat, and nursed oldsters, some of them younger than herself, collected cash and didn't report it. Living with her spinster sister-in-law, Adelina, who was still working full time at the post office, she was hardly going away to starve. Hers was a generation that saw spectacles as an irreparable disfigurement for a woman. Torie guessed the truth of it was Geneva, even at eighty-odd, was vain enough to claim the name of Woman.

Geneva shook her head over the high cost of bifocals.

"Well, dear," she said, to change the subject, "are you coming to the fair?"

Torie hedged. "Thought I might bring the kids for the supper."

Geneva smiled, showing all her dentures. "Freeman Buck's dressing up as a clown. Should tickle the kids."

Torie grinned. It would be worth the price of admission to see dour Freeman in a clown suit.

Geneva's memory was still sharper than her eyesight. It came to her at once that Freeman Buck had come close to dying with Joe Nevers when the Christophers' old summer house had burned down, with that fellow in it that didn't belong there, but what did you expect of summer people, and that the Christophers had lost a boy, not too long ago, at the baseball field, and a good deal else that was gossiped about. She clamped her mouth shut, worried she had already said something indiscreet. The recent history of the Christophers in Nodd's Ridge was like a raspberry thicket, and she was not one who valued that kind of gossip, which was every bit as seedy and tart and liable to stick between one's teeth as it was juicy, and which scratched anyone who got too close. But now the church was in sight, Geneva sighed her relief and gathered herself together.

She refused Torie's offer of help with good-humored indignation. Geneva Porter was no decrepit old poop unable to bear her own burdens from the parking lot to the church hall, even if she couldn't tell eleven from twelve o'clock anymore. Torie settled back to watch Geneva join the procession of middle-aged to elderly women, all bearing baked goods wrapped in foil or plastic wrap, or in baskets, all wearing sensible shoes, from the parking lot to the church.

It was a pretty little church, white and square, sitting on the best view on the Ridge, bar the cemetery, next to the old Meeting House, now used as the town hall. From this height of land, it seemed as if the whole world lay below, wanting only a demon to make an offer. The town was too small to support more than one church, so this one did for the Protestant population, which was nearly everybody, and always had been, the way just about every kid had blue eyes and blond hair. The gospel was bland enough to defuse sectarian passions, and the church provided a social center for the town, in the hall underneath it.

From the back of the parking lot, Torie could see the baseball field. It looked dusty and abandoned, most likely for the town beach. Torie sniffed hopefully for a breeze, but none was forthcoming. Wonderful smells, though, intensified by the heat, that bore the perfume of summer's green, of hot top in the sun, of flaky pastry, and lily-of-the-valley dusting powder. And the smell of her own sweat, beaded salty on upper lip, trickling in her armpits, sticking the small of her back and the back of her thighs to the leather of the seat.

She was tired. She was always tired now, because she slept little and uneasy. Her bourbon was a friendly Hovercraft, keeping her inches above the bottomless, turbulent sea. She functioned as well as she ever had. The worst times were when she dropped into that sea of despair, and then the bottle was a rock around her neck, dragging her down, and she didn't care. The rest of the time she navigated the delicate interface, staying lightly oiled, holding on. It was still before noon, and breakfast's Irish coffee was fading.

Still she floated, a message inside a bottle, surrendering her fate to the elements. She could not quite remember what it was she was supposed to be doing, but she wasn't worried. It would come to her. Sooner or later the piece would fall into place. Her hands rested lightly on the wheel, knowing their place, waiting for the eventual signal to go on. The mail. Picking up the mail. She would pick up the mail and find her way to the next drink.

A shadow fell over her. She looked up. The sun glared in her eyes. She pulled her sunglasses down from her hair with a sigh.

"Cora," she said.

The glasses didn't help. Cora still loomed black between Torie and the sun.

"Nice of you to give Geneva a lift," Cora said.

Cora's arms were crossed at Torie's eye level. They looked serious. It was a pain in the neck to have to stare up at the woman.

"Good deed for the day," Torie said, and laughed as gratingly as only she could.

"I didn't think you were stopping to go to church," Cora said.

"Shit no," Torie agreed.

Cora sniffed. "You're vulgar. You think you're smart or something, but you're not. You're just plain vulgar."

"Oh, dear," said Torie, wide-eyed, in imitation of Geneva. "Well, shit a goddamn."

"I just wouldn't be too proud of it, if I was you," Cora said.

"Oh, I'm not," Torie said. "Christ no. Anybody can do it, they practice enough."

"You think you're so smart, don't you?" Cora said.

"What?" Torie asked. "Christ no. I'm not a bit smart. You don't understand."

"I understand a lot more than you think I do," Cora said. "Just what is it you think I don't understand?"

"Shitloads, actually," Torie explained cheerfully. "But to start with, it's all right about those words, you know, the swears. I just rent them. Anybody can. Rent-a-curse, you can charge it to your credit card. Few bucks a month, you can swear all you want."

"You don't fool me," Cora said doggedly. "I can see right through you."

Torie picked anxiously at her halter and shorts. "Oh, no," she said. "X-ray vision. Good thing I changed my drawers this morning."

"I only got one thing to say to you," Cora said slowly, biting off each word and spitting it out.

"With relief," Torie said. "I been waiting. It's hotter than a whore's watch-a-call-it on a Saturday night, sitting here."

"Keep your hands off my husband," Cora said. It sounded like a threat.

"Oh," Torie said. She thought about it. "Who's that?"

Cora sniffed again. "You know. You're so smart."

"Oh, I guess I could guess, who'd be fool enough to marry you," Torie agreed. "But I'm puzzled. Maybe you could tell me? Why would I want to lay hands on your old man?"

"You figure it out, you're so smart," Cora said.

"I'll work on it," Torie said. "But I can see it's going to be a problem."

Cora raised her voice. "You just leave him alone, you hear."

Torie looked her up and down. "Cora," she said wearily. "Let me explain this to you. I don't want your husband. I already got one that's no goddamn good. Now maybe you want yours, or you don't. I don't know. I couldn't even imagine. And I don't give a shit, either. But really and truly, I don't want him. Not for a minute. Which is probably about what he's good for."

Cora's mouth twisted. "Fire him then."

"Shit," Torie said. "I do that, who'll be my caretaker?"

"I don't care," Cora spat. "I couldn't care less. Try Reuben Styles. He ain't married. You want to," nearly choking on the word, "screw him."

"That's generous of you," Torie said. "But I already did and he's not very good at it. And Cora, watch the mouth. It sounds vulgar, and I bet you haven't paid for it yet."

Smiling glassily at Cora, she keyed the ignition. She was thirsty, and the sun had made her headache fierce. There was a bottle of Wild Turkey in the glove box just for headaches.

"I'll get you," she heard Cora say over the sound of the motor turning over. "I'll take care of you, Missus Garbage Mouth."

"Get fucked," Torie shouted at her. "If you can."

But she didn't care, really. Her heart wasn't in it. The whole conversation was a farce. She sprayed gravel at Cora as she jerked the car around to the road. She was in a hurry to get to the post office. She could park there and have a shot or two of headache medicine before she picked up the mail. Her throat would like that about as well as her poor head. She wondered vaguely if Cora was crazy.

The stitch in her side unknotted, leaving the ghost of a kink in the tired muscles. The burning in her lungs cooled and her breathing evened out. The cut on her hand throbbed angrily. Under the layers of Guy's old hunting pants and long johns, the fine wool of her trousers tickled her raw scraped knees she had crawled across the glassy snowcrust and fallen on. And her joints burned. The painkillers she had taken first thing in the morning were losing their power. She could feel their spell loosening.

The irony of the situation made her want to laugh but the best she could manage was too close to the scraping of a fingernail on a blackboard. She meant to take her leave in a dignified way, and found herself in a race to save the old man's life. Not hers; one way or another, she would be out of it, and it did not matter anymore to her how that happened. But he had managed to entangle himself in her dying as he had in her life, and she could not help being irritated with him, though she knew he had not intended any of it. It was not amusing or romantic because it was fatal, but had to be accepted, like all the other disasters. Bad stars. And all the void between.

But it was nearly over, for which she was intensely grateful. Her fingers groped stiffly for the CB mike, neatly holstered on the dash. A place for everything, she thought, and everything in its place. *Except you don't belong here*, under my goddam car, old man.

There were buttons enough to be confusing but at

least they were buttons and not those wretched elec-
tronic panels with their illiterate runes that one triggered by heat rather than by pressure. She was not
sure there was enough heat left in her, that her fires
were not too low, to make anything work on that
principle. Staring at them didn't seem to sort the buttons out. Her ring hand wavered in the air, near the
end of her nose, three fingers curling to the palm as
her pointer straightened slowly, aimed at the buttons.

"Shit," she said, at last. She pushed one randomly.

And nothing happened.

Grimacing, she pushed each button in turn. And
nothing happened. She pushed herself back against
the seat, angry with herself for being stupid about it.

The old man would have left the operations manual
on the radio in the glove box. He was constitutionally
incapable of not having left it here. She lunged at the
glove box, pawed everything in it out onto the floor of
the cab, and clumsily hooked the proper booklet from
the heap.

She skimmed the directions, turning the pages with
shaky fingers. At the end of it, she realized she had
understood none of it, and made herself begin again,
doggedly. Slumped in the angle of the seat like a
boneless rag doll, she read it over and over, word by
word, until she thought she understood. It was just
like crawling over the snowcrust and under the Cadillac,
she thought, except the scrabbling went on in her
head. She dropped the manual on the seat beside her
and reached for the mike and radio controls with a
shadow of her normal drunk-or-sober confidence. Muttering the directions, well larded with curses to make
them more powerful, she went through each step with
great care. Her immediate reward was a burst of noise
and red dots marching along the panel, no less exciting at that moment than fireworks might have been.
Salvation was only minutes away.

"Anybody out there?" she asked.

She felt in control again, as she had not been in a long time, and heard it in the calm of her voice. Then she realized she had not depressed the talk button on the mike.

"Shit," she said, and squeezed it as hard as she could with a bad case of the chills seizing her, and asked again, "Anybody out there?"

No one answered. Patiently she asked again, and then moved to another channel. And another after that, and then another. She tried the state police channel and heard only static. By the time she had come full circuit and reached channel 11, where she had started, panic was fluttering under her breastbone. The sound of voices made her heart leap. A man and a woman were conversing, gossiping from the sound of it. It was reassuring to know that life was going on its normal way. But the signal was fragmentary, breaking up just as it reached her.

Torie tried to break in.

The woman went on talking, apparently not receiving her.

Torie shook all over with frustration, and cursed the woman bitterly.

Still the woman went on monotonously. Now and again the man answered her tersely, but no more intelligibly. Their voices were familiar, thick and slow with Maine, but Torie could not quite name them. It seemed the more carefully she listened to them, the less she understood of what they said. The weird chorus might have been spoken in a foreign language, except she knew the accent, the cadence, the flat tonalities. Everything but the meaning. It took her back to learning French, when everything was on the verge of making sense, just before she really began to understand it. And then, one brief phrase came into focus.

"You think I don't know," the woman said.

And she might have said how or who, but the rest of her words disintegrated into static.

She sounded like Cora.

Shuddering, Torie threw the mike against the dash and kicked at the radio, unbalancing herself on the seat, so she had to struggle for a moment to stay upright. When she could bring herself to touch the mike again, she handled it gingerly as if her hands were wet and she expected an electric shock from it. She made another slow, painstaking procession through the channels. And silence reigned. No one talking, no one listening, except for her, and she was numb, terrified. Listlessly she paged through the manual one more time, but could not find a way to signal her distress. If there was an automatic SOS signal to be triggered, she could not find it.

"Shit," she said.

She turned off the radio, took back the car keys, and climbed out. The drizzle had thickened. She sneezed.

"Goddamn Joe Nevers," she muttered. "Why does he have to drive a goddamn standard shift? By now, I could have made the road, anyway, flagged somebody down."

It was too cold to stand there and complain. She started back down the hill, needing all her energy and attention to stay on her feet. Somehow she had to find a way to get the old man out from under the Cadillac, before he died of exposure or whatever else had happened to him. She had to do at least that. Then she would worry about getting him out of here.

Her vision grew hot and blurred. She doubled over from a fierce cramp. It spasmed like a serpent drawing back to strike. All thoughts of Joe Nevers, or rescue or death, fled her mind. She had to get to the house. To her blessed pills.

TO THE RELIEF OF TORIE'S PARENTS, her formal schooling was nearly finished. It had been one thing to dawdle through Boston University and then graduate school at Harvard during the war. Eligible men had been scarce, there was little she could personally contribute to the war effort, and little harm she could come to in the dusty warren of the Widener library. They indulged her. She indulged them, unable to disabuse them of the notion she would ever grow up and marry.

As one of the tiny ragged underclass of graduate students, she was older at twenty-six than most of the members of the student body, even the returning vets. University life is necessarily transitory, particularly for undergraduates, whose mayfly generation rarely exceeds four years. Torie Hayes had been there long enough to have become something of a campus fixture, even with eighteen months of archaeological field work in England and Mexico, and a semester in Chicago mucking around with the new radio isotyping. But this part of her life was at an end. She felt herself separating from Harvard, like a cell dividing from another. Her education had trained her as an observer. It was natural and inevitable that she should come to see the university as another microcosmic society, ridden with rules, rituals, and hierarchies. And so seeing it, she found herself outside of it. De-tribalized.

While only a fairy godmother could have granted her a carrel in the stacks that housed her own subject, she had obtained for herself the privilege of a carrel in a neighboring quarter of the library. In summer the little closet was a corner of hell, and in winter colder than an ice queen's heart, but she had grown attached to the dead-and-moldering-leaf smell of old books and to the cathedral silence in that abandoned place.

During the breaks she forced on herself, she poked among the books that walled her in and discovered a section of folios, outsized books, devoted to biology and the healing arts. One in particular seized her fancy. The lifework of one Samuel Biggs Hobson, it was an eighteenth-century compendium of home cures, a stew of witchcraft, sympathetic magic, pure humbug, and folk remedies, some of which actually worked. Hobsom could be relied on for wonderment and amusement when she had read herself into a headache.

On the rare occasions when another scholar penetrated the far reaches of the stacks, Hobson was almost always the object. The book had acquired a certain following among medical students who used it the way English majors and graduate students used *Alice in Wonderland*, as a reliable source of droll epigrams to head their papers, to suggest a spurious breadth of knowledge. But because the book was a folio and an antique, though not at that time an intrinsically valuable one, it was not allowed to circulate. The students had to come to it. Torie came to treat it almost as one of her own books in the long periods in which Hobson went undisturbed.

One late-fall afternoon the embarrassed sound of someone's fumbling among the books became intrusive. When she peered out of her carrel impatiently, the sight of Guy Christopher stunned her. He was squinting at faded and unreadable titles and authors while struggling to keep a pile of folios balanced on a lower shelf.

When at last she moved, pushing her papers away and her chair back, the sound of chair legs scraping the tiled floor caught his attention. He squinted at her as if she were another of the clumsy folios and he could not quite make out her title and author. Then he seemed to take her for the stereotypical spinster librarian, living her entire life like a virgin troll among the books.

"Excuse me," he said, blinking fair lashes against the dust from the books he had disturbed. "I'm looking for a book."

Torie stood up and reached for the slip of paper flopping limply between her fingers. "You've come to the right place," she said dryly.

He stared at her.

"Hobson," she read aloud from the slip. "You're in luck."

She twisted around the carrel, searching for it. It was propped against the tiny-paned window that looked out on an airshaft. A spider had spun a web from its top corner to the reading lamp fixed over her desk. She swept it away briskly with the edge of her hand, which she then wiped on her skirt, and tugged Hobson loose from his neighbors. She faced Guy with the book between them like a large, empty tray.

"Hobson," she said.

Guy's fingers closed automatically over the spine of the book as he peered at her.

"Torie?"

She did not answer, possessed of a sudden urge to baldly deny her identity.

He pressed her, as if he sensed it. "Torie?"

She sighed. "Hello, Guy."

And released Hobson. Guy nearly dropped it. Only

his own natural grace allowed him to recover. She was relieved for the sake of the book, which was stiff and arthritic with age, and easily damaged.

"I can't believe it," Guy said.

She fingered the threads of hair falling loose from her temples, irritated with the awareness that she looked like a drudge. Her hands were distinctly grimy. Her impatience with herself flashed in her eyes; he took it for a glare and flinched. Suddenly his fine, fair features, lit up with discovery, loosened and shifted into apprehension.

She wondered, first, at his seeming initial delight at the sight of her, and then at how quickly it faltered. If she were Guy Christopher, she would not be delighted to encoutner Victoria Hayes again. There are species of embarrassment far more unbearable than deliberate insult. But he had no reason to expect a hard time from her.

"My God," he said.

He shuffled the big book out of the way and forgot about it for good. He reached for both her hands, but while he had been freeing his hands she had crossed her arms. There were awkward seconds while she untwined one hand and offered it to him, stiffly.

"How are you, Guy?"

Though her tone of voice reflected a notable lack of interest in the question, he answered as if he thought she cared. "Fine, fine." He rubbed his hands together with the automatic fastidiousness of someone trained in hygiene. "Working not five miles from here. At Dudley."

"Practicing," she asked, "or have you got it right yet?"

He grinned. "Not on my own, no. I'm in my last year of a residency in obstetrics. See me delivering babies?"

She shook her head. "That's grand. Had your fill of cutting?"

He stared at the floor, sobered by the thought of it. "Saw all the surgery I ever want to, in the war." His lashes fluttered, and he passed a hand nervously over his face. "God, I'm sorry about Tom. I wrote to your mother."

She shrugged. "Yes, I know. Thank you. That was kind of you."

He stuck his hands in his pockets, looking remarkably boyish for a man who must be nearly thirty-five. A man who had finished medical school, gone off straight away to the war, tried one specialty now another, yet he still seemed, in face and manner, unfinished, tentative. Disturbingly like the boy he had been when he was her brother Tom's prep school roommate.

She felt as if she had grown, in the years since she had seen him last, much older than he. Somehow passed him by.

His distress over Tom's death was genuine, and touched her. He blinked away suspicious brightness in his blue eyes.

"Sometimes I still can't believe it," he said.

She closed her eyes.

"I'm sorry," he said. "I didn't mean to upset you."

She blinked at him, and smiled lazily. "No," she said.

She groped her way into the carrel. Wherever her fingers touched, she left fingerprints in the dust and grime. She saw that her books and papers and journals, piled and crammed untidily into this space, were in great disorder. Leaning against the grubby window, she noticed for the first time that the spider she shared the carrel with had laid her eggs in one corner of the glass, like a tangle of angel's hair stuck in the accretion of grime.

"Torie?"

She started. He stood in the doorway behind her, his face set in worry.

"I'm okay," she said. "Just . . . taken by surprise."

He proceeded to further her surprise. He reached out and drew her close in a gentle hug that took her breath away. When he released her, she stepped back in a daze, and groped for the back of her chair for support.

"Come and have a cup of coffee with me," he said. "I want to catch up with you."

She did not want to have coffee with him, or be caught up with, if it was possible for him to catch up with her. What she wanted was a long, cold glass of water, or better yet, beer. But if she stayed in the carrel she could have neither, and as soon as he went away she would cry. She fumbled her jacket from its hook, one-handed, and brushed the loose hair from her forehead with the other, before she remembered how dirty her hand was. But so was her hair, so she shrugged the thought away, economically, she had shrugged on the jacket.

Walking to the coffee shop, and when they were seated and served, he carried the burden of conversation, filling in her silence easily and unhurriedly, as if picking up talk left off only yesterday. She found out what part of the city he lived in, and why he had chosen the Dudley Clinic, why he had abandoned surgery for obstetrics, how he felt when he delivered a baby, which he had a couple of hundred times, several times on an emergency basis. To her surprise, it was all interesting, not just because she was something of a sponge, unable not to absorb new information, but also because he was revealing what he cared about, quite inadvertently, out of the awkwardness of the situation. It was a new and curious light on Guy Christopher. A new respect for him welled in her, and a sudden, almost tender affection. He was trying, after all, to put her at ease.

Her life was a full one. She did not often think of

herself as lonely. But she was isolated, by her own choice. Withdrawn from family, erratic, increasingly abstemious in her social contacts. The feeling that Guy Christopher was spilling his passions to her, a woman he barely knew, had not seen in nearly a decade, and had some reason to avoid, sparked in her the conviction that his were secret passions, and that there was no one in his life to whom he could admit he had passions, that he was serious about something. Perhaps it was only some instinct on his part that his loneliness was safe with a secular nun like Victoria Hayes. She listened without resentment, telling herself she was only being human, not ridiculously grateful for the boon of his company, not enjoying too much.

"So what are you doing?" he asked, at last.

She evaded the question. "Making dirty fingerprints all over this cup."

He laughed "You haven't tasted the damn coffee. What is it, no good?"

"What do you think?" she asked.

Surprised, he examined his cup. "You know," he said, "I don't know."

She nodded. "You drink a lot of coffee."

"No, not that much." Then he changed his mind. "No, that's not right. I guess I do drink a fair amount of coffee."

"Don't you know?" she pressed him. "How many cups a day?"

He opened his mouth, as if he expected a number to pop out, and then laughed. "I don't know."

"People who drink a lot of coffee never know how much they drink," she told him. "Or what it tasted like."

He tipped his chair back and crossed his arms. "I never noticed. But you did."

She shrugged. "Graduate student bull sessions. Got

bored once, started watching how people drank their coffee."

"Interesting," he said. "Think it's true of tea, or cigarettes, or booze? The more you use, the less aware of it you are?"

Ever watch a really fat person eat?" she asked. "Check the hospital cafeteria. I'll bet you'll see some people shovelling so fast they almost choke on it, and I'll bet they'll be obese."

"I will, I will," he promised. "I'm sure it's true, though."

There was still a rose-petal texture to his cheeks. He glowed with flawless health and a naturally sunny spirit. He would bald, she thought, but in a gentle way that would seem natural, as if he were becoming younger all the time, one of his babies. She wondered how many nurses were in love with him.

He was looking at her as seriously as she was looking at him. He reached out and touched her hand, and she understood he had stayed with her through her evasion. "I want to say I'm sorry again, but I don't want you to fade out on me."

She shook her head. "Don't. You're very kind, but it's not necessary."

"Kindness is always necessary," he said. "But this apology is not because I had the inexplicable luck to survive Tom."

She reached for her nearly empty glass of water. "So?"

"I mean about the wedding." He blushed, and seemed younger still.

She touched his hand, lying curled on the table, quickly.

"Nothing to be sorry about," she said.

He nodded. "You seemed so young then. God, you *were* so young. I felt very adult, very grown up. About forty, you know?" His blush deepened. He studied his fingernails hungrily. "God, it was embarrassing. I felt like, like . . .''

"About eight inches," Torie said gravely.

He burst out laughing. "God, you're still a brat, aren't you?"

Her mouth twitched. "Hey, I understand. I understood then, believe it or not. There you were, sophisticated as hell, Big Brother's Friend, and it was a terrible blow to your dignity. You don't have to be so relieved that I'm still a brat. I've lost a lot of my old edge."

"I was worried about that," he said. "I ran into Molly a couple of months ago. She told me you were here. Said you had turned into a bookworm."

"Molly thinks anyone who reads more than two comic books a week is a bookworm," she said.

He stretched and laughed and then signalled the waitress.

"I'm glad I ran into you anyway. I was a little worried at first because you looked so different. But now you look the same."

"Very politely put," she said. "but I do look different. I am not the same. For one, I'm almost as old now as Tom was when he was killed."

Guy was quiet a moment, looking at her. "You need a bath and a hair wash and some lipstick. Some stockings. You need to go sailing and make love, that's all." He blushed again.

"Is that a diagnosis?" she asked. "Or a proposition?"

He grinned. "It's a prescription."

She stood up. "Thanks for the coffee, Guy. It was nice seeing you."

He caught her hand. "Never mind the smart mouth there. How about dinner?"

She didn't know what he wanted, why he seemed to want to make her feel better. She didn't know if he was exorcising some guilt that he was still alive when her brother was dead, or if he needed to show her he was no longer a kid with an uncontrollable erection. And she didn't want to know. He was wrong about her, always had been. She was different, she was older. The Atlantic Ocean and a man weren't going to cure her of the last eight years.

But he wouldn't let go. He stood up and wrapped an arm around her waist to keep her from leaving. She resisted the impulse to slap his face, knee his crotch a good one. He was another goddamn prep school boy with too much of everything, good looks, brains, humor, luck, and nerve. He had written her mother a letter. His manners were better than hers.

"Let's have a good time together," he said. "A decent meal, some laughs. You look like you need it. God knows, I do. I'm a hardworking resident, remember? Bringing kiddies into the world, taking the curse off the poor moms. Don't I deserve a reward?"

"My ass," she said.

He looked over her shoulder critically. "Don't know. You've got it all covered up with that perfectly awful skirt. Could I feel it?"

She slapped his hand away lightly. "Guy," she said patiently. "Are you sure? I mean, I'm not really one of the world's most comfortable, *nice* people."

He nodded. "You're a brat. So what? I like to talk to you. You listen. You know words that are three, four syllables long. I don't have to explain a joke to you. Goddamn it, you're beginning to make me feel rejected."

She sighed. It hadn't been all that hard to have coffee with him. And it didn't seem fair to punish him for making her feel better.

"Okay," she said, and then qualified it. "Just this once."

"Good," he said, and danced a little jig around the

table. It was the kind of foolish thing Tom and his friends had done when they were teenagers and she was a little girl. She shook her head but couldn't suppress a giggle.

It was eighty-thirty. He had said he would pick her up at seven-thirty. She threw down her book and paced the tiny apartment, avoiding her mirror. She would be damned if she would check herself again, like a silly teenager waiting for a date.

There was nothing to see from her single window to the street, no idling taxi or late-model sportscar, appropriate to the resources of a young doctor who was the sole heir to a formidable quantity of mature, if not old, money. She turned her back on the empty street and sat on the window ledge, not caring it was grimy and soiled her dinner dress. Why should she preserve herself like somebody's wedding cake bride for a jerk who was late? A lot late. Except Guy Christopher was not a man who had been raised to be late to anything on purpose, let alone what was no doubt the biggest date of his life.

She snorted and crossed her arms. Her belly gurgled. She was extremely hungry, anticipating a meal, a real meal, in one of Boston's many suffocating, dowdy haute cuisine restaurants. She was actually wearing a brand-new dress, a virgin if she wasn't. It was true that her mother had bought it for her, on a brief visit earlier in the fall.

In one swift, acute glance, her mother had taken in the apartment, which was hardly big enough to turn around in, and rolled her eyes at the sight of Torie's pink refrigerator.

Torie spread her hands to take it all in. "Postwar housing shortage," she explained.

"Christ," her mother said. Theresa Hayes began to swiftly open and close the cupboards in the kitchen. Both of them. "Don't you have anything to drink?"

"No, Mom. We'll have some wine with lunch."

"Oh, all right."

Theresa Hayes had aged rapidly. She was chic and slim and ravaged. She no longer needed a cocktail party or a wedding to justify drinking. Her husband, himself in need of anesthesia, no longer resisted. Drink made Theresa easier to live with because it made life easier for her. Oddly, she seemed more involved in the business of living than ever before. Her house, her clothes, her garden, her friends and their children, her sisters and theirs, all kept her upright if not sober. She had a desire, oft voiced, to see Torie married, to have grandchildren. Torie, it seemed, had decided to be as great a disappointment as Tom's death in the war had been a loss.

Theresa opened Torie's closet and parted the hangers critically.

"Victoria," she moaned.

Torie had changed the old double bed, neatened her heaps of books and papers into something like order, washed the meager, anonymous collection of her thrift-shop dishes, and put them in their cupboard, swept the floor of four months' accumulation of dust kitties and grit, all in honor of her mother's visit. But she had known her wardrobe was beyond hiding or help, and was braced for her mother's groans and exclamations.

"Do you realize you haven't got one single decent dress?"

"What for? In case I have to attend a funeral, Mom?"

"Victoria!"

Torie went into the kitchen so her mother would have room to glare at her wardrobe. She looked into her refrigerator. It was a vintage Greeley Ice Queen, with a fan on the top, and had been painted an embarrassingly biological shade of pink on the outside. The inside was an aggressive spring green, with a tiny icebox done in turquoise, and the three wire racks, now chipped, scratched and rusting, in yellow, the green of watermelon skin, and purple, respectively. It smelled of soured milk so strongly that not even baking powder could eradicate the stink, and it was impossible to keep milk products in it. The only liquids in the Ice Queen were spring water in a rectangular ribbed glass bottle with a green Bakelite cap, ginger ale, and tomato juice. Torie had thrown out the solid food, which had been dried up, molded, gone by, or rancid, just before her mother's arrival. It still perfumed the kitchen from the trash can.

"Let's go to lunch," she proposed.

The haste with which Theresa Hayes snatched her patent leather handbag from the narrow ledge that did duty as a kitchen counter was at once an acidic dismissal of Torie's apartment and a barely restrained lunge for a drink. Torie hardly blamed her.

With two glasses of luncheon wine in her, she allowed her mother to buy her a dress. It was entirely to Theresa's taste, of course, since if Torie's taste had been consulted, there would have been no dress-shopping at all. Theresa's choice was made much as she drove after most lunches—with exaggerated care, not to say extreme calculation. Torie's figure must be shown to advantage, particularly since it was good. She would never want her daughter to be blatantly sexy, the way the girls seemed to dress, more and more, since the war. It looked so . . . desperate. On the other hand, Torie was not eighteen anymore, and must make the most of what she had.

*   *   *

Tonight, the sight of herself in the mirror, wearing that dress, satisfied Torie. To make it clear she was grown up now, she had done up her hair in a French twist. The severity of the style implied no nonsense, and suited the simple lines of the dress, a strapless sheath. It would please her mother inordinately that she was wearing it.

For Guy's sake, since he had volunteered to buy her dinner, Torie was prepared to be as dowdily expensive as she had to be to pass the maitre d' at the Ritz Carlton dining room. No doubt the wine would be the best thing there, but she intended to stay sober and eat heartily, if heavily and unimaginatively, perversity in the name of propriety. Sternly suppressing all her best anarchic instincts, she resolved not to get bombed and dance on the tables, which ought to prove she had matured.

Ironically, all her good resolutions and her mother's efforts appeared to have come to nil. The good doctor had not yet shown. There was a certain amusement in being stood up, except that she had worked so hard at restricting her expectations of this evening to an overpriced but generous meal with a man she liked more than she wanted to. It was hard not to be irritated with the futility of all her elaborate casualness.

She hadn't even bothered to tidy the apartment. Not for some joker who would likely want something to drink that she didn't have, and who would want to hustle her away after a few minutes' small talk. She wasn't about to fall on this man like a desperate old maid. He was merely an old acquaintance and would stay that way. Guy Christopher was an experiment, a way to prove to herself that there was nothing to fear.

She looked at the clock again. "Shit," she said.

She found her book again, forced herself to concentrate, and read a little more. The ploy was successful, it was an hour and a half later before she looked at the clock again.

She laughed. Her first date in what seemed a hundred years, and she had been stood up. Maybe the man had a more bizarre sense of humor than he showed.

It was unkind of her. She was sure of one thing about Guy, and that was that he was kind, far kinder than she, in his flippant way. She supposed she should try to find out what happened. It *was* Saturday, and the time agreed upon *had* been seven-thirty. She did not have his telephone number or address, though he had hers, of course, and had not called her. She did know where he worked, though, and at that instant, she knew what had happened. The man was a doctor. Something had come up that was sufficiently important to keep him from a phone. She looked up the number of the hospital in the phone book and dialed it.

"I'm looking for Dr. Christopher," she told the girl who answered the phone.

There was a pause, and the girl asked, "That's Dr. Christopher the obstetrician?"

Torie agreed it was.

"Are you a patient?"

Torie laughed. "Not his," she said. "Just a friend, and it's not an emergency."

The girl giggled and asked her to wait, but did not keep her waiting long. Breathlessly, the girl reported that Dr. Christopher was in the hospital but was involved with an emergency and had been for several hours.

"Would you like to leave a message?"

"No," Torie said, "and thanks."

She shrugged at the mirror. "Not an auspicious beginning," she said aloud, "but it wasn't supposed to be a beginning, anyway, so there."

She slipped out of her dress, hung it neatly in the closet. There was always that possible funeral. She shucked her undwear, popped into her faded flannel nightgown, and let down her hair. After a moment's thought, she knocked the telephone receiver gently off the hook and dropped a pillow over it.

Her stomach grumbled, reminding her she had had no supper. A rummage in the pink refrigerator turned up some shreds of deli liverwurst, and some peanut butter, in the tall tin pail she habitually bought it in. It was a staple of her diet. She built a sandwich out of staling pumpernickle, the peanut butter and liverwurst, and then stood on one bare foot and then another, considering what she might wash it down with. She drew water into a chipped tea cup and took her supper to bed with a pile of books.

To be sure, she was tired. Determined to make nothing special of the day, she had risen at her usual dawnish hour, swum early at a sorority pool, walked two miles to the library to put in a ten-hour day, and walked home again. The food in her belly and the warmth of her quilts on top of a rigorous day induced torpor and she dozed, sprawled among the books, her half-eaten sandwich spilled down the steep slope of a fold in the bed coverings.

Later, in the damp and quiet cold of the fairy tale hours, insistent knocking and the sound of her name summoned her from the comfortable warmth. She struggled out of bed, still half-asleep, and threw open the door.

Guy Christopher, hangdog and clutching clumsy parcels, stood framed in the diffuse light of the dusty light bulb in the hallway.

"Shit," she said, and spun on her heel to throw herself belly down on her bed.

He came in, hesitantly, behind her, closing the door quietly, flicking on a lamp.

"God," he said, "I'm sorry."

She groaned.

"I guess I shouldn't have come, but I felt like such a jerk. I wanted to apologize."

He certainly sounded sorry. Perhaps if she made think-nothing-of-it noises, he would go away before she woke up past recovering sleep. She rolled over, shading her eyes against the small amount of light the lamp threw. "I figured you were doctoring."

"I just couldn't get to a phone until it was really late. And then your phone was busy."

She closed her eyes, in case he was noticing her phone under the spare pillow. The gesture was open to misinterpretation; what if he thought she was so upset she didn't want to hear from him, when all she had wanted was no interruptions? Maybe he would feel so guilty at the sight of her, wracked with sleepiness, that he would not dare ask about it.

"Anyway," he said, "I already bought these flowers at the hospital florist's this afternoon."

She propped herself up on her elbows, blinking her eyes fast to keep them open, and accepted one of the parcels, an odd triangular object shrouded in florist's paper. She peeled the paper back clumsily. Inside there were chrysanthemums, arranged in a shiny glass baby shoe. The glass shoe laces were inscribed "Congratulations."

"Oh, shit," Guy said. "That's the wrong one."

Torie looked at his face, and was stricken with giggles. Some incredible ball-up had happened.

"That's Mrs. Mooney's," he said. He hid his face in his hands. "My god, she must have gotten your glads."

Torie squeezed her eyes shut as tightly as she could, but tears leaked out at the corners. She sat up, reach-

ing for the drawer of her nightstand where she kept
handkerchiefs.

Guy sank into the straight chair by the dinette, the
only chair in the apartment. He peeked at her, propping his head on one hand, elbow on the table.

"Mary Mooney," he explained, "had such a hard
time. Prayed the whole time, and she was so brave.
She's forty-five if she's a day, waited until her old
mother died to marry a widower with seven kids, and
he put her in the family way right off. I have an idea
she thought she'd gotten the baby from saying a no-
vena during Lent. Oh, God, this is awful."

Torie stopped giggling. She covered her mouth, her
eyes widening as if someone had popped a flashbulb
in her face.

Guy nodded. "You guessed it. There was a card
with the glads that said 'What's a few inches between
friends?' "

Torie whooped and rolled on the bed, clutching the
bedclothes. The arrangement of chrysanthemums, already precariously perched between her feet, tipped
and spilled on the floor. She dove after it, too late.

"Oops," she said.

Guy missed it. He had wandered into the kitchen
proper, where the noise of his rummaging covered the
gentle thunk of the glass baby shoe on the floor.

"Where do you keep your glasses?" he asked.

"Don't have any," she said. "Just the tea cups in the
sink."

There was a dubious pause, while Guy examined
the three dirty cups in the sink. He sighed, and ducked
to look under the sink, behind the dish towel curtain,
for the Ivory Flakes.

"What happened to your refrigerator?" he asked,
while rinsing the cups.

"Don't know," she lied. "It came with the place."

He shuddered. He came back with the tea cups and a foil-wrapped box under his arm. Liquor, or she was Mary Mooney.

"I didn't want this to go to waste either."

The touch of the bottle startled her. It was really cold.

"Brrr."

"Straight from the hospital walk-in. Can't stand warm champagne. And it won't do it any good to get warm again." He began to worry the wire.

"Weren't you worried someone might steal it?" she asked, wondering if she should try to put the flowers back in the baby shoe or just leave them strewn over the floor on the far side of the bed. Would Mary Mooney want them now?

"No," he said. "I put it in the one we keep the blood in."

It was impossible to giggle anymore. She had a stitch in her side.

"What time is it?" she asked, peering at her alarm clock.

"One or so."

She picked up the clock. "Yup, the little hand is on the one, and the big one is at eight after."

"Too late to eat, and I'm starving."

"There's nothing here but peanut butter," she said.

The cork popped gently with a sigh, and the champagne hissed.

"The last time I ate peanut butter," Guy said, "was when Beulah had her gallbladder out. I think I was eighteen, nineteen."

"Beulah?"

"Mom's housekeeper. Old dragon, but a good cook."

He handed her a tea cup of champagne.

She looked at it dubiously. "I feel like the dormouse. Since you've woken me up."

"Here's to Pol Roger," Guy said, and he smiled at her.

"Here, here," she said, and made a mental note to be kind when she kicked him out.

It tasted much better than she remembered. "This is better than peanut butter."

He emptied his cup and went to poke in the refrigerator. "Do you get headaches often from this refrigerator?"

"Only when I look at it."

When he turned around, clutching the tin pail of peanut butter in both hands, she thought of Dorothy and her basket, the one she had carried Toto around Oz in, and got giggling again.

"I'm not surprised you don't keep any food in it. Probably poison it," he said. He pried up the lid and studied the contents. "You know, we had a case in the ER a couple of weeks ago of a kid choking on this stuff."

Torie refilled her tea cup. "Really?"

"Yeah. Is this all you've got, this pumpernickle?"

"Yeah."

He bounced a slice off the counter. "This place is a dump," he said.

"Some guys don't care where they take a girl on a date," Torie said.

He laughed, and sat cross-legged on the bed, eyeing his spur-of-the-moment sandwich. "What are you doing with yourself?"

"Edifying my neighbors by entertaining doctors in the wee hours," she said. She settled back on her elbows and stretched her toes, an operation he watched with interest.

"You deliver a baby tonight?" she asked, suddenly curious.

He nodded. "Balls-up," he said, around a mouthful

of peanut butter and pumpernickel. "Kid was two weeks late, roughly the size of a Sherman tank, and wanted to come out sideways. Transverse, in doctor talk, and he had to be moved around to a deliverable position, or we would have had to do a Caesarean. Which is no fun when the kid is already in the birth canal. Fortunately his mother is a big strong girl who worked hard the whole time and helped us."

"Is everything okay?"

He shrugged. "She's exhausted, and she's lost a lot of blood. The baby's head was big too and he was in the canal a long time. Sometimes that means brain damage. We won't be able to tell for a while."

Torie hugged her knees. "A boy?"

"Yeah," Guy said, wolfing the last corner of the sandwich. He held up one hand, spread wide. "We're on a run. Five boys in the last two days."

Babies had never interested Torie. She glazed over when forced to listen to discussions of toilet training or recitations of labor pains, and had learned to avoid the kitchen at parties, and the baby showers of friends and relations. But Guy's enthusiasm for the business of birthing put it in a new light.

She listened to him talk for twenty minutes while he washed away the taste of the peanut butter and pumpernickel with the Pol Roger. He had most of the bottle, which she thought was fair; it seemed as if he had earned it. Besides, she had her resolution to keep.

"Have you seen Betsy?" she asked, eyeing the bottle ruefully.

"Couple of months ago." Mysteriously, he was blushing.

She was immediately, mischievously, curious. "With Molly?"

"Yes." Suddenly he discovered a need to tidy up, collecting their cups.

"What did you make of Betsy's new spouse?" Torie didn't really need an outsider's opinion. She had made up her mind. But she wanted to relieve him of his embarrassment at having been with Molly.

"Seemed okay."

Exceedingly faint praise.

"Betsy said you called but you were always too busy to come to see her," he added, after a moment's awkward pause.

"It would just make darling Greg unhappy. And Greg unhappy equals Betsy miserable."

She had succeeded too well in distracting him. He was looking at her curiously.

"You don't think it's a happy marriage, Torie?"

"Do you?"

He shook his head.

"Did you meet Twinkletoes?"

"Yeah," he said. "Daddy's little darling."

"Spit image, actually. Just as much of a shit as he is. The two of them walk all over Betsy."

Guy cocked an eyebrow at her. "Maybe you're being a little negative."

"You mean, if I thought Betsy were happy it would be disloyal to Tom?"

He spread his hands.

She heaved the empty bottle off the bed onto the floor. It landed with a clunk and rolled away.

"I wish," she said, "Betsy were happy. I love her. And that son of a bitch is wearing her out. She's had four miscarriages in three years, did you know that?"

Guy shook his head. "You're kidding."

"I wish," Torie said. "Jerk wants a son."

Guy's professionalism was irrepressible. "What's wrong?"

"She loses the babies in the fifth or sixth month. That's all I know about it. She's switched doctors twice when they told her not to try anymore."

Guy winced. "God, that's awful. The timing suggests a number of possible problems. Weakness in the floor of the womb maybe." He thought about it. "Who's her doctor now?"

Torie stared at the ceiling. "Shit. Let me think."

"As long as it's not Hobson," Guy joked.

Torie smiled at him, but her thoughts were with Betsy. An afternoon in spring, at a little cafe on Smith Street, over a hurried glass of wine. Betsy was terribly thin, and apologetic.

"Percy," said Torie.

Guy was surprised, pleased. "Gordon Percy?"

"Yes," Torie said. "That's the one."

"He's the best. She's in good hands."

Torie wasn't easily reassured. "If he's the best, he'd put a stop to it before Greg kills her, wouldn't he?"

Guy chewed his lower lip. "Listen, I'll have a word with Gordon, all right?"

Torie cocked her head in surprise. Damn if he hadn't taken her word for it.

"Hey," Guy said, "I think Greg's a jerk too. I'm a little surprised Molly didn't tell me about the miscarriages. She told me everything else, about how he runs Betsy ragged and lets Linda do the same."

"I don't think Molly knows. I don't know why Betsy told me."

Guy looked at her curiously. "I'm not surprised."

"I suppose, because I'm Tom's sister . . ." Torie said. "Part of her Might Have Been. I wish . . . never mind."

"No fair. What do you wish?"

"I wish I were Betsy's fairy godmother."

Guy was pleased. "See, you're not as hard-hearted as you make out."

"Oh, I'm pretty hard-hearted. Wait and see."

He grinned and reached for her. She slapped his hands away lightly.

"That means you, Doc."

"Never mind," he sighed. "It's been that kind of night."

She threatened him with a pillow. "Look who's complaining. You stand me up, leave me supperless, wake me up in the middle of the goddamn night to bitch about my grub, my apartment and my refrigerator, ruin my reputation with my neighbors and Mary Mooney all at the same time, and you're having a bad night?"

"No, no," he said. "I thought you'd be insulted if I didn't make a pass, that's all."

"Oh," she said. She lowered the pillow. "Now I am insulted."

"I was joking."

"No," she said. "I'm not insulted. I'm disappointed."

"Really?" His face lit up boyishly. Then he yawned. "God, I wish I weren't so tired. Why don't we sleep on it?"

She giggled. It really would be heartless to kick him out.

"Move over," he ordered.

She rolled over gently. He threw himself down next to her with a huge sigh and buried his face in a pillow.

"Wake me at eight, will you?" he asked, into the pillow.

"The hell I will," she said. "Bring your own goddamn rooster."

He lifted his head and looked at her. An expression of real distress had come over him.

"There's something ucky, really ucky, underneath me," he said.

"Good," she said, and turned her back on him.

She felt him roll over onto his back.

"God," he said. "It's some kind of disgusting sandwich."

The springs shivered as he got out of bed. She felt and heard him scraping the sheets with his fingernails. There was a dull thunk in the sink, of something being deposited there, the sound of water running, and then something damp flicking behind her back, over the sheet. She kept her eyes closed and felt heavy and far away.

"Forget it, Torie," Guy said, climbing back onto the bed in a shivaree of bed springs. "I am so goddamned tired I could sleep on rocks right now, but I cannot make love on dirty sheets."

"That's what the last guy said," Torie said.

There was a considering silence. "Brat," Guy said.

"Relax. Just because I'll let you sleep with me doesn't mean I'll let you make love to me. After all, I'll sleep with a peanut butter and pumpernickel sandwich."

He pulled the pillow over his head to muffle his laughter. Presently, his breathing evened out and he began to snore. It didn't bother her; there was something comforting about it. Once in a while, his shoulders shook as if he were still laughing, in his dreams.

When she came in from her morning swim, the apartment was different. The bed was made, the kitchen neatened. The spilled water from the baby shoe vase mopped up, the dead flowers and the dead soldier of the champagne bottle deposited in the trash can, and by the sink, as if waiting to be refilled, stood the baby shoe, blue and glassy. And, as it had never been before, the place was empty.

Where the water puddled on the floor through the night, the wax had whitened and blistered on the linoleum. Dampened towels, the dirty sheets in the bathroom hamper, the water beaded on the shower walls was evidence that he had been there. She hung her suit on the shower head and her towel on the bar, stretched and yawned and shook her head in disbelief. He had been there and was gone. Perhaps she would never see or hear from him again. Something to be devoutly hoped for.

He must have come up the stairs nearly on her heels, for as she left the bathroom there was a light knock on the door. The smell of coffee invaded the apartment before she opened the door.

"Will you marry me?" she asked, and whisked the large waxed paper bag that reeked so deliciously of coffee and hot sugared doughnuts from his hands.

"Only if you promise to evict that refrigerator and quit eating peanut butter and liverwurst sandwiches in bed."

"Where else am I supposed to eat?" With a distracted sweep of one hand, she indicated the apartment. The postage-stamp dinette table had been permanently co-opted as her desk. There was nothing else left except the floor or the bed. She wriggled onto the bed, crossed her legs, and placed the bag in the hollow of them.

He conceded the point by crawling onto the bed next to her.

"You went to Fulton's." She gave him a paper cup of coffee.

"It was so close. I figured you probably ate there. Thought I might even find you there. Anyway, they told me what you like."

She groaned. "Now the whole neighborhood knows."

"Look, they didn't seem too surprised." He relaxed onto the bank of pillows and kicked off his shoes. "Nice of you to run out on me. I felt abandoned waking up all alone. But I figured you had to come back, you live here."

"Well, I'm glad you did." She qualified her enthusiasm. "I'm starving."

"No wonder."

They cleaned up together, Guy shaking out the top quilt in a flurry of crumbs and sugar, Torie disposing of the paper cups, napkins, and bag in the trash.

"Go sailing?" asked Guy, as he leaned over the bed to smooth the quilt.

Relaxed from swimming, and with her belly full of doughnuts and coffee, she could not think what the harm in it might be. It had been a long time.

An hour to the Cape, and they had the sea to themselves. There was wind and chop enough to make work for them, but even that was something to be grateful for, for the exercise warmed them. There was little time for sustained conversation, and little urge to chatter. With a bottle of bourbon to keep their courage up, and a packet of sandwiches from Fulton's Deli, they savored the day and the quiet between them. The boat was borrowed, but the ease they discovered in each other's silence was all theirs, like a birthright.

"I've eaten more in the last day," Torie said, leaving Fulton's after supper, "than I have all year, I swear."

"Good," Guy said, taking her hand. "Thank God Fulton's is open Sundays. It could have been peanut butter. Let's go dancing."

"What kind of doctor are you?" she asked. "Can't you tell I'm dead on my feet?"

He peered at her. "You don't look dead. But okay. I'm a little tired too."

She nodded. "It was a fine day. Thank you. You're very kind."

"No, I'm not. Today has not been an act of charity, Torie. I had myself a good time."

"Oh. Well, thank you all the same, whatever your motivations."

"Charmingly put, but God, you're stubborn. And negative, too."

She shrugged. "I should work tonight."

They reached the stoop of her apartment building. She turned to him, offering her hand to be shaken. He took it and smiled, because now he had captured both.

"I'm off Wednesday night," Guy said. "Let's really have dinner."

Torie shook her head, and tried to pull her hands free. He let them go reluctantly.

"When then?"

She shook her head again. He shoved his hands in his pockets, exasperated.

"You really have changed," he said. "Do you know that? You used to be so . . . so brave."

She looked away. "Well, I'm not anymore. And I have a lot of work . . ."

"That's an excuse," he broke in angrily. "You're hiding behind your work."

"Shit," she said. Her eyes blazed at him. "I can't tell you how goddam tired I am of hearing that shit. If I were a man, you wouldn't dare to imply my work was something to hide behind. It wouldn't ever cross your mind to tell me to smile more, to put on some nylons and lipstick and get laid."

He held up his hands. "Easy, Torie. You're taking this all wrong."

"No, I'm not," she said bitterly. "You all think I've spent the last six years hiding out. There isn't one of you who seems to understand how hard I've worked. I spent three semesters just catching up, for Christ's sake, because I never had a decent course in chemistry or physics or math when I was in high school. They were for the boys. I'm as much a scientist as you, Guy. There's a hell of a lot more to what I do than mooning over old bones and broken pottery."

Guy waited patiently for her to run down. "I believe you. I know what kind of work it takes to earn a master's, let alone a doctorate. Give me credit for knowing you a little better than that. I listened to your brother telling stories about you for three years. I watched you turn cartwheels in a thunderstorm. I never doubted your seriousness, Torie. You're not one to want things casually."

"Thanks," she said, beginning to feel embarrassed at her tantrum.

"But you used to be happy. What good is it, the degrees or the reputation or whatever it is you want from archaeology, unless it makes you happy?"

She stamped her foot. "Happy is nothing, it's stupid. It's the weather, for Christ's sake. Whatever the weather is, you live with it."

"Except it's your weather, Torie. You make it."

"I don't believe that. That's horseshit," she flared back.

"Great," he said. "I can't argue against faith. You want to make a religion out of it."

"Just take me seriously," she said.

"I do," he said, and smiled. He held out his hands for hers.

She trembled, frightened to have him touch her. When she did not give him her hands, he reached out and hugged her carefully, as if she might break.

"I just want you to know," he said, "you don't have to be Sister Mary Victoria of the Holy Bones to convince me."

The mental image of herself in black robes, a fossil thigh bone dangling from her waist like the huge wooden crosses and outsized beads that the nuns she encountered on the streets of Boston wore, overwhelmed her. She had to smother giggles on his shoulder.

When she had caught her breath, she hugged him back, and quickly stepped away.

"Good night," she said.

"I'll call you Tuesday," Guy said.

She did not look back, or out the window to see if he was gone. She felt a sudden panic at letting him go. Splashing her face with cold water, she told herself sternly to get a hold on. It had been a pleasant time after a long period of solitude. It need not mean anything except the oft-touted healing of time was at work. Her life was becoming normal again.

That didn't mean she had to let him get close enough to hear a confession of her clichéd sins. Surely it was a sin to be so stupid as to allow oneself, wide-eyed and cocky, to be seduced by a married professor with a taste for sadistic games. Mark Fletcher, Ph.D., S.O.B.

She stopped at her closet to twitch the gray sheath idly. On impulse, she tore it from the hanger, balled it up, and threw it in the trash, with the dead chrysanthemums and the green glass bottle that had once been full of Pol Roger champagne.

For several days she slept badly, and stayed away from the apartment until very late on Tuesday night, so as to miss any calls from Guy. The following day she left the library at lunch and picked up a bottle of bourbon at a package store. Through the afternoon she nipped it steadily, and left the library at six-thirty with a slight stagger. It was not the first time, but it had been a long time since the last.

Near dawn, she woke suddenly, still more than half-drunk, in a tangle of bed linen. Someone was letting himself into her apartment. For a moment, she was paralyzed, unable to react.

Then the key stopped its rattling in the lock as the wards caught, and the doorknob turned. She scrambled out of the ransacked bed and threw herself against the door. But it was too late.

The opening door slammed into her, driving her back against the foot of the bed. Mark Fletcher stepped inside, light-footed as a cat. He looked around the apartment, lit faintly by the streetlights outside.

"What a slut you are," he said.

She spat at him.

Fletcher slapped her hard enough to knock her sideways to the floor.

He was not a tall man, but he was vain of his body, powerful with weight lifting and amateur wrestling. Just as he scorned the aged tweeds and leather-patched elbows of the academic, and wore expensive, hand-tailored English suits, so he scorned the commonplace physical weakness of his colleagues and flaunted relentless competitive masculinity. Once she had thought him handsome, but in the dim, drunken light of dawn, the flat planes of his face were demonic, and his North Sea eyes were brutal.

"You called me, you little slut. That was stupid. Such filthy words, Victoria. I took it for an invitation."

She shook her head in frantic denial.

"Drunk, of course. Pig drunk. You don't remember, do you? You're such a slut when you're drunk, did you know that?"

She hid her face in her hands. Her stomach hurt.

He took off his jacket and hung it in the closet, pausing to rifle her clothes with long, sensitive, disdainful fingers.

"Where's the bottle?" he asked. "Since you don't have the manners to offer me a drink yourself, I will make my own."

She covered her head with her hands.

He rummaged among the bedclothes.

"Aha." Then, angry, he tossed the bottle to one side. "It's empty. You are a pig."

Her mouth smashed against her wrist, she whispered unintelligibly.

"Speak up," he said.

"Don't hit me," she whispered.

"You shouldn't have called," he said.

He unbuckled his belt and hung it on the bedpost. He picked up a pillow and shook it free of the pillow case. Calmly he twisted the pillow case between his hands.

She threw herself then at the door. He caught her by her hair and jerked her backwards. He threw her onto the bed, stapled her throat to the mattress with one arm, and punched her full in the mouth. As she choked on her own blood and teeth, he whipped her head forward by the hair and gagged her with the pillow case. She bucked under him in one violent convulsion. The heel of his hand found her throat and cut off her wind. From far away, she heard Fletcher scolding her, in the most reasonable of tones.

Guy would not let her sleep. He kept trying to wake her. She told him crossly to go away.

There were other faces, and other voices, but his she knew, and it was constant, goading. He seemed to be in charge. He insisted, often that she wake.

She wanted to sleep, where it did not hurt so much.

"Torie."

Her throat was dry, sandpapery, and swollen. Pushing air through it to shape sounds was like removing some huge splinter.

"Leave me 'lone," she whispered.

He touched her neck, the tips of his fingers light on the carotid artery. She fumbled at his fingers, trying to push them off. Once she rolled her head from side to side, but the hurt exploded, bright and sharp-edged, at the base of her skull.

"Torie."

She squinted at him, hovering over her. His hands

slipped beneath her head to lift it. There was a hard smooth edge of glass and click of water on her lips. It was like swallowing a stone, but soothed as it went down, so she was able to do it again.

"Guy," she said. She closed her eyes.

He showed he was satisfied. He let her sleep.

When he woke her again, she was thirstier, and drank eagerly. At once she was stronger. All her pain flared, as if it were fire feeding upon a rush of oxygen.

"Torie."

She opened her eyes for him. He was pleased.

"Who am I?" he asked.

It did not seem silly that he didn't know. Perhaps he too had been hurt, was in pain.

"Guy."

He held the glass to her lips.

"Do you know where you are?"

Her hand closed convulsively over his, holding the glass as if she were afraid he would take it away.

"Clinic," she said.

He nodded. He let her back down onto the pillows.

"What happened to you?"

She still grasped his hand. She dug her nails into his palm, closed her eyes and turned her head away.

Gently, his fingers on her cheekbone turned her head back. "Tell me."

She rolled her head carefully side to side. No.

He forced one thumb between her curled fingers to massage her palm.

"Who was it?"

She caught her breath and held it, afraid to move.

His thumb on her palm bore down hard enough to make her wince.

"Who was it?" His voice was as tense and hard as his thumb grinding into her palm.

She shrank from him, squeezing her eyes shut tightly.

"What did the son of a bitch stick into you besides his cock?" Guy shouted.

Someone, a woman with a schoolmarm's voice, spoke to Guy angrily. He let go of Torie's hand.

She had not drawn a breath. She writhed in slippery darkness like a straitjacket. Guy shouted her name but she did not answer.

The next time, Guy was not there. The face looking down at her was soft and female, abundantly wrinkled, skin like an aged peach. Bubbles of gray hair spilled out from under a nurse's cap. A soft, talcum-powder-smelling hand stroked Torie's forehead, hair, cheek. A bar pin on an ample uniformed bosom identified her as Edna Worth, RN.

"Better," said Edna Worth, and she was not asking a question.

She helped Torie drink. She did not stop there. She bathed Torie in rose-scented water, massaged her with alcohol, changed her bed linen and johnny. When that was done, Torie felt very like a little girl, home perhaps with the measles, except for the hurts that were so much more than fever and spots. She felt very light. The ease with which Mrs. Worth brushed and braided Torie's hair made Torie think the nurse had been fixing her hair for some time.

Mrs. Worth spoke little, but what she said, innocuous and economical, was as soothing as her strong, sure movements. When Torie fell asleep again, it was with a feeling of safety all the more astonishing because she had not really known she was that afraid.

Guy came again. He sat with her often when Mrs. Worth or the day nurse was not there. He did not ask any more questions beyond how did she feel. He brought her flowers and then delicacies in little boxes that she could not eat but which Mrs. Worth stored in her knitting bag against the day she could. When Guy examined her, Mrs. Worth or another nurse was always there, and sometimes another doctor or an intern. They never spoke of how she was in front of her, and went away with careful blank faces.

The pain scabbed over to a dry cloudy discomfort. She had strength enough to dread Guy's silent visits, because she knew sooner or later he would begin to ask questions again. Edna Worth seemed to sense her unease and tried to shoo him away on pretexts and excuses.

But the day came when Guy sent Mrs. Worth out. She did not argue with him, but her mouth tightened, and she stopped on the way to squeeze Torie's hand and kiss her cheek.

It was only after Edna Worth had gone and left her alone with Guy that Torie realized they were not alone. He had brought another doctor with him, a short middle-aged man, gone prematurely gray, but with a kindly mouth.

"Hello, Victoria," the other doctor said.

Her stomach turned, and she felt a sudden wash of cold and bitter sweat. She turned her face away, to look out the window.

Guy clasped his hands behind his back and faced the window, too, as if to admire the view, which was of the hospital courtyard, glancing at her only occasionally as he made his speech.

"It was very kind of you to refer Betsy to Gordon, and modest of you not to say so. Just lucky coincidence that I ran into him and asked about her. He tells me, by the way, he has had a word with her husband, for whatever good it might do. He did not know you were here, and was very concerned when I told him so."

Torie shivered, her hands twitching on the sheets. She could not bring herself to look at Gordon Percy, who cleared his throat behind her.

Guy stopped. "Are you cold?"

She shook her head yes. He paused to draw a blanket over her.

"I don't want to do this, either," he said, tucking her in.

Her eyes followed his lips warily, but she said nothing.

"Gordon, of course, had to tell me that this isn't the first time," Guy continued. "Much worse, this time, though. We nearly lost you from hemorrhage and shock."

He came close and took her hands in his to rub.

"It's going to happen again, Torie. The next time, the bastard's going to kill you."

She shuddered. She could not prevent a trickle of tears escaping one eye.

Guy blotted it with his pocket handkerchief.

"You know him," he said. "Who is he?"

Holding onto his hands tightly, Torie shook her head slowly. No. She had brought it on herself.

Guy sighed.

Gordon Percy shifted restlessly in the chair he had taken and said, "I've covered for you. Your department chairman thinks you have pneumonia. He's very disappointed for you. I'm sure you know it means a lost semester, and your degree will be that much more delayed. He thinks you can still do the New Mexico dig next summer."

She nodded.

"Your parents think you've taken over the classes of a teaching assistant with mono," Gordon went on. "No doubt they think that's a poor excuse for this long a silence, but if all they get out of this is a case of hurt feelings I thought you'd prefer that to the kind of shock that learning their daughter had been raped and beaten would be."

Her throat closed up in shame. She stared out the window. So many kind lies, as if he thought she was going to go on living.

Guy sat down on the end of the bed, and put one hand on the lump of her foot under the blanket.

"I know nobody's supposed to love such a terrible person, but a number of people do, despite your best efforts to convince them otherwise. So what are you going to do about it, Torie? Let this bastard kill you? Don't you think you owe something to the people who kept the son of a bitch from killing you this last time?"

She groped for her bedside glass of water, and swallowed hard.

"What happens if I tell you?" she asked in a rusty voice.

Guy was eager to reassure her. "I understand you won't want to prosecute. I don't want you to, and Gordon doesn't either. You've been through enough without that kind of ugliness. But we think if this bastard knows other people know, and if he does it again, he'll be caught and punished, then he'll leave you alone. You have to save yourself, Torie. This is the only way. He has to know you won't protect him anymore."

Torie breathed a long, shaky breath. "All right."

Guy smiled and kissed her quickly on the end of the nose. "Good girl," he said.

Gordon Percy clapped his hands. "This is the right thing to do, Victoria. I'm proud of you."

He came over and kissed her too, on the crown of her head. "Brave girl."

*   *   *

She thought of nothing else until Guy came in, the next day, with a spectacular black eye, a split lip, and a splinted finger.

"Jesus," she said.

Mrs. Worth took a deep breath, and gathered up her knitting. "Good man," she said in a low voice, and left the room.

Guy took Mrs. Worth's chair and sat down in it, back to front, so he could lean on the back.

"It's done," he said.

His eyes were tired and a little vague, a look Torie recognized as drug-numbed. She reached out tentatively to touch his swollen face.

"I didn't want you to be hurt," she said.

He clasped her wrist and held her hand against his face, wincing.

"I intended to be civilized," he said. "Wore my doctor hat. Fletcher told me every goddamn lie he could think of, which was a lot. When he realized I wasn't buying any, he tried to lay it off on you. That's when I hit him."

Torie tried to smile. "And he hit you back. What did you tell him?"

She did not want to sound anxious, not when he was battered and bruised for her sake, but could not keep the shakes out of her voice. He understood she needed reassurance, some proof that now she was indeed protected, even in his absence.

"I told him what we agreed on. Next time the cops find out. The department chairman. The president of the university. The newspapers. I told him if you scraped your knee on your desk this winter, I would hold him responsible. If you see him, he's in trouble, he's too close. That means from across the Yard, or down the street. And that means you have to call me at once, you have to call in regularly. There'll be people checking on you. He knows that. I told him if Gordon Percy or I ever saw another girl in your condition in any emergency room in this city, we'd turn him in and testify against him. I also told him if I ever had to treat you again, I'd see something happened to him a lot worse than losing his job or going to jail. I told him in detail how easy it is to castrate a man, especially when you know what you're doing."

Guy tried to laugh, but, clearly, it hurt. Torie held on to him, shivering.

"Blackmail," she said.

"Goddamn right," he said.

They didn't speak of it anymore. He kissed her hand, and went away, to his own bed and healing. She submitted to a flurry of fussing from Edna Worth. The fear was still there, at odds with relief and a pale shade of triumph, but there was also a pervasive sense of wonder. She had questions of her own, and no one to answer them but herself. She wondered if this was the end of it. She wondered if she would ever stop being ashamed. The worst of it would be having it turn out that Guy had saved her not out of altruism, or loyalty to Tom, but because he loved her. That would be unbearable. Sooner or later he would want to know how it began, how she could have put herself at risk, drawn that man's lightning down on herself. Sooner or later she would have to know herself.

She tripped and fell on her face on the back porch. Her breath was driven out of her like air from a popped balloon. With it went her consciousness, like the fragments of the balloon's skin. She was not aware of the blood dribbling from her split lip, her abraded chin, or bruised solar plexus, only of clawing open the storm door, rolling inside, curling up like a frightened porcupine, crabbing to the coffee table near the stove, swallowing a handful of pills. The fire was near, an unexpected comfort. Between its warmth and the narcotics she became sleepy. It was a sleepiness that promised a further velvet and undreaming sleep, and she wanted it. Needed it.

But every stitch she had was soaking wet, and the cold wet of the sleet and snow that had penetrated her clothing met the bitter feverish sweat she had worked up against the pain, and slicked her all over. The layers of her clothing kept it from evaporating.

She pushed herself up against the table. Its surface was a field of shiny multicolored capsules and sugar-candy pills, with the containers scattered like culverts among them. She shoved the capsules and pills back into the plastic bottles with stupid fingers. She remembered the old man. Her fingers shook, and the medicines escaped them, pattering onto the table and rolling around it. When at last she had captured them all, she stuffed the containers into her coat pockets. The old man needed them now.

Still she was afraid to move. But at last she hauled herself cautiously to her feet and groped her way to the back door.

Outside there was enormous peace. Or perhaps only indifference. The Cadillac looked as if it were capsizing in the whipped cream dunes of the snow. Drizzle streaked the clean air, sharp in her lungs, cutting through the mental sluggishness induced by the narcotics.

She crept back to the car, bracing herself against the discovery that the old man was dead. But he wasn't. She could hear his stertorous breathing even before she grasped the car door handle like a chinning bar to lower herself gingerly to the ground. Her own breathing was strained and noisy. The sound of the pair of them, wheezing like the church organ of some reduced and impoverished congregation, suddenly struck her as funny and pitched her into a fit of ragged chortling.

Being underneath the car was like lying just inside a culvert, near enough to an open end for the light to make shadows darker and to reflect in random pinpoints off the snow and off the whites of the old man's eyes. He smiled vaguely at her with his teeth made ectoplasmic by the watery light. Suddenly she was all goose bumps, shivering and shaking. She snuggled up tight against him, and held on to his jacket for dear life.

"Oh, God," she said. "I've never been so fucking cold."

His lips twitched and worked, as if he were trying to form the familiar shapes of his name in the old joke. But the only sound he could manage was a rattling exhalation.

Propped on one elbow, she fumbled for the pills in her pocket. The capsules overflowed her palm and spilled into the snow.

"Shit," she said, and clawed them up, snow, water, and all.

Separating the old man's lips as if he were a horse, she pushed the pills behind his tongue, forcing him to swallow them. She knew she should try to remember what she had given him, and how many, but the facts of it slipped away from her, exactly as the pills passed convulsively down his throat under the fingers she held over his larynx. She felt battered all over, and unsure of herself, but the medication she had taken kept both her physical discomfort and her mental confusion at a safe distance.

The old man's eyes had not left her face. She felt sick to her stomach again.

"I'm going to jack the car," she told him, with a

confidence that was a con practiced on them both. "It won't be long."

She felt in his pockets for his lighter, and showed it to him when she found it. That seemed to please him. He worked hard at the shadow of a smile. Then she rolled away quickly, anxious to be off the cold wet ground and away from his trusting eyes.

The dope had done nothing to restore strength or sureness to her fingers. It took several minutes of cursing to make the lighter work, and then another to heat the head of the key in the Cadillac's ignition, which she had to do half in and half out of the car, standing unsteadily on tiptoe, the car door propped open against her fanny, and her body twisted over the steering wheel. She had to wait for the heat from the head of the key to find its way to the other end. Wrapping one hand in her scarf to get a dry grip on it, she turned the key to the unlock position. Then she was able to remove it. She admired it, it was something that had gone right.

By the time she had propped herself against the trunk of the car, the key had cooled and had to be reheated to enter the frozen trunk lock and turn it. Her eyes wanted to unfocus. It was a fight against the dope to insert the key into the slot at all. When she turned it in the sleet-encrusted lock, the trunk lid remained closed. Sealed with the sleet, she realized, and threw herself onto it, pounding all along its edges frantically. She staggered back a step, delivered a feeble kick to the lock button, and the trunk lid popped up with a satisfying creak, showering bits of ice.

Inside was a mess, her emergency supply dump, all of which had to come out before she could get at the jack. A greasy spaghetti of ropes and chains overlaid road flares and flashlights, none of them in working condition. There was a filthy blanket roll, against the contingency of having to crawl under the car in mud or wet. She slung them all aside, except the blanket. It might be a little extra comfort to the old man. There were two shovels, one for snow, a spade for mud. Two oil cans and a big red gasoline can with enough rusty sludge in the bottom to make a respectable slosh, like a nearly empty tea kettle, when she hauled it out. There was dry gas, a plastic jug of windshield wiper fluid, and broken bags of kitty litter and road salt, with an old coffee can in each. A pair of oily cotton work gloves and a can of Sterno. She put on the gloves, though they were too large for her, and considered the canned heat. It was a shame she couldn't use it to warm up the old man, but the risk of igniting the car he was under was inestimable. Regretfully, she threw it onto the snowcrust where she had strewn the rest of the junk.

The last thing she turned out was her first aid kit, a black metal lunch pail. Inside was a box of Band-Aids, a bottle of rubbing alcohol, a very large green plastic bottle of Excedrin, and a fifth of Wild Turkey. She pried off the cap of the aspirin bottle and sniffed at it. It smelled vinegary. She shook a few into her palm. They were yellowed, crumbling, and granular as the snowcrust. Aspirin, she knew, could deteriorate into strychnine, but she could not recall how long the process took or what the signs were. It was very old aspirin, she knew that for sure.

A couple of years ago the formula had been changed, weakened. One day she had happened on a quantity of the old stock in a pharmacy in a small town in the lakes region she had been passing through, and decided to buy the lot. It was aspirin getting her through the days then, along with the bourbon, before the cancer had been diagnosed.

She piled the dozen and a half boxes of assorted

sizes on the counter near the cash register. The clerk looked at her oddly but began to ring it up anyway. Probably glad to be rid of the old stock.

Behind her a man, clutching a bottle of Pepto-Bismol with a fervor that suggested he needed it as badly as she did her aspirin, looked over her shoulder and whistled.

"That's some headache you got, lady," he said.

"Fucking A," she said, and scooped the lot into her big handbag before the clerk could open a paper bag for them.

Age robbing her of another old friend. She just didn't dare trust it. While she didn't much care what condition her corpse was in when it was found, she had no enthusiasm for going out foaming at the mouth. The pain she had was more than earned. She didn't need any bonuses. And last she knew, the old man wanted to live, so the goddamned things would be no use to him. She scattered the contents of the aspirin bottle over the snow like toxic birdfeed.

There remained her last and best old friend, the bourbon. It never went bad, never failed her. It was she who hadn't the guts anymore. She picked it up, hugging it like a long-lost baby. The fiery light in it always excited her. So beautiful. The drizzle pearled and sparkled on the glass. She uncapped it, sniffed at its bouquet as if it were a bottle of wine. It would not hurt, she thought, just to taste. She would swish it around in her mouth like mouthwash and spit it out.

But once its warmth was in her mouth, it was too much to waste it, and so she swallowed. It was a little swallow, and maybe it wouldn't hurt. She took a second. If the first tiny mouthful hurt her, she might as well piggyback the pain. And it was wonderful, better than it had ever tasted or felt before. But she had not forgotten what she was doing. She stowed the bottle in the lunch pail in the back seat of the Cadillac, out of harm's way.

Now the trunk was empty. She peeled back the carpet and the mat under it, and heaved them out into the snow with a little burst of energy fueled by the taste, more than the scant substance, of the bourbon. The plate over the tire was only loosely screwed down, for her and like her, she thought and laughed. It was hard enough to get the lug nuts off a wheel. She didn't need to start by skinning her knuckles on the butterfly nut on the plate. Not that she had had to change any tires lately. Not in the last millennium. But there was no certainty in this life, no there wasn't. Hadn't she learned long ago to Be Prepared?

The spare itself was hardly used, though fully seven years old. She did not believe in swapping a bad tire for a weak sister. The tire was a big one, hard enough for her to lift before she was sick. She wrestled the bastard out and sat down on it, winded, to regroup.

The physical effort, or the booze, mere ghost of Christmas past though it was, made her more alert. She felt as ready as she would ever be for this job of work, mentally. Half of how good she felt was because she was apparently getting off scot-free with her taste of liquor. Relief, spelled W-I-L-D-T-U-R-K-E-Y. But her physical strength was another question.

She examined her hands. The gloves had layered grease over grime, ground into the morning's abrasions. The bandage over the cut was filthy and falling off. She stripped it away. The cut was swollen and red, hot with infection. Her fingers, though, were skeletal, and whiter than the snow, under the slick of grease. Damned poor tools for the job, she thought.

She shifted onto her haunches to examine the back bumper and peer under the Cadillac. Her rolling around underneath had packed down the snow that had been blown under it during the storm. The slightest pressure made a glassy surface, and the drizzle puddled on it, as it had under the car, and where they had shovelled or walked.

"Goddamn fucking hollow-hearted snow," she muttered.

It was going to be very risky, trying to jack the car. Like trying to climb a glass mountain in a pair of fur slippers. Too easy for the foot of the jack to slip and slide, or the jack to lose grip on the bumper, which was as glassy as every other surface with the sleet. Nevertheless, she was going to have to try it.

The jack was neatly stowed under the spare. Laying out the pieces on the floor of the trunk, she concentrated on putting them together. She felt queasy and sweaty and cold all at once. Scared shitless, she thought.

First things first. She slithered across the snowcrust to retrieve one of the coffee cans, and salted and kitty-littered around the right rear wheel to create a surface for the jack to take purchase on. When the salt had melted in, she chipped at the snow pack to roughen the surface a little more. The chips flew up and stung her face like shards of glass. And it did no good, in the end.

Her hands felt they were bruising just trying to get a grip on the jack. She nearly dropped it, nearly lost it under the car. At last she had it upright and under the bumper, but when she leaned on it, it skated. Just what it would do with the weight of the car on it. She examined the tire iron, used it to chip the surface of the snow pack a little more, but the jack seemed to float. She tried to pack snow around its base to hold it in place. The snow was too wet and would not stick together or to the iron of the jack.

She knew a lost cause when she saw one. The only thing she could use the jack for would be to beat herself to death with it. She heaved the jack and the tire iron into the trunk, where they made an ugly clatter.

She retrieved the lunch pail from the back seat and helped herself to several mouthfuls of bourbon. When there was no immediate reaction, she decided the pills she had taken were somehow numbing what remained of her intestines against the liquor. So they were some goddamned good after all. She put the bottle away against future need, then wandered around to stare at the back end of the Cadillac, hoping for some inspiration.

"Shit," she said, and kicked the coffee can she had left lying on the snow.

It skittered away under the car. There was a dull thunk. The old man made a strangled moan. Afraid she had hit him with it, she dropped to her knees and rolled under the car.

It had come to rest by his hand. There was no mark on his skin she could make out in the gloom. But when she touched the can, it glinted suddenly with reflected light, and it seemed as if a stone had been rolled away. The light of hoped-for-inspiration flooded her mind and heart at once. She clutched the can to her chest.

"Goddamn," she said.

Huddled tight against the old man's knees, she began to chip at the snow under him. Even the sharp metal edge of the can had trouble biting the glassy snow, but soon bits and fragments flew up to sting her face and hands. She did not mind. All at once, she was doing what she was meant to do. Digging. She would dig him out from underneath if she had to move the state of Maine a teaspoon at a time to do it. He was a lucky old bastard to have drawn the best digger there was to get him out.

And then she did not think of him at all. The work possessed her. It was like sculpting, she had often thought, sensing what was within without seeing it, freeing it without damaging it. The can was a gross tool to someone who had worked with fine brushes, minute quantities of acids, and tiny vacuum cleaners, rather like handing a jewelsmith a blacksmith's hammer and anvil to work with, but then she was not extracting something small or delicate or fragile, except in a relative sense, from the snow. Only a goddamned fool of an old man, a fossil to be sure, but not one with any secrets worth discovering.

This was work at which her patience knew no end, and she lost track of the time. But she was too good at it not to recognize when it became clear the idea, so perfect in its manifest destiny, was not working. As carefully and rapidly as she chipped, the weight of the car simply settled just as steadily upon the old man and the snow supporting its right side. The rotten snowdrift against which the car rested was gently collapsing into the space she made with her coffee can.

She hugged the can to her again, as close to tears as she ever allowed herself to come. Here was the proof she was as useless as Joe Nevers. He was mercifully out of it, as lively as the snowbank. She patted him absently, and found him still warm. She crabbed out from under the car.

She opened the back door of the car, hooked the lunch pail out, and closed the door as if there were a child on the edge of sleep inside. Fortifying herself with a careful measure of the bourbon, she studied the situation. Clearly she had only made things worse. Removing snow from under and around the old man had increased the angle at which the car was tilted. The more the Cadillac tilted into the farther snowbank, the more unstable it became. It looked as if it might drop full onto the old man at any moment.

She stared up the hill, a view she much preferred to the empty, forsaken house and the grotesque hulk of the car. At the top of the driveway, the truck seemed to be patiently waiting for her.

She had to assume drifts on the road as deep as the ones around the house. How far would the truck take her through them? How far could she take it, might be the proper phrasing of the question. The last time she had driven a four-wheel-drive vehicle she had burned out the transmission a hundred miles from nowhere. Scratch one Land Rover, no doubt buried under desert sand, waiting to be unearthed by some archaeological expedition of the far distant future. How much of the mile of dirt road, drifted hip-deep, could she hike or crawl in her condition? How long might it take, and how long did the old man have? What else could she do?

She tucked the bottle like a joey in a kangaroo's pocket inside Guy's old sweater she had pulled on over her own, and considered whether she should first go back to the house and change to dry clothes. She felt glassy with the cold, as if soon frost would begin to form on her. Her fingers burned with it, where she had been digging with them. She did not think there were enough of Guy's old clothes left to keep her warm. Once again, she started the uphill trudge. There just didn't seem to be an alternative.

Winter 1949/Summer 1952

"SHIT," TORIE SAID, glancing at her wristwatch. Five minutes late. Her parents were already seated at a table and had drinks in front of them. Guy was nowhere in sight, meaning he was late too. As usual.

She ducked into the coatroom, shaking snow off her hat and scarf and coat. The snow melted cold and wet on her earrings, the diamond studs her father had given her for her sixteenth birthday, which she had worn at Tom's wedding.

In both her smile and her mother's there was the same fixed quality as they hugged and kissed, but it was jitters in her mother, resignation in hers. Behind the mask of her makeup, her mother was trembling. Her father's embrace was as stiff as his neck. She had been right to dread this meeting.

"If Guy's managed to escape the clinic, he's probably tied up in traffic," she said. "Cars all over the road, because of the snow."

Her father, holding her chair for her, grunted. "People in this state drive for all the world like they never had a winter here. Any of 'em ever heard of snow tires?"

"Now, Tom," Theresa Hayes said. "You haven't touched your drink."

"Obediently, Tom Hayes picked up his old-fashioned. "How about you, baby?" he asked Torie. "What are you having?"

She shook her head. "Hot tea would be good. I'm cold."

"Have a hot toddy then," he suggested.

Theresa Hayes nodded wisely. "Just the thing for you, Torie."

"No, no, Daddy. Tea, please."

Tom Hayes signalled the waiter impatiently. Torie's mother took refuge in her drink.

Torie tried not to be angry with them. She supposed she deserved it for all the times she had been contrary for the hell of it. But she couldn't allow them to badger her into a drink to make them more comfortable. Not when she was in one of the longish periods of abstinence that she thought of as fasts. She was damned if she would permit alcohol to become the indispensable prop in her life that it was in theirs. At least there was no pressure that way from Guy, thank God or Whoever it was Who was supposed to Be In Charge.

Theresa Hayes made a valiant effort to fill the time before Guy arrived by bringing Torie up to date on the doings of her aunts and cousins and former neighbors, while Torie listened with as much interest as she could fake. Tom Hayes looked repeatedly and pointedly at his watch but Torie was so used to Guy's now chronic tardiness that twenty minutes seemed hardly late at all. Guy came in blinking snow flakes from his lashes, his cheeks boyishly chapped with the cold.

Torie's mother permitted a buss on the cheek, but Tom Hayes' handshake was abrupt and unforgiving, as cold as all outdoors, even as Guy apologized for being late.

Theresa Hayes tried to ease things by asking after Guy's mother, Frances.

"She's fine," Guy said, relieved to change the subject. "Very sorry not to be able to join us, but her knee's bothering wickedly. She asked me especially to invite you to stop in on your way north."

Tom Hayes nodded firmly. The older generation knew what was proper. He and Theresa would make their manners to Frances Christopher on their way home even if it took them considerably more than strictly out of their way.

When asked, Guy allowed he would have something to drink—Dubonnet—but this did not seem to earn him any credit with Tom Hayes, only another sour look.

Disheartened by her father's pique and her mother's nervous twittering, Torie stirred her spoon slowly through the clear gold of her tea, grateful for its warm steam in the air and the warmth that radiated through the china cup to her hand. They had never been perfect, her parents, nor had she expected them to be, once she was past twelve or so, but years ago they had been young and forgiving and now they weren't. Some elasticity had gone out of their spirits, some hope or joy from their hearts. It seemed as if it were her fault in some indirect way.

But Guy put on his best charm and if he did not succeed in softening Tom, he managed to relax Theresa a little. Guy and several drinks did, that is. She seemed to enjoy the meal more than the rest of them did. Torie relaxed a little too, thinking perhaps her father might be jollied out of his sulk.

This restaurant meal was all of Christmas they would share this year. The elder Hayeses were hurrying home from a vacation in the Caribbean, her father claiming the press of neglected business prevented lingering in the city. Partly, she knew, he was punishing her for refusing to come home for the holidays, and partly, her parents were severely discomfitted at the thought of sleeping overnight in the same town in which their daughter lived a life they judged immoral.

Given the tensions among the three of them, Torie

could just imagine what going home would be like. She loathed Christmas to begin with, resenting the enforced cheer and excessive consumption. Since she was a child, the holidays had degenerated into an embarrassing shopping spree by day, and a round of cocktail parties at night that were little more than excuses to stay drunk for two weeks straight. The tree had shrunken to tabletop size and was artificial. No children's stockings hung on the stair.

Guy, in her place, would have gone home to make the folks happy, but it did not trouble him either that she did not. Could not, he was convinced. It was brave enough of her to sit through this meal with them. He reached for her hand as often as he had one free.

"So what are you two doing for the holidays?" Theresa Hayes asked, when dessert was being served.

"We're going to the cathedral for Midnight Mass, Christmas Eve," Torie said. "Guy's working Christmas Day."

Tom Hayes' face reddened at the casual juxtaposition of Midnight Mass and the wifely statement of Guy's work schedule.

Guy glanced at Torie apprehensively. She had violated the unspoken agreement among them all to pretend she and Guy were not living together.

"Does that mean you're going RC? Has the Catholic Church started condoning fornication?" Tom Hayes demanded.

"Oh, Tom," Theresa said, reaching for her drink.

"Pardon me, Mr. Hayes," Guy began.

Tom Hayes interrupted him. "Never mind asking my pardon. I won't give it. You take a piece of my mind instead."

It was clear he had been looking for the opportunity to speak his piece and was not going to let it pass.

"Daddy," Torie said coolly. "You needn't bother. We can guess."

Guy's hand covered hers, on the table, quickly, a signal to stay calm. But she was calm. She wasn't even angry. It was almost a relief to have arrived at the inevitable contretemps.

"I'll say what I goddamn well please, miss. It's as much a shame for your mother and me as it is for you and Guy. I just don't understand how you can justify the way you're living. You've both had all the advantages. You come of good families. You're educated, professional people, at least that's what you tell me, Torie. For Christ's sake, Guy, you're a doctor. Doesn't that mean anything to you? People look up to you, they expect you to set some kind of standard. Why are you acting like a couple of bums? Unless you want to hurt your mother and me, Torie? And your mother, Guy? How can you do this to her?"

"Mr. Hayes," Guy began again.

"This is not how decent people behave. You're plenty old enough to get married. There's no excuse for this carrying on."

Guy was quiet, holding her hand, watching Tom Hayes. He had known this was coming, too. Torie felt guilt at putting him through it. In his heart, she knew, Guy believed exactly what her father had said. But he betrayed no more than minor exasperation.

"Oh, Tom," Theresa Hayes said again, and began to weep.

"It's my choice," Torie said. "Guy would like to be married. I am the one who won't consent to it."

Tom Hayes slammed his drink onto the table hard enough to splash his shirtfront. They all winced. People around them looked up from their meals to stare at them.

Tom Hayes lowered his voice. "I might have known it."

Theresa Hayes struggled to her feet and stumbled away to the ladies' room.

"Look what you've done to your mother," Tom Hayes said.

"I had help," Torie said. "You were going to have your say no matter what. Besides, she's drunk. She always cries when she's drunk."

Tom Hayes was livid. Abruptly, he pointed a blunt finger at Guy.

"You, mister doctor. What kind of man are you for putting up with this nonsense? Are you so besotted as to let a woman drag you down to live in a way you know is wrong? You're supposed to be the strong one. You make her come round, you take care of her, you protect her honor, if she won't do it for herself."

"Shit," Torie said. "You don't know the half of it."

Guy tightened the grip on her hand, looking anxiously from her angry face to her father's, so very much alike.

"You young people," Tom Hayes said, disgustedly. "You think you know it all. It's your lives. Live 'em how you goddamned well please. But don't come crying home to me when you get hurt, miss, not to me."

He balled up his napkin and threw it on the table. Theresa Hayes, collected at least for the moment, was making her way back to them. Tom Hayes stood up and caught her arm before she could sit down. He marched her out without a backward glance.

"God bless us every one," Torie said.

"Torie," Guy began.

She kissed him quickly on the lips. "I'll only do it for you, Guy. Nobody else."

He scratched his head. "You mean, we didn't need to go through this?"

She shrugged. "Maybe I did," she said. "I didn't know until just now." Then she smiled at him, shyly.

He shook his head. He had given up, she knew, the facile, obvious explanations for her resistance. It was not rebellion against a convention, or some disillusion prompted by her parents' unhappiness. She knew well enough they were not unhappy together, but because of things that had nothing to do with their marriage. He supposed it had something to do with her own unhappy history, but she had healed so well, it was almost as if that had never happened. In any case, he would have expected her to be that much more eager for the refuge of marriage. And he had not been very distressed that she had taken her time, wanted to go a little bit slow. It was inevitable, he thought, that first he should have been her protector, but he had not wanted it to always be that way. It made him uneasy; he would not want a wife who was chronically fearful or timid or dependent.

Still, he never doubted she would find her way. She had a knack for sorting out what she wanted. Once it was done, there was no stopping her. Whatever else might happen, life with Torie would always be interesting. He only hoped he could keep up with her.

The war was well over. The boys back home. Life was normal again. There were cars for sale, and only the British still had to ration. Everyone was getting married. Everyone was pregnant.

At twenty-seven, Torie had not felt old, or an old maid.

Theresa Hayes made it clear that old maid meant too old for breeding. She cast the conventional wisdom Torie's way: "A woman's not fulfilled without children."

Aunt Sissy had a point to make too. "All the good men will be taken if you wait any longer."

The other aunts nodded in solemn agreement. Torie thought about shaving her head and hieing off to a convent. The chorus of relieved sighs from her mother and the aunts when she told them she and Guy were going to get married, at last, was thunderous.

Torie's mother wanted the big wedding. Brazening it out. It seemed a small thing to do for her, at the time. Torie knew other girls who had consented to the hoopla for their mothers. She thought it would be different when it really happened, that the emotions she was supposed to be feeling would surprise her, evoked by the ceremony. But she wasn't nervous, just numb, her doubts veiled as her face, when Guy held her hand in his to put on the ring.

Yet she never doubted she really loved Guy, before the business of the wedding came up, and believed she would love him again when the circus left town, when they were alone again. Nor had he worried during the strange period between engagement and wedding, when she was distant, vague, slippery, when she wasn't sure she was afraid of being married, or of marriage, or of the wedding. Weddings were women's work, and he surrendered her to her mother and the aunts trusting she would be returned to him as his bride.

If at twenty-seven she was on the edge of spinsterhood, at thirty-five Guy was a prime specimen of Eligible Bachelor. No one wondered why he had not married yet. He had been to war and then to medical school. Guy benefitted not only from the height of the physician's status as an authority figure, but as a specialist in gynecology-obstetrics, he was the object of all the awe his countrymen render to the Expert.

Deadpan, Torie told her mother that Guy had "great expectations."

Theresa Hayes nodded wisely, suspecting Torie was joking again. She was uneasy, disturbed by the question of how Torie, with her tart tongue and independent ways, would cope with the institution of marriage.

The irregular arrangement that preceded the marriage could hardly be a sufficient testing ground. It was obviously best for Torie to marry; she could not go on living in sin with Guy forever, and if not with him, what after? That was a perfectly dreadful prospect to consider. Torie's mother shunted all worries right out of her mind on the 100 Proof Limited.

Guy and Torie talked about babies as soon as she gave way to the idea of marriage. Bright young people did nowadays, as a matter of course. Torie understood at once what Guy would never admit: he had the whole first pregnancy planned out by textbook, in his head, from conception to delivery. He wanted nothing less than a baby of his own to deliver. It amused her, which would have shocked Guy to know. Outside of that, all his reasons were conventional. Why else did people marry? It was the thing to do, it was natural. None of that bothered her. She knew he was, in most respects, a conventional man. There were worse faults.

After six weeks of honeymooning, which she spent alternately morning sick and mucking about various archaeological sites as a visiting firewoman, while Guy trailed after her, or when he couldn't stand it anymore, went sailing, they went to live with his mother in the big stone house in Falmouth. Fanny had taken to her, was delighted at the prospect of the baby, and saw to it she was relieved of the usual new-wifely domestic concerns.

Guy's new practice kept him as busy as he had been in the days of his residency in Boston. There was still time, before Tommy was born, for an occasional movie or concert, a weekend in Boston for plays or jazz and Sunday morning in a hotel bed. Guy established a three times a week tennis habit with his best friend from boyhood, Dana Bartlett. Dana and his wife, Jeannie, whom Guy had also known since he was in diapers, were attractive, easy people. Guy and Torie began to see them occasionally. Torie, morning sickness behind her, swam daily at the Y in Portland, and worked quietly on her thesis.

She might have kept the nearly immediate conception of Tommy to herself for a few months, but Guy was anxious and had charted her menstrual cycle. He pounced at once. Nervous and excited until it was time for the test, once the pregnancy was confirmed, he settled down to studying her. What had been amusing in theory became an irritant in fact. At the end of it she was tired of being his lab monkey, discussed interminably and intimately with his colleagues. She was tired of her own awkwardness and bulk, of sharing her body with an intrusive and sometimes uncomfortable presence. She was tired of being Wonderful. She wanted her body back. She felt bewitched, changed against her will into a grotesque fertility goddess.

After the battle of birth, time speeded up, as if to make up for those last months of pregnancy, which had seemed eternal. For the first time in her life, she was unsure what day it was. She didn't read a book for weeks at a time. Her thesis was necessarily set aside.

About the time she succeeded in establishing a nursing and sleeping schedule with Tommy, and began to think there might be something to this business besides exhaustion, Guy's mother had her stroke. The management of the house passed to Torie. She supervised the cook, the housekeeper, the gardener, and Fanny's nurse, and found it fully as much work as if she had done all of it herself. The ground floor of the house in Falmouth had to be remodelled to accommodate sickroom furnishings—hospital bed, wheelchair, a walker for Fanny's good days. Torie and Guy, who had been considering buying their own home, moved into the master bedroom, and converted the sitting room next to it into a nursery for Tommy.

Tommy got her through. Now she was surprised by the advertised emotions. His being, mysteriously, did define hers. She was a mother, whose center was outside herself, for the time being anyway, in this tiny, utterly new, and unexpected person. She nursed him nine months with a satisfaction that nothing else had ever given her, giving it up reluctantly at Guy's insistence. He scolded her for an overanxious, overpossessive mother. She knew he was just tired of sharing her with the baby. His own interest had waned notably with the reality of broken rest and diapers. For the first time she felt possessed, owned by all these people around her, to be fought over and divided up like a pie or an estate in probate.

Summer came just in time. She and Tommy decamped for the lake, with Fanny and her nurse, leaving Guy to commute back and forth weekends. He had the housekeeper and cook to look after him, and the Bartletts when he wanted home life, so she didn't worry about him. No doubt he enjoyed the restoration of quiet and order in his home.

It felt as summer always had to her, as if she had come home. She let her mind idle guiltlessly, her body revel in renewed vigor and youth. The nights that Guy was gone and Tommy and Frances slept, she swam naked across the lake and back. She had time, she knew it now. Soon she would return to work on her thesis.

Guy's old circle, reestablishing itself at the lake each summer, became hers. She was absorbed into the summer way of life. Someone was always having a cookout. The young couples herded droves of kids and little flocks of toddlers. There was an infant on every woman's hip. The evening smelled of charred beef, hot dogs, and burnt marshmallows, and occasionally, acridly, of firecrackers. Someone's kid was always crying. Someone always had cherry Kool-Aid spilled on them. The women talked about babies and kids and smoked cigarettes, even the ones who didn't smoke, to keep the bugs away. The men drank beer and screwdrivers, and talked about their boats, or how the Sox were doing, or how much they would like to spend more time at the lake but how the office just couldn't spare them.

Guy looked forward to his weekends, chockablock full of tennis and water skiing with Dana and Jeannie. The three had grown up together on the lake. Now they seemed to consciously replay those past summers, making a great thing of this tradition or that. They tried hard not to make Torie feel like a newcomer or an intruder, harder than they needed. Of course she felt that way, but without resentment. It was a fact, that was all. She was glad of the excuse of the baby, and sat back to watch.

Since Dana's law office could no more spare him during the week than any other man's office, or Guy's practice, Dana commuted too. Weekday nights he and Guy unwound together in the city, on a tennis court, at a movie, over a few beers.

Jeannie became a regular after-lunch drop-in. While Tommy napped, the two women swam lazily, sunned on the float, and talked about kids. Jeannie was five years older, her two boys old enough to prefer the company of other kids to their mom's. She took a proprietary interest in Tommy, happy in the role of experienced mother. She played with him, and handed him back, invariably saying, "I'm glad he's yours."

One particularly hot afternoon on the float, when a few cold beers seemed the only sensible relief, Jeannie confessed she was casting about for something to do, come fall, now that the boys no longer needed her in that overwhelming way babies did.

"Looking for a job?"

Jeannie sat upright to stare at Torie in mock horror. "Good lord, no. Dana'd pitch a fit. Well, actually his father would pitch the fit."

Torie shaded her eyes with her arm. "Why?"

Jeannie laughed. "You dope. Don't you know hubby's supposed to bring home the bacon? Wifey's place is in the home?"

Torie rolled over and fumbled in the cooler for the can opener. "I'd heard rumors."

"Yeah," said Jeannie. "We don't want anyone thinking Dana's law practice isn't doing well enough to support me in the style to which I'm accustomed."

"Jesus God, no," Torie agreed, and popped the cap off a cold bottle of beer. "What else is there?"

"Another kid," Jeannie said. She tipped her head back to guzzle the last of her second bottle. "Speaking of another, pass me one of those brews."

Torie laughed. "Somehow I sense a lack of enthusiasm for another round of motherhood."

"Jesus God, yes," Jeannie said. She poked an elbow into Torie.

Torie sat up fast. "Shit," she said. "You made me spill my beer." The cold liquid trickled between her breasts.

"Sorry," Jeannie said, and mopped at her clumsily with a towel.

Torie pushed it away. "Leave it alone for Christ's sake. It's cool."

"Whatever," Jeannie said, shrugging. She rolled up the towel to put under her head. "There's affairs," she said. "I could have affairs."

Torie giggled. "I like the way you put that in the plural."

"Damn right," Jeannie said. "No half measures for me."

The two women lay in comfortable silence for several minutes. Ice in the cooler contracted and crackled. Jeannie sat up and dropped her empty bottle into it.

"Who?" Torie asked.

Jeannie fished out a bottle and held it up to the sun. "What?"

Torie admired the way the light went through the bottle of beer, making it liquid gold. It reminded her that the bottle she had spilled down her front was not quite empty.

"Who?" she repeated. "Who are you going to have affairs with? All the men are in town."

Jeannie shrugged. "Shit," she said. "I knew there was a snag in there somewhere." She considered it a minute. "There's Guy," she said, looking sideways at Torie.

Torie blinked at the sky. "I suggest getting pregnant if you want to catch his eye."

Jeannie giggled. "I'm getting drunk. That was really a stupid joke. He's crazy about you."

"Thanks," Torie said. "I guess. Besides, you don't want to mess up a good thing."

"You mean you and Guy?"

"No, dummy. I mean Dana and Jeannie."

"Oh."

"Ayuh," Torie said. "I mean you two."

"You do that good, did you know? I've never been able to say ayuh without sounding like an idiot." Jeannie propped herself up on one elbow. "I hate to disillusion you, kid. It's not that good a thing."

Torie's head buzzed. Too much beer in the hot sun, she thought. Why don't you go home, Jeannie? But she said nothing.

"Dana would just think I was trying to get even with him. I bet he'd say good for you, baby. It would mean I'd be the same as him."

A pair of motorboats towing water-skiers roared distantly by.

"You're not kidding, are you?" Torie asked.

Jeannie shook her head quickly. "Why would I?"

"I don't know," Torie said. "I don't know."

Jeannie dropped back onto her towel and wriggled around until she was comfortable again.

"Listen," she said. "My heart's not breaking. I found out adultery's not fatal. Don't start feeling sorry for me. Someday it'll be your turn."

"What do you mean?" Torie came up on her elbow, staring at Jeannie.

Jeannie balanced her bottle of beer on her flat stomach. "Oh, don't worry about Guy. He's not Dana. With Dana, it's a compulsion. I've known Guy as long as Dana. Shit, you know the whole stupid story about the big teenage triangle, and my choosing between the two of them. It must bore the shit out of you. Just don't forget it was a hundred years ago. I might feel like I made a mistake, but Guy doesn't. He's really in love with you."

"Thanks for the reassurance," Torie said. She stared at the cloudless sky and wondered, not for the first time, what the odds were that Guy hadn't slept with Jeannie, back when they were two corners of Jeannie's famous triangle.

"My pleasure," Jeannie said. "What I meant was, someday Dana will make a pass at you. Your turn."

Torie sat up straight. "Jesus God. You aren't serious. He's Guy's best friend."

"I am, I am. Dana always makes passes at his friends' wives, sooner or later."

Torie flopped onto her stomach, and rested her face on her hands. "I don't know what to say. He's always been such a big friendly bear to me."

Jeannie dropped her bottle into the cooler, where it clinked off others.

"Dana will proposition you," she predicted confidently, "and if you're like every other broad I know, you'll say yes."

"Wait a goddamn minute," Torie said, furious, as much at Jeannie's presumption she knew Torie's mind as well as she did, as at the equally offensive idea Torie was no better than she should be.

Jeannie waved her down. "Don't get all hot and bothered. I know how women react to Dana. I react that way to him myself, worse luck."

Torie's head was full of questions. Was Jeannie paranoid, just imagining it out of an egotistical conviction that, of course, her husband was irresistible? Had she given him some reason? She wondered how much Guy knew of this and why he had not told her.

Dana had never been anything else but sweet and thoughtful to her. She had assumed the attention he paid her was by way of making her feel part of their group, or perhaps because he liked her. Either he was false, and she had been fooled, or Jeannie was a poisonous, sorry bitch.

But Jeannie only sighed sweetly, curled in on herself like a baby, and turned away. In a little while, she broke the silence.

"Sorry. I guess I spoiled your good time."

"No, don't be sorry," Torie said automatically. "I'm just startled. I feel like I wasn't paying attention. I missed something I should have noticed." She picked up the bottle opener and flipped it into the cooler. "If it's true, how do you stand it?"

"It's true," Jeannie said irritably. She turned over and opened one eye. "I'll tell you. First, you're hurt. Then, you're angry. You want to pay the son of a bitch back. Then you're contemptuous. That's where I am now. I suppose someday I'll try getting even. Let's not talk about it anymore."

Torie sat up and tucked her feet under her bottom. "One question?"

"Sure."

"Do you always warn your friends' wives, like this?" she asked.

"Yeah," said Jeannie. "It never makes any difference."

Torie stared at her hands. The only difference would be a soupçon extra of guilt for the sinners, an extra measure of righteousness for Jeannie. Shit. And double goddamn the pair of them.

"I'm going in," she said, and dived into the water, headed for the dock. She had towed the cooler out. Jeannie could tow it in. Maybe it would drown her. This was going to be the last time she did any sunning and drinking with Jeannie. If she wanted something shitty to do in her spare time, she could go get started on her famous grudge affair. By the time Torie hauled herself out of the water she was soberer, but for once the water had not made her feel cleaner.

From the top of the hill, the scattered debris around the Cadillac made it look like one of the abandoned, decaying vehicles that are a species of lawn ornament in rural New England.

Inside the truck seemed colder than out. Torie fortified herself with a slug of bourbon, then slipped the bottle under the seat for safekeeping. When she keyed the ignition, the engine only whined at her. She must have run the battery down some, using the citizens band radio. Stepping lightly on the gas, she keyed it again, and the engine sputtered, turned over, and died. She waited a minute, then went through the motions again, gentle with the gas so as not to flood the engine. This time the engine caught, ran a minute, and just when she started to smile, died.

For several minutes she rested her head on her hands

on the wheel. This was how almost drowning felt. She had come close the day India was murdered, before Joe Nevers had gotten her out of the water. Indeed, he would not have been able to do that if her strength had not reached its limit. It all seemed a long time ago now but it had had a quality of abstraction even then. No fear, no terror, no panic. No emotions at all. Only the calm and certain knowledge that she was not going to make it on her own. And she had not cared.

She had gone on only for David. Even as she was going on for Joe Nevers. She tried again. The engine came to life with a roar, and so did her hope for the old man. She might win this one yet. She felt under the seat for the quadra-traction gear. It was easy to find but impossible to move from the position she was in. She couldn't get a grip on it. Slipping under the wheel, she crouched on the floor between the foot pedals and the seat, the side of her face against the upholstery. It took both hands to move the bastard.

She pulled herself back up onto the seat and was taken with a fit of shivering. When she turned the heater on, it blew cold air at her. She groped under the seat for the bottle. In a little while she felt better, released the emergency brake, stamped on the clutch and threw the gear into drive. The gears ground and the truck bucked, bouncing her head against the back of the seat. She let it inch forward, babying the wheel into the hard right into the driveway. The tires bit hungrily into the snow. The mass of drifted snow pushed back inertly. For the first time, she was grateful for the snow.

The pitch of the driveway was malignant, layered with the drifted snow, now hard, icy, and glazed with the sleet, and rotten underneath with rain and melt. Grasping the wheel tightly, she fought the way the truck wanted to slide down the hill. The snow compacted under its wheels into sheer ice. The weight of the truck shifted against her. The tires began to lose their tenuous grip. The truck wanted its head, she could feel it. It wanted to plunge straight down and off the road where the driveway bent back upon itself for the first time. She let it out, an infinitesimal amount at a time, keeping it in hand, turning its nose into the bend. It took a long, shaky, sweaty time to bring it around. There she set the brake and rested.

The Cadillac was straight ahead, in the drifts at the second bend. The rear end was well up, as if exposed for service by the truck. Over the years she had seen Joe Nevers haul her car out of a number of ditches and embankments. There were chains in the back of the truck as well as in the snow, from her car, for that operation. She planned, vaguely, to chain the Cadillac to the truck and use the truck to lift the rear end of the sedan high enough to free the old man. Then, of course, she would use the truck to drive him out. She had gotten this far, maybe that proved she had only been fainthearted. The mechanics of chaining were not clear in her mind, but she was sure she could sort that out at the proper moment. She was more concerned with finding a way to back the truck into the right position. She would have to pass the Cadillac and back up the hill, she decided.

Carefully, she released the emergency brake and let the truck slide a few more feet down the grade. It picked up momentum; she felt the weight of it before her, dragging her down, and behind her, pushing harder with every inch forward. When she felt she had the truck angled, entering the second curve, to bypass the Cadillac, she let it out a little more. It wanted to go faster. She felt the tires beginning to skate and stamped on the brake. The truck bucked and slued. She lost her grip on the wheel. At once, the truck jumped forward, throwing her over the wheel against the windshield.

She hit it nose first. Blood spattered on the glass and the dashboard, dappled the wheel and spurted over the mink. Instinctively, her hands went to her face, then fumbled for the wheel as she felt the truck skidding out of control. The steering dynamic reversed itself; the tires spun the steering wheel through her bloodied fingers.

Her vision reduced to a slick red fog of pain, she groped with her boots for the floor pedals. What her left foot finally found and floored, in panic, was the accelerator. The sudden slug of gasoline propelled the truck forward hard enough to bounce her off the windshield a second time. The plow blade of the truck bucked through the last drifts and rammed snow into and under the Cadillac's rear bumper. Torie was thrown first to the seat and then to the floor of the cab as the truck shuddered violently at the impact. Shrieking metal sheared and pleated as the Cadillac's hood was driven up under the trunk of the oak, and the rear bumper was flayed by the razor edges of the snowcrust.

Torie curled up under the dashboard. The truck's engine was panting in outrage on the other side of the firewall. Suddenly, the heater came on, blasting hot air over her bloody face.

"Shit," she said.

From under the seat, the bottle of bourbon rolled casually out and came to rest against her hand. She patted it fondly.

Summer, 1941

SHE HOOKED A BOTTLE OF CHAMPAGNE from one of the coolers under the bar and began untwisting the wire *coiffe.*

"Here," said someone behind her. "Allow me."

Thinking it was the bartender back from the kitchen with more of something, or from the bathroom or wherever he had been, she spun around and wobbled dangerously on her spike heels. She found herself eye to broad, tuxedoed chest and looked up into Guy Christopher's face. He had been one of her brother Tom's prep school roomies and had been tapped as an usher at the wedding, for his sins. She had not seen him before the ceremony, had not seen him, in fact, in several years. He had not been at the rehearsal the previous afternoon, but she had had a report from Tom about who made the post-rehearsal bachelor party, and how drunk they had gotten. She could have guessed herself; Guy was disheveled and red-eyed. His tux hung on him as if it were pinned to a clothesline. The roué look suited him. Where there was a modicum of disorder, there was hope of a human being inside.

As he freed the bottle of the wire hood, he wrapped it in a bar towel and applied both thumbs to the cork with care.

"Remember me?" he asked. "Guy Christopher?"

She pretended, for a second, to puzzle at it. "Oh, sure," she said. "Of course."

A smile flashed across his face, creasing his dimples.

She blushed, unable to suppress the memory of mean adolescent thoughts about those dimples. Surely, he must calculate them. Too much, and he would be taken for a grinning idiot, the other fellows would ride him unmercifully. Too little, and they might suspect him of embarrassment. Just enough, and the girls would go all giggly and fluttery.

Back then, she had dismissed him as another one of Tom's ogre-sized friends, overgrown athletes, curiously clumsy off the court or field, obsessed with their sports, and drinking, and sexual experiences they had mostly not had. All vain to the point of silliness, constantly combing their hair, polishing their shoes, challenging each other to feats, and speculating about the effect of their showing-off on the girls they knew. If Guy had seemed, at any time, slightly less the muscle-bound twit, she had labelled him a prep school hypocrite, trying to pass himself off as a human being. All at once, she saw herself as having been a rotten, hard-mouthed, snotty, teenaged brat, and wished Guy Christopher had not remembered who she was.

"Almost didn't recognize you," he went on.

The cork plopped neatly onto the grass. She grabbed a pair of glasses from the bar and held them while he tipped the bubbly into them.

"Had you fixed in my mind about the age you were in the picture Tom had at school."

Torie was mortified, all hope of a fresh start dashed. She remembered that photograph all too well. Portrait of a petty terrorist.

Guy raised his glass. "Tom and Betsy," he said.

Their glasses clinked in a grave toast. Torie looked up at the sky. It was tented in ominous rolling clouds. The air was still and heavy, carrying the voices of the wedding guests and the music of the band across the broad lawns. She touched her hair, arranged in a page boy much against its will. It wanted, in the slightest humidity, to crinkle and curl. The satin of her brides-maid's dress stuck to the small of her back and be-tween her shoulder blades, the dress shields in the armpits already damp.

"At least it's good and cold," Guy said, sipping the champagne. "I hate it warm."

It was indeed wonderfully cold and dry.

"Dance?" he asked.

She curtseyed with a flourish. He laughed, then winced, as if his head hurt.

He turned out to be a good dancer, better than she expected, though a bit distracted by the state of his head. They passed her brother Tom dancing with Torie's mother, who smiled at them glassily.

"My mother's smashed," Torie said.

Guy glanced in the direction of her mother. Theresa Hayes stumbled, was caught by Tom, and laughed.

"So she is," Guy said. "Well, it's a big day."

"She's been looking forward to it for a long time," Torie said.

Guy nodded. She wondered if he knew, from Tom or one of Tom's friends, that her parents no longer went to cocktail parties because Theresa couldn't stop once she was started. Probably he did.

They sat down again, at a table at the edge of the party, and had another glass of champagne. She didn't bother to engage him in conversation; it was clear he just wanted to sit and medicate his hangover.

Betsy was dancing with her father, Tom with Betsy's mother. Torie's parents were dancing with each other, her father holding her mother very carefully, as if he were afraid she would break. Betsy's sister Molly, who had been her maid of honor, danced with her fiancé. As Betsy had before her, Molly had given her promise to her parents not to marry until she graduated college, the June after next. But she and her fiancé, actually the second, her first having been dismissed the previous February, were taking advantage of the essentially sexual nature of the occasion by stealing fervid kisses as they danced.

After a quarter of an hour, Guy held out his hand again to her, and they joined the dance.

"Thanks," he said, as he drew her close.

"For what?"

"Not chattering," he said. His cheekbones reddened.

She grinned at his discomfort. "Hey, I've had a hangover."

He cocked an eyebrow at her. "Have you?"

She shrugged. She didn't have to prove anything to him.

"Why me?" she asked. "I wouldn't have expected to be left in peace, if I were you."

"You mean your little girl with the curl right in the middle of her forehead act?"

She cocked an eyebrow at him. "Don't be so sure it's an act."

"You're getting too old for it, my girl," Guy said, and whirled her around. "I saw my duty as an older man to polish you a bit."

"Sounds filthy to me," Torie said.

"Besides," Guy said behind a confidential hand, "you had the nearest bottle."

Torie laughed.

Tom passed by with Betsy, and slapped Torie's bottom. She rubbed it, stuck out her tongue at him. Guy laughed and shook his head.

She noticed. "Your head's better?"

He nodded. "In fact, I'm getting tiddly again."

"Well, it's a big day," she mimicked him solemnly.

It was a big day. The wedding party reeled under

thunderheads. The heat, the electricity of the imminent storm in the air, formal dress unsuited to the high temperature, an unspoken, emotional acknowledgment that all the world was coming to grief on the rocks of war, and copious supplies of booze combined to make a memorably lively party.

Torie held back, mostly to prove to Guy that she was a mature young woman who didn't need to get puking drunk just because the opportunity was there. But it was a wasted effort. He had no such compunctions himself, seemingly determined to cure his hangover by postponing it. Taking out a loan and paying interest, she thought, watching him with amusement. It made her feel a little superior to him, despite the advantage of his years.

She was surprised that he came back to her, between cigarettes and refills, and courtesy dances with the bridesmaids, the mothers, and three aunts.

"You don't have to," she protested when he bowed foolishly before her, sweeping off an imaginary hat.

"Shut up," he said, taking her hand.

With his arm around her waist, he chucked her under the chin. He blinked his eyes rapidly.

"What do you think?" he asked. "Ol' Tom and Betsy done the right thing?"

"Too bad if they didn't," she said. "Look, it's fine with me. Maybe they'll quit necking on the porch all day every Sunday. It's embarrassing."

Guy grinned. "Boy, you're a tough broad."

She pulled back from him. "Don't call me a broad."

He sobered a little. "I'm sorry."

She shrugged. "Never mind. It's nothing to what Tom's called me."

Guy shook his head. "I'm an only child. I can't figure thse sibling relationships out. Wouldn't it be easier to just get along?"

"Oh, we do. In our way."

"Good," he said. "So it's just feints?"

"Most of the time. We're just about grown out of it anyway. I mean, I can't go around sniping at my married brother, can I?"

" 'Course not." He lost his place. "Sorry. I tread on your toes?"

"Just a little."

He hugged her a little tighter. "Pretty girl. If you were my sister, I wouldn't be mean to you."

"You're getting drunk, you know that?"

"And you can't take a compliment, know that?" He focused his eyes on hers.

"Sorry," she said, and meant it.

The music dipped and ended, there was a pause, during which Guy knocked back the remainder of his most recent drink, and they began again. It was a slow, romantic piece of music, the occassion of much nostalgic embracing by older, married couples, and of seized opportunities by younger couples out to make their own memories.

Torie rested her head on Guy's shoulder. It was a reassuring shoulder, sufficiently broad and muscular and familiar in his similarity to the father and brother who were her chief models of the other half. His arms tightened around her, as if he thought she might escape him, or as if it seemed as natural to him as it did to her.

But the mood of young romance was broken abruptly by the stuff of crude farce. Torie realized that there was something growing between them and while it was directly related to romance, it was not precisely young love. Guy's awareness, though dulled by the booze, was an instant quicker than her own. He flinched away from her, and then gathered her close again, his fair, translucent skin fiery red. The plague of local stiffness seemed to translate itself into an unhappy awkwardness in their dance.

"Goddamn it, I'm sorry," he muttered. His hands were slick with perspiration.

Torie was fighting a violent internal battle to keep from laughing. She thought she might strangle over the low comedy of it.

"Ah," she gasped, "Please."

Then all sensible thought fled her, for the moment.

"Goddamn it," Guy said, gritting his teeth.

Torie sensed from the tension in his body that if he could flee her, he would. At the moment, the option was too embarrassing.

Tom floated by, Betsy, adoring, on his arm.

"Shocking," he said. "Can't you two restrain your-selves?"

Torie shot a searing glance at him. He understood at once he had said the wrong thing at the wrong time and waltzed Betsy hastily away.

Guy's face was a mask. His hands on her shoulder, at the small of her back, were shaking.

"He was joking," Torie murmured. "He can't have seen anything."

Guy peeked at her, more than eager to take her at her word. When he saw she was not mocking him, he seemed to relax a bit.

Torie tried desperately to think of something she could do to help him. No one had ever discussed inconvenient erections with her. She guessed if she threw cold water or champagne on him, that would have a diminishing effect, but it would be just as embarrassing or more so to have the front of his trou-sers all wet.

And then it seemed to her that the problem might be solving itself. Guy sighed with relief. At the earliest possible moment, he let go of her, muttered another apology, and fled to the bar.

She snatched a glass of champagne from a passing tray and slumped over it at the nearest umbrellaed table.

"What did I say?" Tom said.

"Too goddamned much," she snapped, and soothed her tense throat with the icy bubbly.

"Well, I'm sorry," he said in exasperated apology. "I didn't mean to ruin a big romance."

"It wasn't exactly romance," she said. "But it was big."

Looking up at Tom's puzzled face, she could no longer restrain herself and burst out laughing. She smothered it as quickly as she could, afraid that Guy might overhear, or see her, and think she was making fun of him.

Tom sat down next to her. "It's going to rain," he said, flipping one hand at the sky.

Torie did not have to look up. The clouds had covered the sun, shadowing everything. The thick air was shattered with the first audible crack of thunder, still deep in the clouds where the lightning was hidden. A sudden gust of wind tore through the assembly, tearing loose hats and napkins, and leaving a wake of screams from half-soused women. The band members snatched sheet music back from the gust, and began to pack up their instruments. The first guests surged across the lawn toward the big house. A few sought shelter under the tent where the ceremony had been performed, but left it almost at once, as it had captured the heat and was suffocating inside.

Torie watched the party pour across the grass like dry leaves in the fall, until the lawn was empty. Tom started across, turned back to yell at her, but the wind drowned his voice. She finished her glass deliberately, then wandered slowly onto the lawn, still holding it. The first rain dappled her face like tears, and then came in a rush that soaked thoroughly in seconds. She kicked off her spike heels and pirouetted in the downpour, holding her champagne saucer high in one hand. Then she tossed it away. It landed on the rain-slicked grass without breaking. She whooped and dove head first into a cartwheel, all legs and petticoats in one graceful fan over the grass.

Bonelessly, she launched herself out onto the snow-crust. It hurt about the way she expected it would. The sharp granules of the crust flayed the few exposed patches of her hide not already abraded. But the cold was mercifully numbing. She scraped back a pile of dirty snow. Wincing she washed the blood, dried in a stiff mask by the truck's heater, from her throbbing face. She did not dare touch her nose to see if it was broken. She couldn't breathe through it, and it hurt like hell. She scooped a little brackish, tinny-tasting snow into her mouth, to wet the back of her throat. She patted more on her face where she could bear it. For an instant, the impromptu ice pack dulled the burning and ache of her facial contusions.

She worked her way around the back of the truck because it was shorter than going around the Cadillac. Once on the driveway, the tracks of the truck, as well as the old man's footsteps and her own, eased her passage. Then on the snowcrust again, where she could only scuttle like a dry leaf on a winter beach, along the driver's side of the truck. Where the bumpers of the two vehicles were entangled, she sank on her haunches and buried her head in her arms.

She waited, listening. She could not hear the old man breathing. She slipped under the Cadillac like a drowner beneath the surface of the water.

The underside of the car, raised higher by the truck's tail-ending it, formed a roof of a large mouthed cave.

The light reached into its farthest corner, reflecting off snow. The truck had shoved a quantity of snow under the Cadillac, half-filling the space she had made rolling in and out to take care of the old man. It had covered him, head and shoulders.

"Shit," she said.

To get air to him, she clawed snow from his face. One hand on his chest, in three inches of snow over the blanket roll around him, she felt his lungs rattle, and dared breathe herself.

She looked around again. It looked as if he were free. She could make out light between the edge of the car, the back wall of their homemade cave and the snow pushed under by the truck. A quick feel along his lower limbs and she had the proof he was no longer pinned down.

The blankets had taken on the temperature of the snow, stiffening as the moisture in them began to freeze. When she touched them, it was like touching cold stone.

The old man coughed.

"Jesus," she croaked.

She threw herself over him, brushing the snow from him.

He opened his eyes and looked at her as if they had just run into each other at the post office. He turned his head politely to the side and coughed again. She felt the whole rattle of it from his lungs through the blankets to her own body. His face had gone the color of the snow. His skin was clammy, his respiration labored.

"Shit," she said. "Job's only half done. I got to get you inside."

He worked up a ragged smile and tried to speak, but produced only a strangled noise that frightened them both.

"Shut up," she said. "I got you this far, didn't I?"

His body under hers shook. The way his face creased and crinkled, she guessed he was laughing. Unless he was having a fit or trying to get her off him. The very thought sent her sliding to one side, taking the blankets with her.

One gnarled hand snatched feebly after them. He grunted with the effort.

"Ahhh," he said.

"I know you're cold," she said. "Not as cold as you'll be when you're dead."

Spreading the blankets as flat as she could on the uneven surface, she then stretched out on them, and rolled carefully over them to the edge nearest him. She reached for him. He seemed at once to understand what she was doing, and reached, slowly, for her. There was no strength in him anymore, or heat. In the end she did the most of it, because she had to, drawing herself tight against him, then hauling him on top of her by main force. He stared down at her, wide-eyed in sweet surprise. Another try at laughing convulsed him.

She shook against him with her own laughter, grateful for once to be on her back. The tears that escaped her slipped almost invisibly in runlets to the lobes of her ears. She rested under him.

"Last time you'll ever top a woman," she gasped. "Last time underneath for me."

Then she heaved upward, thrusting him off her and onto the blankets. The breath went out of him in a surprised whistle.

She scuttled over him. One clawed hand caught at hers. She stopped to squeeze it with her own fading strength, then reached back over him to pull the opposite edge of the blanket over him. In two swift motions, she had him rolled up like strawberries and cream inside a crepe, at the open side of the Cadillac's cave.

There she left him. She stripped off her fur coat, hooked an old tarp out of the back of his truck, and slung it under the Cadillac. Back under the car, she covered him entirely with it.

"This won't take a minute," she said. "About as long as you're good for in the kip. If you're still good for anything there, which I doubt. I mean, what you used to be good for."

One arm under his shoulders, with the tarp held down over his face with the other hand, she heaved upward repeatedly, until gravity took over, and his own weight carried him over so he was face down on the tarp. He turned his head to cough and suck the air. After that, she had to turn him on his back again. She stopped to feel carefully along the side where the car had pinned him. There seemed to be no obvious break in skin or bone, only prodigious swelling. He flinched from her touch; no doubt it was painful. If his injuries were not extensive enough to kill him, the shock might, or the exposure, or his heart might just give way, unbalanced, like the Cadillac.

She tucked her fur coat around him, inside out, laced the lashings of the tarp across him from side to side, and tied them down enough to hold him in. Then she looped a length of rope through the top, near the back of his head, like the pull-rope to a child's sled. She swapped the old work gloves from the trunk of the Cadillac for an equally greasy, too large pair from the toolbox in the cab of the truck, wrapped the pull-rope around her hands, and slowly hauled him along the trench beside the Cadillac.

Where the two vehicles met, there was a high spot in the snow. At the top of that, she paused to crawl behind and push him, so he slid down onto the driveway. From there, their footprints marked the way to the house, and it was all downhill. One boot in front of the other, she dragged her improvised travois down the hill to where the fire was.

The porch steps were helpfully low. Joe Nevers had cleared them of snow, which made the hauling harder. The cracked glaze of sleet on the treads was little enough assistance in getting him to the back door.

"I'm doing the best I can," she told him crossly, though he had not complained, or even groaned involuntarily at the rough passage.

The sleet fell on the old man's face and pooled in the wells of his eyes like tears. The fastest blinking he could manage could not keep ahead of it.

She looked back where they had been.

The Cadillac and the truck, in their eccentric embrace, made her think of the big black ants in the summer. She had often witnessed one carrying the corpse of another. As a child, she imagined she was observing a rite of passage, a bearer ant delivering the deceased to an ant funeral. The unlovely truth, she had learned in time, was the ants were cannibals. It seemed a fine joke.

The snow was trampled, the wind-sculpted dunes as ruined as the dead vehicles. It had outlived its time. In a week it would be gone, and good riddance. It would be a good thing if this spring, as in so many others, the runoff carried a piece of the hillside into the water and took the Cadillac and the truck with it. The wish was of a piece with the funerary customs of most civilizations that assigned the most loved, useful, or significant possessions of the deceased to the grave or tomb or barrow, along with the body. The lake would make an admirable resting place, and would cover them decently. If it was a good enough marker for her daughter India, it was good enough for her.

She hooked her hands under the old man's armpits, and hauled him over the threshold.

"I'm the undertaker ant," she said sonorously, and then burst out laughing.

She was talking to herself. Joe Nevers' eyes had rolled up in his head, his mouth hung slack. His breathing was shallow and wracked with occasional coughing seizures. His face was as transparent as the sleet. He had lost consciousness again.

Backing through the door, she realized at once the fires inside had not been enough to keep the house warm in the breath of all their comings and goings. She would have to stoke them as soon as she could. But first, the old man must be gotten into her bed, stripped of his wet clothing, and bundled in dry blankets.

With no sleet or snow to slick the way, his weight was dead against her nearly exhausted strength. His hands fell out of the tarp and dragged along the hardwood floor as she made halting progress to the bedroom. A warning twinge of pain nearly threw her into a panic.

At the bedside she released her hold with relief, and turned the linen neatly down. She went to her knees to take his head in her lap. After loosening the lashes of the tarp, she clasped her hands around his chest from the back and hauled him backward out of it, as if to save him from choking. The breath was squeezed out of him in a ragged gasp but she did not let go even when she lost her balance. The weight of him toppled her backward onto the bed and he fell over her. The tarp slid the length of him and crumpled on the floor. She pushed the old man gently off her, grabbing his belt to stop him slipping from the bed. Once on her feet, she lifted his legs one at a time and straightened him on the bed.

It seemed to take a long time to strip him. Getting him into a dry pair of Guy's old red long johns and wool socks was like dressing a huge, slack baby. Like dressing Fanny, years ago, after her stroke.

When she touched his brow to see if he were hot or cold, she realized his hair was damp too. She towelled his head and folded another towel on his pillow. When he was under layers of blankets and quilts, she stripped herself and wrapped up in an old robe.

She knew she should tend the fires. But she was very tired, very cold, and needed her medicine. She dry-swallowed several capsules, thought about it briefly, and then forced a few on the old man by pushing them beyond his tongue. Shivering, she crept into the bed, next to him, promising she would only stay long enough to warm up.

It was the increasing cold that woke her when the day was darkening. She tumbled out of bed in a panic, and instantly regretted having moved at all. Everything ached. Her head buzzed, and her face throbbed. She hopped on the icy floorboards as if they were hot sand under her naked feet. Pinching her fingers on the catch, she opened the Jötel. There were still a few coals among the ashes.

"God," she said, "it's about time you did me a favor."

At the side of the brick chimney that vented the Jötel was a box of kindling, newspapers, and firewood. She dipped a cone of newspaper into the coals. The old newspaper, dried and yellowed, caught at once. She dropped it into the ash and crushed more newspaper into balls to feed the tiny fire. Then she fed it kindling and three small logs.

It was a blow to find the fire in the living room dead and choked with ash. An attempt to clear the ash into an ash can only spread it, like toxic snow, all over her and the room. She was unable to steady her hands on the scoop. No doubt her muscles were starved; it had been a long haul since breakfast. The painkillers suppressed her appetite. She was not hungry but would make herself eat, later.

There were no newspapers close at hand, an uncharacteristic lapse on Joe Nevers' part. She surveyed the room and noticed her puzzle, on the table. Going to it, she turned a few pieces automatically, brushed them clear of blown ash, and pried loose the ones the spilled bourbon had stuck to the table. She found herself seriously considering sitting down to finish it and laughed.

She wondered if they would burn. Scraping them into a catchall made by the skirt of her robe, she took them to the stove and threw them in. In a minute they were burning merrily. She fed the fire until it seemed to have taken hold.

Hugging herself against the cold, she went back to the bedroom.

The old man was blue at the lip. Anxiously she laid her wrist on his forehead. He opened his eyes and smacked his lips drowsily.

"Thank God," she said. "And Sonny Jesus. I thought you were dead."

He smiled weakly. "Not yet," he said in a hoarse whisper. "Don't rush me."

She put her hands on her hips. "Dry?"

He nodded.

When she came back with water, she perched on the side of the bed and lifted his head while he drank. Then she checked the stove and added wood to the fire.

Behind her, he whispered again. "Damp it a mite."

She did. "Okay?"

He rolled his head on the pillow to say yes.

She sat on the bedside again and squeezed his hand. "Do you know what happened?"

"Never did." He tried to laugh at his own joke.

She helped him drink a little more water.

"You hurt?" She wanted to know where and how much.

"Some."

"Well, tell me, goddamn it."

Reluctantly, he catalogued his ills. "Leg's a mis'ry. Chest feels like a horse kicked it. Think I broke a rib or two?"

"Maybe," she allowed cautiously. "What else?"

He looked away from her, at the stove. "Arm."

"Left?"

He nodded.

"It ain't heartburn," she said.

They both knew what it was. She waited for him to brave her eyes again. When he did, she told him the truth.

"I can't get you out of here myself."

"Try the CB?"

She shook her head. "Nobody listening."

He thought about it. "Truck?"

It was hard to say it. "I wrecked it."

He patted her hand.

"Don't matter. You said it. Good a place as any for it."

"Shit," she said. "You ain't dying. You're just trying to spite me. You hang on another night, somebody'll come looking for you for sure Monday morning. One of the old farts. Reuben."

His hands twitched in hers.

"Doubt it."

"Oh, for Christ's sake," she exclaimed. "You goddamn quitter."

He rolled his head emphatically from side to side.

"Ain't so."

The absence of anger, the weight of weariness, in the rebuke made her angrier. He was, of all men, the most apt to know if he were really dying. But she had gone through so much to save his old ass.

"I'm sorry," she said. "You know me, fast mouth, slow brains. Sorry is my middle name."

For once, Guy was not late. She was not ready, but she was glad of his promptness all the same. Waiting any appreciable amount of time, she might have lost her nerve. Not the least of the real pleasure with which she kissed him at the door was a kind of gratitude, a relief. She was surprised in turn by the wholeheartedness of his embrace. He hugged her hard enough to bring her to her tiptoes and make her giggle breathlessly, destroying that hard-won dignity of thirty-six.

But when he released her, he seemed embarrassed and backed away awkwardly. There was the bellman with Guy's suitcase, to be tipped and sent away. She had time to stop shaking. Guy looked over the living room of the suite, furnished with stuffy antiques and strewn with the boys' books and toys. He picked his way through them to look out the windows.

"Where are the boys?"

"With Edna. On the Boston Common. They aren't expecting to see you until later this afternoon. I thought we should have some time together first."

He clasped his hands behind him. "Yes, you're right."

Sometime in the last two years Guy had left his youth behind him and become middle-aged. Ten years of marriage had made him a very different man. He had an air of distraction, of being burdened, about him, as if the thickening of his body, the thinning of his hair, the crinkling about his eyes and mouth and neck required a considerable degree of attention and effort from him. He looked like a man who had regrets.

He looked around the room expectantly. "How about a drink?"

"I'll order one up for you," she said. "Scotch and water?"

He nodded. "How about you?"

"No."

He moved quickly to cover her hand on the phone. "No, don't bother. Not just for me."

It would be easier for him to have a drink or two in him, easier for both of them. She ought to have had something on hand. Why had it seemed important that this passage occur in spitless sobriety?

"You're not drinking?" he asked.

She knew he was asking if she was abstaining again, or merely declining to drink with him.

"No," she said. "As a matter of fact, I've joined AA."

He stared at her. "What?"

"Surely you've noticed I can't handle it?"

He shook his head. "You go months at a time without a drink. I don't understand."

"Take my word for it," Torie said. She patted the sofa next to her. "Sit down, Guy. You look a little wobbly."

He grinned at her. "Hell, it wouldn't be the worst thing in the world if you never drank again. It's just a shock. You don't look like a rummy."

Tommy had left a collection of matchboxes on the coffee table, arranged into a train. She toyed with them.

"In fact," Guy said, taking out his cigarettes, "you look well."

"Thank you."

"Thinner," he said, and got up to look out the window again, as if he might spy the boys on the Common with Edna.

"Some," she said.

"Not that I saw much of you, Christmastime."

"No. I was busy and the boys needed your attention more."

He took the straight chair nearest the window and turned it around to straddle it backward. With a sigh he dropped his chin to the level of his hands on the back of the chair.

"I got the idea you didn't want to see me."

She left off noodling with the matchboxes abruptly and looked at him. "I didn't want you to see me."

There was a strained silence. "What does that mean?" he asked.

"I was pregnant," she said.

He sat very still.

"Her name is India. She's with Edna and the boys."

Torie got up and went to the window. She leaned against it, looking for the children just as he had.

"It's the first time she's been outside without me," she said.

When she looked at him again, Guy was watching her, his face an unreadable mask.

"Whose baby is she?"

She let the question sink of its own weight before answering. "Mine."

He blew smoke abruptly from his nostrils. "And what do you expect me to do about it? Just accept it?"

She was surprised at how little anger he was showing. It was as if he were going through forms, trying on emotions he thought might be appropriate to the occasion.

"Do what you want," she said.

He shook his head disbelievingly. "Goddamn it, Torie."

She touched his rigid jaw. He turned his head away.

"Do you want a divorce?" she asked gently.

"I thought I did," he said. He stared at his cigarette, then ground it out in an ashtray. "I came here to ask if that's what you wanted."

He raised his face to her, confused and yet still hopeful.

"I don't," she said. "The boys need you. I still love you. I don't know if that's enough for you."

He buried his face in his hands for a long moment. Then he took a deep breath.

"Are you going to keep on leaving me whenever there's a dig you want to be in on?"

She sighed. "Are you going to give up delivering babies in the middle of the night?"

He dismissed the question with an impatient flap of one hand. "Of course not. It's my work."

"There's your answer, Guy."

He stood up and put the chair in the place where he had found it. "I wish you hadn't picked right now to join AA. I need a drink."

She laughed.

"Am I supposed to take in somebody else's get every time you come home again?"

"No," she said, meeting the spark of anger in his eye with the cool of ice in her own. "That's done with."

Picking up and putting down his feet with some care, he drifted around the toy-mined room. He stooped to examine one or two and then left them just where they had been abandoned.

"All right," he said at last.

Torie hardly dared to breathe.

"For what it's worth," he said, "there's been no one else while you've been gone."

And then he offered her his hand. When she took it, he pulled her close and led her to the sofa. She crept into the protective crook of his elbow on the back of the sofa.

"I would like some kind of commitment from you, Torie," he said. "I'm admitting my own faults, my own stupidity. I'm admitting I was wrong. I would like to think you were willing to be my wife again, not just an occasional tenant. That means some kind of promise, something, Torie."

"You have it," she said. "No one else, anymore. And I'll give you a half interest in India."

He grinned. "You're outrageous, woman. Tell me, is this child white?"

"I never noticed," she said.

That made him laugh.

He surprised himself. He meant when he came that day to dissolve the marriage, and found himself renewing it. India was first a mystery and then a wonder to him, a girl baby, unlike his boys in sometimes subtle, sometimes stunning ways. He took to her and she to him. It wasn't long before he thought he had the best of their bargain, and generous man that he was, said so.

"I never thought," Joe Nevers said, "I'd live forever, Missus."

She bit her lip.

"Ready as I'll ever be," he added.

She was certain he was trying to be ready, and maybe that was as close as anyone ever got to actually being ready.

Suddenly he stiffened with a little gasp. His eyes glazed.

She clutched his hand in hers.

"Jesus," she whispered. She tried to call him back. "Joe Nevers," she said sharply. "Joe Nevers, don't you dare!"

As if he heard her, he relaxed and closed his eyes. She wiped his face with the towel. His free hand drifted spasmodically to his chest, clawed the hem of the quilt, and lost it. His tongue thrust out of his mouth. His whole body bucked under the covers, and then again and again.

She stumbled backward, located the pills she had left on the dresser, and poured out a handful, most of which escaped her shaking hand and spilled onto the floor.

In the meantime, he had swallowed his tongue and was turning blue.

She dropped the fistful of pills and threw herself over him, as though her weight could force his body flat to the mattress. Frantically, she looked around for something to force between his tongue and teeth and saw nothing. She thrust her fingers into his mouth, trying to catch his tongue, which was as slippery with blood and spittle as a fish in a net. His teeth clamped down on her fingers. She gasped with the pain, and withdrew them. His body heaved upward. She had all she could do to cling to him and not be thrown off.

Suddenly he went slack. His jaw fell open. She rammed her fingers into his mouth and this time was able to pull the tongue out. His color began to improve almost at once. The convulsion appeared to be over.

She picked up some pills from the floor. Tipping his head back gingerly, she forced them to the back of his throat. He swallowed them. She held him tight against her. There were pills within reach, scattered over the covers. She popped a couple, then another for good measure. Then she rested, waiting for them to go to work.

An hour or more later she roused herself from the bed and checked the fires. She took down the last of her brace from the kitchen cupboard and crawled back onto the bed to sit cross-legged next to him. She did a lot of groaning. She thought she had earned it.

When the old man spoke, she nearly dropped the bottle.

"Missus," he said thickly.

His blue eyes were rheumy; the pupils huge with the painkillers she had administered. But he was still all there, the same Joe Nevers he had always been.

"I'll be damned," she said. "And don't bother saying ayuh, either."

His eyes twinkled, though in a distant, faded way, like a star near morning. His mouth worked.

Then, at last, "Ain't fair," he said, and the surprise came through in his voice, which was as strained and knotted as old, waterlogged rope.

"No shit," she said. "Take you all these years to find out?"

He rolled his head on the pillow. *Yes. Joke's on me.*

"Talk," he said. "Blow smoke. Nonesense. Dirty words."

She sniffed in mock offense. "Fuck you, too, Joe Nevers."

"Too late," he said.

She laughed. He grinned crookedly.

"Tell the truth," he challenged her. "Shame the devil."

She shook her head. "Always have."

"Bullshit," he said. "What happened. To Dana."

Taken by surprise, she sat very still. Then she tipped the bourbon bottle thoughtfully and wet the back of her throat.

"Goddamn old gossip, to the last," she said. "How should I know? You want to hear visions and prophecies, you want Our Lady of Fatima. And I thought all these years you were a hard-headed Yankee."

"Never mind," he said. "Tell the truth. Dying man's only kind a secret's safe with."

She wiggled across the bed. "Hold off dying a minute then, will you? Have to pee."

She took the bottle with her. As long as it wasn't hurting, she might as well put it to good use. Maybe the old man would go back to sleep before she came back. When he was convulsing, she thought he was dying. Now he looked good for another ten years. Maybe. Given a doctor and a stay in the hospital. Long, long ways from dead.

He was waiting for her, looking dazed and shaky as an old bear at the end of a dry winter, but still, unavoidably, waiting.

She crawled back onto the bed next to him.

"He was one of those men who wasn't satisfied until he'd proved every woman was a whore," she said.

He nodded.

"Dana?"

"Got it," she said. "That was about half of it. The other half was, Guy and Jeannie were screwing each other."

The old man's eyes widened. Something he had not guessed.

"Yes indeed," she said, "Jeannie and Dana had what David calls 'an arrangement.' Meaning they were cake eaters. Had their cake and ate it too. Great setup for little adventures. Didn't ever cost anybody but who-ever was unlucky enough to become involved with one of them. They were terribly honest, at least to each other. Made a virtue out of it. The only one they lied to was me. You remember that terrible old joke? I was the fuckee, not the fucker." She sighed. "I don't know why anyone would want to go to the Big Post Office in the Sky with this kind of dirt on their mind."

His hand flopped feebly on the cover. Reaching for hers, she realized, and reached for the bottle, turning away so he wouldn't see the tears in her eyes.

THE FIRST THING SHE SAW from the top of the driveway was the smear of white through the evergreens. It was a snowy white, not the aged cream color of the old house. The mystery was promptly and easily solved; at the next turn, the white coalesced into the shape of Dana's new Connie.

She had been anticipating the time without the clamor of the boys and the ravaged silence of Fanny. Time to read, to hear herself think, to savor the abandoned quiet of the lake. The sight of Dana's Connie filled her with unease.

He came out the back door at the sound of her Cadillac and gave her a hug and kiss as soon as she had her feet on the ground.

"Hi, gorgeous," he said.

She laughed. "Hi, handsome," she said.

The brisk wind off the lake ruffled Dana's hair. He was graying with a sailorish, even piratical distinction, and knew it.

He took the bag of groceries she had brought for the weekend. She carried her overnight bag and a canvas bookbag lumpy with her reading list.

"What brings you here?" she asked.

"Thought I might do some hunting this weekend," he said. "Guy said you were taking a mental health holiday."

"It's gorgeous here," she said, stopping in the door to look at the lake.

In the city, the fierce bright day had been almost warm. Here the stripped trees looked naked and cold. The wind-whipped lake water slapped and crashed against the boathouse and the rocks. The air was tinged with the bitter musk of rotting leaves and woodsmoke from the sitting room chimney. No doubt there would be ice scum in the morning and frost on the rusk of leaves.

"Yeah," Dana said. "Guy's crazy to be working."

She shrugged.

In the kitchen, Dana burrowed into the grocery bag and showed her a bottle of new Beaujolais.

"Want me to open this now?"

She shook her head no and started to empty the bag into the refrigerator. It was already running, chilling a pair of six-packs. Dana's fine hand, like the fire in the fireplace.

"Thanks," she said.

"Since I was here anyway," he said, "I tried to be useful."

"You'd make someone a wonderful wife," she said.

"Oh oh, did I trespass?"

"Hell, no," she said. She offered him a beer.

He followed her upstairs and helped her make the bed. The master bedroom had a western exposure and by the tag end of the afternoon had collected a little warmth from the sun. Dana went to the windows to look at the lake.

"It looks cold."

She stood next to him and looked out. The lake was choppy with the wind, uncompromising slate blue, exultantly unpeopled.

"It looks dangerous," she said and shivered. She hugged herself. "I love it when it's like this."

With one arm, he pulled her close to him.

"You would," he said affectionately. "You're just like it."

Startled, she looked at him and then slipped out of his arm. She already knew that Jeannie had not lied about him. She had seen women—the wives of mutual friends—look at him, and seen him look back. She had wanted to be alone, but not with him. It was clear she was going to have to slap him down; it was not an enjoyable prospect. The weekend was fast souring.

She opened a beer for herself and flopped down onto the sofa to luxuriate in the heat of the fire he had built. After the biting cold outside, the heat the fire threw was wondrous and drowsy. She heard Dana in the kitchen, getting himself another beer. He came in and sat down on the rug next to the sofa. One hand fell casually onto her ankle and rubbed it vigorously.

"Mother's weekend off. You've earned it, babe."

She closed her eyes.

He peeled off one of her knee socks and began to massage her foot.

She couldn't help giggling when he got to the ticklish parts. How could she keep her guard up against a man who always knew how to make her feel like a spoiled child? He did the other foot, kissed her little toe, and tickled her instep.

She laughed and struggled against the beer and heat to get up. He let her go, seemingly content with his beer before the fire.

In the kitchen, she rummaged in a cupboard, studying the bourbon she found there, and then shut the door firmly on it. She had promised herself no hard stuff this weekend. She took a beer out of the refrigerator, drank it, and hid the bottle in the trash. It did not help her think of a way to get rid of Dana gracefully.

She brought a bottle back for each of them.

"I'm going to be shit-faced in short order," she said. "What's wrong with that?"

He sat on the edge of the sofa next to her and put an arm around her.

"I want to talk to you," he said.

I bet you do, she thought. Here it comes.

But it took him several minutes to work up to an approach. Finally he said, "Why isn't Guy with you this weekend?"

"He's on call," she said shortly.

Dana's hands gripped her shoulders. "Look at me."

She shook her head no and clutched her beer bottle convulsively.

"He's not, Torie," Dana said. "Why do you think he was so delighted to have you away for the weekend?"

She hissed and tried to pull away from him. He wouldn't let her go. She went limp against him, choking on tears. Tears of frustration, because she was so angry she wanted to beat on him, and could do no more than clench her fists and gasp for breath.

"I've known for a while," Dana said. "Believe me, I hate telling you this. But you're going to find out sooner or later. I feel responsible. If I was everything I should be as a husband, Jeannie wouldn't have needed Guy so much."

He sighed and held her tightly. She shuddered all over and then quieted against him.

"It'll pass," he said. "He'll stay with you. They just need to get it out of their systems."

She believed it but she didn't care. She thought longingly of the Wild Turkey in the cupboard.

"Don't be too hard on them," he said. "Don't blame yourself, Torie."

"Don't tell me what to feel," she shouted, and knocked his hands from her shoulders.

He drooped, and examined his hands. "I'm sorry. I was just trying to help you understand."

"And what are we supposed to be doing here? Tit for tat?" she demanded.

"Come on, Torie," he said, sticking firmly to the high road. "Let's be honest."

She snorted derisively. "It's a little late for that, isn't it?"

"You're angry and you're scared," he said. "Am I right?"

"Yes! Of course I am. And you would be too if you had any sense." She stood up, grabbed a poker and began to punish the deteriorating logs and coals in the fireplace.

Dana sighed. Then he left the room. When he came back, he brought one of her Wild Turkey cache from the kitchen, two glasses and an ice bucket. He sat cross-legged on the rug before the fire and patted the space next to him by way of invitation.

When he had poured bourbon into each glass, Torie picked up the glass with the most in it and carried it, ice cubes clinking, to a spot on the rug just beyond his reach.

"Torie," he said. "Come on over here. I'm not going to rape you. I want to hold you, that's all. I know how upset you are. The best thing for you is human contact."

"No," she said.

"Well, then, for Christ's sake, talk to me." Watching her over the lip of his glass, he tasted his bourbon.

"What do you want me to say?"

"I'd like to know what you really feel," he said.

She hooked a piece of ice from the glass, sucked the surface flavor of the Wild Turkey from it, and then chewed it up.

He shivered. "How can you do that?"

She threw back her head to drain the glass and then

dropped slowly backward onto the rug, untangling her legs to stretch them out straight. She balanced the glass, still faintly tinkling with melting ice cubes, on her stomach.

He brought the bottle over and tipped another two fingers into her glass, then snuggled up against her on his belly.

"Let me get this straight," she said, and fought off a fit of the giggles. That's what they had in mind, the three musketeers, her getting it straight.

He nodded, all patience and understanding.

"You fucked Jeannie. When was it, a hundred years ago or back in the Garden of Eden or something? Then Jeannie fucked Guy. Then you and Jeannie got married so you could fuck legally. Then you fucked whoever. Then Guy and I got married so Guy would have someone to fuck legally. Then Jeannie fucked Guy and now it's my turn and yours?"

Dana had tensed visibly during her recitation. "You're trying to make it ugly when it's not."

He rolled over to leave his glass on the coffee table. Delicately, he pincered hers from her grasp. Then he propped himself on one elbow and settled one hand flat on her stomach.

"There's always been good chemistry between us. I could have seduced you," he said. "I respect you. You're a very smart lady."

"Thanks," she said sarcastically. Suddenly she wanted to cry. She did need to be held and comforted.

He kneaded her belly lightly with the tips of his fingers. He rolled against her to kiss her, no more of a kiss than that with which they commonly greeted each other. She curled her fingers at the back of his neck and drew him back down to a longer, but still delicate, kiss. His tongue brushed the parting of her lips. There was no taste she could call lies, or flavor she could call truth.

"Now how could this be anything but good, lady," he murmured.

She closed her eyes.

His hands were light, modest in exploration. When he touched her breasts, she flinched and caught his hand.

"Don't. They're still tender."

"I'm sorry," he said. "I didn't know. After all this time?"

She looked up at him from under the weight of her eyelids. "Sure."

His fingers traced the relief of her face. He rolled against her hard, slipping one hand under her sweater to press her against him. She pushed her belly into his. The inside of her thighs tightened in response to the weight of his penis between them. She felt the milk start in her breasts and moaned. He mistook the sound for one of passion. Under her skirt, his fingers found the edge of her underpants and the silky threads of hair that escaped them.

Abruptly, she pushed him away and sat up to take back her drink with shaking hands.

He rolled on his back to watch her.

"Easy," he said, when she drained the glass. "You're drinking too fast. You'll pass out on me."

"It's not possible to drink too fast," she said, "and besides, what difference does it make to you?"

He laughed uneasily.

She struggled to her feet. He caught her hand.

"Kitchen," she said. "For the rest of the beer."

He released her. "Okay." He sprawled on the rug, finishing his own drink.

Almost shy when she returned, she offered him one

of the three remaining bottles. When she sank onto the rug, the space between was much smaller.

He tickled the instep of her foot with kisses until she giggled. She twisted and writhed trying to escape, but he held her fast by her ankles. He turned her onto her back and pulled himself over her.

She shuddered against him. She tried to turn her face, but he was quicker and pounced upon her mouth. His tongue invaded urgently. She found a beer bottle by blind feel and poured it over his head and hers.

He gasped and swore, and she was free.

She rolled onto her knees and smashed the bottle against one leg of the coffee table. Panting, she held the broken neck like a switchblade.

He froze on his knees. Then, never realizing how close she was to slashing open his throat, he coughed once. The cough exploded into laughter. He collapsed onto his haunches, rolling on the floor.

She stayed where she was, watching him.

"I give up," he said at last, wiping tears from his eyes. He sprawled on his back again, still laughing, blinking at the ceiling.

For a few seconds she was very confused. Why was Mark laughing? Why hadn't she just killed the son of a bitch the way she vowed she would someday? She shook her head, trying to clear it. Then she threw the neck of the bottle into the fire, and left the room.

The downstairs bathroom off the kitchen was as cold as a British barrow-grave she had worked in during a field trip after the war. She peed and shivered with more than cold, and wished she had a double shot of bourbon to warm her up and drive away her headache so she could think.

If she had any luck, or he did, he would be gone when she came out. But she didn't expect that. He was lying; he hadn't given up. He never gave up. With the slightest resistance, she marked his rising excitement. She sensed it so well because it mirrored her own. It was not chemistry between them at all; it was nuclear physics. The firestorm would be obliterating, the fall-out dirty.

She ought to do it. She had a gilt-edged invitation.

She rose from the icy stool and straightened her clothing. She washed her face with cold water and shook out her hair. It was full of rats and tangles. If she let it go, it would be a bitch in the morning, and she didn't want to face it with a hangover. So she brushed it out. It took a long time, long enough for Dana to have another drink. Or two. She was feeling generous with her booze. It might solve the problem just to incapacitate him.

She stared at the ghost of herself in the mirror. Hugging herself against the chill, she could see no evidence that what she knew now she had not known at noon of the same day. The look in her eye had been there a long time. Wariness. The look of someone hurt bad enough to remain forever poised to flee. She felt dizzy and sick to her stomach. She wished she knew why Guy had done this to her.

When she wound down, the old man seemed considerably more lively than he had a right. His hand, at last, found hers, and squeezed it weakly. She had forgotten how much he loved a story, telling one or hearing one.

He twitched with impatience. "Finish it," he said.

"I figured I had two choices," she said. She knocked back a mouthful of bourbon to loosen up her throat. "I could do it, or not do it. If I didn't, there would continue to be the possibility that I might, which would entail a lot more degrading seduction and resistance and just make more fun for Dana, a bigger hit. Guy and

Jeannie would go on with their affair in the meantime.
Or, I could get it over with. Sober, I could experience
the complete nastiness of it, not the least of which
would be my own enjoyment of it. Drunk, I wouldn't
be responsible, and I wouldn't enjoy it, or very likely
even remember it."

Joe Nevers' eyes did not waver from her face. She
wished he would go to sleep or pass out or something.
It was too much like hard work. She sloshed the liquor
in the bottle and it cheered her up a little.

"I didn't owe any of them anything. Guy had betrayed
me, not just our marriage vows. He'd told them my
secrets, everything about me. Jeannie didn't lie to her
husband, but she had lied without qualm to me and
screwed my husband. And then sent her husband
around to make it all right by making sure I bit the
apple and found out I was naked too. Dana just wanted
another notch on his gun and didn't mind softening
me up first by tattling Guy's infidelity to me. Christ,
what a crew."

Cradling the bottle, she slid down next to the old
man. She sighed.

He rolled his head to look at her. One gnarled hand
crabbed across the covers to pat hers.

"I know what you think," she said. "You've suspected me for years of having murdered the son of a
bitch, haven't you?"

He made no immediate answer. She listened to his
labored breathing for a while, then propped herself on
her elbow to look at his face. Amazingly, he winked, a
slow, outrageous wink.

She laughed.

WHEN SHE CAME BACK he was eager for her. He kissed her forehead, the tip of her nose, her eyelids. He twisted her disheveled hair around his fingers until she could not move her head without it hurting. They stood bound together for a long, lazy time, exchanging easy kisses, swaying like a pair of teenagers at a sock hop.

He was feeling the booze now. She felt it in the way he moved against her, slow and heavy, like an undertow. He talked to her in a low urgent voice. She did not talk back. He knew the things he said were lies and she did too, so there was no need to waste her energy. She floated just beyond his reach. Her own arousal she saw from a distance, with sad contempt. The bourbon mercifully blurred their slow undressing.

She slithered, at last, out of his arms, and began to prowl the room, stark naked. She clawed books from the bookcase and dropped them on the floor. She wrote her name in the dirt on the windows of the French doors to the sunporch. It was the fire dirtied them; she must remember to call Joe Nevers to have a woman in to clean them.

Dana looked up from poking at the fire and called her name. The fire illumined the fine planes of his face.

"Feel better?" he asked.

She smiled into her glass. "Yes," she said. "In my time."

He missed the joke. "Hungry?" he asked.

She shrugged. She had stopped being hungry with the first taste of bourbon. She stirred the ice and bourbon in her glass with her finger. The fire made the liquor's darkness rich with light. She sucked the tip of her finger as if it were bleeding.

He came to her and took the finger from her mouth to suck on. His erection was down a bit, but he hardened quickly against the silkiness of her thighs. At once the wanting him roiled the surface calm of the alcohol in her blood and left her holding her breath.

Their mouths met violently and drew blood. She raked his back with her fingers while his penis dug hard into her belly. He knuckled her crotch clumsily, and she pulled away. This time she did not escape him. His hands clasped her arms tight enough to stop her circulation and when she pulled away, only tightened more, like the straw cylinders she and her brother had called Chinese handcuffs. The hurt enraged her. She tried to draw up her knees between them but he drove the full weight of his body onto hers, forcing her onto her back. His eyes were glazed, and blood from a split in his lip trickled on his chin. She made herself relax, and when he did, fooled into thinking she was no longer fighting, she snarled and bucked, whipping the blood from his chin with her tongue. When he pulled back his head for fear of her teeth, she sank them into his throat.

He cried out, and slammed her against the floor to free himself. Her head bounced on the rug. She rolled away in a daze, and fumbled for her drink. She heard the shaky clink of glass against glass, the bottle being poured, behind her.

"You like being raped?" he asked angrily.

She knew then that Guy had told them her secret history. She was enraged. This was a betrayal beyond adultery. She did not answer Dana, only licked blood from her lips contemptuously. She had to fumble for the coffee table to make it to her feet again. Suddenly tired, she began to gather the strewn pieces of her clothing together. Her head was inside the sweater, her arms snaking through the sleeves when he tackled her, driving her onto the couch.

He was well below her, and she felt the weight of the booze slowing him. She brought a knee up hard, connecting with his nose with spectacular results. He let her go, to cup the gusher from his nose. She didn't think he was going to get it up again for a while.

She finished pulling the sweater over her head. By then he was scooping melting ice from the ice bucket onto his face.

Finished dressing, she went to the bathroom again. From the stool she could see her hair was wild again, so she stopped to brush it out, touch up her eyeliner and color her lips, though it hurt to spread lipstick over the small breaks in the skin.

Dana was rolled up in a quilt by the fire, nursing his nose and the bottle at once.

She took off her wedding ring and tossed it into the fire.

He didn't want to look at her, but when he did, she saw how terribly angry he was. He would never forgive her. That was okay with her.

"You're a goddamn cockteaser, you know that?" he said.

"That's progress," she said. "Just so long as you don't mistake me for a romantic novel. I don't like being told what to feel and when to feel it."

She didn't expect him to understand. If he was capable of that, none of this ever would have happened.

She picked up her overnight case and her bookbag, and hooked the last bottle of bourbon from the cupboard. She was drunker than he was, though he showed signs of catching up, but then, she was used to it.

She liked it that way. Never happier than when she was three sheets to the wind, cruising the interstate at eighty in a big fat Cadillac. To date she had never had an accident, never even pulled down a ticket, at least that she could remember.

The house in Falmouth was dark and quiet when she reached it. She crept in, kissed the boys in their beds, and slipped into her own bed. She woke to the sound of the phone ringing, and David crying. When she came out of his bedroom carrying him, Edna was in the hall, answering the phone.

Edna never blinked at the sight of her, who wasn't supposed to be there, but handed her the phone.

"It's Joe Nevers," she whispered. Tom was already trailing down the hall, rubbing his eyes. "Wants to know are you at home?"

Torie didn't expect Edna to answer that, of course.

She handed David, who was now quiet and interested in what was going on, to Edna, and took the phone.

"Joe Nevers," she said. "What's going on at this hour of the night?"

He didn't answer right away and when he did, he sounded very tired, and very far away.

"Guy with you, Missus?" he asked.

She hesitated. "He's at the hospital," she said. "Is something wrong?"

Joe Nevers cleared his throat. "Could you tell me, Missus, does Dana Bartlett have a new white Connie?"

"Why, yes, I think he does," she said, and fought a yawn. Her head ached fiercely.

"Would he be using your place, Missus?" Joe Nevers asked.

She could see him clearly, his cap in one hand, the telephone held between his shoulder and his ear, scratching behind the other, so as not to have to look straight at her. Joe Nevers.

"Right now, do you mean?" she asked.

"Ayuh."

"Excuse me," she said. "I'm still half-asleep. Of course Dana's at the house. He borrowed a key from Guy. He wanted to hunt this weekend and his father's place is shut up now."

Joe Nevers, who had not shut up the Bartletts' house, knew better than anyone that was a lie. He kept his silence, let the lie take breath, now it was born.

"Missus," he said sadly, "p'rhaps you best give me the number for the hospital so I can talk to Guy now."

"What's wrong?"

Joe Nevers sighed. "Sorry to have to tell you this, Missus. The house burned this morning. Went like a pile of dry leaves. Looks like maybe Dana was in it."

"Oh," she said. "Oh Jesus."

Edna looked alarmed, and reached out to steady her. Torie almost dropped David.

"Joe Nevers," she said. "I'll reach Guy. He'll call you back, okay?"

"Ayuh. That's fine. You ask him to call me at the fire barn. I'll be here awhile."

She broke the connection, then dialed the Bartletts' summer house; Jeannie answered.

"Let me talk to Guy," Torie said shortly.

There was an uneasy silence, then Jeannie said, "Sure."

Guy's voice was guarded. "Torie?"

She took a deep breath. "Something bad's happened. The summer house burned this morning. Dana may have been in it."

Guy gasped.

She was afraid he would soon be beyond response so she talked faster.

"I'm at home in Falmouth. Call Joe Nevers at the fire barn. I'll go over to Dana's to wait with the kids."

She hung up quickly, before he could ask questions of her.

She took David back from Edna. "I have to tell you something."

Edna put her hands on Torie's shoulders. "I heard."

"There's more," she said. "I came home last night . . ."

Edna nodded. "Never mind that. Let me take David. You go back to bed."

Torie shook her head. "I'm going to shower and go over to Jeannie's."

Edna nodded. She approved of Torie doing the hard thing.

Thank God for Edna. Edna had lived with an alcoholic husband for thirty years. She had not been surprised or disturbed to discover, as she almost immediately had, that Torie had a problem that way. She fell in love with Tommy and David, the grandchildren she had never had. She missed her husband, and looked after Torie with the same kind, supportive care she had given him. She was certain that inside, Torie was like Mike, a good person cursed with the drink. David and Tommy were the proof of Torie's essential virtue.

Edna and Guy had worked out their own modus vivendi. Edna's sympathy for Guy was limited. He would not enter his own mother's bedroom anymore, clear evidence of a lack of fortitude. In his turn, Guy found her a barely acceptable replacement for Beulah Clark, who had babied him shamelessly. They got along mostly because Edna was not about to be pushed out when Torie needed her and the boys needed her.

Torie wasn't surprised to come out of the shower and find black coffee waiting for her by the bed, with a decanter of bourbon—hair of the dog—beside it.

"The drink," the old man mumbled. "Blamed yourself."

"Shit," Torie said. "You goddamn old fool. That's why you drank. I'm just a goddamn garden-variety alcoholic. That's why I drink."

He rolled his head back and forth, with noticeable effort.

"You say so."

"I say so," she said. "You think I blame myself because some son of a bitch burned himself up and my house down while he was drunk? Maybe I should blame myself instead of the goddamn bacteria that killed Tommy? Join Gary Buck's club? Maybe I should blame myself because some shithead mistook India for a doe?"

Dry from ranting at him, she chugalugged from the bottle. She spilled some on the quilt, unable to control her shaking hands. She didn't need to read it in the old man's eyes: she was drunk again. Home again. The old familiar territory.

"Shit," she said morosely.

"I know," the old man said slowly, "who killed India."

The bottle slipped from her hands and tipped onto the bed. The liquor spread unheeded, darkening the quilt. She stared at him.

"Shut up," she said. "I don't want to know."

He reached for her hand. She gave it to him reluctantly. He held on for dear life.

W<small>HEN</small> H<small>OPE</small> M<small>C</small>A<small>VOY</small>, on her way out, imparted the news that Cora had had a good day, Joe Nevers thought to himself that meant she was saving the bad for him.

Cora was drowsing, the remote control of the new television set still in her slack hand. He reached over her to push the off button. She opened a baleful eye at once.

"Suppertime," he said.

She smacked her lips, loosening the crust of dried saliva at the corners of her mouth.

But when he brought the soup, she turned her face away. "Too hot," she said, though she had not tasted it, or even felt steam from the spoon close to her skin.

He sat patiently, waiting for the soup to cool. The parlor was stifling. Hope couldn't be trusted not to start a chimney fire, so the furnace was running instead of the parlor stove. Cora looked as if she had melted in the excessive, dry heat, so bony of face and limb had she grown, though her belly was as white and swollen as a bread loaf rising. Mournfully, Joe Nevers checked the thermostat, and tried not to wince. He might as well be burning up dollar bills as oil.

When he picked up the soupspoon again to feed her, Cora shook her head. "I don't feel up to eating tonight."

His big hands closed tight on the handles of the tray. "How 'bout an egg?"

Cora smiled bravely. "Why that would be nice."

He set the timer on it. Cora had to have her egg just so: set, not runny or too hard.

She turned the television set back on while he was in the kitchen, not watching anything but switching it listlessly from one station to the next by the remote control. As her own world contracted to the boundaries of the parlor, television had become extremely important to Cora, a window on the world outside. Joe Nevers had an idea, from the way she talked about them sometimes, that Cora thought the soap operas she whiled away her conscious hours viewing were really happening, that through the magic of the TV set, she was spying on the highly colored, private lives of real people.

It was a brand-new set, with a nineteen-inch screen, the largest available because Cora had such trouble now making out detail. It was installed on the top of the highboy, moved from their bedroom, so she did not have to crane to see it, though Joe Nevers did. No doubt the attendant discomfort prevented his falling into the TV habit.

The highboy spelled the end of the pretense that Cora's presence in the parlor was only a matter of a week or two. It held the linen for her hospital bed, and her nighties, of which there was a considerable quantity, because she was frequently incontinent. One whole drawer held sickroom fixtures that Hope McAvoy considered to be faintly indecent, such as syringes, intrusive reminders of the breakdown of Cora's bodily functions.

Joe Nevers had had to fix wooden dowels along the walls for Cora to support herself by, on the rare occasions when she felt up to shuffling to the bathroom. The bathroom itself had acquired a hospital antiseptic smell. Chrome tubing on either side of the toilet enabled her to get up and down. In the enamelled white steel shower, the enema bag hung like a slack flag.

Cora took no more than a bite or two of the egg before turning her face away again.

"Just not hungry tonight," she said wanly.

When Joe Nevers had cleaned up the kitchen, he moved his recliner near to Cora's bed so he could see the television too.

"What are you watching?"

She shrugged. "Nothing much. What's on tonight?"

She knew as well as he did, as she leafed through the TV Guide many times during her day, but Joe Nevers took it up and went through the exercise of looking up the night's programs.

" 'Peyton Place,' " he said. "Watch that?"

She let him find it on the control, but would not actually let go of the gadget. Her grip on the remote control was a little desperate, as if she were afraid he might pry it from her weak grasp.

"Want the shade lowered?" he asked, before he sat down.

Cora lifted her head to peer at the window. A steady fall of snow winked in the light from the parlor.

"How long's it been snowing?" she asked.

"Since four or so. T'won't amount to much."

She stared at the window, considering the prediction. "Well, leave it up, then. I'll just see how much it amounts to."

While the commercials ran after the firt segment of the program, Joe Nevers made her a cup of weak tea.

"What do you think?" he asked her. "Peyton Place like any small town you ever lived in?"

Cora shook her head. "Too many folks. Look at the size of that bar. Have to go to Lewiston to find a bar that big."

He sorted out her pills. "Too much money, too," he said. "Never saw so much cash in a small town."

Maine or New Hampshire, it was the same. Rural society in both states was founded firmly on a bedrock of poverty and a population as scarce as ready cash. The entertainment for both of them was watching city folks' delusions of rural life acted out.

"You ready for these?" He poured her water.

She was. By the time "Peyton Place" was three-quarters finished with its tangle of sin and bigotry, Cora was glassy-eyed. Otherwise, she would have turned the show off about then, saying she was too tired to watch it through. One of the ways she made sure he didn't enjoy the TV too much. He had given her that power when he bought her the remote control gadget, and she didn't hesitate to use it.

He had to lean over her to push the off button again. She was snoring gently. He dimmed the lights, arranged his reading lamp over his chair, put on his reading glasses, and opened the book he was working his way through, a dog-eared copy of *Harrison High*.

Sometime later, Cora began to talk to herself as she often did, mostly gibberish interspersed with the commonplaces, remarks about weather, recipes, other peoples' children, and the "shows," the soap operas. She quieted again after a while and slept.

Just before midnight, Joe Nevers marked his place, set the book aside with his glasses on top of it, and stood up to stretch, thinking of well-earned rest.

"He thinks I don't know whose get she is," Cora said, outraged, as clearly as the mountains could be seen on a dry cold day.

Joe Nevers froze, hardly daring to breathe. He remembered, all at once, making his hand close on the doorknob, opening the closet door, and seeing his old rifle in its rack at the back of the closet, just where he left it the last time he cleaned it. Almost.

Cora's eyes were closed. He could see the eyeballs rolling grotesquely under her lids. As if they were trying to see everything. She was under, as Hope McAvoy would say.

"I'll fix him," she growled, and then, as nice as how-do-you-do, "he won't . . . have her. Bang . . . bang."

The rifle had been almost right where he left it.

Joe Nevers shook off the spell of Cora's voice and approached her bed. He bent over her.

"Cora," he whispered. "Did you do it?"

She did not answer him, but her mouth twitched in silent laughter, and then her body convulsed, and her tongue thrust out between her teeth.

He stepped back in alarm, cold sweat breaking out on his forehead.

Cora drew a number of uneven, desperate breaths, as if she had lost her breath in laughing, and then steadied, eased, and seemed to drop into a deeper sleep. He watched her a long time, his hands thrust into his pants pockets to keep them from her throat.

He did not sleep well that night.

The next morning, he drove to Roscoe's diner, to use the public phone. He made the arrangements to admit Cora to the hospital in Greenspark, then called Hope and told her to ready Cora for the ambulance trip. He never saw her again.

"Cora did it," he said. "Cora did it."

"That's a lie," Torie spat back at him. "Cora drove a doe into the lake as a cover for murdering India? Did that car fall on your head, old man? Have you gone crazy as well as senile?"

He rolled his head from side to side in denial. "My

rifle wasn't right. Cora was a helluva shot. Church taught her."

Torie fumbled for the bottle and shook it, seeing it had emptied itself onto the covers.

"Tell the truth," the old man wheezed. "India was mine. Cora couldn't stand me having anything 'twas my own. She took her away from me."

Torie tossed the empty bottle aside. "Whose crazy idea was that? About India? Yours or Cora's?"

"I knowed it," he said simply. "She figured it out." The words dragged like rusty runners in the snow.

Torie tapped her chest with one finger. "The truth," she said, "is India was mine."

The old man rolled his head stubbornly.

"Flaw in her eye," he said. "Same as my mother's, my sister's."

"Shit. India's eyes were perfect."

She wanted to stop there but she couldn't. She wasn't drunk enough for any of this.

"And if there were some kind of flaw in her eye, it still wouldn't prove shit," she insisted.

"It does to me," the old man said.

"Listen to me, you just want her to be yours, is all." Her throat tightened up miserably. Her face was hot and throbbing again. "Shit a goddamn," she said, "I don't care."

She shook her hand loose from his and stumbled off the bed. The fires wanted feeding. It was a good enough excuse to wander through the kitchen and hook the last of her brace from the cupboard. She stopped in the bedroom doorway to look at the old man, while she opened it. He struggled to lift his head to see her, then seemed to relax when he did. It occurred to her that he was afraid to be left alone. With her cut hand more hindrance than help, she splashed a little bourbon on her bare feet. Irritated with herself for the clumsiness and the waste, she dried her feet impatiently, one at a time, by rubbing them against the hem of her robe above each heel.

"Joe Nevers," she said, and raised the bottle toward him.

He grinned and followed her progress across the floor as if he were a small boy again, watching his mother coming to take him from his crib.

He fumbled for her hand as soon as it was in reach.

"Joe Nevers," she said, bending over him. "You remember better than I do."

He nodded.

"You think we did it?"

His eyes widened. He tried to say something but could only wheeze. Worried, she cradled the bottle between thigh and chest and fingered the pills still in her pocket. But the wheezing let off, and he relaxed again. His eyes, though, never left her face.

"Well," she said, "you seem to think so. I never heard you subscribe to anything so Popish as the virgin birth. Be damned if I can remember, is all."

"Drunk," Joe Nevers said quite distinctly.

She flopped one hand at him. "What else is new?"

SHE WAS ALONE IN THE NEW HOUSE, and uneasy in the silence. With brandy in her coffee, she drifted through the house, looking at the corners and angles of the emptiness. The last of the wallpaperers and carpenters had left a mess that she and Edna had spent the previous day clearing away. Now the place was spotless, but so sparsely furnished that it looked raw and hard as a green apple. Even the litter of toys in the boys' bedrooms only made the spaces larger and emptier.

Edna had risen early to pack a picnic lunch, and had taken the boys to ride the train in North Conway. Kitchen sounds had wakened Torie, who had slept hard after the previous day's orgy of cleaning and straightening. She put on the cashmere robe the boys had given her for Mother's Day, and saw them off. Trying to sleep again was a useless exercise. She idled through the house to the deck where she lounged in the early morning cool and savored the emptiness of the lake.

This early in the day, the quiet of the lake was almost secretive, hardly more than a breath of water moving against the rocky shoreline, a splash of loons, the whisper of a solitary canoe gliding by. The sound of Joe Nevers' truck in the driveway, his discreet knock at the door, which he did not expect her to answer, the parentheses of entry and exit marked by the slap of the screen door from the back porch, were familiar background noise, not interruptions but part and parcel of the whole.

The builders had torn up the grounds with their heavy equipment when the ground was soft and vulnerable in the spring. Almost from the day the damage was done, Joe Nevers had been at work repairing it, but it was a considerable mess and he was still at it. Most of the work he had done alone, making do with an occasional hired hand from the village, like Reuben Styles, who met his standards of skill and experience.

Sitting as still as the old Victorian sundial he had only the day before returned to its proper position, Torie watched Joe Nevers wheel a barrow of turf, rolled up like a jellyroll, to where he had stopped off at quitting time the day before. There he took off his cap with one hand and mopped his brow. He saw her watching him, and tapped the visor of his cap as he resettled it on his head, by way of greeting, and bent his back to the work.

The night before, Tommy cried out, waking her. She found him shivering, crouched at the door to his room.

She sat down next to him, and hugged him close. "What's wrong?"

"I don't like this room," he said in a low voice.

She sighed. "Why?"

He looked fearfully over his shoulder. "There's something scratching at the window, trying to get in."

She looked up and listened carefully. She heard it for herself. Scratch scratch. The sound of pine branches on window glass.

"It's the tree," she said.

Tommy looked over his shoulder again. He relaxed. "Oh."

"Okay?"

He nodded. She hugged him again.

"Back to bed," she said.

He hugged her tightly. "Can't I sleep with David tonight?"

With a gentle chuck under the chin, Torie lifted his face toward hers. He was still pale and wide-eyed. She sighed. "Okay. Just tonight."

She tucked him in next to David, who was sprawled obliviously in his bed. When she shut the bedroom door behind her, she allowed herself to smile. A fat lot of good his five-year-old brother would be against a tree monster. But it was sweet. She felt a swell of affection for them both, scared seven-year-old and little brother who was this night's charm against a hoodoo.

When the sun was a little higher and began to warm her, she went in to change to shorts and a halter. She pinned up her hair, basted herself with tanning lotion, and found her sunglasses. Methodically, she stacked records on the record player, and a pile of professional papers and books hard by the lounge chair on the deck. She filled an ice bucket, buried a Coke in it, and upended a tall glass over the soda bottle. The spill of cold air from the refrigerator made her shiver, but it was not unpleasant. She held the door open and counted the bottles of beer inside, conscientiously excluding the two six-packs that Joe Nevers had brought in when he arrived.

This was going to be a dry day for her, she had already decided, the second in a row. She ought to tell Joe Nevers to bring in the rest of the case she knew he had in his truck. He would scratch behind his ear, the way he had when she insisted he use the refrigerator instead of the cooler in the back of his truck. It was, after all, a big refrigerator. If it made his life easier to stop Cora harping on the presence of the cooler ("It looks bad, what'll the neighbors think?") in the back of the truck, that was fine with the both of them. Joe

Nevers took her up on the offer, but would only leave half a case at a time in her refrigerator, so as not to hog it. There was time between noon, when he opened the first bottle, and six, when he knocked off, for the last two six-packs to chill. Torie thought she and the two storekeepers in town were the only ones who really knew what Joe Nevers was putting away. The storekeepers were making a profit on it, and Torie lived in a glass house, so they kept it to themselves. Aside from that, Torie counted the space his beer took up in her refrigerator as nothing less than a humane act. Joe Nevers would not be drinking like that unless Cora was making him miserable.

"Joe Nevers," she called to him.

He laid aside his tools and came onto the deck, mopping his forehead with a big bandanna handkerchief.

"Tommy won't sleep in his bedroom because of that tree scratching his window every time there's a breeze."

Joe Nevers shook his head. "I wanted to prune the branches when they was abuilding. You didn't want me to then."

"I do now."

He nodded.

"Besides, it'll improve the view," she added.

"Ayuh," he said, and took his leave.

He reappeared in a few minutes with climbing gear. She watched him belt himself to the pine and cleat his way through its lower branches. He hauled up a chain saw, a handsaw, and rope. Soon branches began to fall like ripe fruit from the tree. The larger ones came swaying slowly and carefully on ropes.

She tried to read, but sitting in the sun made her head ache, and her eyes began to water. She dumped a lapful of reading material on the deck, shut her eyes against the sun, and drank the Coke. It didn't help much.

She went inside to stalk the house again. The old house had been dark, and cavelike, and always cooler than the out-of-doors, but this house was like a greenhouse, magnifying the heat and the light to exotic levels. It was like a stage, lit by banks of suffocating, glaring klieg lights. She felt trapped and restless. She wished she had gone with Edna and the boys to North Conway. She wished Fanny had come, so she would not be alone in the empty house. The summer telescoped into a hot, airless tunnel with no discernible, imaginable end. Without thinking very much about it, she went to the refrigerator and took out a beer.

With the lounge chair flattened out under her, she closed her eyes and gave herself up to the sun. She sipped the first beer very slowly. Gradually, her headache receded. As if on an imaginary rotisserie, she rolled from her back to her belly or from her belly to her back now and again. She did not count the times she went inside for another beer. The first few times she experienced a momentary disappointment with herself, but knew, just as well, that would not stop her.

After a while she went into the house and up to Tommy's room. She opened the window in the sleeping loft, and handed Joe Nevers a beer.

He reached out for it without hesitation, though it unbalanced him slightly. He was pretty safely strapped to the trunk of the pine.

"You want me to fall out a this tree, Missus?" he asked, grinning.

"You couldn't fall if you wanted to, and if you did, you'd land on your feet," she said.

He laughed. "Mebbe so."

"Why don't you take that one," Torie said, pointing at a branch on his left. "And the one next to it."

He grunted and proceeded to sever the branches. When that was done, he took off his cap and wiped his brow.

"Okay?"

Torie frowned. "Well, what about that one?"

Joe Nevers looked at it. "Oh, sure."

He had to rope this one, and when it was separated and on the ground, he gave a great sigh of relief.

"What's the matter, old man," Torie said, "feeling your age?"

He eyed her sardonically. "Be a fool not to."

"Good," Torie said. She leaned on the windowsill, studying the tree. "What about that one?"

Joe Nevers was quiet. He looked at the branch and then he looked at her and then he looked at the branch again.

"Missus," he said, "that branch won't touch this window in a hurricane."

"Just cut it off," Torie said.

He shook his head. "Whyn't I just cut the tree down?"

"Because all that needs cutting is that branch," she said.

"It don't," he said. "Pardon me, Missus, it don't."

"Cut the fucking branch."

"Pardon me, Missus," Joe Nevers said gravely. "You best reconsider your words. You don't want to talk to me like that."

His clear blue eyes showed no spark of anger, or even coldness. Yet she felt herself held by them. She blushed, and dug her nails into the windowsill.

"Of course not. Do what you think best, Joe Nevers," she said, and left the windowsill.

When Joe Nevers came in the back door at noon, stripped to the waist and slick as she was with sweat, she was poking listlessly in the refrigerator, looking for something appetizing without the least stirring of hunger. They grunted at each other over the open door, and she passed him one of his six-packs and the brown paper bag that held his sandwiches.

"Thanks, Missus," he said, but his eye was on the first bottle, and his hand was searching in his pocket for a church key.

He emptied the first one in a couple of swallows and wiped his arm across his forehead before he examined his sandwiches, without enthusiasm. He wolfed them in huge bites, watching her rattle ice cubes into the ice bucket. A good half of what she knocked out of the ice trays skittered across the counter tops and onto the floor, where they began at once to melt and puddle. She ignored them, busy nesting beers in the bucket. He scooched down and picked them up as quick as if he were picking wild strawberries, and tossed them into the sink.

She noticed what he was doing.

"Thank you," she said.

"Much obliged," he said.

He crumpled the paper bag and dumped it into the trash can, along with an empty.

"When's Fanny going to be here?"

"This weekend, with Guy," Torie said. "Will you be ready?"

Joe Nevers nodded. Torie had charged him to restore the grounds to what they had been, to ease Fanny's inevitable disorientation. The new house would be difficult enough to adjust to. The old woman had taken the destruction of the old one very badly, and still wept over it when she thought no one could hear.

When Torie raised her beer in a silent toast, she did not have to tell Joe Nevers it was to her mother-in-law.

"She was a great old girl," he said.

"Wish you hadn't used the past tense."

He shrugged. The Fanny Christopher who had been another mother to him was irretrievably lost, as much a matter of history as the old summer house. It was that Fanny he honored in her ruin.

"Truth, isn't it?"

Torie took up the ice bucket. "Ayuh."

He reached for it. She hesitated, then surrendered it. He hooked the remains of his six-pack from the refrigerator with his free hand and followed her onto the deck.

She dropped onto the chaise and closed her eyes, behind her sunglasses. The sun cooked the yeasty smell of the beer, the coconut scent of her tanning lotion, the water smell of the ice, the acrid resinous smell of the pines. Near her, from where he sat cross-legged on the deck, came the old-fashioned smell of Joe Nevers' aftershave, and his morning's sweat. She heard a beer being uncapped, and then felt a sudden glassy cold against her neck. She flinched and laughed. When she reached for the beer, her fingers encountered his, holding the bottle. She propped herself on one elbow and he released it to her.

"You think," she asked him, and wet her throat to finish, "they make this stuff wetter and colder in the summer?"

"Likely," he conceded.

She looked around her. "I love this place," she said. "The Ridge. It's like a great big secret. The only way you could know it all would be to be born here, and die here, and never leave it in between, not for a minute." She laughed. "Cuts me out, doesn't it? But at least I know it's a secret, and I know some bits and pieces. I can imagine the whole from that."

Joe Nevers shook his head. "I like to think what you said was true, but I been here forever and if there's a secret to the Ridge, I don't know it, Missus."

"You may not now," she said, "but you will. You'll die here, and I won't. By then, you'll know."

He laughed. "Guess we'll have to wait and see." He looked shyly at the deck. He wrapped both hands around his beer.

"You don't wear your wedding ring no more," he said.

"Lost it," Torie said.

"Here?" he asked. "Be glad to keep an eye out for it."

"It's not worth your trouble," she said.

He was startled enough to stare at her. She didn't flinch from his cool blue eyes. It came to her she was tight, and reckless to pass words with this man. She couldn't count on him to be stupid about everything, just because he was notably wrong-headed about women. But she didn't care.

"You'd do well," she said evenly, "to lose yours."

He looked away from her. His secrets to him weren't as interesting as hers.

"I'm getting by," he said.

She laughed. "Liar, liar," she chanted. "Pants on fire."

He blushed, then laughed. He reached over to seal her lips with his fingers. They were broad and calloused against the soft flesh of her mouth.

"Hush," he said. He raised his beer to her. "You and I," he said. "Getting by."

"Oh, sure," she said.

She let herself down onto the chair. Behind her sunglasses she was open-eyed. Keyed up. Her throat was tight, her tongue thick in her mouth. She held her breath. When he stood up, stretched, then bent to kiss her, she was too surprised to react quickly. She wallowed in the taste of beer and salty sweat. She came up on her elbows for more of it. They met only at their mouths. When he let her go, she fell back breathless.

"Jesus," she said.

"Wrong fella," he said. "Name's Joe Nevers."

She was as dizzy as a top set spinning. He reached for her again, and she hung herself around his neck, so he could scoop her from the chair. He carried her into the house, through the glare of the living room. She felt light in his arms, and loose against the dense muscle of his chest. He rolled her onto her unmade and rumpled bed as casually as he unrolled turf to make a lawn.

There were no curtains or draperies, only shades, and these he drew down, so the room was suddenly shadowy and mysteriously cooler.

That was the last easy part. He was in her and gone in less than a minute. Too numbed with the morning's beer to feel the throb of his orgasm, she reacted slowly when he collapsed on top of her.

"Shit," she said.

He turned his face from her.

"Should have expected this," she said.

He started to pull out of her. She hooked one hand round the other at the nape of his neck. He stopped moving and peeked at her. It was easier to guess he had done without too long, as she had, than to coax some satisfaction out of him. She doubted she was up to it, assuming he was. She could not help giggling.

She sighed and released him. She was thirsty. She slipped from the bed to go to the kitchen for something cold and wet, and stooped, without ceremony or thought, to lick his nearest nipple. One lick led, astonishing them both, to another. She did not have to see his eyes widen to know he was responding, for her left hand blindly found his penis. They blundered their way back into each other's arms.

Late in the afternoon, he left her. Half-asleep and half-drunk, still she knew it, from the lightening of the bedsprings, or the sound of his zipper, or the faint rattle of his clothes. The screen door slapped, and she waited for the truck to start, but it didn't.

"Putting his tools away," she said aloud, and fell to giggling.

He must have done that, and perhaps had a beer, just sitting in the cab, before the truck did start, and the house was quiet again, as it had been in the morning after the boys left.

Soon they would be home again. She ought to shower and dress, and throw the sheets in the hamper before that happened. She groped for the nightstand and swung her legs over the side of the bed, but as soon as she sat up, her head hurt and she was dizzy. So she sat a little while, eyes shut tight. She groped by the side of the bed for the bottle she remembered leaving there, found it, and wet down her throat. At last she could open her eyes. They began to adjust to the half-dark of the shaded room. She started to push herself to her feet.

But her hand on the nightstand encountered something cool and hard. She stooped over it, peering at it. It was the gold circle of her wedding ring. Outside, there was the sound of a car coming down the driveway, and the boys shouting to her from its open windows.

She was not that day as drunk as she wanted to be, or said she was later. And he was not drunk at all. Still, she had forgotten most of it, thrown it away like the wedding ring, on purpose. Her memory was full of black holes.

She was the one who went away. He was the one who stayed. The place they shared was nameless and unmapped; they found it only the once, and then could never find it again.

The time for telling secrets had run out. She could hardly summon words anymore. She felt desiccated, dried up and ready to crumble. The old man was wracked and breathless, clinging to her hand. Since morning he had aged, and shrunk too, become a very old man indeed.

She dozed where she was for some time, until she realized that darkness had come round again. A sudden wash of fear sent her stumbling from the bed. The dark had never frightened her before. Now it obscured the old man's face like a veil. Anxiously she patted the length of his arm, felt his forehead, and breathed a little easier, if he did not, to find him still alive.

She groped her way to the kitchen for matches and a kerosene lamp and back again. The old man would have been pleased as punch, she thought, with her extreme care in lighting the lamp. It was strange to see him in the wavering watery light, which did not soften the ravages of age and accident, but lit his face like a skull. The smell of the burning oil, or the minuscule warmth it threw, must have penetrated his private night, for he stirred and opened his eyes with an effort.

He pushed out his last coherent string of words as if they were ballast. "Place finally done me in, Missus."

He coughed violently. She forced more pills on him. She could not remember how many of what she had administered, but she was determined he would not suffer pain while she had a pill to give him. A little extra would do him no harm, not when he was going to die anyway. It never had hurt her.

She curled up next to him. He quieted after a while, and she grew sleepy. She fought it, afraid the lamp might die on her in the night, leaving her in darkness, or somehow set the place afire. It was a fine joke, she reflected, to be a foolish virgin at her age and with her history, unable to keep a lamp lit through the night.

Sometime in the small hours, he woke her with a rush of unintelligible words, as if he were trying to spill all the words he had hoarded in his lifetime. Confused and frightened, she tried to give him more pills. But his tongue pushed them back out of his mouth; his throat seemed closed tight. He convulsed again, violently, and there was nothing she could do but watch and wait. At last the convulsions subsided, and he was still.

She felt wide awake, full of adrenaline, no doubt. She was certain she would not be able to sleep again, though she ached for real rest. She touched the pills in her pockets, thinking it was nearly time for her to take some, that the pain would be coming round again soon.

Then she noticed how very still the old man really was. She turned his face, fallen to the side, toward her with gentle hands. His eyes were open, showing only white. She listened for a heartbeat in his chest, and felt for one at wrist and throat, but discerned nothing. Holding his hand in hers, she sat there a long time, persuading herself that he was dead.

She tried to think what she should do. Hugging herself against the cold, she slipped from the bed to her knees, located her handbag by feel, and found two coins, quarters, to put on his eyelids. She placed them carefully.

Then she took stock of her pills. There was but a mixed handful, a couple of Darvocets, several twenty-five milligram Elavils, three Talwins. She had to hope they would be enough to do the job. She knocked them back with bourbon. She crawled between the blankets next to the old man. The goddamned lamp would have to take care of itself. At least, the Ridge would have something to talk about when the two of them were discovered. The thought made her smile.

When she woke again, the lamp was still burning, but it was unmistakably Monday. The first thing she knew for sure was she felt like shit. The weak sun leaking round the rough edges of the plywood in the windows had a Pentecostal clarity that made the lamp-light irrelevant. The room smelled like a dig, like a mausoleum disturbed, a place where fresh air was something new. There was a faint odor of decay, over-laid with the smell of wet ashes and the oily burn of the kerosene, that combined into the sickening odor of charred flesh.

The old man had stiffened. It would be some hours yet before the rigor passed off. He was still quite as much dead as she wasn't.

She yawned hugely. It hurt, and the back of her throat tasted awful. She moved aching, burning fingers and toes gingerly. Her knees felt as if she had walked to Sainte Anne de Beaupré on them. Her belly felt as if she had been kicked by a horse. Her head felt like Monday.

But behind the scabbed and swollen mask of her face, inside her bodily misery, she felt relieved and then astonished at her relief. She felt as if she had died, and been reborn. Only she knew very well she had not. She still owed God her death, on his dreadful terms. But it seemed as if the death she had come to die by the lake had been died by the old man. Joe Nevers had given her a second chance, just as he had restored, so mysteriously, her wedding ring.

He had not taken away the pain. It was all still hers. It was possible, even likely, that when it came to her again, she would not be able to bear it. The lake for her, then, she decided. But that was yet to come. She had first to see to Joe Nevers' planting, in the cemetery on the Ridge. All the secrets would go with him, for him to take care of. And he would have the best view to be had. She did not believe in heaven or hell but she did believe in ghosts. Surely Joe Nevers, who had never abandoned the Ridge, would not leave it now. She herself did not intend to leave it ever again, not in life or death.

She reached out to touch him.

"Old man," she said. "Joe Nevers." And then her throat tightened, and she couldn't say anything else, not even a cheerful curse word, but allowed herself to weep, quietly, for him.

IT WAS HOT ENOUGH to make her wonder if she were crazy not to be at the lake. She supposed she was crazy. Dream though she might of immersion in the silken coolness of lake water, she had not swum in the lake since 1966. The dream always ended the same way. The arms of a child around her neck, drawing her ever deeper. Somehow it wasn't frightening or disgusting. The experience of drowning in the dream had the calmness of inevitability about it. Nevertheless, she was not at the lake.

If she were crazy, at least she had colleagues in her madness. All of them, like her, absolutely thrilled to be part of a Smithsonian expedition into Jordan, in the middle of a Middle Eastern summer. By June they were all in a stage of extreme silliness; it was clear they were onto something exciting, even significant. It was a carefully kept secret among the professionals that they thought they might be excavating the site of Sodom.

The sun-ridden days tended to blur into one another. One day came, though, that stood out—the day they broke into the burial chamber. In time they would understand they had found a square-mile, six-thousand-year-old necropolis that held the remains of a quarter of a million people.

Torie and her colleagues crouched in a circle above

the chamber, looking down at neatly arranged bones and pottery. After an initial burst of excited comment, there was silence. They didn't know what they had, but they had something, and there was enormous satisfaction in that.

Torie broke the silence. "There's something at the entrance," she said, and gently, with a brush, leaned in to dust the dun-colored shapes in the clay that had caught her eye.

More bones. Only a few large pieces like the one that Torie uncovered first. The rest were shards and flakes. The skeleton within the chamber was complete; it was not a case of remains being disturbed and shifted. All the later chambers that were excavated were quite self-contained. It was a mystery why there should be bones at the entrance of this particular chamber.

Over several months, the shards of bone were reassembled. A skull took shape. Human it was, but it answered fewer questions itself than it engendered.

The last paper Torie Christopher submitted to the Smithsonian before her death of cancer in the fall of 1982 offered not an answer but a speculation.

"I believe," she wrote, "that the individual whose bones mark the entrance to burial chamber One at Bab edh Dhra was a guardian, perhaps deliberately killed at the time of the inhumation of the body in the chamber, and set there as a guardian, or caretaker, in the afterlife."

About the Author

Tabitha King's first novel, also available in a Signet paperback edition, was the well-received *Small World*. She and her husband, author Stephen King, live in Maine.